ALLEGIANCE:
SURVIVING THE
ZOMBIE APOCALYPSE

SHAWN CHESSER

ISBN: 978-0-9882576-7-2

CONTENTS

ACKNOWLEDGMENTS

For Mo, Raven, and Caden, you three mean the world to me... love you. And thanks for putting up with me clacking away at all hours... and then letting me sleep in a *little*. I owe everything to my parents for bringing me up the right way. Mom, thanks for reading... although it is not your genre. Dad, aka Mountain Man Dan, thanks for your ear and influence. Cliff Kane, RIP. Daymon, thanks for introducing me to Grand Targhee *and* Jackson Hole! Thanks to all of the men and women in the military, past and present, especially those of you in harm's way. Thanks to all LE and first responders for your service. To the people in the U.K. who have been in touch, thanks for reading! Thanks to Tom Leeland for help with questions about det cord, your service is appreciated. Thanks to Craig Jeffrey for help with military kit and loadouts. Thanks to Mark Lyon for the awesome image... you make a great Cade Grayson! Lieutenant Colonel Michael Offe, thanks for your service as well as your friendship. Larry Eckels, thank you for your service. Any missing facts or errors are solely my fault. Beta readers, you rock, and you know who you are. Thanks George Romero for introducing me to zombies. Steve H., thanks for listening. All of my friends and fellows at S@N and Monday Old St. David's, thanks as well. Lastly, thanks to Bill W. and Dr. Bob... you helped make this possible. I am going to sign up for another 24.

My idea for the cover was interpreted and designed by Craig Overbey to perfection. Thank you Sir! Special thanks to Craig DiLouie, Gary Mountjoy, John O'Brien, and Mark Tufo. One way or another, all of you have helped me and have provided me with invaluable advice.

David P. Forsyth, thanks for including me in the Permuted Press published anthology, Outbreak: Visions of the Apocalypse. Being published and all of the proceeds going to charity=WIN+WIN.
If I have accidently left anyone out... I am truly sorry.

Once again, extra special thanks to Monique Happy for taking "Allegiance" and giving it some special attention and TLC while polishing its rough edges. Mo, you rock! Working with you has been a seamless experience and nothing but a pleasure. You are the best!
***
Edited by Monique Happy Editorial Services
http://www.moniquehappy.com ⊛ mohappy@att.net

Chapter 1
Outbreak - Day 15
Schriever AFB
Colorado Springs, Colorado

Two days after Pug's execution

Cade Grayson hinged at the waist, snatched the bulky overstuffed duffel bag, and easily flung it up and into the truck's bed where it settled with a solid metallic clunk. Two weeks of running and gunning and surviving on mostly caffeine and sheer will alone had quickly transformed his physique. The small amount of body fat (love handles, according to Brook) that had accumulated around his waist during fifteen months of comfortable civilian life prior to the Omega outbreak had quickly melted away, leaving him muscled and lean. His face had thinned out, the tanned skin taut over his cheekbones where gray streaked sideburns were slowly working their way down to an inevitable merger with his goatee. With the exception of his cardio, which he was gradually building up through daily runs inside the base perimeter, he was in the best physical shape of his life and acclimating nicely to the high desert altitude of Colorado Springs. Thankfully, he had been spared the intense headaches and bouts of breathlessness that had plagued him in the Hindu Kush during his first deployment to that beautiful but Godforsaken country called Afghanistan.

Wiping sweat beads from his brow, he took a covert glance over his shoulder to make sure Brook hadn't been lurking in the hangar, watching, hawklike, as he had just broken one of her many cardinal rules. Inexplicably the petite woman's distinctive soothing voice echoed in his head. '*Lift with your knees, not with your back, Cade Grayson.*' Thirteen years of marriage to a nurse had been challenging at times for the hard-headed only child, and over those years he'd found her ever-changing health-related edicts hard to remember and equally difficult to practice.

***

Ninety minutes earlier when Cade had initially arrived inside the hangar and knocked on First Sergeant Whipper's door, he had been greeted with silence. Then he'd made a good faith effort at finding the cantankerous Air Force lifer. He'd walked the flight line, then nosed around the fuel bowsers and the tool shop, anyplace where he figured a mechanic might be hiding. And after fifteen minutes of searching aimlessly, he'd been back knocking on the first sergeant's door.

There was still no answer, so he'd tried the handle and found the dented and battered yellow door with the sign that read *Authorized Personnel Only* unlocked. Undeterred by Whipper's surly attitude and any fallout he might face from what could easily be construed as breaking and entering, Cade had waded into the cluttered office with one objective: find the keys to the black Ford F-650 in which the now deceased terrorist Pug had arrived days ago.

Locating the keys had been easy; the high clarity diamonds that spelled out *Property of the Denver Nuggets* on the face of the walnut-sized 24k basketball set them apart from those to the other military vehicles. The sheer size of the highly customized 4x4, combined with the super expensive bauble on the key ring all but screamed that it had never belonged to Pug. Who the truck's rightful owner had been, and how it came into the murderer's possession, was a mystery that had no doubt died along with the little psychopath.

No matter, Cade had mused. *It's mine now.*

***

With the rope handles abrading his calloused fingers, Cade straightened his back, let out a loud grunt, and clean jerked the cumbersome pine ammo box from the floor and lifted it level with his sternum. He struggled with the weight for a second and finally perched one end on the tailgate, then used his shoulder to shove it the rest of the way in.

"What's a matter Captain... lost your edge?"

Cade turned towards the direction of the approaching footsteps and found himself face to ruddy face with the man responsible for the verbal barb.

"First Sergeant *Whipper*," Cade said, unable to temper the sharp edge to his words. "To *what* do I owe the pleasure?"

"I want to know who gave *you* permission to break into my office and steal the keys to *this* truck?" the owlish-looking man said brusquely, his pale blue eyes boring into Cade's. Then, corralling an unruly wisp of white hair back into its proper comb-over place, and without allowing Cade time to respond, Whipper continued his rant. "Some nerve you have, Captain. You send a couple of your civilian friends here with a *note* from a *general* ordering me to give them one of my helicopters... and with a full load of fuel to boot. And now you think that gives you the right to waltz in here and take the rig that I had *my* sights set on?"

"Spoils of war," Cade answered matter-of-factly. Because along with the agreement that had him snatch and deliver Robert Christian in exchange for Pug, President Valerie Clay had also granted him an honorable discharge from his Delta Unit along with the promise that he could requisition any ground vehicle that he wanted—thus he chose the dead terrorist's gargantuan truck.

"You *Spec Ops* pricks are all the same—and *Desantos* was no different," Whipper railed. "You pretty boys take what you want and leave the *scraps* for the rest of us to fight over."

With a granite set to his jaw, and a look that said he could do without the headache, Cade slammed the tailgate. He let the echo subside and then shot back. "I had *nothing* to do with you losing

3

one of your helos—that was General Desantos's idea—and a good one at that." He wiped his brow on the sleeve of his ARMY tee shirt.

There was a short silence.

Cade crossed his arms and leaned against the lifted pickup. "Now, *First Sergeant,* are you going to quit busting my balls and walk away, or is this going to escalate?"

The rotund man shifted nervously from foot to foot, his hands disappearing into the pockets of his grease stained coveralls.

"Sergeant Whipper," a voice called from the other end of the hangar near one of the flat-black Ghost Hawks. "Sergeant... you in there?"

After casting a furtive glance in the direction the voice had come from, Whipper remained silent, head bowed as if he was stuck trying to make some sort of a decision. Then he slowly panned his head back around but seemed unwilling to meet Cade's steely gaze. Instead, Whipper studied the gray cement floor.

Cade waited a beat, and then after reading the man's body language and interpreting it for what it was—a sign of weakness—he pressed the attack. He wanted Whipper to leave with his tail between his legs. Even though he would probably never see the angry little man again, he thought that if he left an indelible negative impression on the prick, he would probably think twice before heaping his shit on the other operators and aviators who would continue running missions out of Schriever.

"In case you forgot... *Mike* is dead and can't defend his decision. I should kick your ass just for bringing him into this conversation. Then I should kick it again for leaving Ari and the rest of us hanging in *Indian Country* with our ride staying aloft on nothing but prayers and fumes." He drew a deep breath. *"Really?* An important mission like that and you thought it acceptable to have only one fucking Hercules on the ready line with no other bird standing by as a *backup?"*

4

"I read the after-action reports. But it was out of my hands," Whipper replied.

"*Bullshit!* Because of mechanical failure and *your* poor decision making, we had no tanker rendezvous. Ari was forced to put us down at a municipal airport crawling with the dead. And that was our *second* hot refuel under similar circumstances in as many days because you sent us out light in the first place. And though it might not be clear to your superiors, Mister Cover-Your-Own-Ass, it is *crystal* clear to me where your priorities lie."

"Couldn't be helped," Whipper mumbled.

"*A man died,*" Cade hissed through clenched teeth.

"Sooner or later *all* of these birds"—the Air Force first sergeant made a grand sweeping motion that encompassed the static aircraft on the tarmac outside and the stealth helicopters sitting nearby—"are no longer going to be airworthy. I have limited manpower, and lubricants and spare parts are harder and harder to come by."

"So you have a hard job here, huh? Tell that to Sergeant Maddox—he died so the rest of us could make it home. The fact that you only held *one* Hercules back for us is borderline criminal. And for that I hold *you* fully responsible."

Silence.

Whipper stared daggers at the Delta operator, and then suddenly the 5-foot-5 mechanic rushed Cade, who fluidly pushed off the truck and went into a half crouch with his arms at his sides, hands balled into fists. Then, like a bull and a toreador, the two men crabbed counter-clockwise in the center of the hangar.

With no will to initiate a fight with a superior, Whipper smugly said, "You first, Captain."

"I'm no longer a Captain," Cade stated, a sly smile curling the corners of his mouth.

At once, Whipper's face blanched and his wrathful expression morphed to one of bewilderment. Then his head whipped sideways as Cade's lightning quick rabbit-punch clipped him on the chin. The single powerful blow dropped the first sergeant to the floor, where he lay on his back contemplating the pulsating blue tracers darting amongst the rafters.

"I'd stay down if I were you," Cade said. "Because if you do get up... it will be for the last time."

Glancing at the tall slab-sided rig with its elevated cab and enough ground clearance to drive over a Yugo, it suddenly dawned on Cade why Whipper seemed to covet the truck they had just come to blows over. *Small man syndrome*, he thought to himself. *Just like Pug.* Then he realized why the first sergeant wanted the Ford as *his* bug out vehicle. And it was probably the only thing the two of them saw eye-to-eye on.

"So Whipper, tell me something. Where were you planning to go in this rig?"

Slowly massaging the side of his chin where Cade had delivered his *message*, Whipper lifted his head from the concrete and regarded the operator with a bland look before answering the question. "Nowhere in particular. But definitely away from here when the dead return. And to be honest with you... I just wanted a little insurance. That's all."

"You make me sick, Whipper. So you're telling me that if another herd of dead happens to come this way, maybe from Pueblo or another mega horde from Denver, then your plan is to bail out? Leave the SOAR (Special Operations Aviation Regiment) guys and anyone else that relies on your expertise to just fend for themselves?"

Whipper's eyes narrowed to slits. He stabbed a thumb towards the black truck. "I saw all of the supplies that *you* loaded into the back of that thing," he said accusingly. "You, *Sir*... are the fucking *hypocrite* here."

The truth in Whipper's statement caught Cade by surprise; hitting him like a one-two punch to the midsection. And as bitter a pill it was for him to swallow—the man did have a point—his decision to quit Delta, no matter the motives behind it, did contain a fair amount of hypocrisy. Furthermore, there was no way he could hide behind the fact that Brook had been the driving force behind turning in his captain's bars and walking away from the men he would gladly die for, the very same men that he knew would willingly sacrifice their lives for him on the field of battle.

But he didn't have the time to debate the first sergeant over semantics, nor did he want to bring up one-tenth of the sacrifices he had made for his country while wearing the uniform. In fact, he had nothing to prove to this puke. No need to go there, he thought to himself. Right now, the only thing that mattered to him was to get his ducks in a row and hit the road. He knew that eventually the dead were going to return and in much larger numbers than before. Whether they came from Pueblo, Denver-Aurora or some other direction didn't matter, for he was certain the double-wall of fencing around Schriever had no chance of stopping them. And he wanted to be on the road with his family before they arrived. To go somewhere far from Schriever. Far from the big cities and off the beaten path.

"I'm taking the truck, Whipper," Cade said with a no-nonsense tone to his voice. "And if you have a problem with that, you can take it up with President Clay."

Whipper said nothing. He remained on his back, staring at the shadows in the rafters.

Giving the supine man a wide berth, Cade strode over to the truck and finished stacking the remaining Pelican boxes into the bed, arranging them snugly so they wouldn't go sliding around.

With what little fight he initially had had in him snuffed out, Whipper collected himself from the cool floor, looked disdainfully at the man loading the truck—*his truck*—and trudged silently back to the flight line.

***

Cade stowed the bottled waters and MREs (meals ready to eat) which Shrill had procured for him in the crew cab, on the bench seat behind the driver, leaving enough room for Raven on the opposite side.

He clambered aboard the truck and turned the key. The engine started at once, belting out a dull roar that echoed in the cavernous hangar. He spent a couple of minutes familiarizing himself with the controls and gauges and checked the fuel level. *Full.* He made a rough calculation in his head. Including the gas in the tank, and the extra twenty gallons stored in the four red gas cans in back, he figured the truck had a maximum range of four hundred miles. Then, considering the sheer size of the rig, he took a moment to rethink the probable gas mileage and admitted sullenly to himself that a range of three hundred miles was more likely the case. That they'd have to do a little siphoning along the way wouldn't be such a big deal. After all, that's how he had made it cross-country from Portland to Idaho after the outbreak. And besides, he thought to himself, if they got stuck in the midst of a zombie swarm, being off the ground in the big four-by-four and out of the Zs' reach would be a fair trade-off for a little sucking and spitting.

Once he had motored the seat back, adjusted the mirrors, and was confident that he knew where the important gauges, buttons, and switches were located in the cockpit, he levered the transmission into drive and nosed the truck out of the hangar and into the early morning sunlight.

After a short drive along the tarmac, which took him past the blackened and twisted metal framework that was once the mobile medical until Pug had set it ablaze, he maneuvered the massive black Ford F-650 up to the main gate on the northwest corner of Schriever AFB, braked a dozen feet from the twelve-foot high concertina topped fencing, then powered the window down and waited for one of the guards to come to him.

He cast his gaze to the gate where a number of Zs in various stages of decomposition and undress were clustered together. He noted their bony digits probing the chain-link in a futile attempt to get at the meat within.

Purging the dead from his mind, Cade glanced over his left shoulder to take in the sky show. The sun had just begun to paint the tops of Pikes Peak, Cheyenne Mountain, and the rest of the eastern side of the jagged Rocky Mountains with broad strokes of yellow and orange. As he watched the colors morph and creep down the expansive flanks, a wide swath of burnt umber took over the center of the upthrust prehistoric mantle, leaving the base in darkness, lending the impression the entire range was floating in air.

"How can I help you Sir?" said a voice barely loud enough to be heard over the Ford's idling power plant.

Snapping out of his sunrise-induced daze, Cade yanked the transmission into park and silenced the 6.8 liter V10 engine. He acknowledged the camouflage-clad soldier with a brief nod before producing his credentials along with a sealed envelope.

Shifting his M4 carbine on its sling, the soldier reached up to receive the offering, then cracked a wide smile and flashed a sharp salute upon recognizing Cade, whom, since the Castle Rock and Jackson Hole missions, had become somewhat of a celebrity on base.

"Good to see you, Captain Grayson," the baby-faced 4th Infantry Division soldier said, taking the paperwork from the man whose exploits, past and present, he had heard a great deal about. "My apologies Sir... you're not wearing your cover. I assumed you were a civilian."

"No worries Sergeant," Cade replied quietly, while wishing they would be done with the formalities quickly so he could be on his way before anyone else recognized him.

The guard scrutinized the freshly-minted document closely— so much so that Cade thought he might be memorizing his vital statistics and military ID number—then, after a long minute or two, the sergeant held the identification at arm's length to compare the face in the photo with the living legend perched high in the truck.

"In the flesh," the sergeant added, smiling broadly as he handed back the laminated green ID card. "May I ask a favor of you, Sir?"

"Yes. What is it?" Cade replied.

The young soldier straightened up and ran both hands over his uniform, giving it an impromptu pressing. "May I shake your hand? It'd be an honor."

Palming his face with both hands, Cade sighed audibly then ran his hands through his close-cropped dark hair. He leaned his upper body out the window and gripped the man's upthrust hand firmly. He locked his hard, no nonsense eyes with the staff sergeant's. "What's your name, son?"

"Leeland... Staff Sergeant Thomas Leeland."

"Pleasure's all mine, Staff Sergeant," Cade offered. "Now *I* have a favor to ask of you."

By now several of the men and the only woman who had been manning the gate had grown curious and were forming a loose semi-circle around the driver's door.

A soldier yelled down from one of the towers flanking the entrance. "Hey Sarge! Who is it?"

Cade winced and retreated into the shadowy confines of the truck's cab.

Looking around at his subordinates and still grinning, the staff sergeant replied, "Anything you need Captain... just say it."

"That piece of paper you have in your left hand..."

Coming to the realization he was behaving like a star struck groupie, the young sergeant held the envelope aloft and said with a sheepish look on his face, "This... what do you want me to do with it Sir?"

White and devoid of writing, the envelope was the same type in which Cade used to send out the payment for the lights, gas, and water. Monthly responsibilities necessary to ensure the luxuries that he had taken for granted then, and feared would be of no concern to him ever again—at least not in his lifetime—and maybe not even in Raven's. It felt strange knowing that the everyday commuting to work and bill paying normalcy called life that most people had loathed, yet endured, had disappeared only fifteen days ago—days that now seemed like years. *Old world, different time. The world before Omega. The days before shambling flesh eaters choked the cities and streets across America. A different time indeed,* Cade thought darkly.

Turning the envelope over in his hand, Leeland repeated the question. "What do you want me to do with this envelope, Sir?"

"If for some reason I do not return before o-dark-thirty," Cade said, pausing to let the words sink in before gesturing towards the correspondence clutched in the sergeant's hand, "I will need you to personally deliver *that sealed envelope* to my wife, Brooklyn Grayson."

"Copy that," said the visibly nervous sergeant. "I realize this is way out of line for me to ask you, Captain Grayson, but given the responsibility you are entrusting me with... I have to know just in case. Where are you going?"

"A personal fact finding mission cleared by General Gaines himself," Cade lied.

"By yourself... without backup?"

"Yes soldier, and I need to be Oscar Mike, 'on the move' as soon as possible."

"Wait one, Sir," said the sergeant as he strode towards the gate, wading through his troops while warning them to get behind him and remain there.

Sitting in the cab, outfitted in desert camouflage ACU pants and a black short-sleeved tee shirt, Cade used the time to take a final mental inventory of his gear: his 9mm Glock 17 semi-automatic pistol rode low, strapped to his left thigh, right next door to the Gerber Mk II combat dagger that he never ventured outside the wire without. The Glock 19, a smaller version of the 17, was suspended under his right armpit in a Bianchi quick release holster. He'd brought along six magazines for the two pistols. He reasoned, if a hundred and four rounds wasn't sufficient to keep him alive outside the wire, then he had no business embarking on the upcoming mission, which looked to be the most dangerous one yet. In fact, he had much more riding on it than the life of one man wearing three hats: soldier, husband, and father.

The white sun, now blasting at their backs, cast Schriever's boxy silhouette in the form of stretched out shadows across the desert floor.

The guards looked on in anticipation, Cade included, as the sergeant unslung his M4 and pulled the charging handle. "Going hot," he bellowed, and then after emptying his weapon with controlled accurate shots, the two dozen walking corpses that had congregated overnight were left lying in a tangled knot, their congealed bodily fluids leaking black into the talc-like dust.

"Open the gate," Sergeant Leeland barked as he presented arms and held a salute.

Though not in uniform Cade reciprocated, held it for a heartbeat, and then turned the key, bringing the V10 throbbing to life. Without looking back, he finessed the pedal and coaxed the beast through the parting metal maw and into Indian Country. He turned left and then made another left and barreled south paralleling the fence, dodging random walkers and leaving them in the truck's dust vortex.

***

He drove south for a spell and then east for half an hour, following a laser-straight stretch of highway bisecting the high desert southeast of Colorado Springs. The four-lane black top took him by ransacked convenience stores, their trash-strewn parking lots still teeming with walkers. Along the way, stalled cars containing trapped zombies had become a common sight, and he'd seen too many seemingly abandoned farm houses for him to count. Suddenly he wished he hadn't left his iPod full of classic rock along with his favorite Portland Trail Blazers ball cap inside his abandoned Sequoia on the road outside of Boise, Idaho, though the items were merely reminders of the old world. The world of convenience, filled with meaningless trinkets he'd never truly appreciated; still, he longed for some *Doors* or *Rolling Stones*. Hell, he thought, if it would break the monotony of the never-ending straightaway, he'd even settle for Raven's favorite: *Lady Ga Ga*.

He reached for the dash and punched the stereo on, instantly regretting the action as bass-heavy rap music bounced him in his seat. Blaring from what had to be two hundred hidden speakers—but no less than twenty, he conceded—some long dead hip-hop mogul professed his undying love for bling, women, and New York City. Cade quickly killed the *music,* thereby sparing his ears and ending the unwanted ass massage. Searching for a radio signal in rural Colorado after a zombie outbreak, he learned, was a lesson in futility. Save for a couple of high watt repeaters broadcasting a looping FEMA message telling the public what they had already learned the hard way, the only thing emanating from the rest of the dial was a never-ending droning static of white noise. So he continued on in relative silence, with only the tires' hypnotic cadence keeping him company.

He slowed to zipper the truck through pileups, off-roading only when there wasn't enough room for the Ford's considerable bulk to squeeze by, then after another twenty minutes had elapsed and fifteen miles of highway had unspooled in the rearview, a sign that read *Yoder Population 222* flashed by on the right.

Getting close now.

Cade didn't know Colorado from the dark side of the moon. The only reason he knew that this town even existed was because he had spotted it from his seat in the Ghost Hawk when Ari had buzzed it on their return trip from Sentinel Butte a week prior. And as he neared Yoder on the ground, he hoped the blink-and-you'd-miss-it town wasn't as peaceful as it seemed from the air.

Chapter 2
Outbreak - Day 15
Schriever AFB
Colorado Springs, Colorado

Defeating Brook's blackout job, a scalpel-thin ray of sunshine infiltrated the heavy wool blankets covering the east-facing windows. Lancing into the room, the honey-colored light fell perfectly across her closed eyes.

For a brief instant she thought she might have slept through the alarm and was running late for work—a cardinal sin in the nursing profession. Then a few seconds elapsed and reality set in—she was still stranded on an island of concrete and gravel ringed with barbed wire. The fact that Schriever was surrounded by cities and towns that were slowly but surely being purged of the walking dead and would eventually be theirs to repopulate brought her no comfort. She wasn't unique. A few hundred other survivors, civilians and military, were stuck in the very same situation.

She pushed down the anxiety rising in her chest, sat up, and swung her feet over the edge of the bottom bunk. A *Sealy Posturepedic* it was not, but at least it hadn't been empty the last two nights. A smile creased her face. The memory of her and Cade's tender lovemaking, fresh in her mind, warmed against the

14

morning chill. It had been quite a while since they had been intimate.

First, three thousand miles filled with multitudes of infected had kept them apart. She and Raven had been in Myrtle Beach, South Carolina visiting her folks when the outbreak began and, he had been back home in Portland, Oregon.

Then, after the Grayson family had finally reunited at Schriever AFB in Colorado Springs, the nonstop missions began, tugging them all back into the same kind of existence she had tolerated fifteen months prior to Omega when Cade was still an active member of the Unit—also known as 1st Special Forces Operational Detachment-Delta—or Delta Force for short. They were the best of the best: Tier-1 operators who were pulled from the ranks of the Special Forces or 75th Ranger Regiment.

"Raven... are you awake?"

A groggy-sounding voice answered from the dark, somewhere near the rafters, three bunks away. "I am now, Mom."

Brook stood and did a few toe touches, bending at the waist easily. She put her palms to the floor and arched her back, a move which resulted in a series of soft popping noises. Then she heard the slap of Raven's bare feet hitting the floor followed by a soft patter that echoed off the walls as the diminutive twelve-year-old threaded her way between the towering bunk beds.

"I heard funny noises last night," Raven said, rounding the foot of her parents' bunk. "Did you hear them too?"

"I did not hear a thing, sweetie," Brook replied with a guilty smile that forced her to look away lest her overly intuitive daughter get a sense that a little white lie had been told.

"At least it wasn't screaming like the other night," Raven went on, her eyes widening. "What was *that* all about?"

Brook bit her lip and said nothing.

"Mom... you promised you would tell me."

"After we get up and motivated and have a bite at the mess..." Brook winced at her choice of words. Not the best, considering the carnage that had taken place there earlier.

"What's wrong, Mom?"

15

Brook pulled a clean shirt over her head. "Nothing's wrong, sweetie... I just remembered something. That's all." Then quickly switching subjects she continued on, "So, Raven, after we eat we are going to have some *Mom* and *Daughter* time."

"About what?" Raven asked. Then she thought, *Oh no, I just turned twelve. Am I going to get 'the talk'?*

Brook noticed Raven's face tighten. She hadn't seen a look like that since she'd learned that Uncle Carl had died.

"What is it sweetie?" Brook asked in a motherly voice.

"We're not going to talk about boys and girls and the birds and the bees... are we? Because you don't have to worry, Mom... there're no boys I like here anyway. Well... there's Dmitri. I like him, but not *that* kind of *like.*"

Brook snorted, then covered her mouth, but still couldn't hold back the torrent. And as Raven stared with a mortified look on her face, Brook laughed until her sides ached.

"Mom? Are you all right?"

"Come with me," Brook said. She wiped away the tears of mirth and then cinched the long-sleeved shirt around her waist. Lastly, she reached under the bottom bunk, collected the short barreled M4 and the MOLLE rig—a vest with webbing and pouches containing extra magazines for her rifle—and led her precocious twelve-year-old by the hand. "We're eating and then you get your birthday present."

A little squeal escaped Raven's mouth as visions of a foraged iPod loaded with *'age appropriate'* music danced in her head. Ugghh, *age appropriate.* She hated when her mom and dad said that. It was their way of saying anything safe and bland, usually from the Disney label that was totally devoid of sexual innuendo and any mention of partying or hooking up. They were the two words that just about ruled out every song that had been force fed tween girls prior to the outbreak.

Chapter 3
Outbreak - Day 15
Yoder, Colorado

Squinting against the rising sun, Cade fumbled in his pockets searching for his Oakleys but came up empty. "Shit," he blurted out loud. "You're only thirty-five years old, *Grayson*; you're too damn young to start misplacing stuff."

In the distance, the town of Yoder, population two hundred and twenty-two, arose from the desert. One- and two-story buildings at first, then light standards, indiscriminately parked vehicles, and street signs came into view.

Nothing moved except for the flying rats. In the weeks since Omega burned across the United States, the buzzards, ravens, and crows took over the cities and towns that had once been dominated by living humans. The rapacious birds had also adapted, changing their taste from the occasional road kill to the rotting human corpses that were suddenly in abundance.

Cade eased off the gas and let the truck coast to a stop. His brown eyes flicked over the business marquees atop the deserted buildings. *Nothing.*

He slowly urged the truck forward, weaving around a putrefying corpse inexplicably still gripping the handle of an overturned shopping cart. *Cleanup on aisle five,* he thought

17

morbidly. Garbage was strewn on both sides of the street and glass shards sparkled on the sidewalk in front of what he guessed had been the only bank in town. He caught movement in his peripheral vision as an intact page of newsprint, carried on a wind gust, fluttered across his line of sight. The words '*Walking Dead*' registered in his brain like some kind of warning, and then the litter was gone, cartwheeling down the street.

He parked the truck two blocks in, straddling the yellow line, adjacent to a boarded up hardware store and a greasy spoon diner that he guessed had served its last Blue Plate Special.

Spoiling for a fight, he scanned the buildings on both sides of the street, paying extra attention to the darkened doorways and windows. *Still nothing.*

Keeping his foot firm to the brake, he pinned the gas pedal to the firewall. The power plant roared and strained against the mounts under its hood, threatening to lurch out of the engine bay. He eased off the gas and let the burbling exhaust resonate off of the buildings for a beat and then silenced the engine.

Before long a disheveled looking first-turn stumbled from the narrow alley separating the diner and the adjacent used book store. Meanwhile, movement from the opposite side of the street drew Cade's gaze as a trio of shamblers emerged through the destroyed double doors of a thoroughly looted mom and pop grocery store. Broken glass crunched underfoot with each unsteady step as they plodded into the sunlight, their milky eyes searching for fresh meat.

Adding to Cade's welcoming committee, a handful of flesh eaters materialized from the buildings and side streets a block distant. The morning sun at their backs cast long swaggering shadows, further exaggerating their slow and steady advance.

This situation that Cade had purposefully gotten himself into reminded him of a scene straight out of an old spaghetti western complete with the *Good, the Bad, and the Ugly* theme song playing on a repeating loop in his mind. He was Clint and the desperados were closing in.

He took a mental inventory of the approaching dead, prioritizing each one based on its proximity to him, and what kind of cover he had to fall back on if the need arose.

Who needs a kill house for live fire practice, he mused.

Two twists secured the suppressor to his Glock 17. He didn't mind the extra weight attached to the pistol. In fact, it served to keep down muzzle climb and helped lessen recoil caused by the slide jacking back after each discharge.

In effect, the *can* turned the polymer semi-automatic pistol—already a natural extension of the Delta shooter's arm—into a near silent, yet still, deadly accurate weapon.

In his peripheral vision he perceived the undead trio that had emerged from the grocery store nearing the Ford's passenger side. However, since the dead woman from the alley was nearly at his door, she would have to be dealt with first.

After double checking to make sure the Glock was locked and loaded—which had become the gold standard in the new post-apocalyptic world—he powered down the window and drew a bead between the walker's lifeless eyes.

"You look like hell, lady," he said as the Glock popped once. A pink mist haloed the monster's head and it crashed to the asphalt, limbs askew. The shell casing bounced on the road a couple of times then rolled out of sight.

"I'll be right back. Lock the doors and keep away from the windows," he would remember to tell them.

He sprang from the cab, banged the door shut, and for good measure put another 9mm bullet into the Z's temple. As he stepped over the ghoul's splayed-out body, he made himself a mental note—*always double tap*. Then, like clockwork, the adrenaline surged from his adrenal gland as the fight or flight urge took over, and like energy transiting water, the naturally-occurring stimulant pulsed through his trunk and limbs, snapping him into what his instructors at Fort Benning referred to as '*the zone.*' And as he consciously checked and calmed his breathing, time seemed to slow down, and his surroundings and the emerging threats around him snapped into acute focus.

Crabbing sideways in a combat crouch, he rounded the front of the truck, went to one knee, and waited in ambush for the first of the trudging trio to make his Glock's acquaintance. As he held the pistol steady in a two handed grip, he could feel heat emanating from the Ford's ticking engine—warm on the right side of his face and forearm. A sudden eddy of wind tinged with carrion and heated motor oil blasted his nose, causing him to screw his face up in disgust. A heartbeat later a pair of scuffed Nikes shuffled into view under the front bumper, followed closely by the rest of the lurching creature. Cade lined up the front and rear sights, focused on the soft fleshy spot underneath the creature's chin, and caressed the trigger, sending two 9mm Parabellum slugs screaming upward. Hot shell casings pinged off the grill and ricocheted across his face as the one-two punch lifted the Z off the ground and deposited it into the other two walking corpses.

Failure to feed, Cade thought to himself as he simultaneously dropped the suppressed Glock and withdrew the black combat dagger from the sheath strapped to his right thigh. While keeping a low center of gravity and distributing his weight evenly on the balls of his feet, he waited patiently with the razor sharp Gerber clutched in his right hand. He envisioned Raven, sitting wide-eyed and vulnerable in the truck alongside Brook, who would be clutching her M4 carbine ready to use if he should fall to the dead. He wasn't being chauvinist by insisting his family remain inside the vehicle. He merely wanted a little insurance when push finally came to shove—because if somehow he and Brook got into trouble and both became infected, he knew beyond a shadow of a doubt that Raven would not survive a day outside the wire by herself—she just wasn't ready yet.

Two in front, six to go, he thought to himself, keeping the running commentary going in his head.

He paused for a beat to allow the nearest walkers time to regain their footing, and then he mounted a frontal assault. Sunlight glinted off the ten-inch blade as it flashed forward and up, producing a wet sucking sound as it pierced the first ghoul through the eye socket. Cold fingers grazed his wrist as the pale creature went limp and slid from the deadly weapon.

Momentarily ignoring the half dozen creatures still the better part of a block away, he focused fully on the immediate threat to the front—an overweight Z encumbered by a hanging beer gut and a swinging pair of pallid D-cup sized man boobs.

He shifted the Gerber to his left hand and reached for the butt of his backup pistol with the other. Truth be told, since training exhaustively in the Delta kill house at Fort Bragg— shooting with each hand from every conceivable position and angle—he had no equal when it came to pistol marksmanship.

Seeing as how the compact Glock already had one in the pipe and its safety was integral to the trigger, all that was left for him to do was aim and work the trigger.

The booming reports from the 19 were like night and day compared to the suppressed Glock 17 which he had purposefully dropped to the blacktop by the truck's left front fender. Two bullets travelling at thirteen hundred feet per second cut a V in Man Boob's forehead, and in an explosion of white bone and greasy hair, peeled his cranium up and away. The resulting rooster tail of gray matter squelched to the ground in a wide arc as the corpse collapsed forward, coming to rest face down at the Delta operator's feet.

"Double tap," he said, wiping a bead of sweat from his upper lip. "Does the trick every time."

He straightened up, and feeling a little cocky, bellowed, "Who is next?" He stepped over the cold bodies, trying to decide how he wanted to tackle the remaining six Zs. *Test out the truck or use the pistol?*

He decided to finish the exercise with the thirteen rounds remaining in the compact Glock. He closed the distance, firing as he walked, and after dinging the first two with clean head shots, he dropped the magazine which still held nine shells. Then, with the Zs but a few steps away, he pulled a fresh magazine from the Fobus double mag holder clipped to his belt, slapped it in the well, and released the slide. With the semi-automatic in a two-handed grip, he dropped to one knee and walked fire from right to left. In three and a half seconds he had discharged eight rounds from his Glock, giving each of the remaining Zs a vicious double tap and a much needed second final death.

In less than five minutes, on a lonely road in sleepy Yoder, Colorado, he had answered his own nagging doubts with a solid solo performance. The perceived rust that had accumulated during the fifteen months while he had been away from running hot ops with his Delta unit had been scoured away, and with only his life, and no one else's on the line, he had passed his own impromptu Q course.

Wyatt's back, he told himself as he kneeled to retrieve the suppressed Glock and magazine from where he had discarded them.

Once he was back inside the truck, he punched open the glove box and extracted the Thuraya satellite phone, stabbed out ten digits and placed the receiver to his ear.

Chapter 4
Outbreak - Day 15
Near Victor, Idaho

The two-story clapboard house rested on a flat plat of land at the end of a rutted gravel drive that ran downhill about the length of a football field to the asphalt two lanes that joined up with State Highway 33 a quarter of a mile away.

The turn of the century affair was in dire need of a new coat of white. Several rundown outbuildings dotted the property, and a number of rusting cars waged a losing battle against the elements on the upslope behind the old farmhouse.

On the west side of the property, a picket of conifers stood guard between the house and SH-33 connecting the Teton Pass nine miles to the southeast and Victor, Idaho five miles to the northwest.

With his saucer-sized belt buckle scraping against the pitted porcelain kitchen sink, former Jackson Hole Chief of Police Charlie Jenkins leaned over the overflowing mess of dirty dishes. He parted the yellowed curtains, allowing a shaft of morning sun to splash across the knotty pine table, brightening the drab cramped space. He pressed the binoculars to his face and scanned the asphalt road that ran perpendicular to the gate at the end of the gravel driveway. *Nothing.*

Thankfully the feeder road hadn't seen any zombies since they'd arrived at the house two days prior. He shifted his gaze to the highway. "*Goddamnit!*" he exclaimed. Another large pack of the rotten beasts, numbering more than fifty he guessed, shambled along the road heading towards Victor.

"Whatcha got out there Charlie?"

Jenkins flinched and let the curtain fall back into place. Then he whipped around, instinctively with his gun hand near the butt of his holstered pistol.

"You've gotta cut that shit out, *Daymon*," Jenkins said. "You can't keep sneaking up on a fella like that. Good way to get yourself killed."

"You've been pretty jumpy last couple a days, Charlie. It's a good thing that pistola didn't clear leather," the dreadlocked man replied, nodding towards the lawman's black Sig Sauer. "If it did, I'd have to ask you to cut back on the coffee and donuts."

"Cop joke... very funny. I haven't slept but a few minutes here and there since I left Jackson. Hell, I could use some caffeine right about now. And a big fat maple bar would be heaven."

"That makes two of us," Daymon replied. "What kinda bed and breakfast they running here anyway? Coming down from upstairs I expected I'd be walking headlong into the wonderful aroma of bacon and country gravy."

Jenkins chuckled. "Yeah, I wish these folks hadn't of cleaned out their pantry before they vamoosed. Not much you can whip up with chicken noodle soup, evaporated milk, and pumpkin pie filling." He removed his prescription Aviators and pulled a microfiber wipe from his breast pocket. "What the hell am I gonna do when this square of fabric wears out?" he mumbled, giving each lens a thorough wipe. "'Cause I don't think China's gonna be pumping these things out anytime soon."

Daymon said nothing. He could care less about China or Charlie's second pair of eyes. He just crossed his arms and leaned back against the long dead refrigerator.

"OK, let's cut the small talk and get down to brass tacks," Jenkins said. He replaced his glasses, pushed them back onto his nose and shot Daymon a no nonsense look. "How's Heidi— have you gotten her to eat yet?"

"A little soup, but that's all. Swallowing seems to be her biggest problem," he answered slowly.

"Daymon... she *needs* to eat," Charlie said, concern creeping into his gravelly voice. "That little lady of yours won't get her strength back if she doesn't. And *we* won't be able to go *anywhere* until she can get along on her own. Hell... it'd be even better if she could handle a pistol—or that crossbow of yours. You and I could carry the carbines I took off the NA guards."

"Yesterday she lifted her head and I noticed her eyes trackin' me around the room," Daymon replied, trying to change the subject. "I figure that's a step in the right direction. Whether she can travel soon is debatable. And she's pretty messed up mentally... she barely lets me touch her." He flashed a tight smile that did not go unnoticed by Jenkins.

"I'm sorry to hear that. Based on my experience, victims who have been through what your girl endured all react differently. Some bounce back right away. But most do withdraw for a time. I'm sure she'll come around. You and I both know she's been through a lot... just gotta give it some time," Jenkins said reassuringly.

"The whole thing feels strange... that's all. It's like she doesn't see *me* most of the time. She practically looks right through me," Daymon said with a pinched voice.

"Sorry son," Jenkins said softly. "How has she been sleeping?"

"Not well..." Daymon replied, gazing towards the hall. Straining to hear any sound coming from upstairs, he pinned his dreads behind his ears, wincing noticeably as he did so. "She wakes up a lot... *nightmares*."

Jenkins hefted the field glasses and resumed scanning the road below. "How are *you* doing Daymon... are those gashes on your chest still red and hot to the touch?"

"Yeah, and I'm getting sick of them tearing open damn near every time I sit up quick or make any sudden movements. It's

25

been a *frickin* week and the things are still leaking that green and yellow shit. When do you think it's bound to heal?"

"I've been thinking about that," Jenkins said. He paused for a long while, like he was contemplating something very serious. Daymon could almost hear gears turning in the former police chief's head as he watched the balding man watching the dead down on the highway. "Your wounds *are not* healing," Jenkins added. "And that could become a real problem down the road—perhaps a *lethal* problem. I think we ought to stay here at least a couple more days. Be better so the *both* of you can rest up some more. Do a little *healing*... if you know what I mean."

Daymon moved a step closer and slid a chair from under the kitchen table. "*No*, I'm not following," he intoned. Then, spinning the sturdy chair around so that its back faced his chest, he took a seat and leaned forward, arms folded, and stared intently at Jenkins. "I'm getting real sick and tired of sitting here in this mothball-smelling house and eating cold soup while you watch those things march by. What the hell are you *afraid* of, Charlie?"

Jenkins sighed. "I'm *afraid* of us getting stuck out there with you at half speed and this old man who is slowing down by the second having to pick up the slack. And this mothball-smelling house that *you* picked out... It has kept us warm at night and out of sight and alive for the last two days. And as long as we don't do anything stupid that will draw one of those herds up here, we can stay as long as we want."

"I don't like how that sounds, Jenkins... you're allowing yourself to get too comfortable. I *do not* want to stay here. I *want* to get to Eden where I know there are *good* people, where I don't have to look at dead folk hanging from a cross." He looked at the floor again, trying to determine how much of the information he had just received via the Thuraya satellite phone he should divulge. Finally he decided to offer up the Cliff's Notes version. "I got a call from my friend Cade a little while ago. He's the soldier guy I was trapped with in the farmhouse in Utah. Not unlike this *farmhouse*."

Jenkins perked up. "The same guy who stuck a gun in your face?"

"Yeah... did it more than once." Daymon grimaced at the memory.

"With *friends* like that..." Jenkins muttered.

"He's a good guy," Daymon insisted. "He said he was calling from Colorado Springs and then he gave me the GPS coordinates to the compound."

"So if the call went through, then that means the satellite network is still up and running. And if it is, then the GPS in the cruiser should still work."

Daymon eyed the keys to the Tahoe. "I'm ready to go five minutes ago."

Jenkins lowered the binoculars. "Patience," he said, looking the younger man in the eye.

"Alright *Chief*, I'm good with us staying here another day or so," Daymon conceded. "But that's it." He stared at the floor with his dreadlocks hanging around his face. After a beat he looked up and again locked eyes with Jenkins. "Now that I know exactly where in Utah the compound is, I want to get Heidi there as soon as possible."

"Before we move on you're going to need some antibiotics, or by the time *Heidi* can travel, *you* are gonna be laid up and about as useful to me and her as tits on a boar."

"Sounds like something my Daddy woulda said..."

"I'm just saying. You can't mess with the little itty bitty bugs because they *will* multiply and put you down for the count." His face hardened and he added in a low voice. "Maybe kill you if you don't take care of yourself."

"The compound is only a half-day's drive from here," Daymon pleaded.

"Listen, Daymon, I'm not going to argue with you, but if you take a turn for the worse you'll be taking chances with all of our lives."

"I can pull my own weight," Daymon hissed. "Been taking care of myself for years."

27

"It's not just *you* anymore."

Daymon went quiet.

"Does Heidi know how to handle a gun?"

The former firefighter shook his head because he knew exactly where Jenkins was going with this. "She's a bartender, Charlie," he replied icily.

"This isn't going to be *anything* like Jackson Hole. Those things are going to be *everywhere*," said Jenkins.

No shit, thought Daymon. If only Jenkins knew how much death he had seen during the circuitous route he had travelled from Jackson Hole, to Salt Lake City, to Colorado Springs, and finally ending up back in Jackson Hole. *If only he knew the half of it.*

The floorboards creaked as Jenkins crabbed around the kitchen table and traversed the dining room. Without saying a word he parted the curtains and looked out one of the leaded windows bracketing a built in that was filled with knickknacks, books, and candles.

"Whatcha got *this time*, Charlie?"

"Nothing out of the ordinary... just another group of *walkers*," Jenkins replied, his voice dripping with contempt.

"They on 33... or the feeder road?"

"Still only 33, and it's a good thing we got ahead of them," he added.

Staring the former police chief directly in the eye, Daymon said softly, "It's a good thing we got the fuck out of Jackson when we did. Are you sure you gave the locals plenty of time to escape? Did Gerald get out OK?"

"I called on him myself. Got the feeling he was going to play captain and go down with his ship. Most of the essentials and conscripts defected overnight, and were long gone before the barrier failed. Hell, some even went during the day, openly defying their *great leader.*" Jenkins drew the curtain and turned, facing Daymon. "I saw this coming. Robert Christian started unraveling the second the people of Jackson stopped kissing his ass—and that was on day one. Then the shit really hit the fan when Bishop proposed blocking the passes and setting up the barricade. The truth was that the people were more afraid of the dead than *anything* Christian, Bishop, or his boys could do to them."

Silence.

Rubbing his red-rimmed eyes, Jenkins added, "The dead won... and if I don't go check a few of these farms around here for some kind of antibiotics... you might be joining them. I'm a country boy... you know that, Daymon," he intoned. "So I was sitting here without my coffee and racking my brain asking myself who in the hell keeps antibiotics in the country? Then the answer came to me... a horse farm ought to have a good deal of medicine. They're always dealing with one hoof infection after another."

Daymon nodded an affirmative, then slowly arose from the chair and spun it around so it faced front. It screeched on the linoleum as he parked it under the table. Before going back upstairs, Daymon gave Jenkins a firm squeeze on the shoulder. It was his way of thanking the man without saying something awkward that he might regret.

***

Jenkins's plan was simple. He decided he'd coast from the house to the gate, the Tahoe in neutral with the motor running. The idling engine wouldn't draw much attention, he reasoned, however, he was a little concerned that the gravel crunching and popping under the off-road tires might equate to a dinner bell to the dead. If all went well he would get through the gate undetected, secure it behind him, and then glide quietly downhill until he was in their midst, then wrench the transmission into drive and speed west before the abominations knew he was even there. With any luck the monsters would follow, and would remain oblivious to the house on the hill.

After the jarring ride downhill he parked the SUV near the gate, left the engine running, and slid from the bench seat. Boots crunching a steady cadence, he walked the dozen feet towards the stamped heavy gauge galvanized steel that had, so far, kept out the small throngs of dead traipsing the back roads of Idaho.

29

Being a lifelong cynic, he guessed that whoever had put in the gate did so mainly to keep out roving salesmen hawking weatherproof aluminum siding, or the fly-by-night work crews in rattletrap trucks towing smoldering pots of black goo who came with offers to pave the driveway from road to house—at a 'steep discount' of course—and carrying lifetime warranties which expired the second the half-assed job was *finished* and money had exchanged hands. Surely the thought of an America overrun by insatiable dead never figured into the former owner's decision-making—he was grateful for it all the same.

As he made his way from the truck to the gate he noticed the all too familiar, sickly sweet stench of death. Craning his head, he looked up and down the road before spotting the culprit. Dragging itself along the shoulder, headed for the gate, was the most pathetic thing Charlie Jenkins had seen during his fifty-plus years on planet Earth.

The crawler fixed its clouded orbs on the Chief's slate-gray eyes, then a slow steady rasping sound, like a small dog working a hairball, escaped the monster's putrid maw.

"Talking loud... ain't saying nothin'," Jenkins muttered, his smartass comment punctuated with a sad chuckle, and then, as if the creature somehow knew what the words meant, or grasped inflection or tone in the meat's voice, it repeated the plaintive, soulless sound.

Although the zombie was but a third of its former human self, devoid of everything navel south and trailing yellowed membrane that had once contained its internal organs, somehow its scrabbling fingernails found purchase and it inched forward, a stalwart determination to feed, its driving force.

Charlie had no idea why he was having a one-sided conversation with the writhing mass of carrion. Maybe, he guessed, two days cooped up in a rural farmhouse with a man of few words and a young woman of even fewer—who he feared had a crushed voice box—was beginning to take its toll. In fact, he had spent the last two days virtually alone in his head thinking about his wife's corpse rotting away in the bathtub in his house on the west side of Driggs, and mourning for his daughter whom he hadn't heard from since the first days of the Omega outbreak. He looked at the pathetic creature and a tear traced his cheek as he considered the possibility she was no different than the hissing crawler he was about to dispatch.

As he unchained the gate, and watched the zombie watching him, he realized he had clipped the formerly ambulatory corpse with the Tahoe two days prior. "Persistent one, ain't you?" he said, clucking his tongue.

That the thing had tenaciously clawed its way along the blacktop, following the vehicle that ran it down, scared the bejeezus out of him.

He wondered whether or not the dead had the dexterity to uncoil a triple-wound length of chain as he swung the gate wide. Then he made a mental note to keep a look out for a lock to replace the one he had been forced to lop off in order to gain access to the property days earlier.

After being conscripted by Ian Bishop, disgraced former Navy SEAL and leader of a mercenary force that had descended onto Jackson Hole, Jenkins hadn't had much time to contemplate what the walking dead might or might not be capable of. During the first two weeks of the zombie apocalypse, his sole job had been to watch over the hard drinking local population of *Essentials*, the men and women who, because of their individual skill sets, had been forced by Robert Christian's king-like decree to stay and *contribute* against their will.

The time and energy it had taken for him to keep them in line, while walking on egg shells so as not to rile the crazy man, afforded him little time to dwell on the what-ifs and shoulda-dones.

He looped the chain around the gate and post. "That oughta hold," he said. "And you, my creepy crawler, what to do with you?"

The creature hissed. Still a good distance away, it posed no threat so Jenkins made an addendum to his earlier mental note: he'd take care of the pitiful wretch when he came back. He had no doubt it would still be here—he only hoped more wouldn't show up.

Chapter 5
Outbreak - Day 15
Southwest of Winters's Compound
Eden, Utah

Thirty minutes of his life had ticked away since Duncan wheeled the SUV from the Eden compound's hidden entrance onto State Route 39. And in that span of time, as he drove west, his passenger talked about his upbringing from day one and shared details about every job he'd held since ten years of age—regardless of pay or tenure.

Finally, after Phillip had seemingly run out of minutiae to talk about, Duncan enjoyed the silence while contemplating the motor-mouth's murder.

"Where are we headed, Sir?" Phillip asked.

It was the fifth time in as many minutes the swarthy-faced middle-aged fella had called him sir. Duncan was beginning to think he had been knighted but had somehow slept through the ceremony, and at any moment his southern drawl was going to disappear and he'd revert to the prim and proper syntax of the Queen's English.

"West by southwest," Duncan replied between clenched teeth. Thankfully he still sounded like his normal self.

"We're going to *Ogden?*" Phil said, sounding quite surprised.

"Not all the way to Ogden. That would be like signing our own death warrant. No, I just want to see what kinda shape Huntsville is in. Maybe we'll skirt the reservoir and do a little foraging."

Outside the Toyota's gray-tinted windows the encroaching forest blasted by, giving way intermittently to flashes of fenced-in range before plunging them back into tree-flanked shadow.

"Huntsville was in bad shape," Phillip proffered. "When me and Ed rolled through a couple of days after the shit hit the fan, the rotters were everywhere. Buildings burning. People looting. Heard a fair amount of shooting as well."

Sorry I mentioned it, Duncan thought to himself. The situation he had gotten himself into brought to mind the car scene in the movie Fargo where Steve Buscemi's character Carl Showalter had lost his cool because the silent, stone-faced driver Gaear, who was also his partner in crime, would not engage in the trivial never-ending conversation during the long road trip. And if Duncan's memory served, by the end of that movie, motor-mouth Carl had met the sharp end of a fire axe before finally ending up in the wood chipper as the credits rolled. Thus, by droning on, Phillip was doing himself no favors.

As they neared Huntsville, the winding blacktop took them past a handful of seemingly deserted farmhouses standing sentinel over rolling hills. Then the trees thinned and the landscape turned khaki, and the rolling hills were replaced by a long narrow valley with a looming hill at the far end.

As the air inside the truck got warmer in relation to the sun's upward climb, Phillip prattled on while Duncan sharpened the axe in his mind. The Vietnam-era aviator remained silent until a sign reading, *Huntsville, Population 608*, flashed by.

Looking over at Phillip, Duncan said, "Six hundred souls... better stay frosty."

On the right, a burnt-to-the-ground gas station flicked by, nothing left of it save for the pumps' skeletal steel frames and a familiar yellow and red *Shell* sign. Duncan felt the transmission downshift as the three and a half ton Toyota took on the substantial climb. Then, as the top neared, Duncan had to swerve to miss a lone shambler. Looking in the side mirror and seeing the gaunt form spin and fall face first, the victim of its own failed motor skills, brought a trace of a smile to his lips.

As soon as the Toyota reached the apex, Duncan noticed a ghastly scene a mile or so away on the road below. Without a moment's hesitation he stabbed the brakes, slewing the truck slightly sideways, and then changed gears and reversed until the big white SUV was completely hidden behind the crest of the hill. No sense in crashing the party below, he reasoned. At least not without first knowing who was in attendance.

Duncan wedged the parking brake and slipped the binoculars around his neck. He nudged the door open with his boot, and slid from the driver's seat. "Come with me Phillip," he said as he grabbed his stubby shotgun.

"Yes Sir," replied Phillip as he clambered onto the road, binoculars in one hand, carbine in the other.

In a half crouch, Duncan deliberately made his way to the hill's crest. "Move slowly and keep your head down. *Do not* provide a silhouette for anyone to take a shot at," he called out over his shoulder.

"Got it," Phillip replied.

As soon as Duncan reached the roadside ditch he went to all fours, then laid flat. He shimmied forward until he could see the entire valley to the fore. The Wasatch Mountains formed a picket in the background while Huntsville and the Pineview reservoir were evident in the foreground—the latter sparkling like a diamond tiara above the town.

He braced his shoulder against a gnarled wooden fencepost and took a long look through his Bushnells, walking them slowly from left to right before returning them to center in order to scrutinize the carnage in the middle of the road. From roughly a mile out, the 10-power binoculars brought things into sharp focus. At the bottom of the grade, where the countryside flattened, a military Humvee protruded from the roadside ditch. In the foreground, a flock of blackbirds, sun glinting from their blued feathers, flapped and jostled, competing to feed on a dozen naked corpses. The scene was like something straight out of a war zone. *Hell*, thought Duncan. *With zombies everywhere, what didn't resemble a war zone these days?*

When Phillip made it to Duncan's side he leaned in and whispered, "Whatcha make of it Sir?"

Duncan said nothing and continued glassing forward. His trained eye told him that the black Rorschach patterns painting the gray roadway were spilled blood, and the fact that the pools were no longer reflecting the sun meant they must have dried some time ago.

"Nothing moving down there 'cept the birds. Still, I want to get a closer look at that vehicle before we make a run at Huntsville."

"Who do you think did them in, Sir?"

"No telling 'til we get closer. But the one thing I know for certain," Duncan said darkly. "The two of us are no match for whoever killed those soldiers."

"What do we do now Sir?" Phillip asked.

Having had his fill of being called sir, Duncan bristled visibly. He cast a glare at Phillip, who was surveying the scene below through binoculars of his own. "We go check it out. Haven't you seen enough, Phillip?" he asked.

"Too much," answered Phillip. He lowered the binoculars and shifted his gaze to Duncan. "Sir... I have a bad feeling about this."

"A little fear is a good thing, Phillip. It keeps us sharp." Duncan rolled over, got to his knees, and stood with an audible grunt.

Nodding in agreement, Phillip rose and without saying a word scooped up his carbine, trotted to the Toyota and clambered aboard.

Before climbing behind the wheel Duncan looked down the hill at the zombie he had nearly clipped. It had recovered fully and was laboriously inching its way uphill towards them. Then he looked at Phillip, who, judging by the look on his face, was formulating yet another question.

Why me? Duncan thought as he unslung his shotgun and strode purposefully down the hill. The female creature raised its arms and hissed as he closed in from the high ground.

Utilizing the flip-down vanity mirror on the back of the visor, Phillip watched the melee from the Cruiser's finely leathered confines.

Duncan stopped just outside of the rotter's reach, leveled his weapon, and jabbed the barrel into its chest. He wanted nothing more than to pull the trigger, but couldn't risk the unwanted attention it would bring. Instead, he backed off, creating a yard of separation, flipped the gun around, and swung for the upper decks. The first blow to the head resounded with an earsplitting crack, knocking the shambler to the ground. Duncan stepped closer before it could rise, and with a chopping motion brought the shotgun down repeatedly on top of its head.

One less to worry about, Duncan told himself as he dragged the dead weight off the road. He wiped the shotgun off in the knee-high grass and trudged back to the truck.

"Holy shit," Phillip blurted the second Duncan slid behind the wheel. "What was that all about? Am I getting on your nerves or something? 'Cause if I am I can put a lid on it. Or shut my trap. Or stow it Vera... I've heard 'em all."

Duncan took a deep cleansing breath, eased the brake off, and popped the rig into drive. He crested the hilltop once again and started the long coast downhill, riding the brakes a little, keeping his speed under twenty-five. "No," he lied. "I didn't want to have to worry about accidently hitting the thing on the return trip."

"Good thinking, Sir," said Phillip.

Partway down the hill, Duncan stopped the Land Cruiser on the center line, turned and said, "Phillip, you seen the movie Fargo?"

"No, I haven't. Why?"

"Never mind," said Duncan. He figured after they checked out the Humvee and got back on the road he'd have a chat with

Phillip. And if that didn't work, he'd sacrifice one of his socks. But, one way or another, their drive to the compound would be in silence.

Chapter 6
Outbreak - Day 15
Schriever Mess Hall
Colorado Springs, Colorado

Raven's breakfast consisted of tepid, over-sweetened oatmeal and a glass of flavorless powdered milk that had all the viscosity of air. How anyone choked the stuff down was beyond her comprehension.

Skipping the brown morass being passed off as hot cereal, Brook opted to drink her breakfast. She sipped at the steaming mug filled with what Cade liked to call "Schriever's finest brown water," while her daughter worried the bowl of oatmeal, concentrating intently on what looked to Brook like an intense game of *stand the spoon up*.

Looking around the mess hall, she noticed that the place was nearly empty. Gone were the civilians who'd made the room full of narrow tables and benches a pain to navigate, clogging the place up with their disorderly back-and-forth forays through the chow line.

Suddenly she wondered why the food she had helped liberate and bring back to Schriever wasn't being served. Surely *all* of the Pop Tarts hadn't been consumed already. Then, for a New York second, she entertained the idea of going around the end of the steam table, strutting confidently behind the three-man crew, making her way to the dry storage and *taking* what she had risked her life to help procure.

Though the look on Raven's face would have been priceless, thankfully the thought was fleeting and gone before Brook acted. For the life of her she couldn't put a finger on why she was obsessing about Pop Tarts. The problem had roots elsewhere, and this was how it had started the last time—before she had gone and begged Colonel Shrill to allow her to tag along on the food run. Only that time her ire had been directed first at her husband, who was already onboard a helicopter and halfway to Jackson Hole, and then she had redirected that anger and taken it out on the inanimate objects in the Grayson billet while Raven looked on in horror.

But that small itch needed to be scratched again. The little imp was sitting on her shoulder telling her how exhilarating it was on the outside, and in less than twenty-four hours—if Mister Murphy didn't intervene—she would be getting her wish. For better or for worse, she and her family would be together without extraneous forces poking their noses in where they didn't belong. In a nutshell, the whole wide world awaited them outside the wire.

Finished with her *breakfast*, Raven dropped the spoon and looked up at her mom.

With a coffee mug clutched in a two-handed death grip, Brook stared blankly into space.

Wearing a devilish grin, the bored twelve-year-old waved a hand in front of her mom's slack face. "Hellooo... anyone home?"

The words had no effect. Pulling out all the stops, Raven conjured up her best hypnotic-sounding voice, regal and high in tone, and said, "When I snap my fingers, you will let me eat as much candy as I want." Raven tried her best to snap her fingers but it was one of the many grown up abilities she had yet to master.

Brook snapped out of the daydream on her own, directed a quizzical look at Raven, and then slowly and methodically glanced over her left shoulder and then her right.

"Why were you staring at me?" Brook whispered.

Suppressing a smile, Raven answered coyly, "No reason, Mom."

Brook cocked her head, thought about something for a second, and then let it slide. "Let's go then. We've got family business to attend to."

She extricated her legs from under the low-slung cafeteria table. After all the meals she had taken here, the place still reminded her of elementary school—minus the sloppy Joes of course. What she wouldn't give for a steaming, greasy, tangy tomato sauce and ground beef slathered hamburger bun. And a cold chocolate milk—real—not powdered. Salivary glands kicking in, she rose and shouldered her M4.

With Raven in tow, Brook arrived at the door at the same time a pair of civilians entered. A redheaded girl, who was talking a mile a minute, came through two steps—and a mouthful of uninterrupted words—ahead of the twenty-something male. He wore a military-style boonie hat jammed low over a shock of bright red hair.

Brook recognized Wilson immediately—he was the kid who had driven the Dakota truck during their foraging mission south of Colorado Springs. And because she was still embarrassed at how poorly she had treated him that day, she tried her best to avoid eye contact. *Don't look over here, do not look over here,* she chanted in her head.

Seemingly heeding her telepathic command, Wilson glanced at her weapon and kept his eyes downcast. Meanwhile, like a monkey on Red Bull, the teenager chattered on.

Raven stepped aside to make way for the redheads.

Home free, Brook thought as the pair passed by on her right. Then, as if in slow motion, his gaze flicked up and met her brown eyes.

Her stomach clenched.

He stopped abruptly, and like he had run into an old, long lost friend blurted out, "*Brooklyn Grayson...?*"

She nodded and felt the blood drain from her face.

Raven scrunched her brow and shot her mom the universal look that said, *Who in the hell is he?*

"It's me... *Wilson!*" he exclaimed. With an explosion of scarlet hair, he took off the boonie hat and repeated himself. "*Wilson...* and how have you been, Missus Grayson?"

"I'm fine..." she lied. "This is my daughter, Raven."

Silence.

"Where are your manners, *Raven?*" Brook uttered through clenched teeth.

Raven faced the tall young man and answered shyly with a forced, "Hi."

"Hi Raven, I'm Wilson."

"You said that already... *three* times."

He winked at Raven, then motioned towards the redhead girl on his left. She was half a foot shorter than he and trying her best to avoid the introduction. "This is my *little* sister, Sasha," he said.

"*Wilson,*" she cried. "Did you have to say it that way?"

"Hi," replied Raven, who by now was warming up to the idea of meeting the strangers.

Brook smiled and offered her hand. "I'm pleased to meet you Sasha."

"Yeah... me too," Sasha replied with all of the sincerity of an IRS agent. Then, turning towards Wilson, she demanded they go.

"*Bye sis,*" he said with a smart ass waggle of his fingers that could be construed as nothing but a blatant shooing motion. Obviously glad to be rid of his sibling, Wilson continued on without missing a beat. "I've heard a *lot* of talk about your husband recently." He paused for a tick. "*And...* about what *really* happened to Ted. He didn't die in the barracks *outbreak...* Ted found out from Nash how William really died... and then *hanged* himself. And that was a direct result of your on-the-fly diagnosis of Pug. Hypothesizing, correctly it turned out, that he had that dual personality thing going on, which led to us collectively putting two and two together and then *unwittingly* sending Ted into an emotional trap... at least unwittingly on *my* part."

There was a short silence. Brook's jaw tremored but she remained silent.

"If you ask me," Wilson went on, "Ted should have been allowed to continue believing that William died peacefully... not told that his partner had been shot in the face while in the madman's presence. By Pug... Francis, whoever the hell he thought he was when he pulled the trigger and then set the infirmary on fire."

"I had no idea Ted would learn the truth," Brook whispered. "I wasn't thinking clearly. I wanted revenge, I guess."

"The truth of the matter is that you withheld information," Wilson said sharply. "The *antiserum*, your *brother*, and God only knows what else. Same as lying. So, now it's time for you to come clean. What did *you* know and *when* did you know it?"

Brook swallowed, processed the information, yet said nothing.

Sensing she was being exposed to a whole lot of information that was supposed to remain locked down in the grown up *need to know* files, Raven tried to remain invisible so she could collect more *Intel* as she'd heard her dad call secret stuff.

"I've been *hoping* to run into you for the past two days now," Wilson went on. "Apparently the few of us civilians who survived the *outbreak* can't be seen rubbing elbows with the Army folk. Now me and Sasha are staying where the scientists used to live. Nicer digs... a little *haunted* though. Like someone left some unfinished business. And seeing as how I now know most of what really happened the day after Pug and the rest of us got here...I understand why you've been avoiding me."

For a tick Brook stared at him, and then she breathed out and closed her eyes. She heard the clank of service on ceramic. The sound of an industrial dishwasher, sloshing and whirring on ad nauseam, emanated from somewhere in the back of the kitchen. Voices engaged in small talk, serious sounding words and everything in-between—all drowned out by the sound of her rapidly beating heart and the heavy rush of hot blood flooding her head. Sure she could handle getting dirty. Shooting Zs... No problem. They weren't human anymore. But dealing with the truths that Wilson had just spewed in front of her... Big steaming piles of righteous words that cut to the bone—it was almost too much for her to process, let alone answer to.

"Mom, are you OK?"

Brook tried to breathe normally, to calm herself down so she could respond. Short shallow gulps brought air into her lungs. She longed to sit down but her limbs wouldn't answer the signals from her brain.

Still waiting for a response, Wilson shifted on his feet and moved aside to let an airman, who had just entered from outside, slip between them. He crossed his arms, hoping for an apology. *Anything but silence*, he thought.

"Truth hurts... huh," he stated. "The *outbreak* the other night wasn't isolated to the civilians' barracks. Sash and me were right here,"—he pointed at the floor—" and we saw a man get his throat torn out. People are talking, and it doesn't take an effin rocket scientist to connect the dots—just a former Fast Burger manager—and I've been all ears."

"Yes. Yes it does. The truth hurts more than you know," croaked Brook. "I'm truly sorry. I wronged you on so many levels. Some of those things I wasn't even supposed to know."

"Cade?"

"Yeah," she replied. "If you knew half of the things that I know my husband has done for this country over the years you'd understand why I couldn't say anything." She paused and gazed down at Raven, who appeared to not be listening. She was kind of lost in her own pre-teen world.

Wilson's eyes bored into hers.

"In case you haven't been keeping score," Brook added, "just in the last week the President authorized the use of nuclear weapons on U.S. soil..."

"Forty effin miles from here. And you think that hasn't crossed my mind, lady? I'm twenty, not stupid... but for what it's worth, I forgive you. Doesn't bring Ted back though. But I still forgive you."

Brook drew Raven close and swallowed hard, choking back tears. "Why?" she mumbled.

"Because I saw how you disregarded your own safety and rushed to help that little girl. And then how you handled it when things went sideways... that speaks to your character."

How old is this kid? thought Brook. Because what he'd just said made him seem wise beyond his years.

"Wilson... your breakfast is cold," Sasha called out, her shrill voice carrying across the mess hall.

He said nothing, turned, and reluctantly joined his bleating kid sister.

Then, as Brook and Raven made a second attempt to leave the mess hall, the flat light of summer burst through the door, and in followed another young person. She stood an inch or two taller than Brook, and wore her raven black hair braided into a ponytail that tickled the small of her back. The young woman's silver nose ring, boldly tattooed arms and black painted fingernails shored up Brook's first impression: the beautiful creature had to be nearly two decades younger than her. *Where are they all coming from?* she asked herself. And then suddenly she felt old. Not wise and worldly from her three and a half decades on planet Earth. Not wily and resourceful because she had kept herself and her young daughter alive in the face of so much adversity. No. In the younger woman's presence, she just felt old. Then, out of the blue, she thought about her mom. Not the Omega-infected being that *used* to be her mom. Brook had worked very hard at purging that final awful image from her memory—the one featuring the bloody corpse dragging itself down the carpeted hallway in her childhood home in Myrtle Beach. No, the thought that had just popped into her head wasn't visual. It was her mom's soothing voice repeating a favorite saying that she had never attributed to anyone in particular. It wasn't Ralph Waldo Emerson or Louisa May Alcott, it was simple and to the point just like her mom had always been, and she had uttered it at the last birthday Brook had attended and every one prior. 'Brook my dear,' she used to say. 'I'm not sixty; I'm eighteen with forty-two years of experience.' It was a piece of wisdom disguised in joke form, and always delivered with a happy cackle and a wink.

God, how Brook missed the woman. She pulled Raven close to her hip, giving her a half hug on the move. The action drew a look from Raven that said, *Mom, you're weird.*

Making a concerted effort to hide her emotion as they finally left the hall, Brook looked toward the Rocky Mountains and covertly erased the forming tears.

Chapter 7
Outbreak - Day 15
Yoder, Colorado

After talking to Daymon for a couple of minutes and hearing the encouraging news about his girlfriend, Heidi, Cade spent a few moments contemplating his new reality.

Try as he might, he still found it hard to fathom how suddenly and completely his country had fallen to the dead. He considered that before the onset of the Omega virus there had been upwards of two hundred and fifty million firearms in the United States, and at least half as many citizens ready, willing, and able to use them. That, combined with the vast numbers of people who tuned in to watch prepper TV shows, or were actually actively preparing for a world-changing event like a financial collapse, or for a few more who were on the fringes—the zombie apocalypse—the fact that so few survivors remained was hard to wrap his mind around. It was almost like every man, woman, and child had shit themselves on the spot and then offered up their jugular at first sight of a real walking corpse.

He sat inside the Ford and observed the upstairs windows for any signs of life. After two or three minutes had elapsed and the curtains remained drawn and hadn't so much as fluttered, he was confident that the upper story was free of the dead—he could only hope the same would hold true for the downstairs.

He shifted his gaze to the ground level. *This was going to be a tough nut to crack*, he told himself. The manner in which *Abe's Value Hardware* had been boarded up made the former Delta operator think Scotty had beamed him to New Orleans or Galveston or any number of Gulf Coast cities where hurricanes routinely ravaged the people and structures caught in their path. Here in Yoder, Abe—or whoever had swung a hammer for the store's namesake—had gone to great lengths to protect the contents of the two-story brick building. Quarter-inch plywood covered the front door glass. Four larger wood sheets covered what Cade assumed were massive panes of plate glass flanking the entry on the ground level. On them, a warning had been rattle can sprayed, in black, and it read, 'LOOTERS WILL GLADLY BE SHOT ON SIGHT.' Cade supposed the comedian who posted the semi-humorous message had been witness to the grocery across the street being ransacked, and was merely trying to protect his livelihood from the same animalistic desperation shown by those looters. And judging by the hardware store's front facade, which had been splattered with dark crimson smudges and scores of smeared bloody handprints, Abe's fortifications had spared the store and whoever might still be inside from a fate much more sinister.

The rearview mirror showed Cade that the main drag to his six was still clear. The walkers that he had just dispatched lay where they had fallen, the rotten bodies twisted into various death poses. Lastly, the small throng that had been advancing from the east while he was engaging the others still were half a block distant.

Getting trapped in the store would be massively stupid. Been there, done that, no thanks to Mister Hosford Preston. Big Hoss had paid the ultimate price for leading the dead to the country home in Hannah, Utah—the type of price Cade wasn't willing to pay. *Plenty of things still left to tackle on the ol' bucket list*, he mused.

Cade turned the key and the engine roared to life. He powered down the driver's glass, shifted into drive, and let the idling power plant pull the truck ahead at a walking speed. Keeping his right hand on the wheel, he thrust the suppressed Glock out the window. The F650 had ungodly-sized mirrors protruding from both A-pillars. *Good for towing*, he thought, *but awful for lining up a shot on the move.*

Parking the rig sideways, perpendicular to the half-dozen shamblers in his line of sight, he brought the semi-automatic to bear on them. All but one of the Zs looked to have been dead a long time. Cade's pistol chugged twice. The freshest member of the group lost its head from the eyebrows up, timbered forward and ceased moving. He shifted aim by a few degrees, aligned the sights on the female walker to his right and squeezed off two closely spaced shots. The first 9mm slug left the muzzle riding three hundred and fifty foot pounds, impacted low and to the right from where he had aimed, carving out a shredded fleshy cavern and taking a sizable chunk of cheek and jawbone with it. A millisecond later the unfazed first turn marched headlong into the second speeding bullet which entered its right eye socket and exited out back along with the entire contents of its cranium. The wet mess, propelled by an incredible amount of kinetic energy, spread out and splashed the four remaining monsters with something resembling rancid ground chuck.

Cade moved his aim right but found the telescoping side mirror between him and any kind of a reasonable shot, so he backed off the brake and goosed the accelerator. The truck lurched forward a yard or so, leaving him a better angle on target; as he waited their approach, the creatures started in with their raspy snarls, setting the hairs on his neck standing on end.

He drew a bead on the blinding white pate of the nearest and put a closely spaced double-tap into the center of the horseshoe-shaped clearing atop the Z's head. Then he walked six rapid-fire shots across a flat plane. Halos of pink mist bloomed into the air as the three flesh eaters fell to the blacktop in a moldering heap.

Cade changed magazines with practiced movements, placed the pistol on the seat and powered the truck through a tight one-eighty. He rolled up adjacent to the hardware store with the Ford's pug-like snout pointing west towards Colorado Springs and the thin smudge of mountains on the horizon. Then, with the Ford straddling the curb and blocking the recessed entrance to Abe's, he slid across the leather bench, popped the door, and jumped out onto the sidewalk.

Chapter 8
Outbreak - Day 15
Schriever AFB
Colorado Springs, Colorado

Trying his best to remain calm, cool, and collected—when in fact his guts were churning—Wilson covertly tracked the new girl out of the corner of his eye. The sensation in his stomach reminded him of the teen angst he'd lived with all throughout high school. Wanting so badly to talk to the new girl, any girl for that matter, on the first day of school—the hours spent building up false self-confidence until lunch period—then the shame he'd shouldered because he could never follow through. The pressure cooker build up coupled with the lack of release made him feel like the antithesis of Yellowstone Park's Old Faithful.

"She's coming this way," Sasha said, a little too loud for comfort.

Might as well use a megaphone, Wilson thought. His face flushed hot as he panned his head back to twelve o'clock, then tore his eyes from her, panned them forward, slowly, incrementally, only to meet Sasha's prosecutorial gaze. "Who is *she* and what the heck are you talking about Sis?"

"Her," Sasha said, pointing at the dark haired young woman with a stabbing motion of her spoon. "You've been hawking her

51

since she walked in the door. Like a cheetah watching a gazelle. Heck, if you had a tail, Wilson, it would have been twitching. *Nothing,* and I mean *nothing,* gets past me." Sasha smiled, then shoveled in another spoonful of oatmeal.

"I wasn't watching her..." he lied, dragging out the word *'her'* as if the lithe, toned and tanned woman were well below his standards—she a mutt and he the star quarterback. In reality, a puddle of mental drool an inch deep had pooled around his boots on the Formica floor.

"I'm calling bullshit, Wilson," Sasha blurted.

He stared daggers. "Language, Sash."

Busting his balls in new and different ways was a constantly evolving talent in which Sasha took great pride. The frequency and tone had gotten worse since their mom had gone missing the day Washington D.C. fell to the dead. He didn't understand her. Most kids her age found pleasure in reading. Some even enjoyed lusting over the long dead and gone boy bands. Sasha—she just enjoyed fucking with him. He had to hand it to the fourteen-year-old; she had a knack for getting under his skin. And when she found a chink in his armor—which happened often because there were many—the needling and jabbing and prodding usually commenced until either his Irish temper made an appearance and he made an ass of himself, or he disengaged from the conversation silently, seething. Either way Sasha usually won.

She's coming this way, he thought to himself. He dabbed a paper napkin across his brow and then wiped his palms on his khaki cargo shorts.

Then in that sing-song voice, Sasha said, "What's a matter *Casanova...* you nervous?"

The room seemed to contract and then expand, like it was alive, and the steady thrum of the generators and the whooshing hood system in the kitchen was the sound of its breathing. He gripped the table to steady himself, then shot her an icy glare. Then his mom's voice entered his head, recounting the advice she had given him the day he went for that first Fast Burger interview. *"Remember to be confident. Be in control of the situation at all times. And Wilson,"* she had said, *"be yourself."* The memory of her face and her soothing voice smothered the looming anxiety attack. The events of that day seemed to have happened years ago. In reality, only months had passed since *interview day.* And only weeks had passed since Z day. How he would apply Mom's advice here and now, with the girl ten feet away and closing fast, he had no idea. But he did have a strong suspicion he was about to find out.

"Here she comes," Sasha chided.

"Shhh!" he said as he hunched his shoulders, trying to make himself smaller—to disappear altogether.

She stopped behind him. "What's the matter Red... got a flat?" Her husky voice made him jump, nearly stopped his jack-rabbiting heart.

"Who, me?" he stammered.

"You were the one *shushing*," she answered.

Silence.

"May I join?" she asked. "'Cause everyone else in here's a dinosaur."

Sasha continued to chew her food and motioned to the bench next to her with the spoon.

Wilson gaped at the new arrival, who smelled like sunshine—or a dryer sheet, he couldn't decide. At any rate, his mom's posthumous advice disappeared the moment the girl had spoken, leaving him with a choice to make: run—or as Sasha had so eloquently put it—*"grow a pair and wing it."* He chose the latter.

The breakfast rush was now in full swing all around them.

"You shoulda been here the other day. They had *Pop-Tarts*," Sasha said, breaking the ice. She raised her eyebrows an inch and went on, "Freakin' *cherry* Pop-Tarts... thought I was in heaven."

New Girl placed her tray next to Sasha, and then took a seat on the bench directly across from Wilson, who had a lock on her like a cat on a canary.

"Taryn," she said, extending her hand across the table.

After a few quick swipes against the cool fabric of his khakis, he reciprocated with a clammy offering of his own.

"My name's Wilson," he stammered. He motioned to his sister with a flourish and an upturned palm. Instantly he felt silly. "And she is..."

"My name is Sasha," she said, flashing the brunette a toothy grin. Then, after extending her pale freckled hand, she added, "Wilson *should* have stopped talking for me when I was like... three or four. But I'm not surprised 'cause he's been doing it my whole life." Sasha punctuated the statement by delivering her brother a look that said, *You owe me or I will* ruin *this for you.*

While Sasha and Taryn exchanged pleasantries, Wilson caught himself staring at the skulls and dragons and various dangerous looking things inked up and down the young woman's arms. Full sleeves, he thought. His mind reeled, wondering where the artwork stopped—or whether it continued on under the fabric of her form-fitting black tank. He was smitten, and it showed.

Sasha pushed her tray forward, leaned back in her chair and twirled a long scarlet lock with one hand. Clearly she was enjoying seeing Mister *I'm in charge now that Mom isn't here* squirming under the Klieg lights of life.

Suddenly at a loss for words, Wilson picked at the bowl full of spackle. He studied the wall above the entry where someone had painted a blue badge. A unit insignia he guessed. On it was a white creature with the body of a horse, the head of a dragon and wings like a Pegasus. Written in blue, on a curled herald at the bottom of the shield, were the words: *Master of Space.* And though he hadn't paid too much attention to mythology in school, he had a hunch that the thing might be a Griffin.

Taryn stared across the table and addressed Wilson directly. "Kinda the tall, dark, and quiet type, huh? Only the dark part... not so much." She smiled and laughed at her own joke.

"With skin like this, SPF *two thousand* doesn't cut it," he said. *That was easier than you thought, Wilson,* is what he didn't. Before his mojo disappeared, and while he had a scant amount of forward momentum going in this —*talking to girls thing*—he recounted their journey from the Viscount in Denver to the gates of Schriever.

Seeing an opportunity to bring Casanova down a notch, Sasha elaborated on their stop in Castle Rock and all of the gory details of her run in with Sam the undead butcher and her involvement in Operation Arm Removal.

With a fresh trace of pink painting his cheeks, Wilson downplayed his adverse reaction to the dead appendage clutching his red mane, but didn't waste the opportunity to talk up his skill at driving, which he credited for getting them all to Schriever in one piece. Strangely enough, neither he nor Sasha mentioned Pug's murderous spree or the dominos that had fallen since. Sasha, he guessed, didn't want to expend the energy. His motive was different. He didn't want to spoil this moment by dredging it all up. *Two days was two days*, he thought. Soon he would forget about the past and get on with living. He just wanted to heed Mom's advice and *be himself*.

Sounding neither repulsed nor impressed by the epic tale, Taryn quietly said, "Sounds like you two ran the gauntlet."

"Now that you know our story, how did you end up here?" Sasha probed.

Taryn looked up and fixed her gaze on the redheaded teen.

On the receiving end of a look she couldn't interpret, Sasha squirmed. She was beginning to regret prying into the new girl's business. But Wilson was her brother, she reminded herself, and it was her job to evaluate *anyone* he had eyes for—whether he liked it or not.

Taryn regarded the people around her. The place was hopping now. Then her thoughts raced back to Grand Junction Airport, Dickless and the others who had died after the planes brought the plague. Some were her friends—most were not. She needed a diversion, a second to decide if she wanted to spill her guts here in front of strangers, or choose a more appropriate time and place to recount her week and a half in hell.

"I *totally* understand if you don't want to talk about it. And I'm *really* sorry if *anything* I said upset you," Sasha said. *What have you got to hide, Miss Tattoo?* a silent voice in her head whispered.

Taryn stood up abruptly, looked toward the kitchen, but said nothing.

You blew it, Wilson, the condescending naysayer in his head told him.

Silently Taryn policed her trash, piled it on the tray, and walked towards the garbage cans. And as she retreated Wilson watched, trying his best not to look at her rear end. He failed miserably.

Once Wilson was certain Taryn was out of earshot, he unloaded. "Thanks a lot *Sasha.* I had something good going there until you had to go all graphic about you and the zombie butcher. And you definitely didn't need to tell her *all* about that zombie hand stuck in my hair. Think about it Sash... if you were in her shoes would you want anything to do with me after hearing that kinda stuff?"

Touché, Sasha thought. Then, subconsciously, she reached down to massage her bare ankle which still bore the yellow-green bruising caused by the big zombie's death grip.

An uncomfortable silence ensued between her and Wilson as she observed Taryn dump her tray into a bus tub and then proceed to weave her way through the tables and chairs on her way back to where they all were sitting together. Sasha turned her full attention across the table. "*Wilson...* you need to grow a *pair* and ask her out."

Unsure of how to process the accusation that he was a freaking *eunuch,* he tilted his head back and stared at the acoustic ceiling tiles. Next, the Griffin painting received more scrutiny from him. Finally, as he gazed off into the distance, through the row of small rectangular windows near the ceiling, he broke his silence. "Where do you propose I take her, a drive-in movie? Colorado Springs Fast Burger store number 65?" he asked, his voice a near whisper and his head on a swivel anticipating Taryn's return.

"She is vulnerable, Wilson. Strike while the iron is hot."

"You're *fourteen,* Sasha... where in the heck did you hear that saying?"

"The Young and the Restless."

"Figures."

The same sweet smell accompanied Taryn when she returned. *Definitely not dryer sheets*, thought Wilson as the same heady feeling overwhelmed him. He pulled it together, and as absurd as his sister's advice had seemed, he was a nanosecond from asking her out and proving that he had a *pair...*

"So you want to show me around?" Taryn asked, beating him to the punch. She stood next to him, waiting for an answer. Close enough that her bare thigh brushed his elbow, sending a wave of current through his body. *If this were a comedy on the big screen*, he thought, *her character would have been tapping an imaginary watch.* But this wasn't a comedy, and Wilson's heart knew it, even if his imagination didn't.

He sat there feeling the warmth of her touch and paused for a half a beat, crafting in his head an eloquent way to say yes—but this time Sasha beat him to the punch. *Shit*, he thought. Good thing he wasn't a fighter, because with all of the openings he was missing he'd have been knocked out cold by now.

"We can both show—"

"Not you, little miss," Taryn snapped. "Just your brother and me. My story is rated NC-17."

Sasha glared, but kept her brother's best interests in heart and saved her comments for later.

Ignoring his sister's hurt feelings, Wilson rose. He took a calming breath, then looked into Taryn's dark eyes. "I'd be happy to do you—" He chuckled nervously at the little Freudian slip. "Let me try that again. I'd be happy to show you around." And wondering what the rest of the afternoon had in store, he followed his new friend out into the waiting daylight.

Chapter 9
Outbreak - Day 15
Yoder, Colorado

Cade made a fist and pounded violently on the locked door, putting all of his hundred and eighty pounds behind each blow. He gave the occupants a five count to respond, and when the store remained quiet, reared back and planted a solid kick below the door handle. To his amazement, nothing happened, save for the painful resonance that shot through his size nine Danners and shivered up his right leg. Undeterred, he tested the jamb by putting his shoulder against the decades-old hardwood and leaning in. Sensing a little give, he decided to once again attempt the Danner method of entry.

Boots soles scuffing the sidewalk, he took a short hop and leaned into the kick, this time with a healthy dose of follow through behind it. Two things happened at once: the window sandwiched behind the plywood sheet exploded, depositing a thousand tiny glass kernels out the bottom slot-machine style. Then, the jamb splintered from the impact and the door flung inward, sending the brass bell atop the door jangling. Quickly he reached up and silenced the old-world precursor to the oft used photo-electric eye, and then he paused for a moment to retrieve his tactical flash light from a cargo pocket. His head moving on a swivel and his other senses on full alert, he thumbed it on and entered the hardware store.

The air inside was warm and reeked of death with an underlying trace of fertilizer and lawn chemicals. Disturbed by the violent entry, golden dust motes danced by his face. He stepped out and into the alcove, took two deep cleansing breaths, and then looked east through the slice of daylight beside the Ford, then west, and then east once again for good measure. Nothing moved in downtown Yoder.

After padding over the remains of the destroyed window, he reentered *Abe's* with the Glock's tubular suppressor leading the way. Keeping his eyes scanning his flanks and the aisles ahead, he nudged the door closed with his right elbow. *Anybody here?* he thought as he lowered his breathing and strained to hear anything moving among the shadowy aisles. *Nothing.*

He pointed the flashlight down the nearest aisle, and with two-hundred lumens lancing the dark, set out to fill his shopping list.

After treading through the paint section, he came to a T and paused in front of a wall that held hundreds of metallic key blanks and dozens of colorful fobs to attach them to. He snatched one that caught his attention and stuffed it in his pocket. He had no idea where the impulse came from, but the blue and white Ford oval would be more practical than the gaudy bling currently weighing down his pants.

Feeling the soft give of worn boards underfoot, he padded deeper into the store. As he heel-and-toed his way past a display complete with fake plastic grass and a couple of lawnmowers and rototillers, the air suddenly grew warmer and the scent of carrion grew stronger—nearly overwhelming him. He stopped instantly and listened intently. Nothing moved. Except for the steady beating of his heart, there was silence. His Suunto told him he'd been inside for two minutes. *Time to move.* He didn't want to allow the dead enough time to amass outside.

Black pistol in a two-handed grip, he transited a few more aisles, and where his eyes tracked so did the Glock. Instantly his hackles arose and he froze in mid-stride. The lingering stench had become so concentrated that he could almost feel it. Though there wasn't a superstitious bone in his body, and he knew the sensation was but a figment of his imagination, it still seemed like he had walked into a viscous wall of death. He likened the sensation that caused his skin to crawl to some kind of inbred prehistoric survival mechanism similar to the fight or flight instinct. Similar, he guessed, to the tactic employed by department stores whereby they secretly pumped in pleasant scents like fresh baked cookies, lavender, or jasmine, all in order to subliminally affect their customers' spending habits. Only this pong didn't affect the pleasure center of his brain, it made him want to bolt to the street and inhale another fresh lungful of Colorado air, not bust out the credit card and start buying shit.

Breathing only through his mouth, he pushed deeper into the gloom. As he neared what he guessed had to be the rear of the retail part of the store, he noticed a sound that had become very familiar over the last couple of weeks. For somewhere in the dark, the livewire buzzing of hundreds of insects foreshadowed the scene he stumbled upon next.

His flashlight beam caught the pair of tan work boots first and then he walked the cone of light to the left, revealing the rest of the corpse which he supposed had been there for a week or more. Stretched across the skull, and pulling his eyes to slits, the older man's skin had gone tight. It looked unnatural, waxen-like. The body, belonging to the man Cade assumed was Abe, was prone on the floor and covered by a busy black carpet of common houseflies. Abe's blood had long ago dried black. That he had eaten the barrel of the dull gray semi-automatic still gripped in his hand was clearly evident. His front teeth and lips had been shredded by the blast and peppering the milky white of his chin and cheeks, a constellation of black powder burns. The epilogue to Abe's sad story was revealed as Cade flicked the light up the far wall. Remnants of gray matter and splintered skull and hair had become embedded in the drywall where the blast from the .45 had scattered them. The owner's presence helped explain the gore orgy out front, and Cade knew from experience that once a pack of Zs had cornered some fresh meat they rarely gave up until their hunger was sated—or they died again trying. He eyed the AR-15 and pair of semi-automatic pistols lying near the man's body, knowing full well they were the reason his store still stood while the ones nearby fell. The thought brought back a vivid memory from Cade's youth—glued to CNN, watching Korean shop owners protecting their turf from the mayhem that spread throughout Los Angeles immediately after the Rodney King verdict had been announced. In his mind's eye he could almost picture Abe upstairs, rifle poking between the curtains, fending off the living by any means necessary, and then watching helplessly as the reanimated corpses moaned and growled, announcing their hunger-fueled need to get inside. To get at the meat the primeval part of their brains told them was holed up behind the brick, mortar, and plywood.

Cade knew the feeling of being completely surrounded, dangerously low on ammunition, all hope ebbing. Abe must have been feeling like those Koreans, he reasoned—stuck between Desperation Avenue and Hopeless Drive, out of ammo and with no officers from Rampart Division dispatching to save him—at least Abe had spared one for himself.

With no chance of a working cure to Omega or a way to reproduce Fuentes's antiserum on the immediate horizon, Cade had decided unequivocally that before he became one of them, putting a bullet in his brain would be his final act on earth.

Brushing the unsettling picture from his mind was as easy as shaking an Etch-a-Sketch. He'd cross that bridge when he got to it. Right here and now, he had a task to attend to and little time in which to complete it.

He shook his head as he stepped over the rigor-frozen body. The sudden movement scattered the feeding flies in every direction, their shiny blue and black bodies glinting in the dim light. They buzzed him, making angry Kamikaze dives at his head, pulling up at the last moment before zipping back to their carrion meal. *From whence they came,* Cade mused.

Before continuing on, he looked at Abe's body one final time. *Giving back to the food chain.* He threw a shudder and wondered who the real winner in the room was. *Living, these days,* he thought grimly, *seems to be nothing more than a holding pattern of misery to endure while awaiting the inevitable.*

The next aisle over contained the most important item on his list. For a brief moment he stood stock-still, second guessing himself, wondering if quitting the Unit for the second time in fifteen months was the right move. Leaving Nash high and dry— the one desk jockey who always had his back. Then Whipper's parting barb resonated in his head: '*You're the fucking hypocrite.*' No, he thought, shaking his head. His family was the most important thing, and if he continued putting them second, then Whipper's statement *was* the truth. Family was what had possessed him to go to these lengths to test himself, and his desire to return to his family would see him through.

Pushing the mental flotsam and jetsam from the forefront of his mind, he switched back into mission mode. He grabbed the rectangular cardboard box which had been stored next to the fully assembled demonstration model. He scrutinized the shipping label. The color was correct. *Check.* Size and style, *check, and check.* Satisfied, he hefted the box which was about a foot deep and roughly the size of a larger model flat screen TV. He clamped the tactical light between his teeth, carted the ungainly rectangle through the aisles to the front door, and propped it across the threshold leaning against the splintered wood casing. At the very least the thirty pound container might slow down a walker trying to gain entry and make a meal of him.

The next five minutes blurred by. He stopped at the lawn care aisle to liberate a four-foot length of neon orange garden hose. The Gerber's honed edge made short work and he left the length of hose in the aisle to collect on his way out. He made a right turn, and ignoring the plastic snow discs and toboggans that would never see a ski hill, padded down the automotive aisle. Every type of lubricant, their colorful labels vying for attention, filled the shelves from floor level to a foot above his head. *Where to start?* he asked himself. Once again the flashlight went between his teeth. He opened the lawn debris bag wide and tumbled several quarts of motor oil—and with the last run of hundred degree days fresh on his mind—thought it prudent to include two large jugs of Prestone antifreeze. And then, as an afterthought, he pulled down four Fix-a-Flat canisters from the uppermost shelf.

From the end cap he poached three spare gas cans to add to the ones he'd taken from the motor pool. In fact, most of the items needed for their cross country trek he could have demanded from Whipper, if push came to shove. But seeing as it already had, and he'd gone beyond just shoving the first sergeant, he decided to take what he needed from old Abe instead.

Broken glass crackled and popped underfoot as he deposited the second lawn bag full of supplies next to the entry. He slid the bulky box aside and cracked the door a few inches, causing a new batch of broken glass to cascade from the doorframe. Instantly, hollow moans began echoing off of the makeshift plywood walls flanking the shallow entryway. Cade stuck his head around the jamb and stole a glance at the opening between his ride's undercarriage and the sidewalk. His blood ran cold, then, in his head, he heard Desantos's voice calmly say, *'Make it home, Wyatt.'*

With the specter of being trapped inside with the proprietor's rotting corpse, and who knows how many ambulatory ones on the outside, he kept his feet away from the clutching hands and heaved his ill-gotten supplies over his head and into the truck bed. The bulky box went in last, and though it took a little coaxing, he managed to catapult it up and over where it landed with a crunch atop everything else.

He risked one last foray into Abe's final resting place to take a white silk rose from a plastic vase near the register. He reentered the alcove with a renewed sense of optimism. Then he went to one knee, and with glass shards digging into his patella and at least ten hungry eyed Zs worming their way underneath the four-by-four's protective off-roading skid plates, he aimed at the nearest creature but held his fire. A niggling sense of uncertainty gnawed at him because he was aware that there were a pair of gas tanks mounted somewhere underneath the truck body, but he had no idea where in relation to the wriggling corpses. The last thing he needed was for a bullet to ricochet, hit one of the oversize tanks and send the F-650 up in a blaze of glory, killing him along with it.

But it was a chance he had to take. He went prone on his stomach with the suppressed Glock wavering four feet from the snarling faces. "Come and get me. Dinner time," he called out, urging them forward, hoping to drop a few in the front that would slow down the ones behind so he could get inside the truck. Their hissing grew in volume, a cacophony of insistent cries and snapping teeth. Reacting to the sound of his voice, the creatures that were out of sight crushed in from the back—the whole scene reminded Cade of a Black Friday Walmart mob. He waited a few ticks until the monsters were wedged in one atop the other, smashed shoulder to shoulder, effectively blotting the daylight between the front and rear wheels. Keeping his aim level with the ground, he steadied his breathing and tried his best to ignore the pale hands grasping at the protruding suppressor. With thirty some odd gallons of gas suspended somewhere above the writhing creatures, he decided against the mandatory double-tap and instead walked the Glock methodically from right to left shooting a half dozen of them squarely in the face.

"Look who gets to be a speed bump," he said matter-of-factly. He sprang from the ground and entered the truck through the passenger door, being very careful to keep his lower extremities from the flailing hands. He scooted across the seat and placed the still smoking pistol in the open console next to him. It was hot inside the cab, smelled of leather and still had that plastic new car smell, though not enough to mask the undead stench. Something impacted the door near his thigh, then another resounded. Hollow thumps that told him they knew he was there, and though he really didn't want to see how many of them were on the street side of the truck, he pressed his face against the glass and looked anyway. *Not so bad*, he thought to himself as he quickly counted a dozen or so zombies pressing against the Ford, milky eyes fixed on his window, nails scratching the sheet metal. Reflected in the side mirror, he could see the scrabbling legs of the persistent few still trying to burrow their way under.

He closed his eyes and said a silent prayer, then fished the gilded basketball from his pocket and slipped the key into the ignition. He started the engine running, slammed it into drive, and stabbed the gas pedal. A shrill chirp sounded from the truck's rear end and then the off-road tires clawed into the backs of the dead, churning tattered clothes and putrid flesh into the wheel wells. Cade heard a series of beeps emanate from the dash and noticed a little icon flashing on the instrument cluster as the traction control computer sensed the tires losing their grip in the gore and automatically locked the differential for him.

As the tires grabbed, the brute force torque produced by the howling V-10 was transferred through the bodies and the Ford rocketed ahead. Cade bounced in his seat and the cargo in back slid across the bed and slammed into the tailgate with a resounding bang. He flicked his eyes to the rearview mirror. Thankfully, the box was still in the back but it had come dangerously close to tumbling out. So he stabbed the brakes and brought everything skittering back towards the cab, where it came to rest in a disorganized pile. *Close call*, he thought. To come all this way and then lose the most important item on his list wouldn't have made the trip a complete failure, but it would have been disheartening to say the least.

Chapter 10
Outbreak - Day 15
Ovid, Colorado

It could have gone either way. That much Elvis was certain of. One minute he was helping bag the bodies of folks he had just murdered, and the next he was laying in his bunk at Schriever waiting for one of two things to happen. Either he'd been fingered by one of the survivors and rough men with rifles were going to show up and escort him to a room where he would suffer through a very long interrogation session. Or his new friend Private Farnsworth was going to pull up at the agreed upon time, toot his horn like he had done three days running, and punish him with base gossip and inane conversation all the way to the job site.

In the end the latter won out. But in a way, Elvis had expected the rough men to show up and he had even romanticized the notion that he would wrestle a gun from one of them and go out shooting.

Now, two days removed from his terrorist act and after he'd had plenty of time to evaluate how he had prosecuted it, he would be the first to admit the whole affair had been thought out poorly, but not as poorly as the drive to the mass graves had ended for the Farns. Elvis had waited until they'd reached the job site and Farns had handed over the same .45 pistol from the glove box that Elvis had used to protect himself from the Zs three days running. Then after disabling the dozer, he had lured Farnsworth from his pickup truck with a ruse about needing help to get the machine started. Elvis executed the gullible private from a foot away as he was reconnecting the dozer's coil wire. The big slug did a number on the blonde private's head. In fact his face had been unrecognizable when Elvis buried the still cooling corpse under four feet of dirt. Then to cover up his tracks—literally—Elvis had left the fifty-ton D9 tractor parked directly over the evidence and then drove off in the dead man's GMC pickup.

He drove nonstop one hundred and fifty miles east from Schriever on the 70 in order to avoid the Castle Rock fallout, then he made his way due north following 385 for another one hundred and twenty-five miles along the Colorado/Kansas state line, bypassing the fortified city of Julesburg before stopping for the night in Ovid, Colorado, a stone's throw from the Nebraska border.

***

As Elvis sat in the folding chair in the uppermost story of the abandoned house he had been calling home for the last two days, he had a sudden urge to visit the town of his alma mater. He looked out the dormer window across the flat Nebraska landscape toward where he figured there had to be someone he knew. Then reality set in, and though he bled Husker football scarlet and cream he knew that if he went back to Lincoln with its quarter of a million people—most of them hungering for flesh—he would end up bleeding scarlet for real.

Since arriving at Ovid, as well as the conclusion that the only thing he could do would be to come clean and reconcile the past, he had been dialing the same phone number twice daily—the only number that he knew might get him into contact with Ian Bishop.

He thumbed on the Iridium satellite phone, keyed in eleven numbers from memory, and waited while it rang—after six, a man answered. Elvis was speechless; he hadn't thought this one through very well either, so he just blurted out what he needed to say. "Ian, this is Elvis. You need to know something... The last time Robert Christian called me he ordered me to kill you." He said it so fast he wasn't certain Bishop caught it all, but he was relieved it was out in the open.

There was a moment of silence on the line, then Bishop said, "I know. I bugged the house *and* his phone."

This revelation sent Elvis's head spinning as he tried to recollect what it was exactly that he'd said to Robert Christian after the edict had been issued. Then he rolled with it. "I wasn't going to do it. I promise," he stammered, as visions of rusty nails being driven through his hands and feet made him shudder. "And just so you know, Robert Christian was kidnapped and taken to Schriever by a Delta team led by a man named Cade Grayson. That's all I know... and now that Christian is gone, my loyalty lies with you."

"I know about it all," replied Bishop calmly. "No blood, no foul."

Elvis took a second to process his part in things.

"Still there?" asked Bishop.

"Yes. I heard Jackson Hole fell to the monsters. Where are you now?"

"You heard correctly," Bishop intoned. "Do you have something you can write with?"

"One second." Elvis looked around the converted attic. There was a craft table by the far wall that looked like it had been used primarily for scrapbooking or some other meaningless retiree nonsense. He grabbed a pen from a plastic bin. "Go ahead," he said. In silver glitter ink, Elvis wrote down the GPS coordinates as fast as Bishop rattled them off.

"Got them?" the former Navy SEAL asked.

"I got them," he replied. "Should I dress for warm or cold weather?" Elvis asked, trying to be funny. He didn't receive an answer as the line went dead. He powered the phone off to save the batteries, then looked at the paper scrap scribed with silver numbers, which, without a GPS receiver or an up-to-date Atlas or U.S. map—were totally worthless.

Chapter 11
Outbreak - Day 15
Eden, Utah

The two-man patrol took a circuitous route as they worked their way cautiously down the heavily wooded draw, losing ten feet of altitude every fifty yards or so.

A dozen feet in front of his partner, the stocky point man moved silently heel-and-toeing it while pushing aside creepers and grabby brambles with the business end of his stubby black carbine. As the men padded downhill, any noise caused by their footfalls was quickly swallowed by the lush fragrant flora bracketing the barely discernible game trail. For two hours they had been fighting gravity and the humid summer air which was trapped under the dense canopy of pine and dogwoods. Periodically the point man would hold up a clenched fist, and the camo-clad man bringing up the rear would pirouette a slow one-eighty, eyes and rifle sweeping the forest to their six and then take a knee, ears pricked, listening for anyone stupid enough to be tailing them.

After a few minutes, confident that they were alone, Lev motioned to the point man, and they were on the move again. Another twenty minutes and two more noise checks later, the men found themselves in a small area clear of undergrowth. The soft forest floor was cut through by a small creek running parallel to the trail that had just spit them out; the cool water jouncing over rocks smoothed by ten thousand seasons of spring runoff no doubt a destination for many of the areas' four-legged creatures.

Lev propped his rifle against the nearest dogwood, padded to the creek, splashed his face, and wet his collar. After retrieving his M4, the six foot one hundred and eighty pound veteran of the latest Iraq war took watch so his partner could take his turn.

Holding back his thickly braided ponytail with one hand, Chief plunged his face into the frigid water. Eyes bugged and a grin creasing his ruddy, sunbaked face, the American Indian point man corralled his rifle and without saying a word continued on following the meandering cut in the land while keeping a rapid pace which contradicted his nearly sixty years of age.

In the days since the occupants of the Eden compound had lost one of their own when the perimeter fencing along SR-39 had been cut by persons unknown and then breached by the dead, the more capable among the survivors had been continuously patrolling the heavily wooded acreage surrounding their bug out retreat.

They had been following the creek for a considerable distance when Chief halted abruptly.

"Rotters?" Lev asked. The military style comms gear which he had taken from a pair of dead soldiers a day earlier at an overrun National Guard roadblock east of the compound worked flawlessly, and his query sounded in Chief's ear bud.

Voice amplified and transmitted by the tiny disc-shaped mike pressed to his neck, Chief answered in a hushed tone, "I smell death... but I don't hear any movement."

Lev persisted, "It's gotta be rotters."

Though they had seen the dead migrating in much larger numbers during the past week, Chief answered optimistically. "Since we're still close to the game trail, it may be a dead animal."

"My money's on rotters. We've gotta be close to the neighbor's place," Lev stated, using the term neighbor loosely.

The house that Logan had described earlier, in which the Gudsons, a family of four lived, was more than six miles from the compound. Since the Gudsons' turn-of-the-century farm house and Logan's buried survival shelter were separated by thick woods, two barbed wire fences and a small cliff band of sandstone likely thrust up during an earthquake sometime in the distant past, merely popping by to borrow a cup of sugar was out of the question.

As the two men neared the tree line which abutted the property on the far southwest corner of Logan Winters's considerable plat of land, a fusillade of gunfire, distant and weak, like ladyfinger firecrackers, filtered up through the trees.

Riding on a gust of heated air the pungent smell of death wafted up from below.

"Rotters probably got them trapped," Lev muttered.

"We'll know in a minute," Chief said as he snugged the rifle to his shoulder and levered the safety to burst so that each pull of the trigger would send three tightly grouped 5.56x45 mm rounds down range.

Through the thinning forest Chief noticed flashes of powder blue clapboard and black shingles, and then wavy glass panes in weathered framing to which flecks of white paint clung tenaciously.

"I'm nearing the property line flanking the house... *no rotters yet*," said Chief. "I'm pushing forward... going to end up near the front. You angle to the right and recon the back."

"Copy that," Lev whispered. He pushed forward, slowly, cautiously. Practicing perfect noise discipline, he parted a thicket of waist high ferns and took a knee. He found himself very close to the house. Only a hundred feet separated his place of concealment and the scrappy-looking men who were apparently guarding the back door.

***

After picking a spot between two closely spaced medium-sized pines where he could remain standing yet would not produce a silhouette, Chief glassed the scene two hundred yards distant.

There looked to be some sort of standoff taking place at the Gudsons'. Parked haphazardly, more than a dozen pickups and SUVs choked the gravel drive and occupied every square inch of the expansive front lawn. He could also hear the sounds of gnashing gearboxes and working engines belonging to an unknown number of vehicles still navigating the road somewhere out of sight. Milling about amongst sea of glass and sheet metal, at least two dozen heavily armed men waited, guns wavering menacingly.

A man stood out from the rest. Not because of his stature or hair style or identifiable clothing. He was average height, of average build, and was stuck at birth with an impossibly thin face that came to a point where his sharp nose met with a severe overbite. The thing Chief noticed first was how the others deferred to the smaller man—gave him room to move freely— their body language said it all: the rat-faced Caucasian was in charge and the million dollar question was: *Why?*

Bad guys choose their Alpha leaders differently than real world folks. A piece of paper trumpeting a course of studies completion didn't mean shit. Who you knew... ditto. Usually a rise to power had to do with the severity and cold blooded nature of the crime committed while on the outside. Or the trail of shanked bodies and bloodied hands incurred, without getting pinched, while on the inside. Chief had had contact with many men who had risen to Rat Face's apparent position—up close and way too personal—inside the walls of Northern California's Pelican Bay supermax prison.

Chief panned the binoculars, taking in the Gudsons' home. It was a dingy blue two-story affair, and, like most rural houses built near the turn of the century, lacked any unnecessary architectural detailing. No dental molding, fancy wood scrollwork, or ornate columns gussied up the place—this was not a painted lady in San Francisco—it was strictly an honest workingman's abode in rural Utah surrounded by muddy vehicles and hard looking road dogs.

Hosting a pair of empty rocking chairs, a sloping covered porch that had obviously seen its share of inclement weather wrapped around, stretching toward the backyard where well used plastic playground equipment cooked in the high noon sun. Chief's eyes took in the peripheral details, then lingered on each window searching for movement. The shades at ground level were drawn, but on the second floor they were open revealing only shadows. Designed to provide light for the attic before electric lines stretched to the rural areas, several multi-windowed gables protruded from the roof in front of the house. *A perfect place to remain concealed and observe*, Chief thought to himself.

Meanwhile, in the front yard car park, Rat Face strutted around waving a chromed semi-automatic pistol in the faces of his crew, and appeared to be enjoying immensely his position of authority.

Lev's voice sounded in Chief's ear and a brief flurry of movement caught his eye as a crouching figure passed in front of an uppermost window. "I have six tangos at the rear of the house," Lev stated, "and if the Gudsons *are* inside the house they won't stand a chance against the guys I'm looking at."

"Can't call in reinforcements," Chief answered back, resignation evident in his voice. "We're well out of radio range."

Lev said, "There's gotta be something we can do."

Before Chief could say anything to lessen the younger man's concern, a tinkling of glass reached his ears followed closely by the booming report of what he guessed was some type of shotgun.

"It's on," Lev's stressed voice stated coldly. "Someone just unloaded from the upper window. Dropped one of the bad guys."

"Hold your position."

No shit, thought Lev. He'd be comfortable one on one. Hell, he'd recently survived a frantic two on one gun battle at the nearby hunting cabin just days ago. But one on five—that was stretching it—even taking into consideration his combat experience earned patrolling the mean streets and alleyways of

Baghdad, Ramadi, and Tikrit, the main cities bordering the infamous Sunni Triangle in Iraq.

Before the stricken man had hit the ground, moaning, flesh bloodied and shredded from the hail of lead pellets, his buddies were unloading frantically on the upper story window. An AK-47 chattered on full auto followed by a staggered series of booms as a trio of shotguns and a long rifle entered the fray.

"Permission to engage," Lev pleaded as soon as the firing stopped. Waiting for Chief's response, he remained hidden while bracketing a strapping country boy, complete with a dark beard and flannel shirt, in his crosshairs. With practiced movements the man swapped magazines, slapping a fresh one in his AK. Then, as the blue-gray cordite haze dissipated, an amplified metallic voice broke the calm.

"Give up your guns and come out with your hands up," echoed from the front of the house, followed by a vicious squawk of electronic feedback.

Ignoring Lev's request, Chief patiently waited for the situation to run its course. He knew he was powerless against the gang encircling the house. Furthermore, three tan Humvees had arrived, disgorging another half-dozen men since he and Lev split up.

"Come out or we'll burn the house down around you," the scrawny leader said, speaking through a bulky front-heavy bullhorn. *"I seen the swing set over there... do it for your kids. I give you my word we won't do nothin' to them."*

Chief winced as Rat Face released the trigger, hurling another burst of sonic feedback at his ears. He was tempted to shoot the man for that simple transgression, let alone what he feared was about to befall anyone who willingly exited the farmhouse.

"What's going on up there?" Lev asked breathlessly.

"Stand down," Chief answered. "I've got nearly thirty bodies up here now."

Silence.

"Lev, you copy?"

More silence.

Better not, Chief thought to himself. *You'll get us both killed.*

The screen door opened on unoiled hinges, announcing shrilly to everyone present that the marauders had won.

"The gun first," Rat Face reminded whoever was about to emerge through the front door.

His men drew in around him, their sneering faces and black weapons like pirates waiting to board a defeated Man-O-War.

"Five coming your way carrying one wounded," Lev blurted.

Relieved to hear Lev's voice and grateful that the younger man had wisely decided against taking matters into his own hands, Chief whispered, "Roger."

Ten long seconds passed and then someone slid a shotgun with its breach cracked open, butt stock first from within the shadowy doorway. Next, a man who Chief guessed to be Mister Gudson cautiously stepped over the scattergun and into the light.

"Keep them up," Rat Face ordered, his chest heaving from the adrenaline burst. *"The rest of you... come out or Pops gets popped."* He belly-laughed at his funny and the bullhorn added its own feedback. *"Or if you don't give a shit about him, we can send a couple of zombies in to flush you out."*

His eyes darting about crazily and gasping for breath, the middle-aged man fell to his knees, pleading for the lives of his loved ones, offering to trade his own and every worldly possession for a shred of mercy.

With a casual wave Rat Face ushered two of his men forward.

As Gudson's voice rose to a crescendo, a chatter of words blending together unintelligibly, the screen behind him creaked open and one by one his family emerged. A young boy, perhaps ten or eleven Chief guessed, trudged out, shoulders slumped and shaking with fear. Mom was next. She was fairly attractive, probably closer to fifty than forty. Her brunette hair fell around her face, framing an expression of complete and utter defeat.

The girl came into view at the same time the two gun-toting assholes mounted the porch, zip-ties in hand. She was the spitting image of her mom, only thirty years younger. Probably too young to drive but, certainly in the bandits' one-track minds, she was mature enough for *other* things.

Depositing the bullhorn on the hood of the nearest vehicle, the scrawny leader crabbed between two Jeeps and made his way to the porch, a pronounced pep in his step.

Though he knew Lev was returning to this position, Chief sensed the camouflage-clad man well before he came low crawling from cover. The sixth sense had been a welcome and constant companion since he was a young boy, an innate ability that had saved his life more than once.

"First class shit show happening down there," Lev intoned as he formed up next to Chief.

"Nothing we can do... *right now*," Chief replied, removing the binoculars and fixing a gaze on Lev, who understood fully what '*right now*' implied.

Having composed himself somewhat, Mister Gudson mouthed a few silent words, embraced his kids, kissed them both on the forehead, and then brought his wife into the fold.

Though he couldn't hear what was being said, and reading lips was out of the question due to the angle, Chief could tell by the man's expression and body language that he was saying his final good byes. Then, with painfully slow movements, he straightened and turned towards the henchmen. In seconds he was trussed and had been dragged down the stairs and over to the lawn, his knees carving dusty furrows in the gravel.

Lev, who had been watching through the scope affixed to his M4, stated in a monotone voice, "I think we are about to witness an execution."

"Nothing we can do," Chief reasserted.

Ignoring the dad, Rat Face vaulted the stairs and stopped directly in front of the remaining three Gudsons. After running his hands over the women, giving the younger of them a much more thorough inspection, he barked orders to several of his men. Then he about-faced and descended the stairs two at a time.

Next, he strode towards the prostrate Gudson, pulled the pistol from his waistband, and without deliberation shot him behind the ear.

As the lone shot echoed off the house and through the clearing, mom and daughter began to scream. They were quickly separated and cuffed, arms bound tightly behind them, then escorted to a white van where they were unceremoniously thrown into the back.

The boy, now alone on the porch, sobbed silently his body wracked by tremors.

Once again Rat Face made his way to the porch. He intertwined thin fingers into the kid's straw-colored hair, forcing him to a kneeling position. "Like father like son," he said, his voice booming over the heads of his men before reaching Chief's position.

Chief knew what was coming next but failed to divert his eyes. A glint of sun off steel preceded the crimson torrent as the killer drew a wicked looking blade across the boy's pallid neck.

A leader who is not afraid to get his hands bloody, Chief thought, fighting off the bile rising in his throat. He had seen them before *on the inside* and they were the worst of their kind. The rare human animal who enjoyed and fed off of the pain and suffering of others.

"One less mouth to feed," the man bellowed as he held the convulsing body upright. Aerated blood bubbled and frothed from the gaping second mouth, while, like a baby bird trying to leave the nest for the first time, the boy weakly beat the air with his arms.

Rat Face released the handful of hair, letting the corpse pancake onto the porch face first, then wiped his knife on the boy's tee shirt. "*Search the house top to bottom!*" he screamed, corded muscles bulging in his neck.

Like army ants the men stormed the house, and in a matter of minutes the Gudsons' considerable pantry had been emptied of food. One man emerged, brandishing the only firearms in the house: both pistols of some kind.

War whoops resounded, engines started and the vehicles began a clumsy dance, drivers backing and wheeling, trying to extricate their rigs.

One at a time the vehicles rolled down the gravel drive and were soon swallowed up by the forest.

Incredulous, Lev said, "That's some of the worst shit I've ever seen. And believe me... I've seen some shit."

"It's a close second for me," whispered Chief.

With a sideways look as the white van disappeared from sight, Lev lobbied to go down and make sure the two males were indeed dead.

"No need," replied Chief.

"Why's that?"

"No way we can help them even if they're hanging on."

Judging by what the animals proved they were capable of, and coupled with the blood- and gore-streaked Econoline van, Lev and Chief both arrived independently at the same conclusion: the lawless bandits who had just massacred Gudson and his boy were undoubtedly responsible for cutting the fence near SR-39 and letting the dead onto Logan's property. Considering their numbers and their utter disregard for human life, they could not be taken lightly.

With the exhaust notes receding into the distance and the chilling sound of Gudson's final pleas echoing in their heads, the two men melted into the tree line. Then, after a thirty-yard hike through the dense undergrowth, Chief's voice crackled in Lev's earpiece. "You smell it yet?"

"Yeah," Lev answered crinkling his nose. "Rotters?"

"Not exactly," Chief said somewhat cryptically.

Not in the mood for fun and games after what he had just witnessed, Lev muttered an expletive and pushed ahead. A moment later, after stepping over a crumbling moss-coated snag bristling with up thrust volunteers, he put his boot into the offending deer carcass.

A snicker sounded in his earpiece. He looked up to see the grinning American Indian whom he was quickly forming a close kinship with, and then reciprocated with a reluctant stress-relieving smile of his own.

Chapter 12
Outbreak - Day 15
Colorado Springs, Colorado

Brook pointed out the safety—a sliding lever above the trigger guard on the left side of the carbine—and made sure it was engaged before snugging the rifle to the girl's shoulder.

"Put your left hand on the front grip... like this." She positioned Raven's hand and then put her foot between the girl's heels and moved her stance apart incrementally. "Does that feel stable?"

"I guess."

"Good. Right before you get ready to fire, you flick off the safety... this lever here. And just before you *squeeze* the trigger— and I want you to *squeeze* it just once—you have to press the rifle tight to your shoulder and lean your body forward a tad to counter the recoil. This gun is going to pop your shoulder a bit— that's the *recoil* part—but don't worry, *Mom* has got your back."

"Do I have to..."

"*Yes* you do, sweetie."

Raven finished her sentence. "... shoot the things?"

"They're not *people* anymore. Remember... we talked about it already. They won't feel it and they won't *hate* you for it either."

"How does God feel about it?" asked Raven tentatively.

"God's on board, sweetie," Brook answered matter-of-factly. And deep inside their brains somewhere, they're grateful they are not going to be walking around against their will anymore."

"Really?"

"Yes sweetie, really," Brook said. *I know I would*, she thought.

"I'll try it again... if they won't be mad at me. You promise, Mom?"

"I promise."

Brook's reasons for bringing them to this remote part of the base were many. She had been meaning to tell Raven about her miscarriage and hadn't found the time or the place. Also, she wanted to familiarize herself with the new equipment affixed to her rifle. The day before, Cade had had the armorer fit the M4 with an Eotech holographic optic combined with a 3x flip down magnifier. She remembered what he had said about the new set up. *"The Eotech will be perfect for dinging Zs up close and personal. Then, with one simple motion you engage this magnifier, and voilà, you can reach out a little further. Basically you get the best of both worlds in a tidy little package,"* were his exact words.

"Now this is your sight," Brook said to Raven, trying her best to explain it so her twelve-year-old wouldn't become confused. "And wherever you put the red dot is where the bullet is going to hit. This thing," she flipped the cylindrical optic mounted before the holographic sight up and then back down to demonstrate its range of motion. "It makes things that are farther away look like they are much closer." *I would have made a horrible teacher*, she told herself. She hoped she hadn't sounded condescending like Cade often did whenever he tried to school her in the matters of shooting, basic security, and situational awareness. Furthermore, she hoped she wasn't throwing too much at her daughter at one time.

But unfortunately, the fact that they were leaving at first light didn't leave her with much of a choice. Besides, outside the wire, three shooters, no matter how green Raven was, would give them better odds of making it than just her and Cade.

"Do you get how it works?" Brook asked.

Mimicking her mom's actions, Raven pressed her cheek to the stock and manipulated the slide out function once or twice. "Yes Mom, I see what you mean. Now can I shoot it?"

"You're *ready*?"

"Yes Mom. Now quit asking me if I'm *sure*... or *OK*, or *ready*."

Wow, Brook thought, if this is twelve-year-old sass, what are the teen years going to throw at me? Then she remembered their current situation and the fact that every new day was going to be tougher than she and Cade could have ever imagined. A little over two weeks ago her most pressing concerns had been trivial compared to surviving the Omega outbreak. Choosing an orthodontist—hardly daunting stuff, she mused. Fearing the dreaded talk about the birds and the bees—trumped by explaining why the dead had risen and how it was now OK to put a bullet in their rotten brains. *Hell*, Brook thought, *Raven probably knew more than she let on about reproduction anyway.* Should make the concept of miscarriage easier for her to grasp though. At that, she pushed all of these troubling thoughts down inside and reminded herself that they could be dealt with after she and Raven had put a few rounds downrange. She grimaced at the wording that had involuntarily entered her stream of thought, then smiled at the realization that not only was she beginning to act like her husband, she was starting to think like him as well.

From their vantage point in the guard tower they could see for miles. The only things poking through the hard-baked ground were smatterings of low scrub and tufts of some type of hardy savannah grass clumped here and there. Adding contrast to the ochre dirt, yellowed lace-like tumbleweeds bounced across their shooting range. And though the guards had already cleansed the perimeter of the dead that had been drawn by the commotion caused by the vicious outbreak, there were still a few random Zs lurching about on the horizon. Only three of them were close enough to engage with any chance for a successful hit.

"OK... see the taller one with the necktie fluttering in the wind?" Why the thing had been dressed for success at the onset of the outbreak was anyone's guess. But Brook decided that using generic descriptors like body size or type of clothing the flesh eater was wearing would convince Raven they were less human and more like a walking mannequin. Monikers like male, female, adult, and especially kid were removed from her lexicon when Raven was within earshot.

Raven put her cheek to the smooth polymer stock and her eye near the rubber-ringed glass lens as her mom had demonstrated. "Got it," she said with an air of confidence that belied her age and physical stature.

Good job, Brook thought, and then in order to shore up Raven's four and a half foot frame, braced her knee against the girl's bottom, reached around her shoulders and gently gripped the rifle to lend a little extra support.

"Remember, we do not *jerk* the trigger... we *s-q-u-e-e-z-e* the trigger. Whenever you are ready, sweetie."

Pow!

Smiling, Raven glanced at her mom.

"Very good. Now try three in a row."

Pow! Pow! Pow!

Though the short-barreled M4 offered very little recoil, the consecutive shots jolted both of their bodies. Then, slowly, as Brook sensed Raven becoming more comfortable with the rifle, she eased up on the pressure entirely and backed away.

Geysers of soil erupted around the shambler's bare feet.

"Aim for its head, right in the center." She didn't want to say between the eyes... it just sounded a little too macabre.

Dragging her aim up slightly, Raven paused for a second, barrel wavering, and then '*squeezed*' the trigger like Mom had instructed.

Pow!

Raven remained standing. The decomposing first turn did not. The monster collapsed to terra firma convincingly in a puff of russet dust, knees jutting skyward, its cratered face staring vacantly at the blue Colorado sky.

"See sweetie, it doesn't kick as much as you feared. A little more than the .22, but Mom needs you to get used to it just in case."

"In case of what, Mom?"

In case Mom or Dad dies, Brook thought to herself. Yet another eventuality that needed to be covered but would have to wait.

"We'll sit down and talk about it after we shoot." Brook traded Raven the smaller Ruger 10/22 rifle that she had procured for her a few days prior for the Colt M4. Though Raven had balked at the time, Brook had a feeling that the Ruger would be more to her liking after being exposed to the substantial kick of the M4.

Raven regarded the rifle for a second, then, displaying what she had already learned about the workings of the 10/22, removed the magazine, inspected it closely, and then seated it into the well in front of the trigger guard. She pulled the handle located on the right side of the rifle to chamber a round and double checked, making sure the safety was on.

Good girl, Brook thought.

Finally, Raven looked coyly over her shoulder at Mom and flashed a lopsided grin as if to say, *'See, I got this.'*

Fantastic, thought Brook, noting that her daughter had practiced safe firearm handling by keeping the barrel pointed down range as she went through the motions.

"See if you can hit that one with *your* rifle."

Raven said nothing and shouldered the Ruger. At only four and a half pounds, the polymer-stocked varmint rifle was still not a feather in her grip. Then, without further prompting, Raven squeezed off ten rounds—about one a second—until the gun went silent.

The fallen cadaver had twitched slightly after each good hit.

Six out of ten, Brook thought to herself. Certainly room for improvement, but the major hurdle had been cleared—Raven had stepped to the plate and swung for the fence. So far so good. But as hard as it was for Brook to contemplate, the nagging question remained—if push came to shove, when any one of their lives were in jeopardy—would Raven be able to use the weapon against a hostile human being? It was a question Brook didn't want to have answered. Her heart fluttered and she felt her throat go dry, tightening like an invisible ligature had been placed around her neck. Hot tears welled in the corners of her eyes. *Hell, this wasn't supposed to be happening,* she told herself. School was supposed to start back up in a few weeks, and holding to their annual ritual they should be gracing the doors of Old Navy and the Gap right about now—not blowing away walking corpses in the high desert of Colorado. She fought off an overwhelming tide of nausea and swiped away fully developed tears.

"OK, good shooting," she said, but in her own head the words sounded hollow and distant. "Now reload and see if you can hit the two smaller ones in the distance."

"The kids?" Raven asked.

"The two smaller walkers," Brook said. *Can't sneak one past you,* is what she didn't.

Though the undead pair shuffling towards the fence were still roughly thirty feet away, to the human eye the damage they had suffered prior to reanimating was clearly evident. Both had wounds to the forearms and hands—defensive in nature—indicating they'd fought off attackers. Both had bites around the face and neck telling that those efforts had failed them.

Brook brought her rifle to bear, not to put the kids out of their misery—she would leave that up to Raven if she could get past the fact that they had once been kids around her age. Brook merely wanted to examine them, up close, one at a time, using the 3x scope. Her crosshairs found the boy first, displaying the ghastly wounds in vibrant detail. Nearly every scrap of flesh was missing from the left side of its neck between the partially exposed clavicle on up to its constantly snapping jaw. On the opposite side of the Z's face, the skin and subcutaneous tissue had either been chewed off or rent from its skull by brute force. Brook swallowed hard, and felt her finger willingly moving towards the trigger.

"Mom... why don't you just call them what they were before they got bit," Raven said impassively. She paused to insert a full ten-round magazine into the Ruger. "Those were kids... a boy and a girl," she added. Then, without hesitation, she lined up the iron sights, fore and aft, drawing a bead dead center on the male creature's stark white forehead.

Pow! A single shot from the M4 rang out, causing Raven to jump and lose the lined up shot. A millisecond later, she witnessed the left half of the boy's face dissolve in a gale of putrid flesh and ivory bone flecks. Then, after regaining her composure, the pig-tailed girl shot her mom a sidelong look, sighted on the other Z, and sent a single .22 long rifle round into its cranium where it bounced around, carving furrows through the impulse-sending gray matter. Instantly, like someone had cut its legs, the rotting shell of a young girl that was once someone's daughter collapsed face first onto the sunbaked earth.

Brook grimaced. Her eyebrows hitched up an inch. *Apple doesn't fall far from the tree,* she mused. She turned her back on the twice dead trio then sank to the plywood floor.

Raven engaged the safety and propped her rifle in the corner, then joined her mom on the floor where they sat shoulder to shoulder, lost in their own thoughts. Meanwhile, behind them, out of sight but light years from being out of mind, what may have been three-fourths of a complete family festered in the sun.

Though Brook had planned to lead up to her bombshell admission with a heart-to-heart talk full of hope and encouraging verbiage, instead, she kept it simple by sticking only to the facts. "I lost the baby."

There was silence, except for the wind passing through their perch.

"I knew," Raven replied softly.

"Oh honey... I'm so sorry," Brook said, the tears returning. Only this time around she made no attempt to stem the flow. "I should have told you. But with all of the bad stuff happening and your Dad gone again, I kept it from you—"

"I understand Mom... I'm twelve... not six. I'm not mad at you but I'm still a little sad. I wanted someone to teach things to. To take care of."

"Someday," Brook said. Though in her heart she had a feeling that in her mid-thirties the window for a safe pregnancy was on its way down, and if her family's genetics had any say in the matter it would probably slam shut sooner, rather than later.

Raven put a finger vertical to her lips and shushed her mom—usually a cardinal offense in the Grayson household. But these were different times and called for different rules. Brook had learned to choose her battles differently—and most of those as of late had not been with the living—let alone Raven.

"Mom... is that what I think it is? Do you hear it?"

Brook shushed back, then turned her head towards the direction the high pitched yapping seemed to be coming from.

Like a prairie dog, Raven popped up and scanned the horizon. "It's a dog!" she squealed.

A medium-sized mutt sat on its haunches, equidistant from the three unmoving Zs. Its coloring could easily be described as calico—reddish brown and black spots peppered its predominantly white coat.

Warily Brook forced herself to stand, to see what type of canine had gotten her daughter so riled up. She shouldered the M4 to scrutinize the animal through the scope. "Looks like some kind of shepherd," she finally declared. "I'm guessing it's an Australian Shepherd."

A blur descending the thirteen-foot ladder, hands and feet blazing over two-by-four rungs, Raven was on the ground in less than three seconds flat. She rushed headlong to the fence and stood on her tip toes, fingers poking through the openings, head craning. "Can we keep it?" she called out. Then to further complicate things, she added. "I think he probably belonged to those three out there. So... it's sort of our duty to take him in. *Right?*"

Who am I to say no? Brook thought. She cleared her throat. Not because of the dry air but because she needed a minute to think. "What does *duty* mean to you?"

Looking back at her mom, Raven answered slowly. "It means I'm supposed to help... no matter what. You're talking about taking care of *him*... right?"

"Maybe," Brook replied.

"Duty also means it's the right thing to do." Raven knew the hook was set. Still, she tried to hide the sly smile.

Sounds like something Cade would say, Brook thought to herself.

"Please Mom. Can we keep it?"

"If it's infected, *no way*. But I'm pretty sure only humans are affected by the Omega virus," Brook said, casting a sidelong glance at her daughter. "And come to think of it I haven't seen a cat or a dog since before the outbreak." She turned her gaze on the dog, and then considered the ramifications of traveling with the animal. On one hand if it was a yappy thing they could find a muzzle, or heaven forbid and PETA be damned they could forage around and find one of those shock collars. The sort that some pasty faced necktie peddled on late night infomercials. On the other hand, the dog might earn its keep, she reasoned. It seemed intelligent—most shepherds were. And though she didn't realize it now, she was insentiently rationalizing keeping the thing for her own personal reasons. What if Cade decided to renege on his promise and insisted they stay at Schriever? She doubted it. Something monumental would have had to have happened to make Cade Grayson go back on a Scout's Honor after he had already proclaimed it. After all, he had been an Eagle Scout *long* before Army Ranger School, the Special Forces, and Delta. *Besides*, she told herself, *shepherds have worked and lived alongside humans for tens of thousands of years, so he won't be any sort of a hassle.* "Yes, you can keep it," she said, instantly regretting the five little words.

Clapping her hands rapidly, Raven did a little *happy* dance, spun a few circles then froze completely and slowly panned hear head up, taking in the enormity of the twelve-foot high *double* fence.

"Mom?"

"Yes honey," she answered.

"How do we get to him?"

"Don't look now, but I think he has it all figured out," Brook added, a broad smile creasing her face.

A fountain of red soil spewing between its hind legs, the industrious canine furiously tilled the hard-packed ground, front paws clawing a mile a minute.

After a quarter of an hour had passed, the dog had tunneled under both rings of fencing. The dirt-covered stray sidled up to Raven first and then sniffed at her hands and legs.

At least he's not a crotch hound, Brook thought. Then with a free and easy gait, the pooch approached her, padded twice around the pair, and then leaped into the back of the golf cart.

Brook made a face. "I guess he's keeping *us,*" she said. *Mission accomplished,* she thought. The mother-daughter talk she had so dreaded wasn't as big a mountain as she had built it up to be. Raven had taken the official news about her not becoming a big sister better than she could have imagined. The thing that kind of gnawed at Brook, though, was her daughter's complete one-eighty—the girl had tolerated the shooting better than the last time, and for lack of a better word she had seemed to have *enjoyed* their outing.

Mom and daughter piled into the Cushman cart.

"What are we going to name him?" Brook asked as the propane-powered engine chugged to life.

"How can you be sure it's a *boy* dog?" Raven fired back.

"So you think I don't know my stuff?"

"I didn't say that."

"Then what you're telling me is that it *is* time for the birds and bees... boys and girls talk?"

"*Forget* I asked," Raven said.

"Check his collar," Brook countered.

"It's OK *boy*. I just want to see if there is a tag here." She parted the matted fur and grasped the steel disc hanging from the worn leather collar. "You were right, Mom. It says right here... his name is *Max*."

At the sound of his name, as if confirming what he already knew, the dog let out a short yelp and licked Raven's hand.

Chapter 13
Outbreak - Day 15
Schriever AFB

Wilson would never forget the look that had frozen on his sister's face when he and Taryn abruptly left her all alone in the mess hall. Suddenly at a loss for words, the fourteen-year-old's jaw hinged open, her freckled nose crinkled up, and her eyes narrowed under a hard set brow. Framed by her scarlet mane of curls, her features seemed to be having a meeting in the middle of her face. It was as if the words Taryn had just hurled at her held some kind of weight—a motherly, listen to me or else type of weight. It was the look of utter disbelief when the mind fails to process new information fast enough to come up with an appropriate response. He had seen that look on her face only one other time during the last two weeks—the day a disheveled looking CNN news anchor, wearing a similar expression on his face, finally confirmed that the dead were walking the streets. Wilson wished *his* words had the same effect on Sasha, but ever since Z day when their mom had gone missing during a forced stopover in Washington D.C., things hadn't been the same between them. Lost was the position of authority vested in him and fully backed by his mom. Sasha's respect for him also seemed to have mostly disappeared somewhere between Denver and Colorado Springs less than a week ago.

***

After leaving the mess hall, Taryn and Wilson stayed to the white concrete footpaths which crisscrossed the base. As they strolled side by side, only a few short inches separating them, Wilson tried not to obsess over how warm and silky her suntanned skin had felt pressed firmly against his thigh. That she had purposely taken the initiative further confused the twenty-year-old, setting off a chain reaction of feelings and emotions that up until then had been suppressed and completely numbed by the reality of surviving these last two horror-filled weeks.

Ignoring the real reason behind her decision to ask Wilson to go for a walk, Taryn instead brought up everything *but* her nine days in Hell on Earth. "So, Red... what's your favorite sports team?"

Wow, he thought to himself. This girl is getting cooler with each passing minute. "*Colorado Rockies*, of course," he replied. "*Todd Helton* hasn't failed me yet. How about you?"

"Don't like organized sports. I hated playing them... couldn't take to being yelled at by someone else's failure of a father. And millionaire men fighting and carrying on like spoiled brats in front of thousands of people. That's just wrong on so many levels."

"Baseball's not so bad—"

"Lie to yourself, not to me, Red. No way... never seen a dugout-clearing brawl... *ever.*"

Touché, he thought. Then, struggling to find some more common ground, he tried a different approach. "So what *was* your favorite television show? Or let me guess... TV too bourgeois for you?"

"Bourg— what?"

"It means conformist. Look at your piercings... your tattoos. You don't have a bourgeois bone in your body."

"What's that got to do with TV?" Taryn asked.

"Just trying to figure you out... that's all."

"OK. I'll play along." She looked over her left shoulder—paused theatrically—then did the same on the other side. "L.A. Ink," she whispered.

"*Wow.*" He thrust his arms skyward like he'd just finished a marathon. He spun a tight circle, boots scuffing the path. "She likes reality television no less," he called out to no one in particular. "What... did you like L.A. Ink cause of Kat Von what's her name?" *Come to think of it,* Wilson thought to himself, *Taryn does share an uncanny resemblance to the show's brunette star.* But, in his obviously biased opinion, Taryn was much younger, prettier, and had way better tats than the dead and gone, long-locked reality star.

Wilson's hamming it up elicited a half-smile from Taryn that disappeared quickly.

"OK Mister Judgmental—*your* turn," she said, flashing him a pouty look.

"Well, I *had* a red Mustang. She got trashed in Denver. I had a dream of getting it on Overhaulin'... It's a show about—"

She cut him off. "I've seen the show once or twice."

Then Wilson got caught doing an obvious double take. And though he thought it could go no higher, his affection for Taryn elevated a notch.

"Girls can be gearheads too, you know," she stated emphatically and with a certain sense of pride. Then after a short pause her tone softened. "You know, before this disease, virus, whatever the *hell* it is happened, my dad was building a rat rod in his spare time. He let me and my brother help out a little." She went quiet then added in a near whisper, "I couldn't wait to ride in the thing." Hands held horizontally a few inches apart she added, "It had a real short windshield up front... Brother and me couldn't wait to get the wind in our hair."

"And bugs in your teeth," Wilson quipped. "I loved those things... just the opposite of a hundred thousand dollar *Trailer Queen*. All primered out, peeps could actually *drive* one of those to the car show. Door dings and bad weather... no worries." He glanced over. Tears had welled in her eyes, threatening to spill over. He had little experience with girls—except for the teenagers who worked for him at Fast Burger—and they had a tendency to cry over giving someone the wrong change. Where Taryn was concerned he didn't know what to say.

An awkward silence ensued.

He fumbled through every pocket in his cargo shorts—eight in all—searching for a tissue... anything. *Nothing*, he thought to himself. *Epic fail.*

Taryn tugged the neck of her black tank up to dry the tears and in the process revealed more of her anatomy than she had intended.

Wilson diverted his gaze, but not before he got an eyeful, including, but not limited to the delicate details of her bra. It was black, low cut, and like Taryn—the lace was very complex. He also noticed something fall from her tank. It appeared to be machined out of brushed aluminum, was about the size of a pack of Wrigley's chewing gum, and swung pendulum-like on some kind of clear line. Without looking up she quickly tucked the pendant in and patted smooth the dampened fabric.

He blushed for the umpteenth time since he'd met her. "No Kleenex—"

"That's OK," she said, looking up and meeting his sheepish gaze. "I want to be quiet for a minute. You know... be still. Just think."

"OK," Wilson said. It was about all he could come up with.

They continued on in absolute silence. And when they finally reached the parade grounds—an expanse of brown grass encircled by an oval quarter-mile running track—Wilson steered them towards a fixed set of aluminum bleachers. Low to the ground and utilitarian even compared to the ones at his old high school, they seemed the perfect place to take a break so he could listen *if* Taryn decided she wanted to talk about her ordeal. Besides, he reasoned. With all of the melanin her skin possessed, he didn't think she'd mind sitting in the sun for a while. Hell, from the looks of her olive skin there was no way she could have been trapped inside for nine days. He, on the other hand, pink-skinned ginger that he was—knew from experience that he was going to pay dearly for every millisecond he stayed out in the sun.

They sat in silence, staring at the twelve-foot tall fences separating the base from the zombies' hunting grounds on the opposite side. Out there, a couple of lonely Zs held vigil, eyeing them hungrily, fingers latched onto the outer ring of fencing.

The wind was calm and the sun, nearing its apex for the day, seemed certain to drop another hundred degree day on them. There had already been three consecutive scorchers in a row, and the thunderstorms that the locals swore occurred like clockwork during the waning months of summer had yet to spare them one single solitary raindrop. Wilson decided to quit being Wilson and take charge. "Hottest part of the day is coming, we should probably head back," he said. Then he released his red hair from the confines of his floppy boonie hat and wiped some sweat from his brow. "Maybe we could go inside... someplace cooler," he added. Sasha's voice invaded his head. *'Gosh dang Wilson, take it any faster you might as well just asked her to sleep with you.'*

"That's a great idea," Taryn said, agreeing. "Then I can verbally vomit on you in private. Kinda what I had in mind in the first place. I went through nine days of hell... *alone*, and if I don't talk about it soon I'm liable to go find a gun and quiet this noise in my head."

With the memory of Ted's unexpected suicide fresh in his mind, Wilson couldn't contain himself. "You don't want to do that," he blurted.

"I was just being dramatic, Wilson. I didn't give up at the airport. I'm sure as *hell* not taking the easy way out now."

"Did you make it here by yourself?"

"Yes... and no. It's complicated." She went quiet. They took a few more steps before she spoke again. "Wilson..." her voice cracked. She halted in her tracks, feeling the sun bearing down on her. Heard heavy vehicles going somewhere important, the clunk and roar of engine and exhaust dissipating. She swallowed hard. "When I tell you how I got here I don't expect you to believe me. I still can't believe I made it out alive. And if you think I'm just being a whiny girl fishing for attention and don't want to hear it... I won't hold it against you."

Wilson didn't particularly like the sound of her final statement. Every cell in his body wanted her to hold every bit of her against him. He blushed and pushed aside the romantic thoughts. "You don't have to worry about me passing judgment," he proffered. "You met my sister. She does all of the judging in our family."

"You know... I think I was a little too hard on her considering she's lost contact with your mom and everything she's been through in the last few days. That's all way too much for someone her age to process."

Wilson crushed his hat over his hair. "She's coping... in her own way," he said quietly.

"And *you?* How are you coping? And how much of Sasha's retelling of the arm stuck in your hair is real and how much was due to teenage exaggeration?"

"It all happened the way she said. I've got more to get off my chest. After you, of course. I think I might benefit from a little... what'd you call it? A verbal vomit session?"

"Agreed," Taryn said with a smile. She cast a sidelong glance at the zombies by the fence, and for the first time since her rescue from Grand Junction Regional the enormity of the situation and the true nature of the dead struck her. "What is the government going to do about all of those things?"

"What can they do?" Wilson said dryly. "Before this thing broke out there were... I don't know *how* many people in the U.S."

"I did a report on immigration last fall." Trying to coax the obscure number from her memory, Taryn paused for a beat and looked at the sky. "I think there *were...* I want to say *three hundred million*. But don't quote me."

"Oh no. I'm going to have to hold you to that number, young lady—" Wilson's attempt to lighten the mood failed. He watched Taryn's face go slack, the color flushing from it entirely.

"That means there are a lot more of those things than I ever imagined," she said in a low voice.

"Let's get back. We've got a vomit session to attend." She smiled. "My place or yours?" he asked.

"Mine," she said at once. "I've got something to show you."

Wilson smiled. His imagination was running wild, and for the first time since those initial awkward moments when they'd met, he found himself speechless.

Chapter 14
Outbreak - Day 15
Schriever AFB
Security Pod

The prisoner's restraints clanked against the steel table as he raked soft feminine fingers through his full head of unkempt silver hair. Then, as if suddenly struck by a wayward thought he might be privy to share, he sat upright and shifted his gaze from his open palms and fixed it on the interrogator. After a few seconds he looked away, then began to bob his head left to right, a barely perceptible metronomic shift of only a few degrees in either direction, like he was deciding something of little consequence. Perhaps which three hundred dollar tie he'd wear to a dinner party, or whether he wanted a blonde or brunette thousand dollars an hour call girl waiting in his penthouse when he returned. Over the last forty years, money had not been an issue. In fact, he'd had enough of it to alter elections. He'd even brought a small country to its knees through currency manipulation. He had been able to afford *anything* and *everything* he'd ever wanted. *Immediately.* No waiting. He was the king of self-gratification, and most importantly, he answered to no man.

But recently, things had changed drastically for the ruthless ex-billionaire. In reality, the man Robert Christian regarded across the table from him—the imposing figure whose gaze even he found hard to match for any length of time without looking away—literally held his life in the palm of his hand. And the question his interrogator had just posed contained no uncertain words and had only one truthful answer, an answer that Robert Christian knew would be deemed unacceptable.

He went light in the head. Suddenly, for the first time in three days, he saw the scale tipping in an altogether undesirable direction. And the slide started moments after he had been brought into the cold room and manacled to this very same table. That had been over seventy-two hours ago, by his estimation.

The President had arrived and watched as the interrogators quickly shattered the illusion that Christian could threaten or buy his way out of this predicament. That way of doing business may have worked in the old world. It held no weight in the new one.

His first offer of money had been met with silence by his lone interrogator. His belligerent ranting followed with a flurry of hollow threats earned him an open handed slap, and the last time he had been slapped across the face, he had recalled at the time, had been but a love tap delivered by a nun in accordance with Catholic school rules. The interrogator's sneak attack had been nothing of the sort. He could still hear the roundhouse cutting the air before the crushing blow brought his fantasy world crashing down around him. And before the resounding smack had echoed into silence, he'd had a morbid epiphany: *This hard-edged man writes his own rules and answers to no one.*

***

For Robert Christian, formulating an answer other than the truth wasn't an option. He couldn't lie to this man, he reminded himself. Without a doubt the grim-faced soldier—or whatever he was—had been trained to spot deception. No, he decided right then and there. He'd already told them all he knew, and spinning elaborate lies would only prolong the agony.

He looked at his right little finger. It wandered off at a sharp angle from the others, snapped there by the attached tendons when the knuckle keeping it straight disintegrated. Just looking at the swollen purple digit brought forth a fresh dose of breath-robbing pain.

"You indicated that Elvis was supposed to rendezvous with Ian Bishop and then kill him. As per your orders. Isn't that correct?" The interrogator turned in his chair, looked at his own reflection in the two-way mirror.

"Yes, for the tenth time. That is the truth," Christian stated forcefully. "And Ian Bishop... that Goddamned traitor. He abandoned me. I have no idea where he went, nor do I know where his men took the nuclear warheads he fucking stole from me." The thick vein that snaked across Robert Christian's temple steadily throbbed, seemingly a living thing underneath his skin.

The interrogator shot up from his seat, flipped the metal chair around so its back pressed against his chest, then sat back down heavily. The sudden movement caused Robert Christian to flinch and shrink away. In the attempt to distance himself from the anticipated blow, the former billionaire simultaneously stretched the manacles to their limits and arched his body backwards, away from the table. His chair screeched back several inches, teetered on two legs before coming to rest again, still upright on all four.

The man leaned in close. Robert Christian could see the pores on his nose, the red capillaries in the yellowed whites of his eyes. Could smell the acidic coffee stench of his breath.

"One more time. Tell me who Elvis was working with." He said it slowly, enunciating every syllable. "You give me something that I can work with and then I'll reward you. But if you don't cooperate, I'm going to up the ante. And just to prove to you I'm not such a bad guy... I'll allow you to choose which *fingers* get broken."

Robert Christian looked at his damaged right hand. He kept his eyes downcast. "I have already told you... Elvis *volunteered* to come here," he stammered. "He was supposed to pose as a survivor, try to gain some trust and then wait. Francis's mission was the same... only he was the one who had to smuggle the gun in. I wanted him to kill that bitch *Clay*."

The interrogator bristled. "Why did you want the President dead?"

"So I could have the *United States* all to myself."

Shaking his head, the interrogator said, "The *dead* own the United States for now."

"But *I* had a plan."

"You're insane," the rough man spat. "Just as insane as the fool you sent for Clay. He's dead and soon *you* will be too. "

"No... no... I can help you find Bishop. Get back the nuclear weapons. For what it's worth... everything I've told you *is* the truth. So help me—" He stopped short of saying the three letter word that was nothing but a crutch for weak people. For him, *power* was God. So now, sadly, shackled to the table, he was not only utterly powerless over his situation, he was Godless as well.

Once again the interrogator cast a glance at the mirror, pressed his finger to his ear, adjusted something there and without saying anything more exited the room, slamming the door behind him. The mirrored glass rattled and Christian's reflection staring back at him undulated with it. Then, with a viscous sucking sound, the A/C unit kicked on. A low whoosh came next as frigid air burst through the plastic grill. Somewhere deep inside the box a bad bearing wailed, threatening to silence the beast for good. Having already put up with it for hours on end, and nearly losing his mind as a result, the former billionaire king maker silently prayed for it to fail.

Chapter 15
Outbreak - Day 15
The House
Jackson Hole, Wyoming

Lucas Brother's expression changed from one of mild annoyance to a crunched up sneer. He shuffled the picket of empty liquor bottles, lifting and slamming each one down noisily, and then in a fit of hot rage, upended the black lacquered table sending the empties and a two-day accumulation of cellophane wrappers and caviar tins crashing onto the travertine tiles. "Liam!" he bellowed. "Where the *fuck* is the *clicker?*"

The younger man replied testily, his voice easily carrying from the kitchen and down the hall. "Get off your *ass* and look for it. And I'll be damned if I'm watching *Die Hard* with you again."

It had been a full two days since their boss Robert Christian had been snatched from the mansion in the dead of night by an enemy the brothers hoped they would never have to tangle with again. The infiltrators had been equipped with night vision goggles and armed with silent weapons. To call them efficient killers would be an understatement. Clifford, Hutsell, and Ed could attest to that—their bodies were feeding the worms in a shallow communal grave behind the pool house. Furthermore, the way the *ghosts* had thwarted the estate's security system,

SHAWN CHESSER

picked the locks to gain access, and then disabled the generators spoke volumes to their training and professionalism.

As the credits finished and the '90's synth-heavy music began its fade out, even from inside the soundproofed home theater they could hear clearly the shuffling feet and mournful moans of the dead gathered outside.

The twenty thousand square foot multilevel mansion, once owned by a prominent Hollywood A-Lister, and most recently inhabited by Robert Christian, the self-appointed President of New America, was nearly impenetrable. Perched on a protruding finger of rock and surrounded by steep, undergrowth-choked hillsides, the grand walled compound was only accessible via a mile-long drive snaking up from the valley floor. Ringed by the massive granite Teton and Gros Ventre Mountains, the locals had contemptuously dubbed the prominent display of wealth and opulence overlooking the valley floor, *'The House.'*

"We're out of Scotch..." Liam hollered from the hallway.

"Did you check the butler's pantry?"

"We cleaned it out yesterday," Liam answered.

Lucas gave up the search for the remote, hastily reassembled the leather cushions and plopped back down under the weight of a looming decision.

"That settles it..." Liam exclaimed as he strode, empty-handed, back into the cavernous home theater. "We *have* to leave today."

Tilting his head back, Lucas eyed Liam sideways and said, "I concur." Then he upended one of the bottles that had somehow survived his tantrum and shook it violently over his gaping mouth, milking the last few drops of booze.

Looking disdainfully at the sad lack of willpower currently on display, Liam shook his head. "It's all gone... 'cept a couple bottles of Crème de Menthe, and I'm not going there. *Never* had a Grasshopper... *never* gonna."

Lucas jumped up from the couch, hurled the drained bottle sidearm at the humongous dropdown screen (missing horribly) and said forcefully, "You unlock the gate but don't open it just

104

yet, and then kill the generator. I'll load the Hummer... then we'll be real quiet and maybe the rotten fuckers will forget about us and go away."

"No way, bro. I'm not going out there... it fuckin' stinks. Plus the noise coming outta their pasty pie holes makes me want to shoot myself."

"Get your ass out there or I'm going to shoot you, Liam," he said, fixing him with a steely gaze. "And *please* refresh my memory... where'd you say you saw the minty-tasting stuff?"

Ignoring the last question, Liam unloaded on his brother. "*I* got the wire out of RC's Cadillac. Then *I* jury-rigged the generator *all* so that *you* could watch your precious DVDs. So how about *you* go out there and *you kill* the thing."

Silence. Except for the low level murmuring of the abominations pressing the front gate.

"Tell you what, bro," Lucas hissed. A multitude of silver and turquoise bracelets clicked as he ran his baseball mitt-sized hands through his stringy blonde locks. "OK... I'll do it. Don't wanna... let's call it a trade-off. I'll take care of our *other* problem if you go outside and take care of the rest."

Calculating the value of getting out from under one unenviable task—the messy job neither of the brothers Brother wished to undertake—and instead venturing outside of the mansion, Liam finally conceded. "OK. OK. I'll go out *there*. Just kill that fucking repeating soundtrack," he said angrily, pulling a bulky black semi-automatic pistol from his waistband and gesturing towards the high end Blu-Ray player built into the far wall. "Or I'm going to put a bullet through that goddamn thing."

Stretching his arms to full extension over his head, Lucas clapped his hands. "You've got yourself a deal."

As Liam left the room, still in a bit of a huff, he called out, "Crème de Menthe is in the kitchen by the espresso machine."

"Which kitchen?" Lucas called back as he crabbed sideways between the sofa and coffee table, tiptoeing through trash and broken glass.

"Downstairs kitchen," Liam called back, the echo of his voice quickly drowned out by the calls of the dead the second he opened the outside door.

Wincing from the aural and olfactory bombardment, Lucas grabbed his go bag: a fully stuffed black nylon internal frame backpack, and his AR-15—a semi-automatic civilian version of the military's venerable M-16. He visited the kitchen first to collect the libations, then went to the guest house to make good on his end of the bargain.

***

What's the hold up, little brother, Lucas thought to himself as he manhandled the package into the back seat and closed the door. *Fucker's probably bogarting a bottle of the good stuff.* He was cramming the backpack into the minimal space between the backseat and rear hatch when the overhead fluorescents hissed off, throwing the multicar garage into near darkness.

Good job little bro, thought Lucas.

Diffuse rays from the brutal summer sun infiltrated through the frosted rectangular windows inset high along the far wall, providing just enough light so Lucas could make his way around to the driver's side of the Hummer without banging his knees on the beefy plate bumpers.

He ducked his head and forced his 6-foot-5 inch, well-muscled, two hundred and fifty pound frame into the SUV. His knees crushed against the padding under the dash and the crown of his head brushed the headliner when he tried to sit up straight. *Fucking midget,* he thought to himself, cursing the Hummer's former movie star owner, who, when not on the big screen, was only a handful of inches over five feet and had left the seat all the way forward on its rails and jacked up to the maximum. *The fucker must have looked like a little kid driving this big rig around downtown Jackson,* Lucas mused as he adjusted the mirrors from the Lilliputian's settings to something more reasonable. *Perfect.*

With the truck set up and ready to go, he made his way back into the house and walked right into a wall of questions.

"You put the M-60 back in the truck?"

106

"Yes *Liam*... immediately after you blasted the shit out of everything *but* that silent black helicopter. The *veranda*. The *air*. The air *around* the helicopter. And if I recall correctly, the bad guys killed **Cheeto** Cliff, Ed, and Hutsell, and then took off into the night with R.C. aboard," came the monotone reply.

"Not my fault," Liam mumbled. "That thing was stealth or some shit."

Lucas grimaced and rubbed his eyes.

"Is the ride gassed and ready to go?" Liam asked.

"Yes *Liam*."

Liam stood in the doorway staring down Lucas. "Did you take care of your part of the deal?" he asked.

"Yes *Liam*. Any more questions *Liam?*"

"Was it hard?"

"No *Liam*. We've got a couple of hours to kill *Liam*. Can you please shut the fuck up *Liam*."

"Yes Lucas... where's the Crème de Menthe?"

With a broad smile Lucas closed his eyes.

***

Three hours later at the 'House'

"Wake up," Liam whispered.

Oblivious to his brother's presence, Lucas rolled over and farted

"It's time. Let's go." Words were not going to work, he decided, and against his better judgment he put a hand on his slumbering brother and nudged him. Gently at first, and when that didn't bring Lucas to, Liam resorted to a simulated 5.0 on the Richter scale. The latter approach resulted in him staring down the business end of Lucas's brushed metal .45.

"Relax bro," he said, slowly lifting his arms in surrender. "Let's go."

Shaking off the cobwebs, Lucas inquired about the dead.

"There are a lot less of them now. I told you the generators lured the pusbags."

"Or the heavy machinegun fire. The helicopter. The gunfire inside the mansion. Take your pick, just don't blame it on me wanting lights and a hot shower."

"And Die Hard," Liam added with a wide grin.

"Fuck off," Lucas answered, patting his sibling on the back. "Let's go... the H2 is ready. You unlatch the gate."

"Yes Luke..." and with a sweep of his arm Liam said, "age before beauty."

***

Liam popped the safety lever and with considerable effort sent the garage door on an upward journey.

"Get in the back," Lucas said as he turned the key.

The inevitable questions that began spewing from Liam's mouth were instantly drowned out as the Hummer's four hundred horsepower engine roared to life.

"What the fuck..." Liam blurted when he opened the rear door and saw Lucas's responsibility stretched across the floorboard, unmoving. Greeting him were the yellow-soled black canvas slippers still attached to Tran, who had been Robert Christian's personal chef and sometimes driver. "Why in the name of God did you bring the body?"

Liam looked up, meeting the other man's gaze in the rearview, and by the twinkle in Luke's eyes immediately knew he was up to something.

Lucas replied with a one word answer. "Bait."

"Bait," Liam responded incredulously. "Those things only eat the living... right?"

Ignoring the query, Lucas inched the eyesore yellow H2 out of the garage and let it roll slowly over the cobblestone pavers and around the perimeter of the mansion. As the twelve-foot wall crept past the passenger windows and the gate came into view, the sounds of the dead became more noticeable.

"How many goons are out there?"

"Bout fifty to seventy-five," Liam answered.

Lucas stabbed the brakes, stopping the Hummer just inside of the solid twelve-foot-tall gate. Coming from the floor, a muffled moan sounded as Tran's body rolled forward and then returned to where it had been placed, face down across the transmission hump.

A string of expletives filled the cab and Liam launched off the seat. "*Shit...* he's still alive!"

Lucas chuckled. "I clobbered him good. He went down like a sack of potatoes. He was out cold... plus he's a little squirt. That's why I only taped his hands."

"That wasn't part of the deal, Lucas. He's gonna slow us down."

"Like I said, he's *bait*. Toss him out after I bull the gate open. The goons will go for him and leave us be... at least most of 'em should."

"Good plan, bro. But you owe me one. Cause once again I'm stuck doing your dirty work."

Tran regained consciousness and realized his wrists were bound but his feet were free. He kicked at the door with both feet, inviting a swift kick from his captor's boot. Then a sharp pain shot through his scalp as he was pulled from the floorboards by his hair.

"Go," Liam said as he man-handled the slight Asian man onto his knees and then used his muscular left arm to pin him upright against the seatback on the driver's side.

"Pull off the tape so they'll hear him scream," Lucas called out over his shoulder.

Doing as he was told, Liam wrenched the duct tape from Tran's face, taking with it several days' worth of growth.

Silence... except for the rising crescendo of growls and moans coming from the agitated creatures.

Liam looked into the mute prisoner's almond-shaped brown eyes. Somewhere in there he could sense a smoldering coal of hatred. It didn't register on Tran's slack expression—only in the man's eyes. Suddenly Liam, who enjoyed a foot and a half height advantage and at least a hundred pounds over Robert Christian's former chef, was breaking out with a case of cold feet.

The Hummer's grill met the iron gate with a screech. Slowly, on well-oiled hinges, the thousand-pound gate began tracking a steady arc outward, pushing a number of the assembled zombies with it.

With dexterity and speed that belied their awful appearance, a clutch of creatures slapped at the fenders and hood of the slab-sided sport utility vehicle.

"Almost there," Lucas stated. A gap widened between the gate and the compound wall, and he forced the rig through the undead throng, wrenching the steering wheel left and right.

Liam reached across Tran's writhing body and couldn't help but take another look into the man's narrowed eyes. *Fucker, Luke,* he thought. *This was too close and personal. A bullet would have been easier. Least I'd sleep better.* He opened the door with a click, waited a beat...

"Now!" bellowed Lucas.

It was over in seconds. Lucas elbowed Tran, who barrel-rolled out and hit the pavers amongst bare feet and clawing hands. The door slammed and Liam urged his brother to step on it.

The dead, numbering at least a hundred strong, surged around the yellow vehicle, hungering for the fresh meat.

"Not a sound out of him," Lucas said as he downshifted and maneuvered the H2 through the tail end of the herd, half of which had taken the bait; the rest swiped at the windows leaving a viscous blood-tinged residue.

"Fucking lemmings. Those things are pouring down the bluff," Liam said, stealing a look through the narrow rear window. "Maybe he got away. The look he gave me was like a thousand-yard stare. Like he was on a fucking mission from God."

"Don't matter, he served his purpose," Lucas said coldly. "And you know what, bro... I don't blame him. I wouldn't be makin' lovey dovey googly eyes at you either if you were about to feed me to the goons."

An uneasy silence prevailed.

Sunlight filtering through the high canopy splashed a mosaic of gnarled shadows across the slowly moving truck.

Lucas glanced at the rearview. "Bottom of the hill... what do you think? Should we go left or right?"

Receiving no response from his brother, Lucas thought it over for a second and made an executive decision. "We're going right, over the Teton Pass. I've got a feeling the majority of the goons took the path of least resistance and followed 189. Jackson Hole's probably swimming with them."

"Teton Pass, here we come," Liam said with all the enthusiasm of a *Griswald* on vacation.

"Liquor store, here we come," Lucas added, making bubbles in the Crème de Menthe. "Want some, bro?"

After a millisecond Liam relented. "Why not? It's noon somewhere."

Lucas removed his eyes from the road for a brief time in order to hand the bottle back. And when they flashed forward he immediately knew they were in trouble. The H2's huge disc brakes grabbed as Lucas jumped on the pedal. Smoke billowed from the colossal tires as he wrestled the rig from forty miles per hour to a dead stop.

"What the fuck?" Liam cried.

"Take a look."

Liam poked his head between the front seats. Less than a car length away, in the center of Butte Road, two dozen dead were kneeling around a carcass the size of a compact car. The large three-point rack with the unmistakable rounded edges jerked with each hunk of flesh rent from the bull moose's carcass. One by one, bloodied faces swiveled towards the H2. Then, totally forsaking their cloven-hooved meal, the creatures arose and like lifeless-eyed automatons lurched stiffly towards the yellow vehicle and the meat contained within.

"Go around or go over the top!" Liam yelled. "Do something. Please... just fucking drive."

Stealing a sideways glance at his brother, Lucas was dismayed to see tears streaming down the younger man's cheeks. At a loss for words, Lucas returned his gaze forward, pretended the Hummer was equipped with a cowcatcher, put the transmission into a lower gear and bulled the gathering dead out of his path. Pale hands high-fived the windows and bones crunched under the off road tires as he wheeled the wide Hummer around the seemingly immovable four-legged carcass. Engine groaning, the once yellow SUV parted the dead sea.

"You can look now, bro," Lucas said as the truck gathered a head of steam. "They're gone."

Slowly Liam hinged up from the classic doomed airline passenger position he had assumed. He panned his head right and visibly shuddered at the sight of the sheen left on the window by the groping hands of the undead. He pulled his shirt to his face in order to wipe the accumulated sweat and surreptitiously stole a look through the pillbox-sized rear window—*just in case*.

"You lose a contact back there or something?"

"*Something*," Liam shot back, visibly embarrassed. "Quit busting my balls and drive."

Lucas chuckled as he shifted the whining gear box from four-wheel into normal two-wheel drive, and after three more tight hairpins the gore-streaked Hummer sat idling at the interchange.

Taking into account that in all likelihood Jackson Hole was overrun, there was only one way left to go. Lucas, being the smartass that he was, flicked his right turn indicator and looked both ways before turning onto the Teton Pass highway.

Chapter 16
Outbreak - Day 15
Jackson Hole, Wyoming

With the lurching throng literally nipping at his heels, Tran had thrown caution to the wind and hurled his body face first into the void. And after a landing violent enough to steal his wind, he skidded several yards down the pitch before gravity gave in to inertia and his feet traded places with his head. His slippers flew in two different directions and the underbrush tugged at his pajamas.

Thirty yards flashed by in dizzying fashion, and when he finally came to rest flat on his back, it was nothing short of a miracle that his bare feet pointed south and his trussed arms were not broken. Struggling to draw a breath, he stared at the bluebird sky. Then, reluctantly, he took mental inventory of his injuries. His left ankle throbbed angrily—no telling whether it was broken or sprained. The forked lightning pulsating up his spine brought him the most worry. What if a bone was broken back there and he moved and worsened the injury—maybe pinching the cord, leaving him paralyzed and helpless? His mind raced. The demons would surely get to him then. There would be nothing left for him to do but hope they started in on his lifeless legs. Pushing the worst case ruminations from his mind, he tested his theory and tried to wiggle his swollen and dirt-encrusted toes. *Movement.* A smile crossed his face. He bent his bloodied knees, testing the joints. *Not so bad.* The tartan pajamas that he had been wearing when Lucas had come to get him were in tatters, and adding insult to injury, he could feel a draft somewhere down below.

Strangely enough—though he had bashed his head repeatedly on who knows what on the way down, and swallowed a great deal of dirt in the process—his teeth still remained firmly anchored in his head. If he was going to have any chance of getting off the butte and eluding the undead mob, he had to find a way to free his wrists. No sooner had the thought crossed his mind than the pursuing zombies began to spill into the void. Dozens of pale limp bodies went cartwheeling downhill past him. Many more became entangled in the brambles and low brush on his left and right flanks.

Shocked into action, he rose, and trying his best to ignore the currents of pain arcing from his rapidly swelling ankle, attempted to put some lateral distance between himself and the undead raining down around him.

Maneuvering on the precipitous grade with the luxury of four functioning limbs would have been an achievement worthy of a mountaineering merit badge. Doing so with tightly bound hands that had turned from pink, to white, to a deep shade of purple and had lost all feeling proved to be impossible. After attempting one small step for Tran, he lost purchase, and once again watched sky and earth trade places too many times to count before a writhing drift of decaying flesh arrested his free-fall. Oblivious of the excruciating pain he was experiencing, he pushed up and away from the snapping and grabbing abominations and, as he sensed his body once again rag-dolling down the decline, his world suddenly went silent and dark.

Chapter 17
Outbreak - Day 15
Near Driggs, Idaho

Eight miles from the Teton Pass

Sometimes, when he closed his eyes and the smell of death was downwind or supplanted by the heady aroma of blooming roses as it was at this very moment, he could trick himself into thinking that the world was still somewhat normal. That the Omega virus was a thing from the movies or a figment of some twisted fuck's imagination. That the infected didn't die and then rise and hunger for living flesh. That his *Moms* was going to call at any moment and ask him about Heidi. Ask him if he'd been eating right or if he was getting enough exercise. At that moment, in his manufactured fantasy, he was off duty lounging at his little home in Driggs, waiting for Heidi to return from her nightshift at the Silver Dollar, and soon they would be enjoying each other intimately.

But as soon as the wind shifted and he could smell the stench of the dead and hear their throaty moans inside his little prison on the hill, the reality of his situation came rushing back to him. The dead were out there. His Moms was dead. And he feared that Heidi was never going to be the same woman he had fallen in love with.

115

He craned his head away from the open window. She was still breathing steadily. No doubt asleep again. He didn't know why she was sleeping all the time. His insecure little voice in his head said it was because she wanted nothing to do with him. The rational voice in his head told him she had PTSD—Post Traumatic Stress Disorder— and had slipped into some kind of a depression and would recover on her own timetable.

'*Give her time*,' is what Jenkins kept telling him. It was day three and all he'd gotten out of her was a wan smile and a handful of scratchy muffled words. He didn't know why, but what he really wanted to hear from her were the gory details. What had happened to her while he wasn't there to protect her? What did they do to her? He had nothing but questions, and part of him feared hearing her answers.

He opened his eyes and gazed towards the main highway. Reality was down there trudging lockstep towards Victor and Driggs and other places in the form of multitudes of rotting former humans. And as he shifted his gaze from the lurching dead to a nearby ash tree, he spotted a hummingbird milking a plastic feeder of its last few drops of red nectar. For a half a second he thought he could actually hear the little bird's wings beating the air. Then the sound rose in volume and he could tell it was coming from the east. *Thrumming tires?* he wondered. Then he sensed an accompanying vibration that was so heavy with bass it resonated deep in his chest.

He grabbed the police radio Jenkins had given him. It was set on the same channel as the one the former police chief carried, and had a considerable range—several miles, he guessed. For a second he considered getting ahold of Jenkins and giving him an earful for not checking in sooner and letting him know where he was.

But he decided to heed the man's advice and practice *patience*. First he needed more information about the vehicle with the thrumming tires and booming system that was quickly approaching from the northeast. From the direction of the Teton Pass and Jackson Hole.

116

He put the radio down and bolted for the stairs, took them down two at a time and skidded on the rug in the front room. He cast a cursory look around the room. *Nothing.* Tromped through the kitchen. Quickly scanned the Formica countertops and the kitchen table. *Nothing.* Finally he caught sight of them, sitting upright on the lenses between the decades-old refrigerator and a Felix the Cat cookie jar.

Field glasses in hand, he bounded up the stairs three at a time. He passed the bedroom, giving it a sidelong glance, and noticed Heidi sitting upright with a look of confusion on her face. Like she had come to and didn't remember where she was or what day of the week it was.

"It's OK honey," he said while trying to convey a reassuring look. "I heard a vehicle on the road and I'm going to take a look." There was no time to explain further so he continued on to the end of the narrow hallway, leaving Heidi a bit in the lurch.

He hauled the window up, pressed the field glasses to his face and trained them on the spot in the distance where the highway emerged from between the copse of trees. He braced his shoulder against the window sash to steady himself and waited for whatever was responsible for the raucous rolling concert.

Finally, after a couple of heartbeats, the slab-sided culprit came into view. With yellow paint a tick louder than the stereo, the Hummer straddled the dashed centerline as it closed the distance to the intersection of Bell and 33. And as Daymon tracked the vehicle left to right, it disappeared momentarily behind the grove of trees on the lower part of the property. Trying to match its pace, Daymon kept panning steadily to the right, catching only flashes of the garish colored rig through the densely interwoven branches.

"Better slow down, fool," he said aloud as the vehicle burst back into view and was now rocketing towards a handful of zombies, all of which were now fanned out across the entire highway. It seemed to Daymon, as he watched with morbid fascination, that the person behind the wheel was oblivious to the impending collision and had to be either drunk or high. He guessed the driver had the accelerator pegged and the rig was topping eighty miles an hour—and at that speed, he reasoned, neither the vehicle nor the zombies would be recognizable after the collision.

He lowered the binoculars and continued watching with the naked eye. The undead didn't waver. Though they seemed mesmerized by the booming music and the drone of the engine, Daymon knew without a doubt the prospect of getting to the fresh meat in the vehicle was what held their undivided attention.

His brain suddenly received a jolt of dopamine as impulses, Pavlovian in nature, jumped synapses. He felt his stomach clench and muscles tremor as he braced mentally for an impact he knew would have zero effect on him. He wasn't the unfortunate person about to get a lap full of walker parts when the near-vertical windshield blew inward. There was no danger of him being ejected and eaten by the dead when the Hummer lost control and rolled, becoming a crushed yellow tin can. Still, Daymon's mind raced out of control, matching the speed of the slow moving train wreck below. Then at the last second the driver course corrected, ran the two passenger side tires onto the shoulder and careened through the intersection, somehow managing to clip only one of the walking dead. The creature's right arm lost the battle with the stout brush guard and went airborne, trailing sinew and veins and splintered white bone. Meanwhile, the body of the male zombie completed three full revolutions as it cartwheeled face first into the roadside ditch.

"Fucking close call, dude!" Daymon exclaimed. The last thing he saw was a red flare of brake lights as the tin roof on one of the outbuildings blocked the fishtailing truck from view.

He let the curtains drop and thumbed on the police radio which he used to hail Jenkins.

Chapter 18
Outbreak - Day 15
Near Victor, Idaho

The Three Rivers Horse Farm was four miles up 33 to the southwest of the house that Jenkins, Daymon, and Heidi were squatting in. The expansive property had a massive entry constructed of hewn twelve-by-six timbers that were bolted together with industrial grade hardware. Towering no less than thirty feet over the turnoff from the main highway, the only real purpose Jenkins could see for the monstrosity was that it was a proper place to hang the neatly lettered sign letting everyone who passed by in on the nature of the business. As if the vivid green pastures crisscrossed with blindingly white fences, seemingly transplanted straight from the English countryside, weren't a dead giveaway.

As he made the turn into the equestrian paradise, the handful of walking dead he had just passed took up a slow speed chase.

After a short run out, the drive opened up to a large gravel parking lot contained within the same white three-tiered fencing as the pastures. Save for two late model compact sedans, the parking lot was conspicuously empty. Inside one of the vehicles, a red Hyundai, a putrefying corpse fought against the closed door. The banging intensified as Jenkins nosed the patrol Tahoe in next to the other car, a silver Tercel with Oregon plates.

As he slid from the truck, he thought about putting the former human out of its misery. But he had bigger fish to fry. Daymon was itching to get a move on, and without treating his wounds Jenkins had a feeling they would get worse. Therefore this little excursion was a necessary evil in the big scheme of things. He had even found it amusing when Daymon had had the audacity to question whether it was safe for him to go it alone. Alone was all he knew, he'd told the younger man. In fact, Jenkins hadn't had a patrolling partner for years. And being the chief had its advantages. He was the one who wrote the schedules, so he was the one who always worked the late shift, and he always preferred to do so solo.

Walking by the car, he caught a whiff of the occupant. The sun had made the rotten thing riper than a tomato in August, and suddenly the former chief was pleased with his decision.

The barn doors were wide open, and when he entered a smell twenty times stronger than the car corpse hit him in the face.

Having been brought up on a farm, Jenkins considered himself a country boy. He'd hatched chicks from an egg, raised and tended to cows and pigs, and would even admit (in the right company) that he still was a member of the 4H. But his first love had always been, and still was, for horses—and that was why the scene before him was so hard to accept.

In the barn, which was big enough to board forty or fifty horses, the stench of death hung heavy in the air. He walked down one side of the massive, high-ceilinged building and opened every stall that he came to. A good number of the animals had already died a slow death due to the hot August weather and a lack of food and water. The horses that hadn't were so severely weakened that instead of seeking freedom most of them remained inside their stalls to wait out the inevitable. The youngest and strongest among them trotted out tentatively and then immediately went for the water trough outside in the fenced-in pasture.

After he had opened all of the stalls, only fifteen of the horses had had enough strength to make their way outside. And of those fifteen, five were near death and collapsed after drinking from the trough. Why the owners of the stables hadn't set them free before they left had been nagging Jenkins since he first set foot in the big red barn.

As he walked past the open stables towards the far wall where a number of saddles, bridles, and bits were stored, he noticed that fully a third of the tack hooks were bare and a good number of the saddle cubbies had nothing in them. He thought, perhaps, that the owners took their personal horses and equipment and headed for the hills when all hell broke loose in Boise and Idaho Falls. That would certainly explain why he didn't see a single horse trailer, let alone a vehicle with sufficient enough horsepower to tow one, anywhere on the property. But it still didn't excuse the actions of the dirtbags who'd left the remainder of the horses locked up, thus sentencing most of them to a slow and miserable death.

Jenkins knew the zombies he had passed on the highway would eventually ramble up the drive hunting him, so he unslung his carbine and hustled towards the small room at the back of the paddock. He guessed it would be a fairly convenient place to store the things necessary to keep a number of horses groomed and healthy, and if there were antibiotics to be had, that was where he would find them.

He switched on his Maglite and swung the beam through the entry. The room opened up to the left and was shaped like a rectangle roughly six feet deep by twelve feet long, and was much bigger than he had anticipated. At the far end of the room a half dozen shelves had been installed above a Formica counter inset with an aluminum sink and faucet. Cupboards adorned with basic ceramic pulls flanked the walls at eye level on both sides. Everything save the ceiling was painted a dingy off-white with uneven brush strokes. Tom Sawyer and Huck Finn could've done a better job, Jenkins mused as he swept the bright white beam about the room.

Still fuming over the dying and neglected horses, he began to tear through the cupboards. After working both sides of the room and throwing most of their contents on the floor, he turned his attention to the shelving above the sink where he eventually found several foil tubes of some kind of veterinarian triple-antibiotic.

He stuffed the medicine and a few large adhesive bandages into his pockets and then passed the flashlights beam over the floor to see if he'd missed anything important. As he was doing so, his patrol radio squawked and Daymon's voice filled the air.

"Chief here," Jenkins said out of habit. Then he listened as Daymon informed him about the vehicle headed his way.

"Roger that," replied Jenkins. "I'm at the Triple R and I found your medicine. I'm gonna lay low and hope your friends pass on by."

"You'll hear 'em before you see 'em," Daymon added.

"Roger that. I think I might poke around the house up here before I return... see if I can find us some food and water."

"Just watch out for the fools in the Hummer," Daymon stated. "Chances are they ain't playing for the good team."

"I'm a big boy, Daymon. You just watch out for you and your lady friend, and I'll keep an eye on my own six," he said wryly. He thumbed off the radio and hooked it on his belt.

Just for shits and giggles, he tried the cold knob on the faucet. *Nothing.* Not even a drop. Then, as he about faced to leave the stifling anteroom, he found his way blocked by a walking corpse. The male zombie made one clumsy step forward and swiped for his neck but instead only managed to grasp a handful of Jackson PD uniform. Instinctively, Jenkins pulled away from the flesh eater's bared teeth and poked the monster in the chest with the end of his Maglite. And then, in less time than it took him to bring the hefty black flashlight over his head, a couple of thoughts raced through his mind: he made a quick calculation and figured that a vehicle scooting along at sixty to eighty miles per hour would take less than four minutes to cover the four miles from Daymon's position. Then he remembered that his patrol Tahoe was nosed in next to the two compact cars outside of the barn, and in plain view of the highway. Lastly, he contemplated pulling his Sig Sauer semi-automatic and blowing the thing's head off.

But the Maglite was already on its downward arc. He felt a considerable amount of give that went along with the sound of breaking bone as the knurled aluminum shaft, filled with the weight of five D-cell batteries, impacted dead center atop the zombie's skull. The thing's frigid fingers released and it collapsed to the floor, still moving.

"*Goddamnit*," Jenkins bellowed. "How in the hell did you sneak up on me?" A string of colorful expletives spilled from his mouth as he repeatedly brought his heel down on the abomination's already dented dome, and he didn't relent until the monster ceased moving.

He stepped over the corpse and nearly retched at the sight of all the blood and gray matter glistening in the brilliant white cone of light. The entire melee had shaved a minute off of the time he figured he had left to get in the Tahoe and move it out of sight.

Jenkins peeked around the doorway and into the paddock. *Clear.* He was grateful the zombie had been a lone wolf, but was certain there were more of the flesh eaters where it came from— there always were.

He hooked the Maglite next to the radio, flicked the carbine to safe, and broke into a full sprint with the weapon held at a low ready. In seconds he had covered the length of the barn and broke out into the sunlight. With his head on a swivel, he rounded the front of the Tahoe, quickly wrenched the door open and vaulted inside. As he pulled the door shut, he picked up the thunderous bass notes coming from the approaching vehicle.

The engine fired up and Jenkins backed away, working the steering wheel, accelerator, and transmission in perfect synchronicity—moves learned decades ago at the police academy and perfected since then, patrolling the streets and rural highways of Wyoming. Then, with a spray of gravel, he launched the black and white into the barn. Simultaneously, he put the Tahoe in park, cracked the window, and fixed his gaze on the rearview where he could see a number of zombies ambling up the driveway.

Then, moving fast left to right, he witnessed the boxy yellow Hummer blur by in the mirror and, without slowing, move out of sight and earshot.

Must not be horse folk, thought Jenkins.

A satisfied look on his face, he backed out of the barn and wheeled around facing 33. He sat in the idling vehicle, shifting his gaze between the advancing walkers and the white colonial-style house adjacent to the barn.

Since he'd already dodged two bullets, and with at least a dozen walking dead dangerously close, he powered his window up. He shifted to drive and slowly rolled the two and a half ton vehicle forward, and was greeted with the disconcerting sound of flesh slapping against sheet metal.

At the end of the drive he turned right and, as he steered the Tahoe one-handed northeast along 33, picked up the radio and called Daymon.

Miles away, in the farmhouse on the hill, Daymon's considerable frame filled the upstairs window. Binoculars glued to his face, he passed the time waiting for Jenkins's return, watching the dead trudge up Bell Road.

"That's what I was afraid of," he muttered under his breath. "Goddamn it Charlie." It had become crystal clear to Daymon that the dead had figured out which direction the Tahoe had come from and were now coming to investigate.

Investigate, thought Daymon as he reached for the radio. *Hunt would best describe their actions*. It was his experience that the dead equated moving vehicles with the prospect of acquiring human flesh. And it had also occurred to him over the last couple of weeks that even in the zombies' reptilian minds it was clear that they somehow knew or sensed that *meat* congregated together.

But before he could pick up the radio to warn Jenkins, it emitted an electronic trill.

Unable to tear his eyes from the procession, and with the awful memories of being trapped with Cade in the farmhouse in Hannah propagating his mind, he answered the noisy device. "Daymon," he said tersely.

"I've got good news and bad news," Jenkins stated. "Good news first. The rig passed on by at a helluva clip. And... I think I found you some useful antibiotics."

Daymon made no reply.

Nonplussed, Jenkins went on. "Bad news is I'm going to get myself trapped if I go in the house looking for supplies. It's probably best we do it with numbers when we come back this way. At least then we'll have Heidi as a lookout... even though she can't yell, nothin' to stop her from honking the horn."

Daymon thought about this for a second. "Great in theory, but there are a bunch of walkers heading towards *this* house," he finally said.

"Why dontcha go and take care of them?" replied Jenkins.

"And leave Heidi?"

"A second won't kill her."

"I abandoned her once. I'm not going to leave her *alone* again," said Daymon sharply.

"Understood. I'll be back in a few minutes," Jenkins replied. He removed his glasses and pinched the bridge of his nose, trying to keep the looming headache at bay, and after a tick he went on. "We'll just have to take care of them before we leave in the morning. Shouldn't be too bad." He threw an involuntary shudder thinking about the creature he had just brained and put the boot to in the barn. The idea of putting down a slew of them set his stomach to churning. In the past he'd had no problem blowing away a bad guy—no regrets, no remorse. Those dirtbags never came back to haunt him in his sleep. But these regular folks... the multitudes who had just been in the wrong place at the wrong time, and had gotten themselves bit and then turned— he was finding were the hardest to put down. Since day one of this horrible event, *they* had been the ones haunting him day and night.

Throwing the radio in the console, Jenkins white-knuckled the wheel all the way to the house on the hill, utterly dreading the fact he was going to have to deal with the dead.

Chapter 19
Outbreak - Day 15
Huntsville, Utah

Duncan let the Land Cruiser coast most of the way down the hill, then braked a few feet shy of the supine bodies they'd spotted from the rise. He put the e-brake on, and out of habit started the flashers ticking. "Remember to keep your head movin'... 'On a swivel,' as a good friend of mine likes to say. And one more thing... those 'rotters' as you all like to call them... they don't always let you know they're comin'."

"Yes, Sir," Phillip replied. He exited the truck, then looked left, then right, then back like he was in grade school and the crossing guard was AWOL.

Duncan smiled—clearly his advice had sunk in. Remaining vigilant himself, he craned his head around the Humvee's buried rear end. "Clear on this side," he called out. Because he had seen walkers that had appeared to be truly dead rise and attack, he approached the nearest body with a great deal of caution.

Mouth agape in a final silent scream, shadowed sockets where his eyes had been, the dead National Guardsman glared blindly at the morning sky. The cause of death was obvious: like a kindergartner's unfinished connect-the-dots, purple entry wounds riddled his abdomen and left leg. Contrasting sharply against alabaster skin, coal-black tribal tattoos spiraled up both arms before finally coming together an inch above his sternum. On his left shoulder, encircling a soldier's cross—an M4 rifle standing vertically with a pair of boots at the base and a helmet perched on the buttstock—were the words *Fallujah, Never Forget*, and a unit insignia he didn't recognize. To Duncan, it was painfully obvious that the young soldier's last seconds on earth had been spent suffering with immeasurable agony. He had seen dozens of men, the same age, and in similar poses—usually minus their manhood as well as their eyes—on the muddy and bloody battlefields of Vietnam. The fact that the Guardsman had escaped joining the ranks of the walking dead seemed to be the only bright spot to the man's final day on earth.

"Fucking savages that did this," Phillip said, contempt dripping from the words.

Duncan regarded the statement, nodded, but said nothing.

"Hey Sir... over here," Phillip called out. "We got some more dead soldiers in the ditch and a whole lot of head-shot rotters on the road."

Duncan looked both ways before crossing the two-lane blacktop—a habit not entirely necessary for survival in the zombie apocalypse. Then he skirted the front of the Humvee, giving it a wide berth, all the while looking underneath to ensure a grabber wasn't lying in wait and ready to ruin his day—a habit he found *very* necessary for survival in the zombie apocalypse.

Duncan stood alongside Phillip, who was kneeling and peering down into the roadside ditch where a dozen more guardsmen, their bird-pecked bodies frozen in various death poses, had been unceremoniously dumped.

"Bunch a shit," Phillip muttered sullenly as he stood up straight. "They were just doing their jobs." He shook his head.

A few silent seconds passed.

Phillip sat on his haunches and poked a stick at one of the dead zombies that had been left where they fell by whoever had gunned them down. "What do you think went down here *Sir*?"

Duncan envisioned his hands around Phillip's scrawny neck. Squeezing the seeds from his Adam's apple. He had heard one too many *sirs* uttered by his talkative road dawg. *That's it*, he told himself as he revisited in his head the hours' old exchange he'd had with his brother.

"*It's not wise to go out there by yourself*," Logan had said, suggesting that Duncan take a handful of men with him.

"*I work best alone*," he had countered.

Little brother finally relented, but did so with one condition attached: excluding Gus, Lev, or the Chief, big brother had to choose one of the men from the compound to ride shotgun, and for once, age hadn't trumped persistence. The fact that he was a loner by nature and usually eschewed travelling companions—especially ones with a sidekick mentality—made Duncan wonder what the hell he had been thinking when he agreed to Logan's *one* condition.

"*Sir...*" Phillip said again.

Cursing Logan under his breath, Duncan squared up to the walking stick bug. He looked down into the man's closely-set eyes and said in his best John Wayne, "Phil, I don't carry a rank any longer... and callin' me *sir* just makes me feel old. I'm no math major, but I figure I've only got ten—maybe twelve years on ya—so I'm not your elder either." He paused for effect, and stroked his silver mustache which was trying to grow into a goatee. "So how bout we stick with Duncan or Winters... you do that, and before you know it—you and me—hell... we'll be thick as thieves." *And if you don't, it's the wood chipper for you.*

"Understood," Phil said, breaking eye contact. At a loss, he pressed the binoculars to his eyes and slowly turned a full circle. "We've got six rotters coming from the west. Also there are a few of them in the field over there... couple hundred yards off."

"We've got time," Duncan stated. He removed his Aviator's glasses and wiggled the ear pieces, testing the tiny screws holding them together, then produced a handkerchief and polished each thick lens with meticulous precision before squaring them away on his face. "To answer your question, Phillip, these soldiers died more than a week ago. Probably closer to ten days, give or take." He turned and walked along the edge of the ditch towards the Humvee. "Let's take a closer look," he added, covering his nose and mouth with the handkerchief.

Trying to determine what had happened to the small patrol, Duncan eyed the desert-tan rig. Half in and half out of the ditch, with one knobby tire clawing the air and a wicked-looking gun barrel stabbing skyward, the metal beast looked like a stricken Cunard liner about to slip under the sea.

He turned his scrutiny to the roadway and angrily kicked at a mound of shell casings. The four-inch long, finger-thick brass threw the sun and tinkled like chimes as they skittered and bounced along the flat surface. He guessed that these dead men had been deployed to this weather-beaten stretch of road to either set up a checkpoint or to block its passage altogether. Whichever the case, it appeared to have been hastily constructed. There were no Jersey barriers—those 42-inch high modular concrete slabs usually employed on freeways to re-route traffic. He also thought it odd that the troops hadn't strung up concertina wire or employed sandbags. These two observations, when combined, led him to believe that this had been set up not only to allow people out of Huntsville, but more importantly to keep looters from going back into the city. To say the checkpoint and the troops manning it had been dangerously exposed—to the infected but also to human threats—would be overstating the obvious.

"Phil... Come here, I wanna bend your ear."

"Whatcha got, Duncan?"

"See these shell casings?" He nudged a small pile with his boot.

"Lots of 'em," Phil observed. "Different calibers, it appears."

Good job, Duncan thought. "Yep. We've got 9mm, 556 Nato, 7.62x39mm... *Kalashnikovs*." He raised his brow an inch. His glasses hitched up too. "AK-47s probably. The bigger shells are from that mounted .50." He gestured to the long-barreled gun atop the high centered Humvee. "I figure these dead boys—they probably knew the people gathered. Probably even knew the ones who did this... ate lunch with 'em at the diner in town on occasion. Never forget, Phil... when push comes to shove, people change... *allegiances* shift."

"So the Guard let their guard down—"

"And let the bad guys get too close before they engaged. Lethal mistake, because the .50—she ain't designed for accurate close quarters combat," Duncan said, finishing the younger man's thought. They'd held their fire, probably as a result of compassionate human nature overriding self-preservation, he guessed. Hell, he would rather be eaten alive by army ants than be stuck in the same position. He couldn't fathom having to follow orders that said he had to shoot his fellow countrymen— especially with the world going to shit around him—that would have been a hell of a moral dilemma. For anyone with a sense of fairness it'd be hard to wrap a mind around, let alone actually follow through. "They went through all of the ammo for the .50. Musta been a shit show." This got Duncan to thinking. He picked up a handful of the metal clips that linked the .50 caliber bullets together. There were hundreds of them littering the floor and footwell in the open-backed vehicle—a by-product of the disintegrating ammo belts fed into the Ma Deuce by the gunner. *These need to be repurposed*, he said to himself.

"Duncan... check this out."

"Whatcha got Phil?" he drawled.

"A pile of bloody uniforms. This one belonged to Corporal Howard of the Utah National Guard... apparently he was O-negative," he said with a frown as he displayed the punctured ACU blouse so that Duncan could see. "Says so right here."

"Unfortunately that info's not gonna help him... wherever he is now."

"There are more uniforms than bodies. That makes no sense. Why would they take prisoners but leave their vehicle?"

"Probably to use 'em for slave labor. Make them do the things you don't want to... clear a house of infected. Burn bodies. Cut firewood. You name it. Or worst of all... you infect them—and we've already seen it at the compound—then you got yourself fire-and-forget weapons. Rotters don't need to be fed or watched too closely. Can't think or reason... therefore they're not scheming on how to escape," Duncan proffered. Then he pointed at the grass near the far shoulder. "There were a couple more vehicles parked on the side... there. Probably Hummers judging by the tire impressions. And all of these cars stretching down the road, see how they're loaded up with crap, camping gear and what not? Look closely, Phil. You've got mostly Utah plates, but damn near all of 'em have either Salt Lake City or Ogden automotive dealerships advertised on their frames. The people who left these vehicles *did not* continue forward on foot, otherwise we'd have passed all kinds of discarded things they tired of carrying... so I'd be willing to bet someone forced them back into Huntsville."

"And?" Phillip said.

"And most of them are probably rotters by now," replied Duncan. "Roaming the interstate and the back roads. I think that goes a long ways toward explaining why we're seeing so many undead visitors outside the compound."

Phillip turned his gaze towards the town and the glittering reservoir beyond. "So, the other day... why in God's name did they cut the wire and let in the rotters and then not follow them in and attack us?"

"Easier for them to loot what they need from unguarded soft targets in the area first. As I said before, they wanted to flush us out to the road... to get a ballpark idea of how many we were and whether or not we were armed. I god-damn guarantee you that they're thinking twice about comin' in... seein' as how we chewed up the mess of rotters they sent in."

"So why didn't they ambush us at the fence?" Phil queried.

"For all they know we have a small army inside the forest. What would you think if a military type helicopter was flittin' around the countryside that you previously thought you had all to yourself?"

"Well, if I had anything to do with killing National Guard soldiers," Phillip nodded to the eyeless cadaver to his right, "I'd be suffering from a very tight sphincter, and wishing I had eyes in the back of my head."

"So what choice do *we* have then?" Duncan asked.

"I dunno."

Come on, thought Duncan. *Use the brain God gave you, Phil.*

Fracturing the quiet, staccato bursts of gunfire rolled across the reservoir coming from the nearby town.

"AK-47," Duncan stated confidently.

"How can you be so sure?"

"Vietnam. Been on the wrong end of 'em more than once. They have a slower cyclic rate than the M-16... they've got a distinctive chatter that I'll never forget." Then, playing into the whole democracy thing Logan insisted the group practice, he decided he'd delve further into Phil's brain. "So what do *you* think we should do... do we sit in the compound and assume they aren't going to return? Do we get into an arms race with an enemy we know nothing about? Or should we go and hunt them down?"

As if saying, *Beats the hell outta me*, Phil shrugged his shoulders and waited for Duncan to enlighten him.

Flunked the test, Phil, Duncan thought. Then he said, "They'll come. When they need food, bullets, or women." He kicked at the shell casings again and locked eyes with Phillip. "They'll come. So we have to be ready for them."

"That's it?"

"No... not exactly. They've already declared war. We'd be stupid to fight this on their terms. We need to go and hit them where they sleep... get them on their heels and either run them out or kill 'em all. And if it's put up for a vote... mine goes for the latter."

Looking around nervously as if the bullets might start flying at any moment, Phil summoned up the courage to ask Duncan what he thought they should do right this moment. As if on cue, another hollow-sounding burst of gunfire rang out in the distance.

"They're coming this way," Duncan said assuredly. "Quickly... we need to get this thing on the road."

***

After reeling off fifteen feet of cable from the Humvee's winch, Duncan positioned the Land Cruiser pointing east—the direction of the compound—and hitched the spooled-out cable to the towing receiver underneath the Toyota's rear bumper.

"The rotters are getting close," stated Phillip.

Duncan stood on the Toy's rear bumper and looked west down 39. A trickle of walking corpses approached, weaving in and out between the mass of stalls. Then he gazed east, the way they had come. More of the creatures, only these were separated from the road—kept at bay by a farmer's fence.

Phillip prairie-dogged up. Looked up and down the road. "Shouldn't we be going?" he asked nervously.

"Yes, but we're taking the Hummer... if it'll start."

Phillip cast a weary eye at the shambling dead. "What can I do?"

"Get in the Toyota, put her in the lowest gear you can, and when you hear me holler, stomp on it."

"OK. But why do we need it? You said the gun was out of ammo."

"I've got an idea," Duncan replied as he mounted the listing Humvee. He applied the brake and turned the switch on the left of the dash towards the start position. Then held his breath. With a loud *Braap* the open-topped truck's diesel engine turned over and thrummed to life. Out of the corner of his eye he noticed movement, and then two things happened at once: gunfire rang out—seven or eight tightly spaced shots. Then the two first turns that had apparently emerged from between the vehicles and had been flanking from the left—out of his blind spot—fell to a heap five feet from him. He shifted his gaze to the front where he could see the upper half of Phil's body protruding from the Toyota's open moon roof; he flashed a thumbs up and then cursed himself for the lapse in security. More shots rang out before he could un-ass himself to assess the situation. Phil grinned, flashed a thumbs up back at him and yelled, "All clear," before he and his AR-15 vanished back inside the Land Cruiser.

"Now!" Duncan bellowed.

The Toyota's power plant whined and strained, trying to pull the nearly three ton rig from the ditch. Like an enormous Salad Shooter, the Hummer's meaty tires chewed up grass and gravel, sending chunks of sod blasting the barbed wire fence to the rear. Slowly but surely, with the Land Cruiser tugging, the effort paid off as the 200 horsepower and 380 foot pounds of torque transferred from the Hummer's 6.2 liter engine to the tires grappling with the road's edge.

Duncan was nearly launched from his seat when the front end came down with a resonant bang. As quickly as his old bones would allow, he leaped out, shotgun in hand, and following his own advice put his head on a swivel. *Clear.*

He hastily rewound the cable into the front-mounted winch, then retook his seat in the Hummer. Being careful to avoid driving overtop the Guardsmen, he conducted a three-point turn and sped off to the east.

With the white Toyota filling the rearview mirror and thankfully blotting out the macabre scene, he thought about the soldiers and lamented the fact they would never receive a proper burial. That they would molder in the elements until the birds and wild animals had picked their bones clean only made their fates harder for the old veteran to accept.

Headed east on 33 with only the thrumming of the big tires for company, one of the motor mouth's lines from Fargo popped into his head, bringing a smile to his face. *'Would it kill you to say something?'*

Duncan looked in the mirror and spied Phil with his hands at the proper *'ten and two'* on the wheel. "It almost did you in Phil, old boy," he said aloud. Then he drove on in silence. A totally glorious vacuum of space type of silence.

Chapter 20
Outbreak - Day 15
Schriever AFB
Colorado Springs, Colorado

Taryn took a sharp right and bounded up the steps of a much nicer structure than Wilson could have imagined she would call home. "We're here," she proclaimed proudly.

He waited patiently, kicking an errant pebble with the toe of his boot as she worked the lock. He could feel the subtle twinge as the sun cooked his pale dermis. Suddenly he was self-conscious of his appearance. What really worried him was that maybe the brim of his hat hadn't provided adequate coverage for his nose, and when he removed it he might be mistaken for Ronald McDonald. *Oh well*, he thought. At least there was one positive thing about having a sunburned face. It provided good camouflage for a blushing fool like him.

He admired the row of squat pre-fab buildings. All were painted the same battleship gray as most everything else on the sprawling base, and with their rectangular angles and flat roofs he thought they belonged inside a prison's walls. In a way, the entire base had become quite penal to him these last few days.

"This thing is tricky," she said over her shoulder. Then, after fiddling with the lock for a few seconds, the tumblers fell and she made her way into the shadowy interior. "It's dark. Watch your step."

Wilson noticed a slight drop in air temperature when he reached the top step. Then, as he crossed the threshold into the spacious living quarters, a refreshing blast of conditioned air enveloped his body, causing a wave of goose bumps to break out on his pale arms. He whistled, a long drawn out note that commingled with the low thrum emanating from within the room.

"*Surprise,*" Taryn said, her arms spread wide like Vanna White giving away a new car. The air inside her quarters was at least thirty degrees colder than the air outside, and through her black tank Wilson couldn't help but notice her nipples reacting to the shock.

Surprise indeed, he thought. Reluctantly, he tore his eyes away, turned and crossed the room. "How in the heck did you score this?" he called out as he spread his arms and wallowed in the cold air blasting him. Shoehorned into a window, two feet above a row of desks lining the wall to the right of the entry, the boxy modern unit looked out of place—like some kind of an afterthought that had been added recently.

Taryn parted the curtains flooding the room with natural light. "It was already there when they assigned this trailer to me. It's funny though, I keep waiting for them to figure it out and send me packing. That's one of the reasons why I haven't gone out much since I got here."

"You've been here three days—right?"

"I did the mandatory twelve plus hours of quarantine first. Followed by two and a half days of self-imposed solitary right here." She shrugged. "Might as well call it three."

"When you arrived here did they give you the TSA pat down and the full naked search?"

Taryn nodded. "You?"

"Yep. I received the full on drop the shorts once over. And the whole '*have you been bit?*' yada, yada, yada," Wilson said.

Taryn nodded. "I've never felt more violated... and I've been through my fair share of airport security."

"I wouldn't think that would rattle you. You seem really confident to me. Like you could handle yourself before all of this. You know, with guys and stuff. But against the monsters, how'd you pull that off?"

"One day at a time."

"Sounds like one of those twelve step slogans."

Taryn didn't get the reference but laughed anyways. Then she suddenly became aware of the climate's effect on her anatomy, and folded her arms across her chest and smiled sheepishly at Wilson.

"I have a sister, remember... I've seen 'em before."

"*Gross*—" she cried.

"No, no, no..." he stammered. "I didn't mean *outside* of her shirt. At least not since me and her were kids." The more he said the deeper the hole got. So he clammed up. The last thing he wanted to do was get on her bad side.

Taryn glared from across the room, arms still clamped in front.

He blushed, but thankfully the red badge of embarrassment was masked by the second degree sunburn that made his face feel like he'd been bobbing for apples in a tub of Tabasco.

Trying to salvage any modicum of respect she might have for him, he quickly changed the subject. "You want to talk about... *things?*"

"I'm ready." She crossed the room and took a spot on the lower bunk, her thigh resting a few inches from his. "Where to start?"

"From the beginning," Wilson said in a low voice.

She drew a deep breath and began by describing how the two passenger jets—one from Salt Lake and one from Vegas—had delivered the Omega virus to Grand Junction Regional. She went on about witnessing her family, friends, and the entire world outside die over the span of a few short days, in real time, via Facebook, Twitter, and YouTube, brought front and center on the Retina display of her iPhone. She described her glass-walled prison at the airport—her undead boss's office—as a skybox seat to the end of her old life. She recounted how her boss, Richard Lesst—also known, not so affectionately, as Dickless—had constantly harassed her when he was still alive. Then she gleefully recounted how the nonstop nitpicking and sexual innuendo had finally died when he did, going so far as to describe in painstaking detail how his rotting, lifeless corpse had stared at her through his own office door for nine straight days.

"So what happened to *Dickless*?" Wilson asked.

"I shot the *fucker*."

Struck by the irony of the situation, Wilson lost it. And wracked by uncontrollable laughter, he collapsed onto the bunk which jounced under them after each of his full body spasms.

"I'm sorry," he said, wiping the tears from his eyes. "You killed *Dickless*. The Cohen brothers couldn't have written a better ending."

"That's not all."

"There's more."

"It's not as funny."

"Lay it on me."

Taryn stretched out on the bunk next to the redhead, gazed up at the loadbearing slats above her, and finished telling *her* story.

"So after you survived the fall from the airport terminal and shot Dickless dead, a silent helicopter full of soldiers scooped you up."

She reached up and drummed her fingers on the bunk bed overhead. "That's what happened."

"Sounds like something out of a Michael Bay movie. But I believe you."

"I'm done spewing, Wilson. I'm not kicking you out. In fact, as cliché as this may sound... I *need* you to stay and just hold me."

He shifted his gaze, looked into her eyes.

"Just hold—" she said, and then quickly looked away. But before she did Wilson noticed a crack in her brave facade. She

139

seemed embarrassed by the simple request. Hell, he couldn't blame her. After a long moment she regained eye contact and the corners of her mouth upturned into a half-smile. "At least for now," she cautioned. "And I'm going to warn you... I'll be thinking of my dad at first."

Wisely, Wilson said nothing, and there was silence except for the low hum from the wall unit.

"Why couldn't I have died like everyone else?" Taryn asked. Then her body went into convulsions as those final words crossed her lips. She rolled over, facing away from him, and with sobs wracking her body drew her legs and arms into a fetal ball.

He wrapped his gangly arms around her and drew her body closer. Abruptly his own survivor's guilt reared its head. His thoughts turned to his own father whom he hadn't had much contact with since he was a little boy; for all he knew he was probably dead before the outbreak started. Then he shut that part of his past away and thought about his mom and all of the things that he had been meaning to tell her, but thanks to the dead would never have the opportunity to. And as he lay there spooning with the young woman he wanted to get to know better, his throat constricted and his own bottled emotions welled to the surface.

***

Shivering and disoriented, Wilson woke up first. He dodged his eyes around the room. After a few seconds he remembered where he was, but since his watch was on his left wrist and his left arm was trapped under Taryn's dead weight, he had no clue what time it was. Not being used to sleeping during the day had left him feeling groggy and hung over. Like someone had jammed cotton balls into his cranium, his thinking had gone fuzzy. So he closed his eyes, lay still, and tuned in to the rising and falling of Taryn's chest, let himself be comforted by the calm steady tempo to her breathing. *Still sleeping*, he thought. Then the realization that he had left Sasha alone to fend for herself, God knows how long ago, hit him like an electric current. While holding Taryn's head off the pillow with his right hand, he tried

140

to worm his left arm out from under her limp form. *Almost there*, he thought. *Don't wake her up. Because if she's anything like Sasha*, he thought to himself, *there'll be hell to pay if I do.* His arm was almost free, when suddenly he found that he couldn't move it any farther. Good job, Wilson. He supposed his watch was snagged on her long braided hair.

He lowered her head to the pillow. "Taryn," he whispered.

She mumbled something unintelligible, then rolled towards him, curling his arm up in the process.

As he recalled *Operation Arm Removal*, a morbid smile crossed his face. Oh how the tables had turned, because this time it was his arm that had become stuck in someone else's hair.

He tried again, a little bit louder this time. "Taryn, wake up."

Nothing. He couldn't coax a twitch out of sleeping beauty. *"Taryn!"*

Two things happened simultaneously. She came up swinging, landing two well-placed blows to his chest, thus freeing his arm which hadn't been entangled in her hair after all. However, the thin filament with the thumb drive hanging from it had been. The clear line snapped, resulting in the metal drive going airborne and finally coming to rest underneath one of the desks.

"What the heck, Wilson!"

He tapped his Timex. "I didn't want to wake you but your necklace was hooked on my watchband." He rubbed his chest through his shirt. "Gonna bruise up good."

"Well you scared the shit out of me. Up until today I've been sleeping with one eye open."

"Because of your boss?" Wilson asked her.

"Mainly him and Karen. She worked at the Subway at the far end of the concourse. They've been visiting me in my nightmares. I'm *sooo* afraid to close my eyes."

"Could have fooled me. You were out, *o-u-t*, out. Almost like you had been drugged or something."

"I felt safe, Wilson... for the first time in a long time... I felt secure in your arms. And I have only you to thank for that."

Wilson's eyes went wide and he nearly threw up in his mouth. Not because her words seemed trite or insincere, but because he sensed that he was venturing into uncharted waters. Then another one of his mom's favorite sayings popped into his head, *'Be careful what you wish for, Wilson.'*

"Let me get this for you," he said, changing the subject while at the same time trying to deflect her praise. He crossed the room and retrieved the brushed aluminum thumb drive.

Taryn went silent as she observed the redhead turn the device over in his hands, giving the thing more scrutiny than a thumb drive in a world with few operable computers deserved. And when he walked his gaze over to meet her eyes she noticed that the color had drained from his face—sunburn and all.

"What's the matter, Wilson," she asked, worry cracking her voice. Fearing that he was suffering from a touch of heatstroke and was getting ready to pass out or something, she bolted to his side. "Are you OK? You look like you've just seen a ghost."

"I think I just did."

Taryn made a face, then stared at him trying to decide if she needed to get him to a doctor—*if there were any left*, she thought to herself. He ignored her. Just stood there staring at the drive resting on his open palm. Then, after a few seconds of quiet layered atop the subliminal rumble of the hardworking A/C unit, he spoke up. "Where did you get this?"

She grabbed his elbow, guided him to one of the U.S. Air Force issue metal chairs, and parked him there. "I found it sticking out of that top bunk," she finally replied. "Wrapped up with some Oreos. Why do you ask? It's probably filled with nothing but country and western music anyway."

From his seated position Wilson had to look up to meet her eyes. "Take a look at this..." He held up the drive and pointed to the words 'Property of the C.D.C.' "The C stands for Centers, the D is for Disease—"

"The other C stands for Control," Taryn said, finishing Wilson's sentence. "And why would that be here in Colorado Springs?"

He turned the drive over.

"Do you know who *Fuentes* is?" Taryn asked.

"I recognized the name but the letters didn't make sense... at first. Now, I think I know the answer to both of your questions... but I need to go see somebody to be certain." Gripping the drive between his thumb and forefinger he held it in the air. "And I need to take this with me."

He snagged his boonie hat off of the desktop, crushed it over his hair pulling it down tight, and then in passing gave Taryn a quick peck on the cheek.

"You'll need this too," she proffered.

Wilson turned back to see what he was being ordered to take. She was holding the silver key that worked the lock to her lonely quarters.

"Come back and stay the night here. And please bring Sasha if she'll come... let her know that she's welcome here too."

He glanced at his watch. More than three hours had passed since they'd left his sister in the mess hall. "OK," he said. "I'll see what she says. But if she doesn't accept your olive branch I won't leave her alone. She's family." He paused for a second and then jounced down the steps. And with that the door closed after him, cutting off the stark white light streaming in from outside.

Taryn stood alone in the trailer, stock still, allowing the cool conditioned air to flow over her. "You better come back to me Red," she said aloud. "Or I'm going to have to come and get you."

***

Twenty miles east of Yoder, Colorado

The needle edged past eighty. *Smooth*, Cade thought. He abruptly changed lanes and marveled at how the F-650's body exhibited a lot less roll than expected.

Next, still clipping mightily along the laser-straight interstate, he steered directly towards an unmoving human form laying spread-eagle perpendicular to the centerline. And as the truck passed over the supine Z, its stout suspension shrugged off the rotten obstacle as if it hadn't even been there.

In the distance, the Rockies were becoming more pronounced, meaning that Schriever wasn't far off. Farmhouses blurred by, rusting farm equipment and old cars languishing in the sun.

But the clear straightaway didn't stretch on forever. So Cade chose an arbitrary spot which he guessed to be about a football field's length away, and then, gripping the wheel tightly, he eased off the gas and stood on the brakes.

A violent judder rocked the truck, vibrating from the road through the massive tires, ran through the frame and right up his spine. It lasted for a fraction of a second and then the ABS—antilock braking system—began to automatically pump the brakes faster than any human being could.

The massive pick-up slewed minutely and then stopped short of the pair of wrecked SUVs he had chosen as the imaginary end zone of his imaginary three-hundred-yard run out. "I'll take it," he said jokingly to the imaginary salesman sitting in the passenger seat. "Put it on my AmEx." He let himself enjoy a rare moment of uncontrollable laughter.

As the blue-gray smoke from the superheated rubber wafted by the driver's side window, he reached back and gripped his M4. He popped the door and slid out of the cab. Once he was standing on the hot asphalt, he shifted his gaze, letting his eyes follow the dual black stripes painting the road some seventy yards behind the idling Ford.

Keeping one eye peeled for Zs, he hopped up onto the rear tire, collected the empty gas cans and the length of hose from the bed, and then jumped back down, his Danners sticking slightly to the sun-scorched asphalt.

Returning his attention to the tangle of American iron, he strode purposefully toward the back of the vehicle that did the rear-ending. Noticing some movement up the road to the west, he propped the M4 against the rig's rear tire and set the hose and cans in the shadow of the big red Suburban. He popped open the filler door with his Gerber and twisted off the cap. He inserted a couple of feet of hose, and as much as he hated this part of a necessary evil, sucked until the vile-tasting liquid hit his lips.

One after the other, he filled the four extra cans while ignoring the handful of walkers that were now only a dozen yards away.

"Bring it," he growled at the noisy monsters as he returned to the Ford and deposited the liberated fuel into the bed.

Without a moment to spare, he turned back to face the creatures. He snicked the M4's safety off, and in his best Eastwood said, "Not your lucky day." Starting with a leathered first turn, he worked the muzzle left to right, emptying the entire magazine one accurate head shot after the next into the moaning crowd.

Barrel still smoking, he tossed the carbine on the seat ahead of him and clambered aboard his new ride. Leaving the interstate littered with twice-dead zombies, he set a course west. *Next stop Schriever.*

Chapter 21
Outbreak - Day 15
Winters's Compound
Eden, Utah

Grateful only for the bulging white clouds scudding through the summer sky and the brief shade-filled moments each one afforded, Chance squinted against the sun and took a long pull from the olive-drab surplus canteen. For reasons unknown, he fully expected the last few ounces of water to be cool and refreshing. But after sitting in the elements for hours, the super-heated liquid might just as well have been Earl Gray tea. Cursing under his breath, his thirst far from sated, he slammed the empty canteen against the ground. *If only P.J. wasn't Dad's favorite*, he thought, *then I would be the one riding around in the air conditioned SUV doing the shooting and looting.* That he had been sweltering in the same spot since dawn only added insult to his injured pride. It almost seemed like Dad was further punishing him for being a fat ass with a shoe size IQ. And now, well after noon, he was bored to death, drained of energy, and unable to keep his eyes peeled.

***

The low growl echoing up the valley interrupted his afternoon siesta. And like a triple shot espresso, the adrenaline surge that followed quickly brought him to his senses. Mouth spewing

146

expletives, and thoroughly pissed at himself for nodding off, he brought the spotting scope to his eye.

Though still out of sight, he could hear vehicles approaching from the west. As the engine sounds drew nearer, he recognized one of them as belonging to the Toyota that had exited the woods hours earlier via the cleverly hidden access road. The second vehicle had him stumped, and though he thought of himself as a car guy, for some strange reason he couldn't place the torque-heavy low-end growl and gearbox whine that he was hearing.

He shifted slightly to the left to make for a better viewing angle. Took his eye from the lens for a moment to make sure his AK-47 was within arms' reach, then reacquired the vehicles just as they emerged from the tree-lined curve in the road.

He had been dead-on about the first vehicle. The Land Cruiser that had left earlier with two men inside now appeared to have only a driver behind the wheel. His heart twisted in his chest as the second vehicle emerged. "Chance, you dumbass..." he muttered. "You know what a Humvee sounds like." *Dad's not going to like it when he hears about this*, he thought. And considering the military vehicle had what he guessed was some kind of a large caliber machine gun mounted on top, Dad was really gonna be pissed off.

The two vehicles stopped unexpectedly a hundred feet short of where Chance believed the hidden gate was located. He watched the Humvee driver open his door and step onto the shimmering blacktop. Though he was terrible at guessing a person's age—and equally as bad at remembering first names— Chance supposed the man had to be somewhere in his fifties.

While keeping the tree line at his back, the Humvee driver walked towards the zombies with a distinctive swagger—or limp—Chance couldn't be certain. And to say the man seemed at ease against the lopsided odds he faced would have been an understatement. With the short-barreled shotgun resting on his shoulder, Chance thought the man looked like some kind of stagecoach driver or maybe even that guy Mad Max from those post-apocalyptic movies Mom wouldn't allow him to watch as a kid. *Yeah, Mad Max*, the eighteen year old decided. Minus the spiked leather jacket and the ever-present mutt, that's exactly whom the guy brought to mind.

After communicating something to the driver who was still sitting inside the Toyota, Mad Max sidestepped to his left, keeping the zombies off to the right.

Looking like workers on strike, albeit rotting and disheveled, the dozen or so zombies paced the road. It was the same staggering uncoordinated lot that had been patrolling the same quarter-mile stretch since the lone Toyota exited earlier in the day.

No sooner had the vehicles reappeared and Mad Max emerged from the Humvee, did the shambling dead begin to move in unison towards the meat. Chance's eyes widened when he realized that even though he was a couple of degrees uphill, he would still be in the gunman's line of fire. And if the man was shooting with shot shells then there was a slim chance he could catch a deadly dose of lead pellets. So with self-preservation at the forefront, he flattened his offensive lineman-sized frame and tried to be one with the earth.

But the ground was unyielding and Chance was not a gopher. Truth be told, he was closer to two hundred and fifty pounds. *Fuck it*, he thought. *If a golden BB catches me right here, then so be it.* He raised his head a few inches and trained the scope on the action, and as he watched the melee unfold three things happened simultaneously: Mad Max leveled his weapon at the advancing dead, a lick of red-orange flame vented from the shotgun muzzle, and the nearest rotter's head erupted, sending a slow motion arc of liquefied gore airborne. Chance shuddered at the ghastly sight. He still hadn't gotten used to the damage a firearm could inflict on the human body—living or dead— especially point blank and to the head. A fraction of a second later the booming report rolled uphill like a thunderclap, then quickly echoed to silence. Chance kept his eye pressed to the scope and watched, wholeheartedly rooting for the monsters to prevail. The fewer men with guns that he and the others would have to deal with when Dad finally sent them in, the better, he reasoned.

As he continued to observe, he found it amusing how the monsters jostled against one another to get to the shooter, who merely sidestepped and backpedaled while keeping a good amount of spacing between him and the hungry throng. Dude probably had some kind of military training, Chance concluded. "But why the hell aren't they using the big machine gun?" he wondered out loud. After all, Dad had shown him firsthand what something similar could do, and he never ever wanted to be on the receiving end of one of those flesh shredders.

As he worked the scenario over in his mind, it suddenly dawned on him what the two were trying to accomplish. Mad Max was luring the monsters into position, and while they blindly followed, another man, who was very thin and looked to be middle-aged, had emerged from the Toyota and was silently flanking the zombies in order to put them in some kind of a crossfire. "Goddamnit," Chance muttered. The more he saw of how these guys handled the rotters, the less he wanted to tangle with them.

A cold void formed in his gut as he contemplated what Dad had in store. He said a little foxhole prayer, easing away from the scope. He pushed his fledgling blonde dreadlocks from his face, then dabbed more sweat from his brow. He could feel his tee-shirt, wet with alcohol-infused sweat, sticking to the fat rolls on his back and sides. A gust of hot wind rife with carrion and exhaust fumes ruffled the brittle grass surrounding his hide. And then, when he finally put the scope back to his eye, Shotgun Guy's back faced him squarely. For just a split second he entertained the idea of popping up and screaming "*Wolverines!*" and hosing them down with his AK. But that brilliantly crafted idea dissipated instantly when the thin man opened fire and had already dropped three more of the dead with accurate double-taps to the head before the shotgun rejoined the chorus.

Chapter 22
Outbreak - Day 15
Jackson Hole, Wyoming

Tran came to, fearing that he had become a meal for the dead. He had no idea what time it was or how long he had been out. Tree branches rustled in the wind, and somewhere above him in the lush canopy a murder of crows engaged in a noisy debate. Despite the fact that he didn't yet have a craving for human flesh—the pain flooding his body could mean only one thing— he had died and was reanimating as one of them. Then a chilling sound drew his attention, like the desperate spit of an angry tomcat cornered by a menacing Doberman. A dozen feet to his left and half that distance uphill, a first turn was emitting the noise while doing a sort of clumsy mechanical looking breast stroke—a pitiful thing to watch indeed. The pale, one-eyed demon would thud one arm forward, lancing the dirt with bony fingers, scrabble its knees like some kind of insect, and then slowly pull itself along, advancing only inches at a time. Clearly, gravity combined with the steep grade was giving it fits.

Suddenly it occurred to Tran that he must *not* be one of them. Because from what he had seen firsthand in the Elk Refuge—the dead didn't eat the dead.

He spent a few agonizing minutes breathing deeply, trying to get oxygen-rich blood flowing to regain the equilibrium he'd need to confront the threat. Meanwhile, the simple act of tracking the thing with his eyes brought on agonizing pain—like someone jabbing an icepick repeatedly with metronomic precision into his brain. So intense was the pressure behind his eyes that he began seeing double—like looking through someone else's prescription glasses. *Concussion*, he thought to himself. And as he lay there fighting to remain awake, the events leading up to this moment came rushing back to him with acute clarity. The mental movie picked up a millisecond after he had been shoved from the moving vehicle, when every nerve in his body instantly came alive—the adrenaline blasting through his body urging him to act on the fight or flight instinct—the life-saving mechanism that had been hardwired into humans since saber-toothed tigers were the alpha predator. In that do or die moment, he'd decided that flight was in his best interest. He remembered taking the full brunt of the fall on his shoulder, and then recalled seeing the big off-road tires whir by at the edge of his vision. And as he scrambled forward on his hands and knees, searching for a sliver of daylight amongst the sharp knees and shredded feet, he had yearned for nothing more than a shot at revenge against the two brothers who were sacrificing him to ensure their own survival.

The tomcat hiss resounded, dragging his attention to the present. Fully aware the one-eyed zombie was near, and with every intention of fleeing, he rolled over onto his chest and tried to stand. It started out well, but by the time he was on all fours, an all-encompassing tsunami of nausea slapped him back down. And like a kid determined to see the ball drop on New Year's Eve, he fought to stay awake—to somehow stay in the light. The last thing he remembered before succumbing to the subdural hematoma pressing against his brain was the sickly sweet stench of death and the steady, seismic thumping of ol' One Eye coming his way.

Chapter 23
Outbreak - Day 15
Winters's Compound
Eden, Utah

Duncan staggered to the left, putting himself at the top of an imaginary L, and Phillip moved right in a tight arc so he was at the toe.

The dead followed dumbly, finding themselves bunched up at the heel of the invisible L, near where the painted yellow dashes bisected the road.

A steady *Pop! Pop! Pop!* erupted from Phillip's smaller caliber AR, followed closely by three rapid-fire booms from the combat shotgun. Sandwiched between the ear-splitting blasts was a metallic *schnick-schnick* as Duncan racked each new round into the chamber.

One left, Duncan thought to himself. The Mossberg belched fire one final time, then clattered to the ground at about the same instant the Colt Model 1911, firmly clutched in Duncan's right hand, cleared leather and swept up and forward. He noted the sensation as the webbing between thumb and forefinger depressed the automatic safety. He tracked his outstretched arm at the closest threat. The first turn suffered from a bad maggot infestation. The dermis covering its bare upper body rippled and undulated as the colony of fly larvae fed on the deceased host. Duncan's pistol boomed twice as he fought against the substantial recoil to keep the muzzle down and on target. The report from the discharged .45 caliber rounds drowned out all else and set his ears to ringing. The middle-aged female rotter's head exploded behind the iron sights—whether from his pistol or Phillip's rifle, it didn't concern him—he just shifted his aim and worked to empty the Colt into the dead, a few which were still staggering his way when its slide locked open.

Without taking his eyes from the stragglers, he dumped the spent mag, rammed a fresh one home, and let the slide *snik* forward to chamber a new round. In the time it took him to perform these nearly autonomous functions, Phillip's AR had gone silent, and all of the creatures were down.

A thick cordite haze tinted the atmosphere a curious shade of gray around the battle space. The color reminded Duncan of the smog-filled skies over Beijing, Mumbai, or Mexico City before those mega metropolises fell to the dead and the multitudes of cars and factories ceased spewing pollution forever.

Once the gunfire ceased, Chance pulled the waterproof Birder's notepad from his hip pocket. He had stumbled upon it recently inside one of the rural homes that he and his brother had been tearing apart in their quest for ammunition, food, booze, and most importantly prescription medications. It was the solution to his most pressing problem, and hopefully he would never have to revisit the thorough ass kicking he had received from his dad upon turning over a soggy paper notepad complete with running ink and unreadable words. He wiped the damp sheen from the first plastic page, pulled the black grease pencil from the spiral loop, checked it for a sharpened point, then proceeded to add his findings of the day to the notes already jotted there. Right below the time when the lone vehicle left, he wrote in big blocky numbers what time the men returned, described the Humvee and the one-sided undead ass kicking he had just witnessed, and detailing, with a series of arrows and numbers, the tactics the men had employed. And even though he used to be a self-professed Military Channel junkie—before *all* of the stations went black—he didn't know a pincer maneuver from a frontal assault. Therefore, the poorly drawn diagram relayed less information than a preschooler's scribbling.

***

"Let's get these things off the road," Phillip offered. He slung the AR-15 over his shoulder and proceeded to make sure all fourteen of the rotters were down for good. He used his Beretta only once, taking out a crawler, its spinal cord already severed by one of their bullets. He bent down and hauled the dead thing off to the side, being mindful of the leaking brains and their proximity to his boots.

Duncan hinged over and retrieved his shotgun and the lone empty magazine for his .45. "Be careful," he said. "These things have been known to play a little game of possum on occasion. You and I know they're not the sharpest tools in the shed... and even though they don't make for good dinner conversation..." he winced at his choice of words, then went on, "I'm afraid somewhere behind their dead eyes lurks a certain bit of cunning... maybe even cooperation at times."

Thanks for the lecture, Dad, Phillip thought to himself, while at the same time wondering how difficult it had been for 'Oops' to grow up having a ball-busting big brother who was also old enough to be his dad.

He grunted from exertion and pushed the corpse's bare spindly legs over its head, causing it to perform an upside down and backwards somersault, the impact at the bottom of the ditch leaving its limp arms folded across its chest. Jaw hinged open, skull, hair, and most of the frontal lobe lost to a .45 slug, it looked as if it was about to offer him a lecture of its own. "I don't see it your way, Duncan," he said, tearing his gaze from the glaring eyes. "These things aren't people anymore."

"A small part of them *still* is," Duncan countered. He made a face at the smell and put his back into his work, dragging the one that had suffered decapitation by shotgun, not by the hands, but by the heels so he wouldn't have to look at his own handiwork.

Still, the headless corpse spilled a brackish blood trail over the road from where it first fell to the ditch where it would finish decomposing.

Blood trails were nothing new to Duncan. During the war in Vietnam, the Viet Cong always came back for their dead. Sometimes the blood trail was as good as a body to the lieutenant, which in turn was as good as ten bodies to his higher ups—who coveted a high body count. Then that number was taken by the politicians, who in turn picked another arbitrary number to get the figure they thought the President wanted the public to hear. Just thinking about politicians made him angry. They were one of the few denizens of the old world that he would never miss. There were a few others on the list but none caused his blood to boil quicker. No more two- and four-year election cycles. No more damning ads. Hell, if he hadn't seen so many good people die since Z day, the tradeoff would almost be worthwhile. *At least the dead were predictable*, he mused. *They tried to eat you, not screw you when you weren't looking*. The visual brought a rare morbid smile to his face. Yep... in Nam, winning had been nothing but a numbers game—a fake war of attrition that had been destined to fail. There were simply too many Chinese, Viet Cong, and North Vietnamese throwing themselves into the fray to be stopped. Defeating the dead was going to be a much harder slog, Duncan concluded. An ongoing war of attrition from which mankind could never walk away from—and probably wouldn't survive.

***

The two men worked in silence, both eager to clear the road and return to the compound before more walking dead arrived.

Once the road was corpse-free, Duncan took a load off. He was still favoring his lower back, and heaving the dead weight hadn't helped matters any. What he really needed was to lie down for a spell and take something to kill the pain and inflammation. His only hope was that baby bro had something stronger than a Tylenol.

Casting a glance towards Duncan, and noticing that the old man was in a considerable amount of pain, Phillip took it upon himself and policed up the shotgun shells and all of the brass he could find. "Why didn't we just pass these things by and get on through the gate?" Phillip asked. He paused for a second, expecting an answer.

"It's not that simple."

"But there were so few of them... and as slow as they are... we would have had plenty of time to lock up and put the camouflage back in place."

"If we stop yakkin' and get off the road before more of them come around to see what all of the commotion was about, then we'll be OK. But if just one of them staggers around that bend," he stabbed a thumb westward, "and sees us go inside, it'll hang out, and sooner or later we'll have a posse of undead waiting for us *next* time anyone exits here. This goes back to what I was saying about there being something human left upstairs." He tapped a finger to his head. "Some of 'em have long memories. I've been in places with better fencing than this. I *barely* made it out of that scrape alive... and that necessitated a Black Hawk. So Phillip, my boy, in a nutshell that's why I stopped short of the entrance. We cleaned 'em out... but we're not home free. Let's get off the road. Cause if we let another bunch of rotters start hanging around here again we might as well just put up a sign showing the bad guys exactly where the hidden entrance is."

"Good call, Sir."

Duncan grimaced but didn't let Phillip's verbal slip alter his mood. Because no matter how annoying the younger man could be, today, he'd come through when it mattered. *Hell yes*, Duncan thought. He'd go to war with *Slim* any day.

***

With his bladder compressed against the cool ground, Chance figured he could hold the piss another five minutes, tops. Just enough time to let the two gunslingers slink away, thinking their secret entrance hadn't been compromised. *Jokes on you, bastards. When we come rolling in there*, he thought, *you bunch of dummies aren't going to know what hit you.* Just the thought of a little violence started a dull ache below, and adding the possibility of a female or two as spoils of war really put some lead in his pencil. He grabbed his AK with one hand and, grunting, pushed his considerable weight off the ground.

His plan had been to take a piss in the woods and see if he might rub a quick one out. He never made it to the woods. In fact, he was on all fours when he got the piss part of his plan out of the way. The second he sensed the cool metal pinch his neck, warm urine spread from his crotch, seeped down both pants legs and turned the denim a darker shade of blue. His head slowly ratcheted up, dreads partially covering thin slits for eyes. "Hell are you?" he demanded.

The rifle jabbing him in the neck protruded from a bush. The bush remained silent, unmoving, deadly. His eyes tracked along the barrel. *A large scope on top. Fingers inside some sort of gloves.* He had been holding his breath. He exhaled sharply and realized his erection was gone. Being on the wrong end of a gun could do that to a guy. First time for everything, he figured.

"Who are you and what the hell do you want?"

"*Shut up!*" said a disembodied female voice from somewhere nearby just inside the tree line.

Then a burst of static, followed by a soothing female voice, emanated from behind the rifle currently crushing his jugular. "Old Man... come in. This is Jamie."

Chance recoiled as a second human-shaped bush emerged from the woods and waved one foliage-covered arm at the men he had just been spying on. *Ghillie suits*, popped into his mind. *Those aren't bushes*, he thought to himself. *Just a couple of bitches dressed like snipers.*

He tried to rise. "You have no right—"

A boot caught him in the ribs, blasting the wind from his lungs. "Lay back down," the rifle-wielding woman hissed.

Chance complied, then cried out when a bony knee with a hundred pounds driving it speared the soft spot between his ribs and spine. He wheezed and fought to clear his head, but before he could regain his wind and fight back he felt his already fatigued arms being wrenched behind his back, and then heard the unmistakable sound as the zip tie cinched his wrists together. Soft hands brushed his face. A strand of rough burlap covered his eyes, blocking out everything, and then those same supple hands cinched the blindfold tighter than he had anticipated. He grunted, waiting for the gag he knew was the next logical addition to the fucked-up mess he had gotten himself into. It arrived a second later, and then to add insult to injury the cool muzzle returned to his neck.

The walkie-talkie or whatever it was spewed soft static, then a gravelly voice spoke out between short blips of white noise. "This is Duncan. What's going on up there?"

"Looks like we have ourselves a secret admirer. Twelve' o clock, past the fence up here on the rise," one of the female voices replied.

Once again the radio hissed to life. "How long have you two been hiding up there?" Duncan inquired, sweetening his drawl on account of the ladies.

Jamie removed her knee from the jiggling rolls of fat, patted the man's sticky back, and nodded at bush number two. "We've been watching *him* for about ninety minutes. Took us half that time to sneak up on him," she replied over the two-way radio. "Not to worry though. We had your back all the way, Sir."

Duncan winced, shook his head side to side, and with a devilish grin spoke into the radio. "We were up to our asses in alligators down here. Least you coulda done was added a couple of more rotter kills to your name."

"I was tracking them but you boys kept getting in the way... wouldn't have wanted to accidently bag one of you two. Besides... looked like you and Phillip had it handled."

"Roger that," Duncan replied. "You two coming back to the compound with us?"

"No... we'll herd this *watcher in the woods* down to you. Meet you at the fence in two shakes."

Duncan said nothing, just watched the spectacle as the two five-footers—fully clad in camouflage suits made up of burlap, twigs and grass—marched the much larger man-boy towards the road. His kinked and matted locks flopped atop his head, keeping tight cadence with each labored step. A poor man's dreadlock job, Duncan mused. If that's what you call 'em on a white guy. He hoped to see Daymon again. Posing that question would make for one hell of an ice breaker. Maybe it'd even allow the old man the opportunity to apologize for referring to the ex-firefighter's fine mane of dreadlocks as a spider. At least he hadn't named it Charlotte, he thought. That would have really gotten things started on the wrong foot.

As it was, if Duncan's memory served, Daymon had been like a little clam when they'd first met—quiet and wound tighter than the Blue Angels flying in formation. He warmed up slow, but once you got to know the kid he was all right. The kind of guy you could call solid.

Pushing the thoughts to the back of his mind, he stepped to the barbed wire, placed a boot on the bottom strand and pulled the middle up, creating an opening half the size of their sunburned prisoner.

Getting the blindfolded biggun through the fence was easier said than done. With Phillip pulling far less than his weight, and the girls pushing on far more than theirs, they finally got it done. The whole endeavor made certain Duncan would be taking a handful of Tylenol later— quite a few more than "*the doctor's recommended dose.*"

"So, darlin'," Duncan drawled. "What was this sack of shit doin up there?"

Jamie removed her boonie hat; the overlapping foliage peeled away with it. Then she handed over the small yellow notepad. "He's been keeping tabs on us."

"Phil, why dontcha double check him for weapons, then help Jordan jam him into the back of the Hummer."

"Yes, Sir."

"Fuck Phil—"

159

"Sorry Duncan."

As Phillip gave the white Rasta a thorough searching, a few muffled grunts, most likely an argument of some sort, escaped the kid's mouth through the oily scrap of burlap clogging his mouth.

Duncan regarded the notepad. Turned it over in his hand. "And what am I to do with this?" he drawled. "Go on an Audubon Society outing?"

"Just look inside," Jamie said. She donned her hat minus the ghillie overlay, helped Jordan over the fence, then effortlessly scaled it herself, joining the younger woman on the other side.

Duncan read the last two pages, made a face, then stuffed the journal in a cargo pocket. "I'll take this to Logan and the others see what they make of it."

"We'll hang out here a little while and see if anyone comes looking for this turd," replied Jamie as she arranged the foliage-covered net over her head until just her eyes were visible. "Let's go, Jordan. Good job up there."

Duncan watched the two women walk uphill and crest the rise, noting that they had taken a slight deviation so their tracks wouldn't be as obvious in the tall grass.

Moving gingerly, he slid behind the wheel, then keyed the two-way radio. "Ladies... be sure you shoot first and ask questions later."

"Copy that Sir," said Jamie, who by now had melted back into the forest.

Duncan's brow knitted. Somewhere in the background, overlapped by the woman's voice, he thought he could hear someone breathing, low and steady. "Logan, that you?" he queried.

Silence.

Duncan keyed the radio. Repeated himself. "Baby bro... that you?"

"Yes," a voice replied.

"Gotta let her go. She's a big girl."

More silence.

"And she's probably listening in right now you *moron*," Duncan added. Just a little brotherly jab. Then he gazed to the west. *Clear*. To the east, *clear*. At Phillip, who by now was in the Toyota, head scanning the road, waiting patiently.

"She knows how I feel," Logan conceded.

"Well Romeo... harden your heart. We're on our way with a present."

"I know," Logan admitted. "I overheard your entire conversation."

"You were *eavesdropping*?" Duncan joked.

Changing the subject, Logan said, "So what do you mean by *harden my heart?* Are we going to *torture* him?"

"We'll see," Duncan said darkly. "If he doesn't cooperate... what was it that Malcolm X said? *By any means necessary—*" He made it a point to speak loudly so the kid in the back seat had something to think about on their *long* drive to the compound.

A rustle of clothing and some grunting emanated from the back of the Humvee.

Duncan smiled and fired up the engine. Then he got Logan back on the two-way. "One more thing— I know you were a good little packrat before the shit hit the fan— but what I'd *really* like to hear is that you went and stocked up on a good amount of ammunition for that big Barrett sniper rifle of yours."

"I've got *some*," Logan said.

Duncan smiled. He knew Logan's favorite store had always been Costco. Therefore, Logan's idea of *some* had always been a little different than most everyone else's.

"How many is *some*," Duncan asked.

"Five... maybe six hundred rounds. Why?"

"If this new toy of ours makes it down the road without getting wedged between a couple of trees, you'll see." Duncan stuck his arm out the window and waved Phillip ahead. He kept track of the Land Cruiser in the rearview, watched as it passed on the right, then stopped short. Phillip moved quickly; he opened the hidden gate and hopped back inside. He drove the rig through and waited for Duncan, who tucked his ride close to the

161

Toyota's bumper, entrusting Phillip to batten down the hatches behind them.

Again Logan's voice crackled through the radio. "What is this new *toy* you're bringing back?" Then he cleared his throat dramatically. "I'm afraid to hear an answer though. If a Department of Homeland Security Black Hawk is not enough toy for you, old man... what is?"

"You'll see," Duncan intoned. He smiled as he pictured Logan sitting in the communications area back at the compound, wondering what in the hell his older brother was up to this time. And even though the story of a cranky Air Force first sergeant freely giving away a helicopter so he could ferry himself to Utah was one hundred percent above board, he was certain Logan hadn't bought it. Furthermore, Duncan knew without a doubt that in Logan's mind, his retelling of his flight from Portland, Oregon to Schriever AFB in Colorado also required a tall pair of hip waders.

Duncan's smile turned to laughter as he visualized his much younger brother madly twisting his handlebar mustache, which, while they spoke, was probably slowly turning gray from worry. After their mom—who had perfected the art—Logan was the next biggest worrier in the family. Always had been. And at times Duncan wondered how crazy the Winters's household would have been if him and Logan had been closer in age. The one thing he was certain of, his dad would have gone crazy with two worrywarts in the house while he was tear-assing all over southeast Asia with a Huey Gunship strapped to his ass. Because Lord knows their mom's constant worrying had been more than enough to age their father prematurely, and then the new baby coming along when the two were in their mid-forties had vastly accelerated the aging process.

A pall fell over Duncan as he reflected on their passing. Both were in their mid-sixties when they'd passed, much too young considering all of the Hollywood pukes who lived to be in their nineties while still banging girls in their twenties. He shook his head. Hell, the world was an unfair motherfucker.

162

Yep, his parents lost out. They had barely inched into their golden years when the Reaper took them, six months apart—inexplicably, both in their sleep. Hadn't even made a dent in their retirement savings. In the end, the nest egg had been split between him and his brother. Logan built the compound with his half of the inheritance. He believed the Y2K bug was coming and was destined to knock the world on its collective butt; consequently, this worry nurtured within him an overwhelming urge to spend it on something tangible. And a handful of Conex shipping containers and the land to plant them seemed reasonable at the time. Especially since Logan feared that money would soon become worthless—nothing but unreadable data contained on dead hard drives within dead computers.

Duncan, on the other hand, burned through his cash in a blur. Two hundred and fifty grand. Vegas, Reno, Lake Tahoe—pretty much anywhere he could drown his sorrows and gamble away the money, which had become a constant nagging reminder of yet another cruel cosmic joke played on the Winters's family. *If only I was as emotionally mature as Logan*, he thought. *Then maybe I'd have something to show for all of Mom and Dad's hard work.* He wasn't proud of many of the things he had done in the past but he *was* proud of Logan, and when they had been reacquainted a handful of days ago, he had never been happier. The kid had his unconditional love and that wasn't a one-way street. In fact, their parents' deaths had brought them closer together for a spell, until life had once again separated them. Duncan was not only grateful for how Logan had spent his inheritance and the relative safety the compound afforded, he also considered himself lucky that he'd found his last remaining kin. Now that they were reunited, he'd do anything to ensure baby bro's safety—even if it meant making the ultimate sacrifice.

After the last few crater-sized potholes sent spasms through Duncan's lower back and elicited pain-filled moans from the trussed and blindfolded prisoner in the back seat, the gravel feeder road finally spit the Humvee into the clearing-cum-makeshift-airstrip.

163

Chief, Gus, and Lev stood in the sun looking like kids on Christmas morning, eagerly awaiting their parents' blessing to tear into their presents.

But Duncan didn't stop. Instead, to confuse his prisoner, he drove the length of the airstrip, then spun a U-turn when the packed dirt stripes ran out. He sped back towards the mystified trio, zig-zagging to and fro across the runway. For good measure he made two more similar passes and finally parked near the waiting men and killed the engine. When he emerged from the military Humvee he pressed a vertical finger against his lips and gestured for the men to approach.

Chapter 24
Outbreak - Day 15
Schriever AFB
Colorado Springs, Colorado

Bang! Bang! Bang! The three sharp raps, loud enough to wake the dead, rattled the screen door.

Brook padded across the room and snatched up her M4. Since she wasn't expecting anyone to drop by, her mind rapidly flicked through every scenario she could think of. Annie didn't like to venture out with the baby, especially with the Elvis guy still not accounted for. Cade had said he wouldn't be back until around dinner time. She flicked her gaze to Raven, who was staring wide eyed from a top bunk five feet away. She checked the safety. *On.* Flicked the lever over to *fire.* The rifle is now *hot,* she thought. Only it wasn't *her* inner voice that she heard, it sounded more like Cade was speaking in her head. She kept the barrel trained on the floor, eyes riveted to the door.

"*Who is it?*" she said, lowering her voice a few octaves so as to sound intimidating. She stole a sidelong glance at the stray Australian Shepherd that she had somehow been convinced they *had* to adopt. Max was on his belly, white teeth bared, hackles raised. So far he hadn't growled or barked and seemed to be focusing on the door handle. *Good dog,* Brook thought to herself.

165

Following the urgent knocks, a muted male voice called out, "I'm looking for Brooklyn Grayson."

Bang! Bang! Bang!

"*Who* is looking for Brooklyn Grayson?" she said, this time without altering her voice. She brought the rifle to her shoulder and trained it at the door, midway between the handle and the middle set of hinges. Exactly where she assumed center mass would be on her gentleman caller.

Again the voice called out, much louder this time. "It's *Wilson*. I ran into you in the mess at breakfast time."

Amazing, Brook thought. *Now the kid's stalking me.* "What do you want?" she bellowed.

"Open the door. This is *effin* important!" he hollered back.

She lowered her rifle, flicked it safe and motioned for Raven to unlock the door, all the while her face conveying a look urging the twelve-year-old to be careful.

Raven flashed her usual '*I got this, Mom'* smile. Meanwhile, Max let out a lone growl that Brook interpreted to mean that he also had their back.

Bright light cut into the room followed by the gangly redhead. He removed his hat, and nodded at Raven first. "Thanks," he said to her. Then he skipped the formalities and addressed Brook. "I have something *very* important to show you." He kept his eyes locked with Brook's, reached a hand into the hip pocket on his cargo shorts, and came out with the thumb drive, its metal case reflecting the sunlight streaming in the open door.

Brook stared at him, then at the metal object that he was holding in her line of sight. "Come inside," she said. Raven closed the door, maneuvered around the visitor and plopped down on her mom's lower bunk.

Wilson handed the device over. "If this is what I think it is... everyone on this base is going to shit a brick." He smiled, a big toothy grin made whiter by his sunburned face.

Brook couldn't begin to fathom the importance of the item the kid had just handed her. She turned it over in her palm. PROPERTY OF THE CDC was etched into the aluminum case on one side. After a beat, which gave her mind the time to process the acronym, her jaw fell open.

"What is it, Mom?"

Brook's eyes flicked to Raven and then over to Wilson, whose face was still plastered with that satisfied Cheshire Cat-like grin. Then, after she flipped the device over, it was she who nearly shit a brick. Because, scrawled there freehand in bold block letters in black sharpie, was the name FUENTES, and just seeing it nearly stopped her heart. "Where did you get this?" she gasped. But before Wilson could answer, Brook's mind blazed through the ramifications—99.9% of them were good but the other one-tenth of one percent troubled her. And the root of that worry had to do with how Cade would react if the information that everyone had assumed was lost forever was actually stored on the thumb drive that she held in her hand.

"My friend Taryn found it hidden away in her quarters. Which apparently is the same building that the medical personnel stayed in."

Brook nodded. "When did she find it?"

"Three days ago after she got out of quarantine."

"*What...*" Brook cried. "Why did she sit on it for so long?"

Obviously taken aback, Wilson paused for a tick. "She told me it was probably filled with MP3s... you know—*music.*"

"I'm young enough to know what an MP3 is, *buddy,*" Brook shot back.

"It's not Taryn's fault. She didn't know what CDC stood for or who the hell Fuentes is... err... *was.*"

"I can see how that could happen. The initials CDC didn't ring a bell with me when I first saw them." Brook made a face. She remained silent for a moment, turning everything over in her head.

Raven had been following the conversation like a spectator at an Olympic caliber ping pong match, her head swinging to and fro after each verbal volley.

Max, on the other hand, appeared to be oblivious to the conversation. He was curled up under Brook's bunk, head tucked in with one brown ear probing the air.

Brook cocked her head to the side and worked at taming her medium length locks. She wrapped a band multiple times around a thick shock of her brown hair, leaving it up in a high ponytail. "Raven, get your boots on," she said. Then directing her attention at the dog, she added. "Max. You're staying here... lots of golf carts and trucks zipping around out there." The dog's head gophered up. He fixed his bicolored eyes on Brook, wagged his tail as if in agreement, then reburied his head.

Brook grabbed two loaded magazines from the metal table near the door, stuffed them in her side cargo pockets, and fastened the Velcro so they'd stay put.

Finished lacing her boots, Raven pulled a tan ball cap low on her head, leaving her pigtails poking out the sides.

"Where's your sister?" Brook asked Wilson.

"Sasha's being a baby. She's back at our trailer. And she's pissed because Taryn stole a few hours of my attention."

"Who is this Taryn girl?" asked Brook.

Wilson's brow hitched up. "Your husband and his men saved her from an airport somewhere in western Colorado. I think Taryn said it was in Grand Junction. Anyway, she was the only one who survived the outbreak there. *Nine* days all by herself."

"How well do you know her?"

Wilson nodded and a smile formed as he spoke, "Me and her are pretty close."

Brook noticed that same toothy grin again. *How close?* she wondered. "I'm taking this to Shrill. He'll know what to do with it."

"Can I tag along?" Wilson asked.

"I wouldn't have it any other way," Brook said. She followed Wilson and Raven out the door and locked up.

Chapter 25
Outbreak - Day 15
Jackson Hole, Wyoming

Tran came to once again—only this time he knew without a doubt that he wasn't one of them. Though he had no idea how long he had been unconscious, when he opened his eyes and sat up he was pleased to note that the pressure in his head as well as the sickening vertigo that had accompanied it had lessened somewhat.

He had escaped the blonde brothers, this he also knew. He had tumbled downhill out of control and had been knocked unconscious somewhere along the way. And it appeared that miraculously he had come to rest on a shallow, but relatively flat shelf jutting out from the steep hillside.

As he sat on the shelf taking inventory of his injuries, he caught a whiff of carrion and instantly remembered the one-eyed demon that had been stalking him. And as his vision sharpened, he realized that the answer to his most pressing problem was right there, protruding from the volcanic soil, staring him straight in the face. Reddish ochre-colored and shaped like a clamshell, the flat obsidian shard was roughly six inches long by four inches wide, thick on one end and tapered off to a sharp edge on the other. In another time and to another culture, after a certain degree of shaping and sharpening, the stone would have made a fine hide scraping tool. Or affixed to a hickory haft—a crude, but deadly hatchet. Tran needed it for one purpose and he hoped it was sharp enough to do the job.

Meanwhile, just a few feet away, his one-eyed nemesis clawed its way towards him.

Trying to decide which course of action to take, he shifted his gaze downslope. The zombies trapped in the brambles hadn't forgotten about him. They eyed him raptly, their dry throaty moans carrying uphill, snapping the hair on his arms to attention. The amount of damage the vipers nest of thorns had done to their ashen skin was appalling. A road map of gashes crisscrossed their bodies, rivulets of red the highways and byways.

Tran thought it through. He could fling himself over the edge, roll down the hill and risk ending up in the brambles with the struggling creatures. Or, he could cast aside his lifelong vow to shun violence, somehow get the rock and free himself, and then kill the one-eyed demon.

Surely that wouldn't be the same as killing a human. It wasn't murder, he reasoned.

With his mind made up, he pressed his cheek against the cool earth, summoned the needed strength, and flipped over onto his back. After catching his breath and then swallowing a great amount of pain he hinged up into a sitting position, (remaining conscious this time) and then scooted backwards on his butt to a spot where he could reach the rock with his numb hands. One look at the ghastly black and blue extremities caused him to wonder if there might be a couple of metal hooks in his future. Then, after fumbling the stone multiple times, he finally got it clamped between his trembling knees.

The birds suddenly went silent as One Eye's hissing morphed into guttural animal-like growls.

Tran ignored everything around him, and with a laser-like focus worked his bonds back and forth over the rock. After a dozen passes the obsidian cut through the silver tape, freeing his deadened hands.

He cast a sideways glance.

One Eye was an arm's length away.

He folded his legs underneath him Indian style, nearly losing consciousness from the pain the simple action incurred.

The demon lunged—displaying a quickness Tran hadn't expected. Both clawlike hands scraped the earth where one second ago his battered feet had been.

Tran grasped the rock as best he could and stared into the demon's eyes. It continued to advance, snapping its yellowed teeth—wanting his flesh. It took a herculean effort from him to raise the two-pound hunk of volcanic glass overhead. His shoulders blazed deep inside where the ball rotated in the cuff. Millions of nerve endings flared to life as oxygen-rich blood coursed through the veins and capillaries servicing his hands. And as he held the rock aloft waiting for the demon to move a few inches closer, the opening words from a Mahatma Gandhi quote resounded in his still throbbing head: *Non-violence does not signify that man must not fight against the enemy, and by enemy is meant the evil which men do, not the human beings themselves.*

His arms trembled, muscles threatening to fail him. *It is not man nor woman*, he thought to himself. *It is a monster created by the evil inherent in man.* With that, he brought the rock down, adding what little energy remained in his muscles to gravity's pull. A hollow thud resonated as the obsidian shard glanced off of the thing's temple and struck the pliant ground.

Undeterred, Tran wrapped one hand around its neck and straddled it, being careful to stay clear of its snapping maw. He felt the monster's body compressed under his hundred-pound frame. The stench expelled from the demon's lungs caused his eyes to tear. And as it lay on its back like a turtle, arms and legs rowing the air, teeth clacking out a soul-shuddering Morse code that he that would take to the grave with him, he gazed into its one good eye. He studied it momentarily, a little afraid but not terrified. He contemplated the skeletal face, wondering: *Is this what my fate holds? To become a demon stalking the earth?* Then he summoned all the strength he had left. He could feel the obsidian now, in his right hand, cool and smooth and wet. The hand was bleeding where it had cut in. *It doesn't hurt.* The other hand still held the beast by the neck, firm to the ground. One hundred pounds worth of firm. He aimed for the spot where the upturned nose separated the creature's one good eye from the wet socket full of splinters. For a moment he imagined the missing orb hanging from a slender switch somewhere upslope—like a lonely marshmallow waiting its turn in the campfire.

He brought the obsidian down with all the force he could muster. He watched the demon's one good eye roll back and track the crushing blow. Then Tran chopped away until the creature's brains leaked from the fissure cleaved into its head.

He stripped the clothes from the cadaver and realized after seeing the gaunt creature's dehydrated breasts that he had killed a woman. How could he have known it was a woman? The wisps of hair remaining on its skull didn't offer a clue. Nor did the cargo shorts and button up cotton shirt. Tran didn't know which side the buttons rode up a man's shirt, let alone a woman's. That bit of sleuthing wouldn't have helped. But now that he knew the awful truth, that the living corpse had been someone's daughter and maybe even someone's sister or mother, it caused him great anguish.

It couldn't be helped, he reasoned. He'd had to kill to survive, of that he was certain. He scraped the largest chunks of brain and hair-covered skull over the ledge, took one last look at the dead woman, and said a silent prayer asking for forgiveness before rolling the naked corpse into the clutching briars below.

Chapter 26
Outbreak - Day 15
Schriever AFB
Colorado Springs, Colorado

"Come in, Brook," Major Freda Nash said with the charm of a bed and breakfast owner welcoming a new guest. She held the door to her office open and pointed the way with her free hand. "How have you been?"

Brook nodded. "I'm getting along OK," she said. *Holy hell, you look awful,* is what she thought. Standing in the doorway less than a foot away, Nash looked like she'd just returned from being out on tour with a hard partying rock band. The usual press to her uniform was gone. Dark circles hung like banners of mourning under her eyes. A royal blue Air Force ball cap with the angular eagle and star logo embroidered in silver on the front panel was pulled down low over her eyes. Sticking out from the back, her black ponytail showed streaks of gray. The only thing about her that seemed squared away was the way she carried herself. She had the attitude of a six footer despite her small stature and obvious fatigue.

"Come on in out of the heat, young lady."

Brook smiled and said nothing as Wilson came ambling in behind her.

173

She noticed the Air Force officer's demeanor change and the smile go away at the sight of the young man with the sweat-stained boonie hat atop his head.

"Wilson... I believe."

He removed his floppy camouflage hat. "Yes, Ma'am."

"Sit down. Sit down," Nash urged as she removed reams of paper from the two chairs fronting her desk.

Still a little intimidated by anyone wearing a uniform, Wilson did as he was told, selecting the chair furthest from the door and nearest the buzzing wall-mounted A/C unit.

"Flick that thing to low, would you Sir," Nash said to Wilson. He reached a sinewy arm upward and punched the button marked '*Night Mode*'. The major nodded a thank you in his direction.

Being fully aware that Nash and General Ronnie Gaines had gotten their noses out of joint because Cade had cashed in the capital that President Clay had offered him in exchange for snatching Robert Christian from Jackson Hole, Brook opted to remain standing. She wanted to retain any advantage she could in order to steel herself against the overtures Nash was about to throw at her. "I'm OK right here," she said.

"Suit yourself." Nash worked her way around the desk and sat in her own high-backed leather chair. "So how's Cade? Haven't seen him around the last couple of days."

"He's getting things ready. We're heading to Utah tomorrow." Brook smiled with her eyes. Her lips remained pursed, a thin white line bisecting her tanned features.

Nash made a face. "He's really going through with this... going to quit the Unit again?" she said, adding a slight tilt to her head.

"Already has," Brook countered.

"How unfortunate for America," Nash muttered.

In an obvious attempt at cutting the tension between the two women, Wilson made his presence known by clearing his throat loudly. "*Ahem*... Brook... did *you* forget why we're here?"

"Wilson's..." Brook furrowed her brow and looked at Wilson, trying to decide what to call Taryn. "His lady friend found this." She placed the thumb drive on Nash's desk. "This thing had been stashed in her bunk."

"What is it?" Nash asked. She picked up the device. Turned it over in her hand just like Brook had a few minutes prior. The reaction was similar and happened instantly. The color drained from the major's face. She remained silent and wheeled her chair to the right, plugged the thumb drive into the USB port of the Panasonic laptop, and hinged up the screen. Then after a few seconds had elapsed, Brook noticed a stark glow illuminate the major's face as the computer's LCD screen lit up. She watched her jaw clench and the corded muscles running the sides of her neck bulge noticeably.

"Does it have any of the doctor's notes on it?" Brook asked Nash.

Nash stayed quiet for a beat. Brook watched the color slowly returning to Nash's face.

"Brook... I know you are aware of the sensitive nature of this information. It got your brother killed, and for that I'm sorry." She turned her gaze to Wilson. "I appreciate your vigilance in this matter, Sir, and on behalf of the President of the United States I want to thank you for bringing this to our attention." Nash stared at him for a moment. He cracked a half smile as the importance of the information contained on the drive hit him. Nash cleared her throat. "But I have to ask you to leave my office so we can have some privacy," she added with a firm delivery. Without hesitating, he planted his hands on the chair arms and rose up off of the seat.

"You're not going anywhere, Wilson," Brook said icily. She gripped his forearm firmly but her gaze remained locked with Nash's. The A/C warbled on. Nobody spoke for a minute, and Nash continued to stare. Her gaze passed from Brook to Wilson before finally settling back onto Brook.

Finally Wilson nodded imperceptibly, swallowed hard, and settled back into his seat.

"I have to make a call," Nash stated. She plucked the handset from the brick red telephone that looked like it hadn't seen action since the Cold War. The computer continued running through some kind of sequence which cast a green flicker on Nash's stoic features as she waited for someone to pick up.

***

Cheyenne Mountain Complex

In the span of thirty minutes, the number of dead pressing the fence topside had doubled. Secret Service Special Agent Adam Cross's hand hovered near the black phone. He was just about to call topside security and have them deal with the problem when the shrill ring of the emergency hotline caused the usually unflappable man to visibly start. Without a second's hesitation, he reached for the red phone that fellow agent Eckers had taken to calling the *Bad Phone*. It had earned the nickname for good reason. The throwback to the Cold War was connected to a fiber optic cable that ran underground from inside the Cheyenne Mountain Complex—also known as NORAD—to multiple identical red telephones in various locations at Schriever Air Force Base eighteen miles to the northeast. The phone had sounded off on three separate occasions since President Clay's arrival in Colorado Springs, all in the last week, and coincidentally all on Cross's watch. And not once had the news on the other end been good.

As Cross enveloped the receiver in his massive left hand, he said a silent prayer. He wasn't holding his breath, but he hoped that the old saying—*bad news comes in threes*—would hold true in this instance.

"NORAD," he said crisply, "Special Agent Cross here. The line is secure."

Cross nodded intermittently, phone pinned to one ear, his pen moving furiously over the yellow legal pad in front of him. After a few seconds he cracked a rare smile, slapped the handset down without a parting word and picked the sleek black handset off the phone next to it.

"Madam President, this is Adam Cross speaking," he said into the receiver. "Major Freda Nash just rang on the direct line. She wants your permission to initiate Operation Slapshot. She needs to reposition the remaining satellites immediately so she can start working up the pre-mission briefing. She indicated the entire package, men and assets, can be wheels up by zero six hundred." He went on to inform the President how the thumb drive with Fuentes's notes had been recovered. Then he went silent and listened to the President's instructions. Finally, a couple of minutes and a half page of notes later, he covered the mouthpiece and looked across the aisle at Special Agent Lawrence Eckers, who had been sitting in front of a phalanx of flat-panel monitors, flicking through the video feeds transmitted from the many security cameras peppering the flanks of Cheyenne Mountain. "Eckers, get on the horn. I want Major Ripley and her crew topside ASAP. Have her spool up Marine One... the President wants to go visit Schriever."

"Copy that," Eckers said. He seized the black phone nearest him, punched a three-digit code, and rattled off a series of orders to someone on the other end. He then replaced the handset and addressed his boss. "You can let President Clay know Marine One can be wheels up in five."

Cross removed his hand from the mouthpiece, relayed the message, and ended the call.

"Let's go," he called out. He took one last look at the large TV monitor, noting the zombies were only two deep and posed little threat to the President's safety. Still, he made a mental note to self to have them thinned out before she returned. Then he jumped up and snatched his ballistic vest from the swivel chair next to him, slipping it over his head and fastening the Velcro as he walked towards the massive steel blast door. He collected his weapons which had been hanging next to the foot-thick slab of metal. Still on the move, he donned his Secret Service-issued sidearm, chambered in .357 SIG. The semiautomatic Sig Sauer P229 always rode under his left armpit, easily accessible in a Gould and Goodrich shoulder rig. Then he threw the single point sling over his head, letting the small MP7 machine pistol dangle where it was within easy reach on his right side. Under normal circumstances he would have donned a lightweight windbreaker to conceal the armament, but these were different times and being discreet was no longer tantamount to the job.

With Special Agent Eckers in tow, Cross escorted the President from her quarters to the topside entrance, donning a pair of black Oakley sunglasses during the short elevator ride up. In less than four minutes, all three of them were onboard the Osprey that had been assigned the call sign Marine One shortly after the former President had gone missing and Clay had been sworn in to succeed him.

Agent Cross leaned in towards the President. "I brought your go bag. In case you have to pull an all-nighter," he said, loud enough to be heard over the aircrew's pre-flight chatter.

She simply nodded in return. Considering the nature of the information Nash had relayed, time was not on their side. Getting the mission spooled up quickly had to be priority number one, she reminded herself. Therefore, if an all-nighter was what it was going to take, then it made no sense to waste valuable time ferrying POTUS back and forth between Schriever and the Cheyenne Mountain Complex.

By the time Cross had briefed the other four Secret Service agents in the detail and strapped himself into a seat nearby, Major Loretta Ripley had finished the pre-flight and coaxed the dual turbine engines to near maximum RPMs. The airframe groaned slightly as the rotors punished the air overhead. The whine from the engines grew to a crescendo and the massive tilt rotor aircraft freed itself from gravity's strong pull. The ship had gained a hundred feet of altitude by the time Ripley set the twin nacelles rotating forward and the craft began switching from vertical to horizontal flight mode. And as the airspeed swiftly picked up, the seasoned aviator banked Marine One hard to starboard, making the Rockies disappear behind them and putting the bird on a course that would deliver them to the sprawling Air Force base just over the eastern horizon. "Two mikes out," she announced over the ship-wide comms.

***

Schriever Air Force Base

Brook's eyes followed the handset as Nash replaced it in the cradle. *Here it comes*, she thought to herself.

"President Clay is on her way here," Nash stated in a low voice. "In a few minutes I'll be briefing her, and I hope I'll be able to tell her what she expects to hear."

"Goddamn it," Brook said, shaking her head. "I knew I should have taken this thing to Shrill, because I know what you're thinking and I don't even want to go there."

Nash removed her cap, plopped it on the desktop. "Are you sure you want your friend to sit in on this conversation?"

Brook had a feeling it would be better to hear Nash out sitting down, so she took a seat next to Wilson. Once she had settled she regarded Nash with a bland look but said nothing.

The petite major took the silence as permission for her to continue.

"I am going to be forthright with you Mrs. Grayson. I *will* make an appeal to your husband that under normal circumstances he'd probably rebuff. But nothing is normal about the hand we have been dealt." She paused for a moment. Her eyes flicked over at whatever data was displayed on the laptop screen. "It's hard for me to wrap my mind around the fact that only two weeks into this shit show and Omega is already well on its way to erasing humans from this rock forever. Brook... time is precious. Every day, untold numbers of humans are falling and joining the ranks of the dead. I've spent nearly every waking hour watching it unfold in real-time through satellite imagery. If we don't act on this newfound gift soon... the human race may not recover."

"Nice speech, Major, but Cade *will not* be swayed this time... even if the President tries her fast-track promotion to General *bullshit*," Brook stated defiantly.

"I resent that, Mrs. Grayson. Both Desantos and Gaines were deserving of their battlefield promotions."

"I'm not taking anything away from *them*. It's just that I'm still resenting Clay's tactics. Using Cade's unwavering patriotism—which is his only true Achilles' heel—to lure him back to the teams. We had a great life before Omega, and very soon we will get to enjoy that again."

Nash shifted in her seat. "You going to hide on a mountain top?"

"If we have to."

"Gaines, Cade, and the rest of the team are rested."

"He turned in his captain's bars. Told me so himself. He's out now." Brook felt her resolve beginning to crumble. Still she finished her sentence while trying her best to sound convincing. "He won't go." Brook shook her head vehemently. "Not now... not even if the President begs."

There was a long stretch of silence. Then the heavy sound of rotors beating the air usurped the low hum of the A/C unit.

"I hate to burst your bubble, but if I know Cade the way I think I do, he *will* agree. Especially if I mention all of the times both Shrill and I have helped *you* along the way. Sneaking onboard with the Ranger chalk. Crafty, but dangerous. Furthermore, you would never have had access to the medical gear you used to deliver Mike Junior, and you mustn't forget the antibiotics that saved your brother's life." She paused as an aircraft passed nearby. Then they all sat in awkward silence until she said, "And I'm sure there's more Colonel Shrill can add to the list if we're keeping tabs. He's on board with this. And this time I'm certain he's no ally of yours."

Brook buried her head in her hands. "That was *me*, not Cade. You can't extort *me* like this... and make him put his life on the line," she mumbled.

"I have to," Nash said in a funereal voice. "And it doesn't make me proud."

Wilson sat slumped in his chair, totally silent, the boonie hat pulled low over his eyes.

Brook looked at Nash through red-rimmed eyes. "Why the big rush?" she asked softly.

"We've been moving various surveillance platforms around the country since Robert Christian's terrorists struck and destroyed Fuentes's hard work, and most of the sense of security the people on this base had grown accustomed to along with it. Replicating the antiserum has been priority one since. So we have been working around the clock in order to find a facility similar to the CDC in Atlanta. Not a far stretch, considering all of the different types of bio labs scattered about the country... or so we thought. Every facility east of the Mississippi: Fort Detrick, NIH—National Institutes of Health—in Bethesda, the CDC, of course, and even Plum Island, as isolated as it was, have already been abandoned or overrun. Two days ago—" she paused for a heartbeat, unsure if she dared continue considering that the kid lacked a security clearance—"we finally found what we were looking for. A bio-lab that was working with the CDC before things got out of hand. And most importantly—the linchpin to the whole deal—it appears there are still people trapped there. Living, breathing scientists, if we are lucky. Come on *Brook,* work with me. You know as well as I do that the data on this drive is worthless without the brainpower to decipher it."

"So send General Gaines and a couple of detachments of his 10th Special Forces," Brook proffered.

"Not possible. Most of the 10th is out in the field hunting NA stragglers."

"Where is this facility you want to send Cade?" asked Brook resignedly.

"Canada. Not too far from here. Ten-hour mission there and back... *maximum.*"

Brook grunted. She knew from experience how things worked in the Army, and she doubted the Air Force was any better. Nash's guarantee of ten hours could easily become twenty-four. A day could devolve into two. Or worse, Cade wouldn't come home this time.

"So call their *Premier... the President of Canada...* or whatever they call them up there," Brook said. She swallowed hard. Wanted to punch something in the worst way. "Why don't you have *them* rescue the scientists and deliver them here. I'd call defeating this plague well worth them taking the initiative."

"*Brook...* nobody is answering the phone up north. The same thing down south... Mexico, Central and South America. No one is picking up... there is nobody left *to* pick up." Silence dominated as the major's profound words echoed to silence.

"We - are - all - alone," Wilson said softly, drawing each word out.

"From the mouths of babes," Nash said under her breath.

Brook looked away. Suddenly she felt a familiar sensation that always originated behind her navel, then spread from there like a multi-tentacled symbiotic creature probing her insides. And at that moment, with that icy ball making her sicker by the second, she knew there was nothing she could say or do to keep Cade— the Eagle Scout, decorated former Ranger and motherfucking Delta warrior—from going down range again.

"Tell the President I won't get in her way... *this time*. But if she ever comes between me and Cade again, there will be hell to pay. And when Cade gets back from Canada I do not want you to have contact with him. Leave us the *fuck* alone."

One of Wilson's mom's sayings spewed from his mouth. "Brook, you shouldn't burn your bridges."

"I didn't ask for your two cents, Wilson," she said, glaring in his direction.

"It's a deal," Nash said. "Your sacrifice won't be forgotten."

"And then we're even," Brook said icily. She pushed the chair back, gripped her rifle, and strode towards the door.

"You aren't going to wait for *President Clay?*" Nash said incredulously.

Pausing with one hand on the door handle, Brook searched for proper words. *Fuck it*, she thought. "I better go *now*. Because if I don't, I have a feeling I'm liable to do something I will regret later." She turned away from the door and squared her body towards Nash, who had gotten up and was standing beside Wilson. "Cade has told me how much you care about him and the other operators, and I don't have a doubt that every word he said is true." Brook ground her teeth and then went on. "But if *anything* happens to my man, both you and the President are going to have to answer for it."

Wisely, Nash remained quiet, and with mixed emotions watched Brook file out ahead of Wilson, who glanced back with a sheepish expression on his face, shrugged his shoulders, and mouthed a silent, "*I'm sorry.*"

The door slammed shut behind Wilson. He pulled the floppy brim of his hat lower over his eyes to ward off the sun, and hurried to catch up with Brook. *Damn*, he thought. *For someone wrapped up in such a small package the woman sure had a hell of a stride.* And when he finally caught up with her, he said, "Took a hell of a beating in there—"

"She's right, you know," Brook said without slowing or looking back at him. "I always tell Raven to do the right thing even when no one is looking. I just went against one of my own tenets."

"What do you mean?"

"Nash had a *Helluva* point. If she's that short on personnel, who am I to stand in the way... try to change the outcome behind closed doors. Cade will do what he wants to do. He's a *fucking* only child. That's all I need to say."

Wilson glanced at his watch. "What are you doing after you get Raven—you hungry? Because I'm sure we can rustle up a Spam sandwich."

Brook chuckled.

Mission accomplished, Wilson thought to himself. "So do you want to meet her?"

Brook shortened her strides until he caught up. "Meet who?"

"The woman of the hour... Taryn," he said proudly.

"That would be nice. Then I can thank her for opening this whole *saving the human race* can of worms." Brook's smile was lost on Wilson. He made no reply and just stared at some kind of noisy aircraft approaching from the southwest.

"Sorry, bad attempt at a joke," she proffered. "Sure, I'd love to meet Taryn... maybe I can rebuild the bridge I burned with Sasha."

Wilson shook his head. "You got your hands full there."

"I'm sure I do," Brook conceded. She looked into the distance and picked up something moving fast and getting closer, barely visible over the top of the massive airplane hangars. In just a few seconds the aircraft had gone from a distant black speck on the horizon to a full size black airframe that had begun to slow, finally ending up in a steady hover suspended under two wildly spinning rotors, both of which looked to be the size of a backyard swimming pool. "That's the President's Osprey," she added.

"Let's keep moving. I don't want to have to watch you kick her ass."

Brook made no reply, only thought how nice it would be to get her way once in a while. She was tired of telling herself: *some day*. Then, as Marine One settled on the far side of Schriever near where Desantos was buried, they reached the Quonset hut that the deceased general's family still called home.

Chapter 27
Outbreak - Day 15
Jackson Hole, Wyoming

For a man with a wrenched back and an ankle the size of a cantaloupe, Tran felt that he had negotiated the last stretch of hillside like a mountain goat. Along the way he had been forced to use his makeshift obsidian weapon against two more of his former fellow human beings, crushing both of their skulls while they struggled helplessly to extricate themselves from the brambles that had stopped their initial free-fall. Killing them had gone against all of his pacifist beliefs, but just the thought that they might somehow succeed and end up hunting him overrode any feelings of empathy. Tran was in survival mode and had been since the big blonde tried to sacrifice him to the dead.

He stopped short of the gray, sun-splashed road which was barely visible between the aspens. As he stood there and listened to his heartbeat and the blood rushing through his ears from the added exertion, the wind set the trees quaking, bringing with it the rank odor he had gotten to know all too well. Painful as it was for him to do so, he eased down to a kneeling position and then to all fours. A wave of nausea pummeled his body and his vision grew flat at the edges. He put his chin to his chest and managed to overcome the urge to throw up by taking a few deep breaths. He waited for his head to spin back to normal, and then slunk like a dog to the road's shoulder. Once there, he poked his head from the undergrowth to see where the stench was coming from. He spied something very large and very dead occupying the middle two-thirds of the road. Though the carcass seemed to have been mostly stripped of its flesh, he counted half a dozen zombies still working for a meal.

Tufts of fur still clinging to scraps of the animal's hide littered the road, and from his vantage point he could clearly make out one of the demons furiously digging its clawlike hands, trying to get at the meat sandwiched between the beast's giant ribs. The frenzied tugging and gnawing sent tremors through the dead animal's knobby vertebra, causing its elongated skull, complete with a full rack of antlers, to rock back and forth on the roadway. Tran didn't know an elk from a deer, but judging by the looks of the elongated flat spot closer to the skull and the stunted spikes on the upper ridges of the antlers, the remains on the road had once been a very large bull moose. He truly felt sorry for the grand creature, but at the same time he was thankful for the diversion its death had created.

He supposed there would be no better time than now to cross the road since the things had their heads buried inside of every available orifice. He quickly stole one last sideways glance at the grisly scene. Suddenly he had a feeling that the eyeless skull, which continued to shimmy side to side, was an omen of some sort telling him not to cross the road.

No time for superstition, he admonished himself. His first few tentative steps went unnoticed by the hunched-over creatures. But by the time he had limped to the yellow centerline, one of them had gophered up. Its yellowed eyes peered at him from behind a blood-slickened face. It tilted its head at an angle like a confused dog, staring like it knew he was there, yet unsure of what it was looking at. He guessed the thing had to be blind or somehow visually impaired. Either that or he had suddenly turned invisible.

Ignoring the abomination he continued on, shuffling his bare feet along the blacktop, focused entirely on the tree line across the way. *Almost there*, he thought. Then, acting against every instinct in his body, he stole one more glance to his left. The sight that greeted him took his breath away. The creature that had been staring at him had inexplicably gone back to mining meat from the road kill.

With a word of thanks to his ancestors, he melted into the growth, intent on making it to the Teton Pass highway without being eaten.

Chapter 28
Outbreak - Day 15
Schriever AFB
Colorado Springs, Colorado

Robert Christian jerked awake. Whoever said "prayer works,
worry doesn't," he thought bitterly, didn't know what the hell
they were talking about. Because his prayer hadn't been
answered. The A/C was still belting out cold air and the lopsided
ball bearing was still as noisy as ever.

Abruptly the door opened and in walked someone he hadn't
seen since the very first session. The man was taller than the
others, a little over six feet, and looked like he would be at home
on a surfboard, not working security for the new President of the
United States.

"Hi Robert," Special Agent Cross said.

Christian said nothing. He bowed his head, letting his chin
rest on his chest.

"One more time," the man asked. "What was the *real* reason
for the dead drop?"

"*I told you.* They didn't know each other... never met. The
drop was so Francis could receive information pertaining to the
President's comings and goings."

"And that's why they didn't meet face to face?"

Tired of hearing the same question posed from a different angle, Robert Christian threw his hands into the air. They made it only eight inches from the table top before the links tightened, and like a dog that's reached the end of its chain, they crashed back down with a hollow thud.

"It's how Francis always operated," he stated. "Safer that way, he said. He almost always worked autonomously. This time was going to be the exception to his rule. Unfortunately, before they could meet face to face and set up the hit, Francis had his episode and went rogue. I don't know what happened because I wasn't here. And I'll say this for the last time..."

Cross brought a closed fist down on the table. "I'm calling the shots," he spat. "I'll let you know when you are done talking. What was Francis's mission?"

The prisoner sat up straight, regained a semblance of composure, and continued where he had left off. "The *President* was the target."

"So, Francis or Pug, or whoever he was at the time," Cross intoned. "He was coherent long enough to set up the dead drop before he went... I think *rogue* is how you put it earlier?"

"I wasn't here," Christian said again.

"That other thing—infecting the civilians. That was Elvis's doing?"

"Entirely his idea. I gave him the go ahead, though."

"I appreciate your honesty. Who else did you say was here with Elvis?"

"Just Francis."

"And after Francis went rogue, Elvis was your only remaining asset."

"Yes. Put me on a lie detector if you don't believe me."

No need. I believe you, the interrogator thought to himself. "I have one final question to ask you," he said. "And if I don't like the answer..." he nodded towards Christian's gnarled hand.

"Oh, again with the fingers. Since your friend already ruined my pinky... how about we go down the line. Break these two."

He wriggled the index and middle finger on his right hand, and nearly passed out from the pain.

The A/C unit made one last coughing sound and then shut down.

Silence.

"You want a drink?" the blonde-haired interrogator asked in a nonchalant manner.

The question hit the prisoner harder than any blow. He straightened up. Could taste the scotch hitting his tongue. Burning his throat. Warmth coursing through his limbs. Every response subconscious, and Pavlovian in nature. The uncontrollable shakes began instantly.

The interrogator produced a fifth bottle of some type of Scotch that was far from upper shelf. He poured a half an inch of the amber liquid from the bottle into a white coffee mug, and placed the bottle on the table. He pushed the well-worn mug forward until it sat on the outer threshold of the prisoner's reach.

Christian lunged for the offering but came up half an inch short.

Cross regarded this with satisfaction though he didn't let it show.

Christian dipped his head to meet his hands and proceeded to massage his eyes behind drooping eyelids.

"I'm not a bad guy," Cross said. "I'll let you have the contents of that mug if *you* tell me who Elvis was working with."

Looking the interrogator in the eye, Christian exhaled sharply. "Only Elvis knows, and that *is* the truth."

Cross lifted the mug off the table. "You want this?"

"I *need* that," Christian answered, his voice wavering. Then the shakes hit hard. In fact, his detox had begun minutes after the soldiers had shanghaied him from Jackson Hole.

Excluding the multiple interrogation sessions at the hands of rough men who claimed to be President Clay's personal security detail, he had spent most of his time shaking, vomiting, and begging anyone within earshot for a drink.

Breaking up the routine, the President had visited him twice. The first time she strolled in had been mere seconds after his arrival. And that was when he spilled his guts about the ex-Presidents and their involvement in his Guild. When the President finally left the room, he was rewarded for the information with a two count pour of some sort of rotgut Scotch. By his standards, any spirit aged less than fifty years was unacceptable. Still, he greedily consumed every drop.

By the second time the President came calling, he had already blown his wad of information. Even after the other interrogator mangled his finger, there was nothing in his hazy memory left for him to add. In fact, the two weeks before the United States fell to the dead were a blur of black tie parties, fundraisers with politicians past and present, and booze—lots of booze. A never-ending torrent of the only thing that made him feel less the failure for not seeing his dream of a one world government come to fruition. He wasn't getting any younger, and with the Internet Age his old ways of doing business were becoming more difficult. It had become too easy for Joe Blow to access personal data via the Freedom of Information Act and see developing patterns in banking and influence peddling and then connect the dots. Before the fall, there had been conspiracy sites devoted to picking apart the Guild. He had even sent Francis to quiet the worst offenders among the ranks of bloggers. A handful of them had disappeared as a result of their meddling, and Francis was the only one who knew where the bodies were buried.

The two weeks following the fall had been heady times. For if he thought there were no rules before, now with FEMA and the federal government fighting to contain the Omega outbreak, and local and state governments also finding themselves massively overwhelmed, that left nobody to stand against him and his twisted vision of a New America. The timing had been perfect for him to make his move when he did. And all had gone to plan except that he had underestimated the true nature of the dead. They had become wildly unpredictable, moving in large numbers, herdlike. The government hadn't been forthright with their initial assessment of the Omega virus. Its high virility and the nature in which it was transferred helped to swell the ranks of the dead exponentially with each passing day. So he circled the wagons in Jackson Hole, hoping to let the virus run its course and the dead to rot and eventually become nothing but environmental biohazards that would merely need to be cleansed from the countryside. In the end, he didn't have the patience to wait for Omega to run its course. Nor could he go a moment without a drink. Those two character flaws proved to be his downfall. In an inebriated state, he decided to send Francis to Colorado Springs to eradicate the new President, Valerie Clay, the former Speaker of the House whom he loathed, and was the only person he thought who truly stood in his way. And that decision, which was the result of years of having everything his way, set forth the chain reaction of events which resulted in him being in this cold room begging for a drink of ten-dollar scotch.

The interrogator nudged the mug incrementally, torturing the prisoner with anticipation until it crossed the invisible line of demarcation on the table top that Christian had burned into his memory. Finally able to grasp the handle, he shakily brought the mug to his lips, then downed the contents in one quick motion.

"I hope you savored that," the man said with a smile. *Because it's your last*, he thought grimly. Then he stood, grabbed the bottle and left the room without a backwards glance.

The door banged shut and as if on cue, the A/C belched to life.

Chapter 29
Outbreak - Day 15
Near Winters's Compound
Eden, Utah

P.J. stood just inside the first row of trees, knee deep in a natural hedge of scrub oak that delineated the forest from the softly undulating grass field unfolding before him. He looked at the ground directly in front of him. A good expanse had been trampled. *More than one person did this*, P.J. told himself. A large circle stood out from the rest, matted and crushed. He had no doubt that this is where Chance had set up shop. His gaze flicked over flattened grass. There were no obvious signs of a struggle. No blood. No shell casings.

Where the fuck are you, Chance? Dad told you to stay put until I got here, he thought. As he stood there trying to decide what to do, he suddenly wished he had inherited the same genes Chance had. Sure, the size was wasted on the dolt, but considering the alternative, he was fairly content with being smart and small.

P.J. took after Dad, who wasn't the biggest hombre in the valley. Years of being on the wrong end of mean-spirited taunting, hazing, and later on good old fashioned whippings at the hands of the bigger kids in high school had hardened P.J.'s hide. A hell of an asset to have in times like these.

Somewhere above his head a birdsong played out, a soft warbling that gave him an idea. He pursed his lips and whistled three times. Short trills, close together. To a normal person the calls were no different from the real thing. But if Chance was anywhere nearby, he would decipher them for what they really were: a secret code shared between them and one of the few rare things they held in common. Growing up they had relied on the unique call to warn each other when Dad was drunk. A clever defense mechanism devised by two young kids to avoid the belt, boot, or during the worst of Dad's benders—bruises and broken bones.

The fake bird call didn't slip by Jamie unnoticed. And when it came again, she focused on the spot, twenty yards to the west, where they had overpowered the dreadlocked kid. Dressed head to toe in woodland camo, a kid, or young man, she couldn't tell because of the baggy fatigues and drooping boonie hat, was standing very still just outside of the sun's reach. A pair of black binoculars were pressed to his face, and some sort of rifle was propped next to one of the gently swaying conifers.

The figure called out one more time, with the same three short trills, and before she could get on the radio to hail the compound he had backed slowly into the forest and was gone from her sight.

***

After the three warning calls had gone unanswered, P.J. had finally decided discretion was the better part of valor. Truth be told, he was scared as shit. He held an opinion that the folks Chance had been sent to watch were way above their league. It wasn't an educated guess. It was something in the air. Like a sixth sense he supposed, trying to tell him something. Suddenly he felt another sensation. He was being watched. *No doubt about it*, he thought as he hefted the Romanian AK-47 and retreated deeper into the shadows.

Ten minutes later he was back at the forest road where he'd left the silver Land Cruiser he had pilfered brand new off the lot on day three of the outbreak. It was parked bumper to bumper with the black 4Runner Chance had taken from the same lot.

He paused in the tree line and tried the bird call one final time.

Two or three minutes later, after no reply, P.J. hopped in his eighty thousand dollar ride, turned on the gravel road and headed west, a billowing trail of dust the only evidence he'd been there.

Jamie parted the trees just as the engine noise and scrabbling tires were receding out of earshot. Though neither she nor Jordan had gotten a good look at the kid or the vehicle he'd left in, the black SUV sucking in the sun directly in front of them was rather intriguing.

"Call it in," Jamie said to her protégé.

Jordan hailed the compound and reached Seth, who was pulling a stint in the communications container. She relayed all of the pertinent information, and after a moment or two their instructions came back: Don't touch the truck, and get back to the road. Gus and Phillip were coming up to relieve them.

With that, the two women became one with the trees, and with the brush grabbing at their ghillie suits, trudged the quarter-mile back to the sloped clearing.

Chapter 30
Outbreak - Day 15
Schriever AFB
Colorado Springs, Colorado

Creeping steadily towards an inevitable merger with the craggy Rocky Mountain range to the west, the relentless sun had dropped another hundred degree day on the airmen and soldiers tasked with guarding Schriever's main gate.

A single bead of sweat ran down the bridge of Staff Sergeant Leeland's nose and curled over the tip, wobbling there subtly but refusing to fall. He ignored the urge to take a swipe at it and instead kept the binoculars trained on the lone truck barreling along the northern fence line. The jittery tan vehicle he was tracking looked like it was being pursued by an angry ochre snake. Shimmering heat waves further distorted the image, adding to the illusion that the vehicle was breaking some kind of land speed record on the Bonneville Salt Flats. Soon the roar of the engine had alerted all of the guards, sending them sprinting from the guardhouse towards the gate, carbines held at the ready.

As the truck rapidly closed the distance, the two guards in the tower swiveled their Browning machine guns in its direction, gaping black muzzles eager to hurl massive .50 caliber armor-piercing rounds at it if the need arose.

Donaldson fine-tuned the Bushnells, bringing the driver and truck clearly into focus. "Stand down," he called out. "It's Captain Grayson returning. Stand down everyone."

Without missing a beat, the soldiers lowered their weapons and backed away from the double gate as it rolled open on big rubberized wheels. A murder of crows exploded from the pile of zombie corpses piled a dozen yards from the entrance as the F-650 shot through. The gate was already closing behind the rig before its rear bumper had cleared the threshold. The entire operation appeared choreographed, like it had been performed hundreds of times.

"Corporal Mouton," Leeland bellowed. One of the soldiers near the guard house looked up but made no reply. "Get on the horn and see where that Dead Sled is. I want those rotten Zs out of here five minutes ago."

"Yes Sir," replied the soldier.

A few seconds later, Leeland had descended the stairs and was approaching the Ford on the driver's side. Cade powered down the window, grimacing from the squelch it made as the fine powdery dust invaded the window channels. The staff sergeant threw a crisp salute Cade's way. Then, after a moment's hesitation, Cade broke a couple of laws and returned the salute. He didn't have the heart to tell the eager staff sergeant that he was no longer in the Army, and neither was he a captain, thus the age-old courtesy was no longer necessary.

"Welcome back Sir," Leeland said as his right arm fell back to his side. "Looks like you need to take this thing through a Water Works. It's a shame they are all closed down."

Cade presumed Leeland was referring to some local car wash chain, but didn't ask for clarification. "No... she needed a little camouflage anyway," he replied.

Leeland chuckled at the joke. "Where did you go—and what's it like out there?" he pried. There was a certain urgency in his voice. Like everything he heard on the base had to be taken with a grain of salt. "I'm going stir crazy stuck inside here. Watching people come and go."

By now, just like they had when he'd left earlier in the day, the guard detail crowded around the dirty truck. "Nothing has changed much out there," Cade called down from the cab, loud enough so everyone could pick it up. "I just wanted to put this girl through the paces. Do a little off-roading."

"What's the verdict. Is she mission capable?"

"More than you know," Cade said, adding a conspiratorial wink.

Leeland grinned ear to ear. "Copy that, Sir." He fished a hand in a cargo pocket and retrieved the white envelope Cade had given him hours ago, then strained to full extension handing it up to the former Delta operator.

"Thanks for hanging on to this for me Staff Sergeant," Cade said with a deliberate nod.

"Any time, Sir. Permission to speak freely, Sir."

Cade nodded again. Said nothing.

"Are things getting better out there?"

"A little better, Staff Sergeant."

The same big grin returned to the guard's sun-bronzed face. "So maybe with a little luck we'll have the dead cleaned out of downtown Springs before winter, and all of the Water Works opened by spring."

"You soldiers from the 4th ID—Fourth Infantry Division— have done most of the heavy lifting. Colorado Springs will probably be cleared sooner than you know," Cade said. *But If I were you, I wouldn't get my hopes up too high*, is what he didn't. He'd leave the telling of the hard truths up to the man's immediate superior. He looked at all of the heads bobbing in total agreement. *A little boost to the morale never hurt anyone*, he thought to himself.

Chapter 31
Outbreak - Day 15
Jackson Hole, Wyoming

Tran had no idea why the zombie had ignored him up on Butte Road, but he was grateful all the same. Why the thing had gone back to feeding on the moose instead of setting the whole clutch chasing after him was a mystery he had been turning over in his mind every agony-filled step of the way since he'd crossed the road.

The lower third of the towering peninsula which the mansion commonly referred to as the "House" lorded over proved easier to navigate than the part he had tumbled down. The pitch had lessened and the underbrush thinned out dramatically. With the afternoon sun boosting his spirits, and eager to get out of the woods and onto flat ground so he could assess his injuries, he quickened his pace from a steady limp to a sort of old person's shuffle. Soon the forest and undergrowth gave way to knee-high grass, and not twenty feet in front of him a sturdy looking fence strung through with horizontal strands of rusty, barb-filled wire halted his forward progress. Twisted from years of seasonal change, and held upright by hard volcanic soil, the multiple gray posts spaced roughly ten feet apart appeared to run the entire length of the Teton Pass Highway. He looked right—the road stretched on straight as the ridge on a wild boar's back. To his left the shimmering blacktop met up with I-189 before curling off left to downtown Jackson Hole; a right turn would take him to Hoback Junction and the Snake River crossing.

That the interchange was choked with dozens of shambling undead, and led to nowhere he wanted to be, quickly solidified his decision to go right and trudge up the pass road.

Wavering on unsteady legs, he gripped the wooden fencepost for balance. He lifted his right foot and inspected it from the big toe to the heel, then plucked a handful of inch-long thorns from the cracked and bleeding flesh. Thought about performing the same maintenance on the other foot—the one attached to the ankle he feared was broken—then dismissed the idea since there was no kind of feeling in it anyway. Flies bombed at his head then alit and skittered around with impunity on his mask of dried blood. With both hands he gingerly walked his fingertips along the inches-long gash running from just above his left eye to the crown of his head. His short-cropped black hair had soaked up a good volume of the blood lost, along with dirt and twigs, and then had dried thoroughly, stiffening up like a helmet. He looked at his fingers. "No blood," he said aloud. The sound of his own voice, hoarse and gravelly, caused his heart to skip. Aside from the murderous brothers who'd left him for dead, he hadn't spoken or heard another voice for quite some time.

Ignoring the buzzing and flitting insects, he about faced and kept to the inside of the fence line. He limped along at half speed, passing dozens of the crude wooden crosses on which noncompliant Jackson natives—whom Robert Christian had decided were no longer necessary—had been crucified alive, then left as morbid examples for all to see: a warning of what would happen to anyone who didn't buy in lock, stock, and barrel to his dystopian version of a New America.

Chapter 32
Outbreak - Day 15
Schriever AFB
Colorado Springs, Colorado

Throaty exhaust notes reverberated in the confines of the metal airplane hangar as Cade wheeled the gore-covered dust-bomb past a half dozen static aircraft in various stages of maintenance.

Like everyone else on the base, from the handful of doctors on down to the airmen fixing chow at the mess, the crew chiefs and flight engineers were working with what they had—practicing their own version of triage on the small fleet of aircraft that now called Schriever home. The helos and aerial refueling birds received the most attention; the rest of the fleet received spit and a band-aid if the manpower became available.

He backed the big Ford into the same spot where it had been parked earlier in the morning, set the brake and looked through the open hangar doors at the aircraft sitting on the tarmac just beyond Whipper's office. One of the pair of charcoal-black Ghost Hawks—larger, but stealthier and nearly silent versions of the venerable H-60 Black Hawk helicopter—sat crouched on the apron. Its carbon fiber blades were tied down and both of the mini-guns had been retracted inside the bird, giving the appearance it was taking some sort of nap while the SOAR pilots who put it through its paces so capably were enjoying their seventy-two hours mandatory stand-down.

Beyond the Gen-3 "Jedi Ride," he could see the unmistakable outline of Marine One, the President's hulking twin rotor Osprey. The bird's V/STOL—Vertical and/or Short Take-Off and Landing—capability, paired with its 275-knot top speed and the fact that it carried a much larger fuel load than most helicopters made it a no brainer to ferry President Valerie Clay to and from the super secure Cheyenne Mountain complex. For a moment Cade stared, wondering why she was here at the base. Then he zeroed in on First Sergeant Whipper's stomping grounds. Though it was at an oblique angle, he could just make out the taxi-yellow door which he expected would fly open any second and disgorge an angry mechanic hell bent on revenge. After a few seconds had elapsed and the wrath of Whipper hadn't descended on the road-weary operator, he unfolded himself from the truck and hopped out.

The tailgate hinged down with a gunshot-like bang and a puff of powdery soil. Shooing the dust from his face, he removed the cardboard box that was almost lost in the middle of Yoder's main drag. He made short work of the strapping tape holding the rectangular box together, then unfolded the sides flat to the floor, revealing a host of chromed and multi-colored parts. He looked at the components for a few long seconds. Undeterred, he set off on a quest for a toolset.

***

Two hours, several scraped knuckles, and a host of salty curse words later—most of them fully accredited to the late Mike Desantos—Cade stood back to view the finished product. Fully satisfied that he had done his best with what he'd had to work with, he stowed the tools and locked the Ford. Finally, he righted the shiny new contraption and headed for the Grayson billet.

Chapter 33
Outbreak - Day 15
Near Driggs, Idaho

"Let's hope the fourth time's the charm," Lucas Brother said as he put the H2 into park.

"We won't know until we get inside," Liam said. "After the last three you'd think this is a dry county or some shit."

Lucas rubbed his temples. The cold sweats had returned, and his headache was getting worse by the minute. This search for booze and a place to stay was beginning to wear him down.

"Quit yer stalling," Liam said. "It's your turn, bro... get out and ice those things."

"Hell, you mean get out?" Lucas spat, throwing Liam a sidelong glare. "I'm driving, dumbass. I thought we agreed... the driver always stays in the truck. Didn't you learn anything from the 189 Junction? We almost bought it back there."

"Yeah, right. The driver stays in *unless* I'm the driver," Liam muttered under his breath.

"I heard that," Lucas shot back.

The house at the end of the driveway was unremarkable. It was one notch up from a mobile home and appeared to have been a one-level '50's ranch style before someone decided that adding an unsightly second floor on top to double the square footage seemed like a good idea. Painted beige, with lavender trim that screamed "old folks live here," the humble abode seemed to be unoccupied.

"Looks promising," Liam said. "And that old pickup might have some gas in it we can siphon."

Lucas squinted. Took a long look at the burgundy older model Chevy. Checked out the house trying to detect any movement. "All right... get out and pop the gate."

Liam looked out the rear window in the direction of the road they had just turned from, staring hard at the three creatures stumbling along the blacktop. Then the wind shifted and their moans carried uphill along with the smell of death. He looked over at Lucas, who was grinding the wheel with his palms. "I'm *not* getting out here. It's *your* turn," Liam declared. He crossed his arms and pressed his body hard against the seatback.

"Suit yourself, Liam. I'll push that fucker in with the bumper."

"No sense in smashing it up if we don't have to," Liam whined. "Besides, I've never had anything as nice as this thing. Shit... never had anything with leather seats."

"Who says it's yours?"

A staring match ensued. Neither brother so much as blinked.

Finally, with the zombies drawing nearer and his eyeballs drying to the point that they were beginning to sting, Lucas relented. "Fine... let me show you how it's done, *bro.*" He snatched the entrenching tool from the back seat. It was a medium-sized military shovel with a serrated edge that folded down small and compact. Ian Bishop had no doubt left the thing in the Hummer and it had already proven useful at killing silently.

He unfolded his long frame from the Hummer and slammed the door behind. And with a swagger that belonged in the *Octagon*, he loped towards the undead trio. "You're trespassing, fuckers!" he bellowed, veins on his neck bulging. The zombies answered back with muted hisses of their own.

He chose the smaller of the three, a teenager he presumed, judging by the video game-inspired tee shirt. *Modern Warfare didn't prepare you for this*, Lucas thought darkly. *Hardest war this kid ever faced was against puberty*, he mused. And that was before something chewed half of his face and a goodly-sized chunk of his neck away.

Lucas stopped mid-stride, and then when the former gamer was at arm's range, put everything he had into swinging the entrenching tool. It traced an arc parallel with the ground, and with a gut-churning crunch struck the creature just above the ear, delving a half a foot in before the serrated edges seized on bone. He held the limp body up with one wavering arm, planted a boot on the soldier silhouette painted in the center of the soiled black tee shirt, and kicked the limp body from the shovel. Then he pivoted on one boot and squared up for the next two combatants. His nose crinkled at the stench wafting off of them. Only clumps of gray hair remained, dotting their skulls like furry islands in a white sea. *First turns*, he thought. *Probably a couple of travelers who got stranded after the outbreak.* An eerie wet rattle emanated from the nearest one, setting the hairs on his neck to attention. He raised his arms overhead like some kind of medieval warrior and brought the tool down in an overhead chopping motion. The blow missed by a fraction, glanced off of the Z's skull, and severed its ear, leaving a wet hole where the decaying lump of flesh and cartilage had been. The ear plopped to the ground and the remaining inertia sent the shovel's sharp edge plunging deep into the monster's clavicle, severing muscles and tendon along the way. The arm, now rendered useless, hung limp at the creature's side while it continued flailing and grabbing with the other. Cold fingers grasped at Lucas's shirt as he struggled to pull the makeshift weapon free. "Motherfucker..." he cried out. He released the handle and felt a rising panic taking over. Then, against his better judgment, he pulled the .45 from his waistband and fired a single-jacketed hollow point into the walker's head. The thing's forehead imploded, spraying blowback in Lucas's face. After a long couple of seconds it finally released its frigid grip and collapsed to the ground.

Lucas shifted his aim and squeezed the trigger twice. The first round blew clean through the second zombie's upper chest but did nothing to halt the abomination's plodding advance. Things slowed and Lucas tracked the brass shell casing's tumbling arc with his eyes. The second lead slug hit six inches higher, shattering its jaw into a hundred pieces and propelling teeth and bone upward through the soft palate, effectively destroying its brain. The body hinged back and struck the asphalt violently, producing a hollow-sounding thud. And as the booming reports rolled away to silence, he shifted his gaze towards the Hummer where Liam had thrown his arms into the air—a universal gesture silently asking his older brother—*"what the fuck did you just do?"*

Lucas shrugged. He walked past the gas-guzzling symbol of excess and flipped his brother the bird. Standing on his toes, he reached over the fence, feeling for a lock. *Nothing.* He removed the six-inch cotter pin holding the gate in place, opened the clasp, and let the gate swing wide aided only by gravity. "Hurry up!" he bellowed, banging on the quarter panel as the Hummer squeezed by.

Liam spun the tires, launching the truck over the threshold, and without missing a beat Lucas closed the latch to lock the dead out and vaulted into the idling truck.

Pinning the accelerator to the floor, Liam barreled up the unimproved drive, keeping the truck's tires glued to the well-worn ruts while the strip of grass growing in between slapped the underbelly of the SUV, producing an eerie swishing sound and leaving a turbid plume of husk and seed in its wake.

"Nobody home..." Liam said as they neared the house with its darkened windows and closed front door. Whether it was a question or a statement Lucas couldn't be sure. "No one's shooting at us," Liam added with a dumb grin pasted on his face.

Lucas couldn't resist. "Yet," he replied.

Liam turned the wheel sharply, decimating a family of garden gnomes with the Hummer's off-road rubber. He smiled, obviously happy with his handiwork. He finished off the three-point turn without destroying anything else and backed the yellow rig up to the tiny front porch.

The doors hinged open simultaneously and the brothers jumped out, weapons in hand. "You go around back," Lucas called out, motioning with the AR-15. He jammed the dull gray .45 between his waistband and the small of his back. "I'll stay here... give you a minute or so and then I'm going in. If there *is* someone inside they heard the gunfire and know we're here. Watch for them rabbiting out the back."

"How far you think they're gonna get?" Liam said, pointing out the AARP sticker displayed on the Chevy Silverado's rusted rear bumper.

"Don't take 'em for granted, bro," Lucas fired back, pointing to the NRA sticker pasted on the rear glass slider. "*Now git,*" he snarled, and without any attempt at being stealthy mounted the stairs, taking them two at a time.

Three strides and he was standing on the square porch. It was four-feet wide and nearly as deep. A sticker that read "NO SOLICITORS" was affixed to the inner door at eye level. "Ohhh... I'd better leave now," he said in a smartass tone as he tried the outer screen door. He found it locked, but the metal mesh screen was nearly rusted out. He easily thrust his thumb through, enlarged the hole and angled his wrist so that he could reach the lock and pop it. To his amazement, the pair of ancient-looking hinges didn't screech out an alarm as he eased the flimsy thing open.

He peered through the inset glass. At first glance, the interior of the house seemed unoccupied and didn't offer many clues. There was no movement in the living room, and he could see no farther than a shadow-filled hallway leading into the back of the house. The furniture was plain. A low table containing dozens of dust catchers displayed on yellowed doilies sat against the far wall, alongside an emerald green davenport. Dominating the opposite wall, the television sat on wooden legs, dark and quiet. It was an old console model of some sort, made from dark wood with a rounded glass screen that had probably displayed its fair share of *Leave It to Beaver. Bingo*, he thought to himself. *Old folks.* He jiggled the doorknob. *Locked.* In his mind's eye he could see

Liam standing in plain sight out back of the house. A bullet catcher if there ever was one.

He brought the AR-15 level with his head, preparing to break out the leaded glass. But before he could follow through with the intended blow, a single gunshot, sounding like it came from Liam's Beretta, rang out. He froze with the AR's collapsed butt stock wavering an inch from the pane.

Then someone began to shout but the words were garbled. Distant. Lucas grimaced because he couldn't make out whose distressed voice he was hearing nor what was being said. He eased the screen door closed, backed off the porch, and instead of following in his brother's footsteps he peeled off to the left, keeping his head below the windows as he padded past a number of chest-high bushes. He halted at the rear of the house, pinned his blonde hair behind one ear and listened for a second.

But by now the shouting had ceased, and the only thing he could make out was the noise of some sort of fabric flapping and popping in the wind. He risked a one-eyed peek around the corner. Liam stood in the center of the yard, roughly thirty feet away, his face a mask of worry. The black Beretta clutched in his right fist was trained on an elderly woman who in turn was pointing a derringer-style pistol of her own directly at his midsection.

A gust of wind ruffled the sheets on the line, revealing a man's body lying near the woman's slippered feet. He was splayed out, pale and unmoving, atop a pile of white sheets that had been splattered crimson with his blood.

"Put it down," Liam barked as he looked over his shoulder towards the front of the house.

Lucas crouched low and sprinted a dozen feet to his left, keeping the line full of flapping laundry between him and the gun-wielding granny. He glanced over and could see the look of distress on Liam's face change to one of recognition and then calm as their eyes met.

"OK... I'll put mine down if you put yours down."

The lady shook her head. She began bleating, "*Why?*" Saying it repeatedly, her scratchy voice rising in volume until her wails nearly drowned out everything else. The wind. The clothes on the line. And Lucas creeping up behind her with his pistol in a two-handed grip.

The small gun trembled in the woman's skeletal hand. Everything slowed down for Lucas as he cut the angle, taking his brother out of the line of fire. He pulled the trigger on the move and watched her head hinge sideways at an impossible angle as the slug impacted behind her left ear, splashing chunks of brain and ruptured skull onto the drying wash. The supersonic slap from the .45 caliber projectile lifted her from the ground and out of her fuzzy slippers. Death had come so quickly that the tiny Derringer remained unfired and was still clutched in her fist when her body fell back to earth.

"Liam... you OK?"

"I don't know," came a shaky reply as he checked his torso for bullet holes.

"So why did you ice the geezer?" Lucas said as he stood over the man's body. "He doesn't even have a gun."

"Shit... you look at that face, it's all pale and skinny. I shit you not, I thought the dude was a zombie."

"I can see the resemblance."

"Let's see what they left us in their will," Liam said. Chuckling, he stepped around the corpses, climbed the back stairs and entered the house through the open back door.

Chapter 34
Outbreak - Day 15
Schriever AFB
Colorado Springs, Colorado

Cade gave the door two light raps, then waited a beat. *Nothing.* He knocked two more times, putting a little more muscle behind them. *Still quiet.*

He expected to find his family either at the mess or hunkered down here trying to keep cool, and he hadn't seen them when he popped in to the former. *Strange*, he thought. A hundred degree day had a knack for driving people inside and keeping them there. Still, he wasn't worried—Brook could take care of herself and Raven. She'd already proven that many times over. He just wanted to make sure when he opened the door he wasn't greeted with the business end of his wife's M4.

So he knocked one more time, waited a second longer, and then fished a hand into his cargo pocket. He rooted amongst the truck keys and the gilded basketball. *Nothing.* As he'd suspected, Brook had the only key to the hut.

Even though he was pretty certain the person or persons responsible for infecting the civilians and setting off the outbreak inside of Schriever had already fled, keeping the door to the

Grayson billet locked at all times was their new SOP—Standard Operating Procedure.

He propped his rifle against the jamb, shrugged off his combat pack and rifled through the side pockets looking for his lock-gun—a highly effective lock-picking tool that could easily defeat most standard tumbler locks. In fact, he realized that since he had been running ops with the new Delta team, the soft spoken Maddox had dealt with every secured door they had encountered. To say the deceased operator had been a magician with a lock would be vastly understating the truth.

Finally his fingers brushed the plastic grip; somehow the thing had worked its way to the very bottom of his ruck and was mixed in with the unpalatable discards from the awful MREs that had kept him going at times. That the tool wasn't immediately accessible would have earned him an ass-chewing from his mentor, the late Mike Desantos.

During the few seconds it took him to gain entry into his own quarters, he made a mental note to square away his ruck before setting course for Utah in the morning—and put the lock-gun where he could get to it at a moment's notice. *From here on out I need to be on my A-game*, he thought to himself. Because tomorrow, there would be no team of shooters backing him up.

After hustling the shiny contraption through the open door, he found a bunk far away in the shadows and hoisted it on top, pushing it back far as he could and then spreading a thin sheet over the sharp angles.

He ventured back into the bright afternoon to collect the rest of his gear, set everything in a pile in the center of the dark room, and locked the door. Unbuttoning his ACUs on the move, he made a beeline for the toilets.

He'd been holding this one in for half an hour, and as he stood in front of the urinal with one arm propped on the cool tile and blasted away at the fragrant little pill, he detected subtle movement out of the corner of his eye. He dropped his Johnson and drew the compact Glock from his shoulder holster, swept it to the right and bracketed some kind of dog within the tritium sights.

"You gotta be kidding me," he said aloud as he holstered his weapon. "And how did you get in here, pooch?" Though he was merely thinking aloud, the answer to his question hit him at once—*the girls.*

He finished his business at the urinal and put everything away in its proper place. Then he knelt in a submissive posture and clucked his tongue. "You a girl or a boy, you hairy rascal?"

Cade watched the dog regard him for a tick, then the seemingly fearless shepherd padded forward and sniffed at his upturned palm. While the dog was busy vetting him, he gently grasped its collar and glanced at the quarter-sized tag hanging there. "Your name is *Max.* That's what it says on your dog tag," he said in a sing-song voice. "Look... I've still got mine." He tapped at his army issue dog tags through the fabric of his sweat-stained tee shirt. The dog went prone, eyes intently focused on him—one blue and one brown. The brindle shepherd received a thorough scratching behind the ears. "Where did the girls find you?"

Cade shrugged out of his shoulder holster and peeled away the damp, rank-smelling tee shirt and chucked it into one of the many sinks lining one wall of what used to be a communal lavatory.

"You must think I'm crazy talking to you like we're long lost buddies." In the event the girls had snuck in and happened to be watching, he looked over his shoulder before continuing the one-sided conversation. "I've been outnumbered two to one for the last twelve years. So I welcome you with open arms... you can be my *wingman.*"

Max sprang to all fours, turned a circle and let out a single muted yap.

"OK—let's get out of the bathroom. Or else someone's going to think we're light in the loafers," Cade said as a wave of fatigue suddenly welled up within him. A full day's worth of adrenaline highs and the inevitable valleys on the back side of those peaks was finally catching up. He made his way to a bunk and plopped down with his boots still laced, feet planted firmly on the floor, and the rest of his torso stretched across the thin mattress—and that was exactly how Brook and Raven found him when they came back from visiting with Wilson, Sasha, and Taryn.

Chapter 35
Outbreak - Day 15
Winters's Compound
Eden, Utah

The blindfold peeled off with a dull pop, and like something alive, the man's greasy dreadlocks splayed out over his shoulders. Duncan chucked the burlap strip to the floor, and placed himself between the prisoner and the single hundred-watt bulb they had strung up for this occasion. He figured he'd look all the more imposing if they played it that way.

Twirling his waxed handlebar moustache, Logan had struck a somewhat sympathetic pose, arms at his side and slouched in the folding metal chair. He had one leg propped across the other and his black bowler hat concealed his eyes.

This room would do, Duncan thought to himself. It wasn't a jail cell or an interrogation room, but neither was it the Embassy Suites. Row upon row of food stuffs jammed the room from the plywood-covered floor to its low metal ceiling. Shiny cans tilted sideways, their contents and a date scribbled in the hand of either Logan or Lev, lined one wall. A wall of rice and pinto beans stored in plastic five-gallon buckets loomed behind the seated prisoner. The latter not so good in an underground bunker, Duncan mused. Aside from the booze-tinged sweat oozing from the young man's pores, the room had a certain unique odor about it. A mild metallic nose with an underlying dampness. The more he thought about it, the more the smell reminded him of an unfinished basement.

Duncan noted the man's wild eyes darting about the room. He allowed him a moment to stew in his situation and then removed the gag. "What's your name?" he demanded. Then he stepped closer, hovered over the young man, invading his personal space.

"Since when is it illegal to watch somebody?"

Duncan reared back and threw the yellow notepad. It hit the watcher squarely in the chest and ended up on the floor near his scuffed boots.

"Take it easy on the guy," Logan said. He got up from his chair, pushed the bowler to its proper place, and glared at his older brother.

"Says the peacenik in the family," Duncan said, emitting a sad-sounding chuckle.

Logan took one step closer. "He's all of what... *seventeen*? You don't need to *hurt* him."

"*Eighteen*... and my name's Chance," the prisoner said, twisting his head in Logan's direction.

"Old enough to go to war. Old enough to vote... but not old enough to drink. Why do you smell like a brewery, kid? Is that all you're doing now that the end of the world is upon us?" Duncan asked.

"What the hell does that have to do with anything?" Logan spat. "Give him a break... you've been out there. You've seen how hellish it is."

"Quit sticking up for the kid!" Duncan bellowed. He regained his composure, and in his syrupy southern drawl addressed the kid. "Now, Chance." He paused for effect. "I'm only going to give you one *chance* to tell me the truth. Then I'm going to ask Mister *Gives a Shit* here to leave us alone so we can get better acquainted."

Chance swallowed hard. His eyes flicked to Logan looking for any sort of help. Received none. Logan had the bowler hat once again pulled down low, keeping the stark white light of the single exposed bulb at bay.

Duncan cracked his knuckles. Sat on his haunches so that he was seeing eye to eye with Chance. "I'm going to make this easy for you to remember. I have three questions that start with a W. Why were you watching us? Where are you staying when you're not taking notes about our comings and goings? Who else is there with you when you aren't watching us? I may have follow up questions if I don't like your answers."

"I'll talk to *him*," Chance said. He motioned with his eyes, rolling them in Logan's direction.

"You'll tell *him* everything?" asked Duncan.

"You'll *really* let me go?" the kid asked tentatively.

"I want to *kill* you," Duncan said matter-of-factly. "You were watching us. Taking notes for some reason. Furthermore... you had a gosh dang AK-47—"

Logan cut in. "I will escort you to your ride personally." He held the young man's car keys aloft. "But only if you *promise* you won't come back."

Duncan snorted. Shook his head and stared at the floor. "You're making a big mistake," he murmured. "But it's your call."

"Yes it is. And it's a fair trade by my estimation," Logan added. Then he revealed his eyes. Looked squarely at Chance. "You have my *word*... I'll let you go. How'd you get here?"

"*He* has to leave," said Chance. "Then can you cut me loose?"

Duncan spoke up. "Yes to one. No to two." He walked past Logan, and on his way out the door added a parting shot, "If you don't tell him *everything*... and I mean every little detail. Then I will be back. Before I leave I have to ask you one more thing…"

Chance wormed around and looked towards Duncan. "What?"

"You seen the movie Pulp Fiction?" asked Duncan.

"Who hasn't?" the kid quipped.

"Good. Then you remember what Marsellus Wallace said to the hillbilly rapist."

It was silent inside the storeroom.

"Let me refresh your memory. Marsellus had just suffered some unspeakable shit at the hands of the hillbilly *and* the gimp. So Butch saves Marsellus's ass and Marsellus says... I'm paraphrasing now, so bear with me... he says to the hillbilly rapist, '*I'm gonna have one of my friends get medieval on your ass.*' You following, Chance?"

"I'm the *hillbilly*," Chance said resignedly.

"Bingo. I'll be back if you don't answer every one of this man's questions to the best of your ability." Judging by the beaded sweat on the kid's lip and brow, and the size his eyes had gone, Duncan didn't need to repeat the medieval line. He rose to his full height and flashed a covert wink at his baby brother, stepped over the raised threshold and clanged the door shut behind him.

***

Ten minutes later

Logan emerged from the store room, shut the door and leaned backwards, pressing his hundred and fifty pound frame against it. After a beat, a broad smile formed on his face.

Duncan pushed off of the wall that had been supporting his weight. Eyebrows inching up, he gave his brother a look that said, '*spill yer guts.*'

Holding up an imaginary statue, Logan began to recite a made up acceptance speech. "I'd like to thank the Motion Picture Academy first and foremost—" A chorus of raucous laughter from the brothers filled the confined space.

"He told you *everything*?" Duncan asked.

"*Everything* he wanted us to think," Logan answered under his breath.

"You think anything he said was truthful?"

The low murmur of someone talking in one of the other subterranean rooms floated past them. Logan crossed his arms, and swiveled his head back and forth. "No way. First off... I don't think it's just him and a few relatives camping thirty miles east of here like he says. And secondly, I don't buy his bullshit story that he didn't know anything about the cut barbed wire, the two infected dudes and the rotters that followed them in. He was all jittery and diverted his eyes more than a few times. He was *lying*," Logan said confidently.

"Doesn't matter, when you go back in there take this with you and ask him to sign it. Furthers the illusion... know what I mean?"

Logan studied the single sheet of paper. "Effin peace treaty. Good call. Makes it look all o-fish-ul. So, Bad Cop... you really are going to let him go?"

"Keep him locked up until about an hour before nightfall and then blindfold him. Drive around the airfield for about five minutes. Doesn't matter which way you turn or how many times. Just confuse the kid. Make him think the compound is farther in than it really is," Duncan said, flashing a shit-eating grin at Logan. "It's what I did when I brought him in here. Shoulda seen the look on Lev's face when I kept doing laps and figure eights. Then after you get his head spinning, you take him to his vehicle." Duncan handed over the dented and scratched AK-47.

"Where the hell is his vehicle?"

"Black Toyota about a quarter mile north of the clearing. The ladies saw a fella come looking for the boy. They tried to get to him but he knew how to move quiet and fast."

Logan flashed him a bewildered look. "And then what?"

"Then you make a show of it... tell him we won't be as forgiving if he comes back around. Then give him back his rifle."

After checking the magazine and seeing his reflection staring back at him in the shiny brass casings, Logan shook his head doggedly. "I can't do it. Not this way. What's going to keep the *shitbird* from putting a couple of rounds into my back when I'm not looking?"

"Go with Lev or Gus. Give the kid the rifle after you reach his vehicle."

"*You sure?*"

"*Positive.* When you were in there playing Good Cop I ruined the firing pin." Duncan smiled, removed his aviator glasses and buffed each lens with a deliberate circular motion. Fogged them with his breath and repeated the process.

"You're a wily bastard, Dunc. Playing him like that. And then that Ving Rhames shtick— '*medieval on yo ass*'—effin priceless, brother."

"Sometimes a flash of brilliance shines through all of my bullshit," Duncan drawled.

"Don't sell yourself short, bro. You've always been the brains of the family. After Dad, of course. You know, if there's one thing I'm grateful for it's that Mom and Dad didn't have to see this shit happen to the world."

"Dad woulda been OK," Duncan said. "Mom— she wouldn't have gotten on very well, what with only a rolling pin and her acid tongue against the dead." He clapped his brother on the shoulder. "I promise you. This is going to work out just fine. Best case scenario is ol' Chance stays away. Better case, he brings his *family* back and we're ready for them. Take care of them once and for all." He embraced Logan in one of his trademark bear hugs. Whispered in his ear. "I kinda hope they do bring it... cause there's a couple more tricks up this old dog's sleeve."

He fleshed out the rest of the plan for Logan, and when he had finished, Good Cop reentered the storeroom to cross the T's and dot the I's.

Whistling a few notes of Skynyrd's Free Bird, Duncan walked down the connecting corridor. "Phillip," he bellowed. "I've got a job for you."

Chapter 36
Outbreak - Day 15
Schriever AFB
Colorado Springs, Colorado

The sun was making its downward slide over the Rockies as Brook worked the key in the lock. The hottest part of the day was behind her, and now she was looking forward to a little family time. Time to clear up a few things. Time to cleanse her palate for a steaming plate of crow.

She took another look at the sky going red, pushed the door in and stood back. "Cade... you in there?"

Nothing.

She turned back to Raven. "I want you to stay right here while I check things out." Raven nodded. Mouthed a silent OK.

Brook entered the dim room holding the M4 at low ready, with the barrel at a forty-five degree angle between horizontal and the floor, just like Cade had taught her the first time they'd hunted pheasant together. Before Raven was born and well before brandishing a weapon against danger, real or perceived, had become a part of her normal routine. Just like eating or breathing—two things necessary to sustain life—toting around seven pounds of forged titanium and machined metal had become nearly as important for her survival.

She had one boot in the door when Max confronted her, muzzle against her leg and his stubby tail wagging a manic hello. Ignoring the dog, she pushed in further. And once her eyes had adjusted she saw her shirtless husband, chest rising and falling, splayed out on the bunk opposite the two they had pushed together to serve as a sort of mini-queen bed. She noticed his M4 amongst his gear near her feet, but she didn't see the ever-present pair of Glock pistols.

"Cade—" she said in a low voice. She watched him for a tick. He stirred, but didn't respond. She called out to Raven. "Come on in sweetie... but be quiet, your dad's asleep."

***

Cade finally stirred after a couple of minutes. He opened one eye to recon the room. Except for a trickle of light coming in around the covered windows, it was gloomy and he appeared to be alone. He propped his head up on one elbow and shifted his gaze behind him.

"Hi Dad."

"Hi sweetie," he said to Raven, who was sitting on the adjacent bunk. "I was wiped." He ran his hands through his dark hair. Rubbed his eyes, squinting against the fading light.

"Time for a haircut, Dad," Raven said. "Maybe a shave too? Sure looks itchy."

"No, it's not so bad sweetie. I think I'm going to let it grow out a little."

"I liked your face before this... when it was smooth. You know, like Uncle Mike's—" she stopped mid-sentence. Made a face, clearly wishing she could take back the words.

The three of them said nothing for a couple of minutes.

Finally Cade broke the silence. "It's OK, Raven. Even though we can't talk to him, Uncle Mike is still with us. Right in here... in *spirit*," he said, touching his chest over his heart.

"How do you know?" she asked, screwing up her face.

"I read about it in the *old people* hand book. You'll have to trust me. Can you do that?"

"Yes Dad."

He stood and stretched. "I'm going to go on a quick run before it's full dark," he said. "Want me to take the *dog?*"

"Not so fast, *Captain* Grayson. Wouldn't want Max to get *lost* now, would we," Brook said, adding air quotes with her fingers to the word '*lost.*'

"I *love* dogs," Cade said, suppressing a grin.

"*Sit down,*" Brook commanded.

He dropped his tennis shoes and did as he was told, planting his butt on the rack.

"We need to have a family conversation, and honey, I have a confession to make," she said softly. She paced the floor for a few seconds. Took a deep cleansing breath and went on. "I left the reservation while you were on your way to Jackson Hole. Went on a food run along with General Gaines, some of his 10th Special Forces guys, and a few of the civilians."

Cade's eyes narrowed. "I know," he said matter-of-factly.

Brook stared into his brown eyes. "Who told you... I mean how did you find out?"

"Your boots gave you away."

"My boots?" she asked as her gaze shifted unconsciously down the length of her body towards her feet.

"The mud caked on those things wasn't from around here. Too many minerals. Smelled like manure. No kind of soil like that around here."

Brook chuckled. "That was *gated community* dirt," she said. "*Rich folks dirt.*"

"Like I said before. We live and die by the decisions we make, and we're not going to live forever."

"*Dad...*"

"I'm only speaking to the truth, Raven. Your mom and me are trying to prepare you for that day, and it starts right now. Keep it on your mind so that when it does happen you'll know exactly what *you* need to do."

"And then?" she asked softly, her head resting on the bunk's vertical post.

"You *survive*," Brook added. "You forget about us and you save yourself... that's what it's going to take for you to survive. You'll have to detach—"

"Detach?"

"You know. Like I had to do in Myrtle Beach. Those things were no longer your Grandma and Grandpa... and I didn't think of that thing crawling down the hall as my Mom when I pulled that trigger." Brook paused to let it sink in. Watched Raven's brow crinkle. *Too much too soon*, Brook thought to herself. Then she changed the subject. Went on to explain to Cade where she and Raven had been and what they had been doing. Over the course of an hour she told him about Wilson and Sasha and their entire story—from Denver on up to their unanticipated mess hall meeting after breakfast. She went over the horrors Taryn had endured inside of Grand Junction Regional until she was rescued by him and his Delta team. Finally she dropped the thumb drive bombshell in his lap.

Cade visibly tensed as he listened to the improbable news coming out of her mouth. He sat up and gently extricated himself from Brook's embrace. Exhaled audibly and looked her in the eye for a beat. Shifted his gaze over to his daughter.

"It's true," Raven said rapid-fire. "I believe Taryn. She's nice. Wilson... he's kind of old and annoying..."

Brook whispered in Cade's ear, "He's twenty."

Raven went on, "—and Sasha... she's kind of full of herself, but I think sooner or later she'll come around."

"You've got 'em all figured out," Cade said, feigning surprise. "Except for the dog... If I were you I wouldn't get too attached to anyone. Because we're not going to be here much longer."

Raven smiled.

"We'll cover that in part two of our family meeting," Brook said rather tentatively. Then she laid out her proposal. "We'll all go to Eden. You, me, and Raven. Sasha. Wilson and Taryn, from the sounds of it, will pull their weight."

"Don't forget Max," chimed Raven.

"And the dog," Brook said, shooting a reassuring look at her daughter who was standing hands on hips and glowering her way.

There was silence as Cade just stared at Brook with a sour look on his face. He shifted his gaze to Raven, then the dog. He was outnumbered.

Brook and Raven stood before him. Smiling.

The whole thing had been a cleverly crafted and properly sprung ambush. Cade fought off the small curl of a smile working on the corners of his lips.

Brook continued. "If they go with us there will be someone close to Raven's age. Plus," she whispered into Cade's ear. "Young people like Taryn and Wilson are going to be necessary to repopulate. To keep us going. Keep us fighting back against those things."

Cade was speechless. The word *incredulous* crept into his mind. Rarely was he at a loss for words, so he merely stared with a firm set to his jaw.

"Bed time, Raven. I need to work on your father. Set Max up on one of the bottom bunks."

Max heard his name and emerged from the shadows. Raven scratched behind his ears. Then she pecked Mom and Dad on the cheek. "Come on boy," she said as she headed to the bathroom to get ready for bed.

***

One hour later

"So it's settled then—you'll at least show up at the briefing at zero-five-hundred? Give them your two cents' worth?" Brook wrapped her toned arms around her man. Wrestled him flat to the bunk without receiving much of a fight in return.

"I'm not sold yet," Cade replied. "Plus it depends on where they're going."

"*Bullshit,* Cade Grayson, you're too much of a *patriot* to let the objective stop you from going. There's *so much* riding on this. Like Nash said to me in not so many words, 'Time is of the essence'—*cliché* but true."

"I'll go and sniff around. See what kind of mission they are planning."

"Take these," Brook said, holding out her right hand. It was balled up into a fist, her knuckles facing the ceiling. "You'll need them."

He held his hand out palm up.

She dropped two squares of desert tan fabric into his ready hand. Velcro on one side—captain's bars stitched in black on a field of desert camo on the other. "Nash said for you to keep them whether you report to the briefing in the morning or not." Brook grabbed Cade's other arm, looked at the Suunto strapped to his wrist. She looked into the gloom towards Raven's oasis. Cocked her head and listened for a beat. She heard nothing but rhythmic breathing. "Looks like we've got a window of opportunity," Brook said in a soft sing song voice. "Don't worry... I'll leave you a couple of hours to decide on the mission." She kissed him hard on the mouth. Felt him pressing against her, an urgency rippling through his muscles. They stopped simultaneously. Twisted around to face the back of their quarters. A few words of gibberish echoed from the dark. "Talking in her sleep," Cade said as he rolled Brook from her side to her back.

They made love in the dark. Stopping only when both of them were winded and spent.

Brook dabbed the sheen from Cade's cheeks and upper lip. Ran both hands through his damp hair. Then she abruptly kissed her man on the forehead, rolled away and was asleep in less than five.

That was it, he told himself. He had just witnessed Brook's ritual. She had started to compartmentalize. To ready herself for another stretch of being alone while he was outside the wire. That simple act—rolling over and switching off like a circuit breaker being thrown—after they had just shared an hour of intimacy. An hour of true feelings exchanged without words. Her body language told him it was OK for him to go. Told him she understood. Told him she had known what she was getting herself into thirteen years ago when they married. And it assured him that she hadn't forgotten.

He lay there staring at the mattress above him. Contemplating the waffle pattern the springs cut into the dingy green fabric. Imagining what would have been if he had left Taryn to the mercy of the zombies at Grand Junction, just like he had left the survivors from the capsized barge at the Flaming Gorge dam. For if he hadn't rescued her, he surely wouldn't be wrestling with the decision to once again forsake his family and put his life on the line for the sake of the many.

He fell asleep with the unanswered questions ensconced in his mind and the fabric captain's emblems clutched in his hand.

Chapter 37
Outbreak - Day 15
Near Winters's Compound

"Goddamnit, what a pain in the ass," Phillip muttered. The task he had started in the back of the Humvee had quickly grown old. His spindly legs didn't altogether fit in the cramped back end, and he kept whacking his head on the pistol grips hanging from the big machine gun. So now he sat in the grass with a slowly diminishing pile of metal links, meticulously relinking them with loose fifty-caliber rounds. He'd lost count at two hundred but he still had one and a half ammo cans full of the inch-thick cartridges that were topped off with armor-piercing lead.

"Hey buddy," Duncan called out from his blind side. Phillip's head jerked up. He dropped a pair of the links he had been holding. "Shit," he exclaimed. "What are you doing sneaking up on a fella like that?"

"Sorry... take this." Duncan handed the lanky man a longneck Bud. "It's warm—still wets the whistle though," he drawled. "Pass me some of those... I'll give you a hand."

"Why do we need so much belted ammo?" Phillip inquired.

"You remember the machinegun fire we heard down by the roadblock—coming from inside the city?"

Phillip looked up from his task and nodded.

"AK-47... heard that kind of chatter gun poppin' off in my direction more times than I care to remember. Mostly in Nam. Been on the wrong side of 'em a couple times in the last couple of weeks though. But that's not the point. If those hombres have Kalashnikovs, then no doubt they have bigger stuff. Hell, that Chance kid we let go had an AK-47. Leads me to believe our bad guys are calling Huntsville home, and like I already said... sooner or later we'll be facing off against them. Rather do it on our terms out in the open. That Ma Deuce there... she packs a Helluva punch. Thing can swat a Huey outta the sky. Just makes sense to have her as an *equalizer*."

"Good thinking, Sir. At least we got *something* out of our little excursion." Phillip grabbed the last olive green ammo can. Looked inside and made a quick mental calculation. "There are about seventy rounds left. How many does Logan want me to leave him for his Barrett?"

"Better leave him fifty or so," Duncan said. "I can't wait to see Oops shoot that thing and get his skinny butt knocked to the dirt."

Both men worked in silence for a few minutes. Duncan stopped to shoo away an armada of buzzing gnats. "Saved my ass back there at the roadblock," he said out of nowhere. He looked over the top of his aviator glasses. "Thanks," he added sincerely. "I figure I owe you one."

Phillip took a long pull off of his Budweiser. "Wasn't nothing. I just hope you get the chance to pay me back is all."

"Alternative sucks." Duncan smiled and let out a low chortle. The kind of sound someone makes after they've stared down death and survived.

"No disrespect Sir... I mean Duncan... you didn't see those rotters flanking us today, did you?"

"'Fraid I didn't," Duncan answered demurely.

"Those thing's prescription?" Phillip asked, tapping at his eye as if he were the one wearing the glasses.

"Yes Sir. I was supposed to go to the VA hospital up on the hill in Portland to get my eyes checked about a year ago. Kept putting it off until finally a week before the feces hit the oscillating thingy I finally made my appointment. The shit part of it is... my appointment was yesterday." He upended his amber bottle and looked for its replacement.

"Newsflash Duncan. You ain't getting new glasses, so I better stick close to you from here on out. Wouldn't want you to get eaten."

"*Shiiiit*," Duncan drawled. "This old boy's flesh is *tougher* than a deep fried chicken gizzard—good luck with that, rotters."

Both men shared a few moments of morbid laughter.

"You know somethin, Phillip," Duncan said as he regained his composure.

"Lay it on me," Phillip replied.

"You're an OK guy when you aren't calling me Sir."

Chapter 38
Outbreak - Day 16
Teton Pass
Jackson Hole, Wyoming

Am I dead? Tran had asked himself after that first uneventful encounter with the pack of feeding zombies as he crossed Butte Road. And now, hours later, trapped on the straight stretch of Teton Pass Road, barbed wire flanking both sides, with nowhere to go and surrounded by zombies, he surrendered completely. He said a few silent, solemn words to his maker, collapsed to the smooth warm roadway, and waited for the inevitable clawing nails and gnashing teeth.

After a few moments had passed and his blood hadn't been spilled, he willed his legs to support him. He stood on the centerline, hunched over, with a spasm hammering at his lower back. His eyes tracked the walking carrion as they took the path of least resistance. He was like a rock in a stream splitting the oblivious throng down the center. His mind had been playing tricks on him. For reasons unknown to him at the time, the zombies wanted nothing to do with him. He didn't know why, nor did he care. With nothing but the dead and the steady slapping of his own bare feet for company, he left the crucified behind and tackled the curving mountain road with renewed vigor. He spent the next several hours trudging uphill among them, an achingly slow and silent procession, during which he began to question his humanity —for the second time since the big man named Liam threw him from the moving truck, he wondered whether he had turned, and was now one of them.

***

As Tran neared the sign proclaiming the elevation of the Teton Pass to be 8,431 feet above sea level, he couldn't help but think someone's altimeter had been malfunctioning the day they recorded the measurement, because to him, it seemed like he had been trudging Mount Everest all day, not this mere pimple on the earth. Without a watch to consult, he guessed he'd made a respectable mile an hour in forward travel—ten hours, he supposed, of putting one foot in front of the other while rubbing elbows with the dead. A feat to a tortoise maybe, but to a biped with a severely swollen ankle and a throbbing skull, surely it was some kind of world record.

As he pushed on, the foundation of hatred he had been trying to ignore strengthened with each tortured step. He tried to block out the fact that, for more years than he cared to admit, he had been head chef and sometime driver for a murderous madman. Instead, he tried to spin his situation into the realm of the positive. To reflect on his proper upbringing. To strengthen his belief that there was a certain order to the way the world worked and he had just been playing his role by working for the crazy billionaire. Truth be told, until the takeover of Jackson Hole, Robert Christian's true nature had remained hidden. Sure, he could have run like all the others after the first group of resistors had been executed, but he hadn't. There was no changing the past, and the harder he tried to distance his thoughts from the evil that had taken place in the valley, the more it became evident that by association he had played a small part in so many innocents' misery. In fact, until this epiphany, he had been adrift in a river of denial, and in a way he wished the demons would have eaten him. Put him out of his misery. Made the looming decision moot and inconsequential. And as he tried to purge the

231

two brothers' scowling faces from his memory, he had a psychic shift. Suddenly *an eye for an eye* made perfect sense to him. He had missed what the one-eyed demon he had been forced to kill symbolized. Was she sent as some kind of message—a portent of things to come? Was he fated to survive and somehow stop the two men from further madness and mayhem?

With these questions preoccupying his thoughts, he failed to see the zombie directly in his path—until he collided face first into its sternum. The creature gazed down on him with cloudy indifferent eyes, then turned and shambled towards the looming cluster of burned-out vehicles. The largest among them looked to have been at one time some kind of school bus. It had been parked so that it partially blocked the road from the guardrail on his left to the far shoulder on the right, and it was going nowhere because it rested on blackened, bare rims which appeared to be fused to the road.

Tran stopped and leaned against a stalled-out SUV in order to watch the lone monster shuffle through the ten-foot gap that remained between the sloping shoulder and the hardscrabble mountainside. That the thing hadn't eaten him came as no surprise. He limped around to the driver side of the green, two-door Scout. Hinged at the waist to look at his image in the side mirror. A monster peered back. Blood had dried black, leaving his already thin face resembling a grinning skull. A jagged fissure snaked through his hairline. It bulged with glistening, swollen flesh, and oozed a viscous yellowed fluid. In the failing light of dusk he could see a stark white strip of his skull underneath the festering mess. Not only did he look like one of them, the infected wound made him smell like one of them. The morbid-looking face reflected back at him was a hundred times worse than he had anticipated.

He backed away. *I'm not one of them*, he thought to himself. "I'm alive," he whispered under his breath, the words doing little to convince him. He evaluated the situation, trying to decide on his next move. Looked at the truck—something about the black E spray painted on it seemed familiar. He'd seen other vehicles in town that sported the same markings. It gave him hope that there might be something inside that could be of use to him. The door was unlocked, and inexplicably a set of keys still dangled from the ignition. *Another omen*, he thought to himself.

Chapter 39
Outbreak - Day 16
Near Driggs, Idaho

After losing the fourth straight round of Rock-Paper-Scissors in a row, Liam rose from the low-slung couch and ambled on unsteady legs to the '50's-era kitchen. As he transited the dark hall using the walls and jambs for guidance, he tried to place the unusual odor. Mothballs maybe. Octogenarian farts? He couldn't be sure, but it seemed that twenty years of retired living had had a way of imparting something malodorous into the furniture and walls and carpet of the dead couples' home.

With only the moonlight filtering between the sheer curtains to see by, he poured a few fingers of Scotch into each of the coffee mugs. Then, for good measure, he tipped the clear bottle of Claymore, swallowed hard, twice, making bubbles form in the amber liquid. Made a sour face and wiped his lips with the back of his hand.

He returned to the living room with the mugs and the partial bottle. Set everything on the coffee table between the burning candles and the half-eaten plate of corned beef and hash. "Lucas!" he bellowed. "There's a bunch of those rotting fuckers at the gate. I can see their white faces from here."

"What the hell do you want *me* to do about it?" Lucas called back from the bathroom. "Piss on 'em?" he added, laughing.

Liam drained his mug and reached for the booze. "Your popping those two deadheads on the road didn't do us any favors," he intoned.

Lucas hitched up his pants, grabbed his pistol, and headed back to the living room, talking as he walked in the dark. "Don't worry bro... they *won't* get in." Staying clear of the flickering flames, he crabbed by Liam's knees and nearly broke the couch when he sat down too heavily.

There was a long awkward silence as Lucas tried to get ahold of his thoughts. Then, fighting through the short term memory-stealing buzz, the point he had been trying to make returned to him. "I put the pin back in the gate. Those things can't turn a doorknob, let alone pull out a cotter pin and work the clasp and then reason which way the *fucking* thing needs to swing." He finished the statement by throwing his brother a wild look. A look that said: *do not question me when I'm loaded.*

Liam ignored the glare he knew all too well and went there anyway. "You're sure? Maybe we oughta park that old truck against it... for a little extra *insurance.*"

"It'll be OK. We'll get up at first light and get back on the road. I'll drive right *over* the bastards."

"What about the old folks... see that plaque over the mantle?" Liam didn't allow Lucas the five minutes he needed to process the complex question. "Old guy was a World War Two vet. I think we oughta bury them. You know— out of respect."

"He lost this war. Plus, I oughta piss on both their bodies for this," Lucas slurred, holding up the nearly empty bottle. "Crap's probably been in their cupboard since Prohibition." He laughed hard. Kept it up for a minute or two while Liam tried to engage him.

"We still trying to find Bishop?" he finally asked.

Lucas pulled it together. Took a belt from the bottle before replying. "I figure we head northwest. Sooner or later we'll bump into some of his boys. Either that or some of our old friends."

"I'd rather it be our old friends," Liam stated in a low voice. "Bishop fuckin' bailed on us."

"*No*, that dumbass Paul lost the frickin' satellite phone at the Cowboy bar. You seen all the dead. I figure Ian had no choice... we'd been nothing but loyal to him. Hell... I was a good lieutenant... except for the booze run into Wilson, I followed his every order to a T," Lucas declared proudly. His head nodded, chin to chest, then jerked upright abruptly.

Liam shook his head. "If you really think we'll be safe here tonight I'm going to sleep."

"*In there?*" Lucas said incredulously.

"Bed smells better than this couch. Or that nasty shag rug for that matter."

"Suit yourself," said Lucas. "I'm gonna work on this." He filled his mug half full.

Liam gazed through the picture window. Stole one final long look at the gathered dead. Threw a shiver that chilled his spine and lingered for a moment. It still creeped him out how they stared and stared. *On autopilot, every last one of them*, he thought. There didn't seem to be more showing up, so he shrugged his shoulders and headed into the gloomy crypt of a bedroom. "Put out the candles before you nod off and burn us to death," he called out, his voice echoing down the hall.

Lucas said nothing. His eyelids felt like they were attached to lead fishing weights. He set the empty mug aside. Laid back on the couch, his boots shooting off the end, heels on the armrest.

The bottle calling to him, he grabbed it by the neck and took a long swig as a nightcap. He slid the bottle onto the table. Then, as a very important afterthought—a survival-hinging-on-it kind of postscript—he grabbed his .45 from the table and stuffed it in his waistband right next to the Brother's family jewels.

***

Teton Pass

Tran panned his head slowly, made certain that he was alone, and then slowly turned the T-shaped handle and allowed the pressurized gas shocks to push the rear window open. He fumbled around in the dark, trying to figure out how to lower the tailgate before finally finding the latch and letting it down softly.

Grateful that the dome lights hadn't flared on, he rifled through the various compartments, mostly by feel. His hands touched over a ribbed metal helmet, and what he guessed was a full face respirator. He unfolded and then put aside a heavy canvas jacket with some kind of metal clasps, and a pair of pants with wide belled bottoms that matched the top. He continued digging, and underneath all of the firefighting gear he found a very sharp double-bladed axe and a scuffed up pair of boots. Stiff leather, steel toes, cork soles and four sizes too big. *These will do*, he said to himself.

In a side compartment mixed in with discarded fast food wrappers he found a roll of tape. It was three inches wide, thickply, and commonly used on duct work. *Perfect*. He scanned for unwanted visitors, then gingerly pulled himself up and sat on the tailgate. He used the majority of the tape to splint his ankle. He started with half a dozen strips, running them like a stirrup under his heel and up both sides of his lower leg, then spun the roll around his ankle a dozen times. At first the improvised cast hurt like hell, but eventually the pain pulled back to only a dull ache.

Next, he covered the shredded soles of his feet with the sticky silver stuff, pulled the boots over his swollen feet, and laced them tight. He looked over his shoulder in the direction of the roadblock. *Clear*. Then looked down the ten percent grade where he could see the small grouping of walkers he had left behind just rounding the corner several hundred yards down mountain.

Risking calamity, he hoisted up the gate. It closed with a dull clang and latched with a click. Risked one more look behind him. The creatures had picked up their pace from a slow shuffle to a jerking half trot. The moans and hissing began a second later. Leaving the glass window yawning open, he hobbled around the left side, his heavy new boots scraping a cadence. He folded himself behind the steering wheel and said a prayer while he worked the key in the ignition.

After a few valiant cranks from the starter, the engine finally relented and turned over. *It runs,* Tran thought to himself gleefully. Suddenly the day that began with a gun being thrust in his face started to look up. The engine idled, nothing like the near silent power plants crammed under the gleaming hoods of the Cadillac and Range Rovers he used to chauffer his old boss around in. This engine sounded precisely how Tran felt—like it was on its last legs and about to throw in the towel. It ticked and wheezed and then the RPMs would ratchet up unexpectedly though his foot was nowhere near the gas pedal.

Another peek in the rearview confirmed his worst fear—the demons had heard the raggedy engine roar to life and were now closing the distance fairly quickly. Suddenly his only chance of survival hinged on whether a vehicle that rolled off of the assembly line in the 1970's could carry him a hundred feet to the downhill side of the pass. After that, gravity would relieve the engine, and he'd be at the mercy of the vehicle's last brake job and however much tread remained on the tires.

He looked forward just as the flesh eater that had shown indifference to him a moment ago lurched through the narrow passage on the road's shoulder. He put the truck into gear, wincing as he worked the pedals underfoot.

The old green rig gathered speed slowly at first. Working against gravity and a general lack of upkeep, the tired engine propelled Tran's new ride uphill towards the lone zombie and the apex of the Teton Pass which was only a handful of yards beyond the burnt-out bus.

The monster didn't flinch. It didn't leap out of the way like a stuntman in an action flick. It simply held its ground in front of the rapidly accelerating truck. Then, like a little girl's worn out dolly, it folded at the waist where it was met by the tubular brush guard, head-butted the hood with an explosion of sound and crimson, then disappeared from sight.

Tran didn't bother looking in the mirror again as he squeezed the Scout by the makeshift roadblock. He focused only on the spot on the moonlit road where the centerline seemed to disappear into the inky black horizon. Once there, he flicked on the headlights and let off the gas, figuring he'd save whatever the old girl had left under her hood and in her tank and use it to hunt down the two brothers.

Chapter 40
Outbreak - Day 16
Near Driggs, Idaho

"No, no, no," Heidi mumbled. Then, as she stirred from a deep sleep, her right hand shot from under the threadbare sheet and went to her neck where she caressed the sore muscles and tendons. In his failure to choke the life from her, Robert Christian had inflicted a large measure of damage to her skin in the exact shape of his clasped hands. The thumbs were crossed at the base of her neck, and the faint outlines of four fingers encircled both sides before meeting over her spine. Angry blue and purple bruising was going yellow around the edges. Subconsciously she dug her heels into the mattress and arched her back until the springs protested. This continued for some time as she battled something or someone in her nightmares.

Finally the foreign noise roused Daymon, who had always been a bit of a heavy sleeper. So much so that he had even been known to wake up to a Glock in the face on more than one occasion. He opened both eyes. *Still dark.* His hand went to the nightstand. Grasped the pistol grip of his combat twelve gauge. It felt heavy and powerful in his hand. The reassuring smell of gun oil hit his nose as he lay there in the dark, eyes open, ears straining to hear.

"I don't want to. No. Leave me alone." She drew a lungful of air in.

"Heidi... Shhh, you're OK. It's just a nightmare," Daymon whispered. Although Robert Christian's brutal attack had muted her voice like Marlon Brando's in the Godfather, he still reached across the bed and placed his free hand over her mouth.

Her eyes flicked open, wide and white in the dark. She forced a raspy yelp through his strong rough fingers. She fought back at first, flailing and punching until she realized who was staring her square in the face. It *was* Daymon and *his* dreads were brushing her cheek. His breath tickling her neck. Not one of her former captors—breath rank with alcohol—leering in her face after having done God knows what to her against her will. Simultaneously she nodded in recognition and relaxed her muscles.

Daymon felt the fight leave her, then saw her eyes ask a question he couldn't answer. At least not until he did some investigating. He rolled out of bed to his right, weapon braced against his leg. No need to check—there *was* one in the chamber. He stood rooted, listening to the night again. Something had his sixth sense tingling. When Jenkins turned in he indicated he was a La-Z-Boy sleeper, and that's where Daymon placed him based on the low timbre snoring emanating from downstairs.

Daymon made his way to the window. It was still cracked halfway as he had left it, and the screen was wholly intact.

Except for the occasional cricket or coyote, the night sounds had changed profoundly since the outbreak of the Omega virus two short weeks ago. The skies had been quiet twenty-four/seven since the jetliners were no longer flying their usual patterns. Furthermore, the several hundred-ton multi-car freight locomotives that used to deliver food to the majority of the population living on both coasts were now reduced to the world's largest paperweights, and no longer roared cross-country adding to the noise pollution. Right now, everything was still outside. The silence was enormous—quiet as the dark side of the moon.

241

Then he heard an engine laboring. Bad lifters clattered out a metallic discordance somewhere in the distance. As he pulled his dreads back and listened closer, he could tell that the vehicle was approaching from the east—travelling the same road they had come in from. *Survivors from Jackson?* he wondered. *Maybe Gerald had escaped from the Silver Dollar*, he hoped.

Whatever the case, he would know shortly. The vehicle was getting closer, and for only the second time since leaving Jackson Hole the prospect of coming into contact with other survivors was close to becoming reality.

He pressed the binoculars to his face, hoping to pick up the oncoming vehicle through the trees at about the same spot he saw the Hummer pass by earlier. Though his hopes weren't high that he'd be able to tell who the driver or passengers were, the fact that the moon was bright enough for him to discern the make and model did lend him some solace. As he waited and listened to the engine noises approaching the rise, he wracked his brain trying to remember what kind of truck old Gerald drove. Suddenly a pang of remembrance struck him, followed by a strange feeling of familiarity. Even on its last legs and obviously going through its final death throes, he knew who the vehicle belonged to. The problem was that he had no idea who was driving her.

Lu Lu broke the crest of the hill, one dim headlight lighting the way. Resisting the urge to rush downstairs and roll Jenkins for the keys to his Patrol Tahoe, Daymon just watched his old green Scout as it made a few slight detours around the smattering of walkers patrolling the main road. He continued taking in the sight for sore eyes until she was out of view and the sad-sounding engine was no longer calling his name.

He didn't remember leaving his keys in his old truck when he had left her for dead at the apex of the Teton Pass, but neither had he seen them since. In fact, there were many details about the last few days that he had lost or had conveniently forgotten about. He was good at survival, and purging the attention-robbing clutter from the forefront of his mind was a fall back mechanism that had kept him focused and one step ahead of the game.

Chapter 41
Outbreak - Day 16
Near Driggs, Idaho

If the vehicle had been any other make, model, or color, Tran was certain he would have driven on by without giving the property a second glance.

But it wasn't, and he didn't.

The truck was sitting in the open at the end of a long uphill driveway which naturally drew his eye to it. The yellow paint, augmented by the high riding moon, shimmered like a neon glow stick.

Tran knew that if the truck was there, then so were the animals who had left him for dead. Ignoring the demons walking the road, he slowed momentarily. He suddenly felt irresistibly drawn to the house. Like a moth drawn to a flame or Gollum to the ring, he needed to get to the house.

But he resisted the urge to jump on the brakes. Instead, he peeked at the odometer and watched the far right dial tick off five-tenths of a mile. At three-tenths he passed a small knot of undead that initially had had their backs to him. Their reaction time stunted, they were only able to reach for the truck as it passed them by. When the odometer ticked by the half-mile mark, the road took a slight bend to the right. He slowed his borrowed ride to a crawl and checked the mirrors. *All clear.* There were no demons in sight, so he stopped on the right shoulder, snuffed the one headlight, and removed the keys.

After clambering from the Scout and onto the road, Tran turned and waited for the demons to come. And when they didn't appear around the bend at once, he began to walk in their direction. His oversized boots beat a clunky rhythm on the lonely moonlit road as he followed the left-sweeping curve He could see the house in the distance, but he couldn't see the brothers' truck. He knew it was there. There was no doubt about it, he had seen it up the hill, and for reasons he couldn't explain he knew the brothers were inside the distant house. The evil the two men radiated was palpable.

He marched ahead, and as he cut the corner by degrees the zombies he had driven around came into view. They watched him coldly. He imagined they were choosing which part of him they would eat first.

But what they did next caught Tran by surprise: the entire group inexplicably about-faced, and as soon as he had cut through their ranks he could hear their clumsy footfalls—the scuffing chorus of worn shoes commingled with the wet slaps of putrefying feet—as the throng fell in behind him.

Walking through the wavering corpses was one of the hardest things he'd ever forced himself to do. Though his every instinct screamed for him to turn around and flee, the need for vengeance somehow overrode the impulse and compelled him to keep moving—to keep putting one boot in front of the other no matter how awful the smell of their decaying flesh.

He followed the road, trailing undead wingmen for twenty minutes; then, as he neared the gated driveway where he had almost plowed down the zombie congregation, his boot kicked a nice sized rock, causing the monsters to turn and regard him with their clouded pale eyes. At first he sensed some sort of recognition on their part, but it vanished as quickly as it had manifested.

He dug deep down inside searching for the courage to ignore their scrutiny and trudge into their midst.

Limbs hanging limply at his sides, he wove his way to the metal gate. He was careful not to touch any of the gathered dead. Partly because they made his skin crawl worse than a pillowcase full of scorpions. But mostly because he had no idea whether their sense of touch remained. He harbored a fear that one brush with his warm body or a simple puff of his breath on their frigid exposed skin would cause them to turn on him. He hadn't come this far to be torn apart yards from his first taste of sweet revenge.

Moving mechanically, Tran reached his blood-caked arm through the gate and pulled the metal pin from the slide bolt. He snicked the bolt open and replaced the pin so the chain wouldn't clank and alert the brothers. Then, feeling the cold steel through his pajama top, he leaned into the gate. It opened effortlessly. *Almost there,* he reminded himself.

With cold runners of anticipation coursing through his body, he hobbled painfully along the worn dirt road, point man of the undead procession. Once he was half way between the gate and the house, he picked up his pace to put some distance between himself and the pack. And as he skirted around the yellow SUV he stumbled purposefully into the left front fender. With his left hand he brushed the hood and found it was cold to the touch.

He fought his desire to use the handrail and gingerly climbed the stairs to the front porch, stopping for a tick on the landing in order to catch his breath. The gash on his brow began to throb and sting as sweat cascaded over his bloody face. He ignored the urge to wipe the perspiration from his eyes as he gazed through the glass pane inset at eye level in the center of the door. Nothing moved except for the shadows cast by the flickering flame atop a partially melted candle. The house was quiet inside, and if the brothers held true to form, Tran thought optimistically, by now they would be their usual inebriated selves, passed out and dead to the world. He smiled at the prospect. Dead to the world— *soon, my Neanderthal friends.*

He checked the screen door. It was unlocked.

The wooden steps creaked behind him as the dead continued to follow his lead. He reached an arm inside the crack between the jamb and the screen door and worked the ornate brass handle. Inexplicably, this door was also unlocked.

***

The door swinging wide made no sound. And as the dead crossed the threshold between the porch and the living room, their footfalls were instantly absorbed by the oriental rug covering the hardwood floor.

Lucas's eyes fluttered behind closed lids. He was in the midst of a nightmare that had suddenly become all the more real in his mind. Because now, not only could he see and hear the monsters that had amassed outside of the gated walled compound manifested in his dream—he could *smell* their carrion stench.

The nightmare had become so vivid that his subconscious finally had had enough, and he awoke with a start. He put his palms to his eyes and rubbed the sleep from them. Then, when he rolled sideways and tried to rise from the sofa, he was slammed back down onto the worn out springs with three hundred some odd pounds of hungry snarling zombie on top of him.

It took half a heartbeat for him to realize that his nightmare had been supplanted by the real thing. But half a heartbeat was too late. He found himself in a fix with his arms pinned near his face and the butt of his pistol inaccessible and being ground into his gut. Pushing up against the cold dead weight, he craned his neck at an ungodly angle in order to protect his face from the snapping teeth. He kicked his boots at his assailants and found only the partial bottle of scotch, which crashed to the floor, and the still burning candle that followed it.

Unbeknownst to him, the evasive move exposed the fingers on his left hand from the second knuckle down to a goon's sharp canines. The sound of crunching bone reached his ears before the pain signals made it to his brain. And when they did, he let out a shrill howl. The surge of adrenaline following the loss of his middle finger gave him the strength necessary to arch his back and roll out from under the crush of pallid bodies.

He hit the floor cussing and screaming, and crawled on his hands and knees. He made his way past a patch of rug that had just caught fire. Kept pushing forward, staying low to the floor, towards the hall leading to the old couples' bedroom. The only room in the house with a bed—the room Liam had commandeered for the night.

The zombies wormed along the floor after the meat until their bony fingers found purchase.

Lucas kicked at the dead, oblivious to the fact that his fate had already been sealed when his digit was severed. He rolled onto his back and grabbed at his pistol with his good right hand. As it cleared his belt buckle, his finger brushed the sensitive trigger, sending the hammer down. The discharge was deafening in the enclosed hallway. The large caliber slug entered Lucas's inner thigh, shredding everything in its way and then punched through the rug before embedding an inch deep into the old growth oak floor. Flesh and muscle was instantly pulped and the femoral artery was severed, resulting in an immediate large scale loss of blood from the gaping through and through.

***

Having just been awakened, not from the initial ruckus, but from the scream and the string of expletives coming from the living room, Liam rolled off of the bed. His knees hit hardwood and he found himself nearest the window and away from the dresser he had propped his rifle against.

The doorway opened up to the hall that was amplifying the sounds of a life and death struggle happening in the living room. Those telltale grunts and hisses combined with the eye-watering carrion pong told him all he needed to know: Lucas had let his guard down and the house had somehow been compromised.

"Lucas," he yelled. "You in there?"

Nothing.

Boom!

The unmistakable report of his brother's handgun rolled down the darkened hall.

One shot? Liam thought incredulously.

Then, spurred into action by his brother's apparent lack thereof, he dove across the bed, arms outstretched. He landed on the soft queen mattress and sunk in immediately, rolled off, landed on his knees and commando-crawled towards his rifle.

But the dead beat him to it. As they barged into the room, one of the moaning creatures careened into the dresser, causing Liam's AR to fall to the floor out of reach.

As Liam stared at the gun, stiff hands tore into his flesh. He heard fabric rip and felt every vertebra in his back pop as he was slammed face down against the floor. A searing pain stabbed his skull as one of them tore into the exposed nape of his neck.

"Lucas... help. Help me!" He bawled and pleaded for his life. He begged God. Called out for his mom. During his final moments on earth, the sounds coming from his mouth were unintelligible and had been reduced to an inhuman, high-pitched warble.

From his spot behind the screen door, Tran witnessed the demons pour into the house and pounce on one of the brothers. Their weight pushed him from the couch to the floor, where he let out a howl like that of an injured animal.

Tran's skin crawled from the shrill sound which was followed by a litany of swear words, and then simultaneously the man kicked a candle to the floor and his gun went off in an explosion of light and sound.

Then he watched with grim satisfaction as the man crawled through the flames to the back of the house with the demons in pursuit. From his spot on the porch, and over the stink of the dead, the metallic smell of hot blood hit his nose.

As the first man crawled for his life, another voice, baritone and distant, called out from the rear of the house. It only served as a siren song for the dead as they flowed down the shadow-filled hall towards it.

Having seen enough, and not wanting to get caught in the middle of the feeding frenzy, Tran waited a beat for the last of the zombies to file into the house. He cast a quick glance down the stairs. Surveyed the lawn and the drive. *Clear*, he told himself as he eased the screen door shut. He descended the steps as he had climbed them—slow and deliberate. He followed the drive to the road with a sense of satisfaction after having fed the brothers to their own bad karma.

With the screams finally silenced and the fully engulfed house lighting up the night sky, Tran concluded his lonely trek down the rutted road. After two right turns he was on the smooth blacktop heading for the green SUV. And as his boots scraped out a slow steady cadence, his thoughts turned to the brothers. He couldn't fathom why, with the world in the state that it was, that the two had relied only on the gate by the road to keep out the demons. Hubris rolled down hill he supposed, and like Robert Christian their overwhelming sense of entitlement ultimately led to their downfall. Tran's only hope was that there was a hell, and that the sadists were already there.

Chapter 42
Outbreak - Day 16
Schriever AFB
Colorado Springs, Colorado

The numbers glowing green on Cade's Suunto read zero-four-thirty. He had been awake since zero-three-hundred, and save for the soft steady breathing of the two loves of his life, everything was quiet in the Grayson billet.

He sat in the chair by the door, lacing his boots and thinking about how he was going to handle the Whipper thing. There had been no witnesses. No security cameras recording his lapse in judgment. So what it boiled down to was that it was between him, Whipper, and the wall, and the only thing he had to answer to was his own conscience. That and the man's word, of course. The fact that he was taking up Nash's offer—with a little added encouragement from his family—dictated he would have to make up for his transgression sooner or later. Furthermore, Whipper seemed like the type of individual who might take something like this "*up the chain.*"

The main thing Cade had going for him when he had decided to play a little chin music on the crotchety first sergeant was the fact that, at the time, he hadn't technically been an Army captain. Therefore, he supposed, the likelihood that he would be

251

summoned before General Gaines for a disciplinary hearing hovered somewhere between slim and none—especially taking into consideration the high priority nature of the pending mission. So, for now, the only fallout that he feared would be a loss of respect amongst his peers. And the sad fact of the matter was, that was the consequence he feared the most.

He passed the bottom bunk he had been sharing with Brook as he made his way towards the rear of the building. Sharing not being the optimal word when under the covers with his *bed hog* of a wife. She seemed to be sleeping soundly as he padded by. Then he marveled at how just a few days and a new numerical title had changed his daughter as he heel-and-toed it past the *twelve-year-old* section of the family dwelling where three of the bunk beds had been pushed together (with a little forced Dad labor) and now formed a sort of elevated island sanctuary within the sea of adultness that Raven indicated their living conditions had become.

He counted two bunks over. Reached up, feeling around blindly in the gloom, and pulled the sheets concealing his secret onto the floor. He stepped up onto the lower bed so he had a better angle and an added measure of leverage, grabbed one of the shiny painted aluminum tubes in each hand, and lowered the mountain bike to the floor. He didn't want to wake anyone prematurely, so he carried the thing to the front door with one hand on the knobby rear tire to keep the noisy freewheel from giving him away. The purple and white belated birthday present went propped against the wall next to the door where Raven would see it. Then he placed the white envelope addressed to Brooklyn Grayson on the small metal table near the entry. On top of the envelope he left the single white rose for his wife.

Then he shouldered his pack and strapped on the black combat dagger. Grabbed the M4, clicking it onto its single-point harness, and then holstered both Glocks. And then as he left the billet, he blew a kiss towards his sleeping family.

***

0500 Hours - 50th Space Wing Satellite Operations Room

To Cade, the air inside of the low-ceilinged room where Major Freda Nash and the men and women of the 50th Space Wing would be presenting their briefing seemed like it had been piped in from hell. A run of three uninterrupted hundred degree days, with a possible fourth just dawning, had made even the nights in the high desert muggy and barely tolerable.

Trying to compete with the phalanx of humming computers, dozens of warm bodies and the multiple heat-emitting monitors scattered about the room would have given the commercial-grade roof-mounted A/C unit a workout, let alone the jury-rigged little wall-mounted box in the corner currently waging a losing battle. And with the base still at the mercy of the half-dozen aging diesel backup generators, and the power hungry electronics inside the TOC—Tactical Operations Center—already a major drain, running the internal air conditioning had been out of the question.

He ran his fingers between his neck and collar, letting the trapped body heat escape, then took a quick inventory of the room. Next to Nash, standing at rigid attention, his bald ebony pate gleaming in the diffuse overhead lighting, Colonel Cornelius Shrill tracked the moving images on the flat-panel with an intensity Cade had yet to see the base commander exhibit. To his right—a foot and a half shorter, petite, brunette, and with a firm set jaw—stood President Valerie Clay. Though she was unarmed, dressed in desert tan fatigues she could have been mistaken for any one of the female soldiers or airmen who called Schriever Air Force base home.

As he finished his sweep of the room, his gaze passed Clay's Secret Service detail and fell on General Ronnie Gaines. The tall SF operator's attention was focused laser-like on the hundred-inch flat-panel—and the look on his face matched the others in the room—businesslike and deadly serious.

Cade's attention wavered momentarily, then returned to the briefing. Nash's voice faded in and out as the images of insurmountable suffering and wide scale death flashed across the

LCD screen. He was becoming numb to it all. He had seen the carnage wrought on the United States by the roaming packs of dead from every angle. Beamed in from a Reaper drone orbiting at ten-thousand feet. From the safe confines of a helicopter roaring by a hundred feet off the deck. He had seen real-time satellite imagery of zombies, six hundred thousand strong, shambling lockstep out of Denver on a collision course with his family. Monsters tumbling like lemmings off of the Golden Gate bridge, much of its span dangling into space, didn't even register. Nothing was new for the hardened Delta Force operator. A new image graced the flat-panel in front of him, but unfortunately the thousands of watercraft, all shapes and sizes, a sort of floating morgue that dotted Sydney Harbor, failed to make a blip on his give-a-shit radar. The horrific image splashed on the screen was nothing different than the death and misery he had seen recently on the Flaming Gorge Reservoir—just a greater measure of it. Every person out there was suffering—worldwide—and he had seen enough of it since the dead began to walk to last ten lifetimes.

Death came in many different guises. Yeah, the Pale Rider was an underhanded bastard, Cade mused. The humorless fucker kept coming up with new and extraordinarily horrific ways for man to make his acquaintance.

He was drawn from his *Many Faces of Death* moment by Freda Nash's voice. "This next image was taken by one of our three remaining KH class satellites," the diminutive major stated. She looked over at Cade, nodding her head ever so subtly. "Watch for the glint in the lower right corner. That *is not* one of our birds."

Cade made a face. *Three left?* he thought incredulously, as the new image on the screen caught him flatfooted. To his knowledge, the Department of Defense had more than a dozen of the billion dollar crafts in orbit at all times. For early warning as well as an orbital spying platforms. But what the birds were really capable of was way above his pay grade. He had assumed this briefing had been called to go over what was on the newly discovered thumb drive. Maybe touch over any actionable intelligence the President's men had coaxed or hopefully beaten out of Robert Christian. Instead he was looking at an HD video taken from a low earth orbit in outer space, at what appeared to his untrained eye to be the International Space Station. And as the silver and white speck grew larger, he discerned the monstrous array of solar panels and finally the white cylinders that were fastened together to make up the space station's living and working areas.

Nash dabbed beads of sweat from her face and then continued. "Although the Chinese have not contacted us since they spread the Omega virus, we believed at first that they *had* some continuity of government. However, after this incident happened four days ago, our assessment has changed." She clicked a button on the remote sending the image moving. "Watch the station closely. There are six crew aboard. One Israeli, one Chinese national, and four Americans. Most of you know the commander of the ISS..." She paused, bowed her head momentarily, then continued on. "Many of you *knew* Colonel Chris Mashfield," she corrected herself. She wiped her eyes and turned to face the flat-panel.

Cade marveled at the image captured by the Key Hole satellite. The Earth was a brilliant blue, and the continents and islands looked abandoned and lonely surrounded by vast oceans. As viewed through the high-flying lens, the contrasting white clouds seemed to be randomly frozen in place. And contrary to how fucked up things really were on the surface, the Earth looked peaceful and inviting from two hundred miles up. Then, after roughly ten seconds had elapsed, and with the South Pacific passing slowly underneath the space station, a shiny foreign object moved into view. The KH-12 satellite's high resolution optics zoomed in and it became clear to Cade that the second object was some kind of satellite. It kind of looked like a kid's homemade robot costume, square and shiny, like a box wrapped in tinfoil, with shiny sails and bristling with what he assumed were sensors. It seemed to decelerate as it rotated on axis. Either that was the case, Cade thought to himself, or he was mistaken and the difference in size between the trailing satellite and the ISS in the background made the intruding craft only *seem* like it was making some kind of closing maneuver. Suddenly the screen froze and Nash resumed her commentary.

"The attack occurs at the forty-two second mark," Nash intoned. "The newly arrived second vehicle is a Chinese Yuan class killer sat. Watch closely."

She turned back towards the flat-panel and aimed the remote to put the image back into motion. The tension in the room became palpable. Gone was the shuffling of feet and the hushed conversation. All eyes were riveted on the flat-panel display awaiting the inevitable.

Cade watched the elapsed time running in the screen's corner. He had never witnessed any kind of space-borne laser being discharged either during a test or used in an attack of this nature. And though he knew this footage was days old, he still felt a twinge of sorrow for the people onboard the ISS—even the lone Chinese national.

The numerals crawled forward, and when they hit the forty-one second mark he felt a sudden overwhelming empathy towards the crew, all of who were totally oblivious that they had only one second left to live. Every muscle in his body went rigid as he waited for a green or red laser beam to lance from the Chinese sat and then some kind of huge fireball to bloom as a result. In his mind's eye he saw an X-Wing Fighter being obliterated by the Death Star's ion cannons.

Instead, two things happened at once: some kind of cylindrical object—probably made from titanium, Cade reasoned—flashed diagonally from the Chinese Yuan hunter-killer satellite, transited space on a razor-straight trajectory, and then disappeared without any kind of a fireball or cataclysmic explosion, sound, or light show, into what he guessed was the crew compartment just aft of the fully deployed solar sails. The impact tore a rapidly widening black wound into the station's pristine white skin.

Next, a burst of propellant shot from the thrust gimbals located on the rogue satellite's flank, changing its attitude and setting it on a digressive tangent, taking it away from the slowly disintegrating space station. A tick later, the Chinese Yuan craft fell victim to a similar attack, as multiple projectiles of like size blurred by the optics of the KH-12 and dissected the unmanned Chinese sat into several smaller pieces, which in turn spun off in different directions, trailing a glittering carpet of flash-frozen fuels and lubricants intermixed with thousands of minuscule pieces of shimmering exotic metals. The entire aftermath, minus the planet in the background, reminded him of how the lights of Los Angeles use to sparkle at nighttime.

The room came alive as every person took a collective breath. Then went silent as the fate of the doomed crew aboard the ISS became evident. Finally on the upswing of the emotional rollercoaster, a cheer went up as the Chinese satellite was destroyed.

Emotion-filled conversations erupted around the room and increased in volume until Nash cleared her throat into the *hot* microphone. After a few seconds, she stopped the footage. It was replaced with the 50th Space Wing's logo on a bright blue background. The room suddenly fell silent, and Nash's commanding presence took over.

"The attack that you just witnessed was *not* initiated by the Chinese government as we know it. At least not *recently*. Like Russia and most of Europe, China has gone black. The entire country is quiet. Their military is idle. As for their Navy, we're certain their sub fleet is intact—at least the ones that were underway when things went south for them. Nearly every vessel in their surface fleet—littoral and blue water—was either in port or returned home by Z-day plus two. The direct line to Secretary General Jinlong has been silent since Z-day, and we have had *zero* contact with *anyone* in their government since. So the fact that no one contacted the President after this heinous act—either to confirm, deny, or apologize is not surprising, and says more than the act itself. I don't want to sound cliché, but ladies and gentlemen, *the silence is deafening*. The only communication we have had with mainland China *was* with a handful of people operating Ham radios, and that ceased days ago. Every single one of those interactions indicated what we had already suspected: the dead have taken over and their government has failed them. So this begs the question: why are their space-based assets targeting our platforms?"

She paused for a moment, noticed several people looking questions at her. Took a drink from her bottled water.

"The Chinese programmed their hunter-killers with Dead Hand protocols similar to the way the Soviets had their ICBMs set up to strike if the USSR was attacked. Essentially, all of the attacks on our assets were ordered—preprogrammed if you will—well before Omega escaped from their BSL-4 facility. That every one of us are still breathing is the reason why we are certain Jinlong and the generals are dead. If they were not, the second phase of any attack we have ever war gamed would have come next. A wave of ICBMs would have been launched against us... and snuffed the rest of humanity out in the process. The bang following the whimper at least. I'm going to step aside now— President Clay wants to say a few words."

As Cade processed the major's briefing, the proverbial light bulb went off in his head and the reason Nash hadn't been able to provide real time satellite blanket over Jackson Hole was now crystal clear. *You're forgiven, Freda*, he thought to himself.

He watched Clay come to the podium. The way she moved suggested she had a ballistic vest strapped on under her ACU blouse. Her security detail lagged back, watching everybody's hands. Their training dictated they watch for telltale clues that might precede an attack. And hands going into pockets were one of those signs.

Nash shook the President's hand and then stepped aside. The President didn't need to adjust the microphone or take a drink of water. She didn't have a fistful of notes, nor did she look nervous. She wasted no time and dove right in.

"I want to commend General Ronnie Gaines first and foremost for the stellar job he's done in place of Mike Desantos, whose boots were big enough for two men to fill."

She looked Cade's direction. He shifted his gaze to Gaines, who just happened to be staring in *his* direction. *Shit*, Cade thought. *Don't do this here. Not now.* Suddenly he regretted affixing the captain's bars to his uniform.

"All kudos go to the 4th ID and the 10th Special Forces who have been under his command. Downtown is nearly clear of the dead," Clay added. After a few seconds of applause she went on. "They have also moved a number of shipping containers south to construct an improvised barrier. Something to slow the dead that have been a constant trickle up from Pueblo." She paused. A ripple of subtle movement made rounds of the room as excited people processed the added snippet of good news. A sort of poor man's wave sans the sporting event. "I also want to recognize Captain Cade Grayson for his continued allegiance to the flag and to the country," she said, meeting his gaze.

Here it comes, he said to himself. He nodded. Smiled. It was forced and tight. He watched her step from the podium and stride in his direction. He thought about bolting. Then a quick burst of flash traffic from *Egoville* entered his thought process. *General Grayson does have kind of a nice ring to it.* But the G word carried way too much baggage for his liking. And as the President squared up less than a foot in front of him, he asked himself: how in the hell am I going to politely decline *this*?

Like a Secret Service agent, his eyes tracked her hand as it delved into her pocket. Out came a black velvet box.

With his gut doing flip flops, Cade stood at attention. Too late to say or do anything. For lack of a better word—he was *trapped*.

She unsealed the box. Inside was a light blue ribbon that appeared to be folded over on itself more than once. As the lid hinged fully open, President Clay rotated it towards him. Nestled atop the ornate ribbon, decorated with a field of tiny white stars, sat a gilded five-pointed star surrounded by a green laurel wreath. He'd seen this before in books and once in person at the

Smithsonian in DC. His throat clenched upon noticing the American eagle sitting atop a gold herald, on which the word VALOR had been inscribed in bold, important-looking letters.

"You earned this," she whispered in his ear as she stood on her toes to place the Congressional Medal of Honor over his bowed head. "And this one is for Mike," she added, covertly slipping an identical black box in his blouse pocket. "Had to look high and low for these, but that's a story for another day." She backed away a couple of steps and offered up a professional looking salute. Cade reciprocated. And as he held his arm at the proper angle, he noticed on the edge of his vision the rest of his peers go rigid and do the same. His throat was closing in on itself. He felt on the verge of tears. And not a single one of them could he attribute to his situation. They were all reserved for the Desantos family.

***

Twenty minutes later, after Clay had concluded her pep rally and Shrill had touched over an impending nuclear crisis which most of the facilities in the country were sure to face in the coming weeks and months, the majority of the people in attendance were politely asked to leave by Major Nash.

Once the TOC was cleared of all nonessential personnel, she launched into the real meat of the briefing. "I'm going to keep this short, gentlemen... and lady," said Nash, nodding towards Major Ripley, who in her navy blue flight suit stood apart from her male counterparts. "First of all, Captain Grayson, congratulations. Don't let it go to your head." She smiled at him and then moved her gaze around the room. "As all of you know, a thumb drive containing notes taken by Sylvester Fuentes, who was working on the Omega antiserum, has been located. Not to put any undue pressure on the men and women who will be going downrange... but finding the right people to interpret the data contained on the drive *is* the linchpin to producing more of the antiserum Fuentes used successfully one time. I'm not going to go into all of the details of how it came into my possession, but do know that without decisive action taken by Captain Cade

Grayson this may not have fallen in my lap. It's real," —she held up the brushed metal device for all to see— "and your mission to the CDC's counterpart in Winnipeg, aptly named Operation Slap Shot, may be the linchpin to mankind's survival." Nash paused as a low murmur circulated the room. Then, to infuse some hope in the support crew as well as the operators, she offered up an extra nugget of information. "As of 1500 hours yesterday afternoon, we have proof of life inside the facility. The general has all of the details and he'll share those once you are underway."

The briefing lasted another twenty minutes. Call signs were issued to the air and ground elements. The Ghost Hawk would go by Jedi One-One, the original title bestowed upon the black helo the day it rolled out of the Skunk Works facility at Area 51. The name had stuck like glue, and no one, not even the desk pilots who loved coining new and sometimes silly call signs, had ever attempted to change them. And considering the fact that the Gen-3 helos were now affectionately called Jedi Rides by the elite warriors who rode the stealthy helicopters into combat, the paper pushers knew better than to ever broach the subject.

The President's Osprey, call sign Jedi One-Two, with a chalk of Rangers aboard would accompany Jedi One-One on the mission.

Nash went over the refueling logistics, which seemed to have multiple redundancies already put into place—just in case. *Good to see the little—but very important—details were being attended to*, Cade thought to himself. He glanced at Lopez, Tice, and General Gaines. The three operators seemed to be listening closely as the feisty major continued going over contingencies and emergency procedures. They would have limited sat coverage, Cade was pleased to hear. *Better than none.*

"What about drone support?" he asked.

His interruption received a chilly glare from Nash but she obliged anyway. "Not as of now," she said. "We're still trying to reconstitute those forces."

"Copy that," Cade intoned. He subconsciously fingered the medal he had just received. Then, feeling a little embarrassed, he slipped it off and dropped it into his pocket next to Mike's posthumous award. He looked around. Thankfully, it appeared his action had gone unnoticed. He glanced sidelong at Ari and Durant, then shifted forward in his seat and regarded Hicks, the oftentimes quiet flight engineer/door gunner, who rounded out the crew responsible for keeping Jedi One-One in the air.

After the Jackson Hole op, Gaines had ordered everyone who had gone *"down range"* to take a mandatory two-day stand down. That, in Cade's opinion, had left all three of the SOAR members looking well rested and raring to go—at least as good to go as a person could appear with ninety-plus percent of the populace walking around hungering for flesh.

Ari busted Cade eyeballing him, cracked a wide smile, and flashed a thumbs up.

Someone likes his mission profile, Cade mused. *He can thank me later for the extra refueling tankers.*

Cade put his hand in his pocket, felt the medal sitting there. Touched the points of the star just to make sure he hadn't been daydreaming. So it was decided. Coming to the briefing had been more than a gesture. In fact, the moment he Velcroed the black captain's bars on his ACU's and strapped on his weapons there had been no turning back. *Brook knew what she was doing*, he thought. She knew he could never say no to this mission. She had seen the pull of duty drag him back in too many times to count during their thirteen years of marriage. He *was* too much of a patriot to turn down something on the order of this magnitude. The far-ranging implications of the mission's failure were too many to calculate and too cataclysmic to ignore. He had nobody to blame but himself that this mission to Canada's version of the CDC had been dropped into his lap. After all, he was the one who'd yanked the tail of the cosmic tiger. It had been his decision to rescue the girl at Grand Junction Regional—the girl who had found the thumb drive. A fair amount of serendipity had gone into the events leading up to this moment. Therefore, he concluded, who was he to decide that his part in God's plan was over?

Chapter 43
Outbreak - Day 16
Logan Winters's Compound

"If I would have known then what I know now, this is the first prep I would've done after I bought this plat of land. Only I think I would have gone with surgical steel—ground the bastards down to a sharp point before sticking 'em in the ground."

Duncan stabbed his dagger into the earth and handed Logan another finished product. "Woulda, coulda, shouldas don't carry much weight these days, baby bro. How'd it go escorting the kid to his vehicle?"

"Did just like you said. He about shit himself when I handed him his AK. Coulda swore he was thinking about turning it on us."

"Gus pick up on that too?" Duncan asked. "Him being law enforcement and all."

"Yeah, nothing untoward happened though. Gimme one of those," Logan said, motioning to the sticks Duncan was whittling. Working by the sterile blue-white light of his headlamp, Logan gripped the first foot-long branch firmly with both hands. It was alder, and about as big around as his thumb. He worked the blunt end into the mud and clay wall of the two-foot deep hole, making sure that the whittled point slanted downward at about a forty-five degree angle. He planted a dozen more of the sharpened sticks into the walls of the hole, pointing in from all directions of the compass. When he was finished, he policed up some dried foliage and used it to conceal his handiwork.

"These things effective?" Logan asked, a measure of skepticism in his voice.

"Punji traps?" Duncan nodded, the beam from his headlamp moving lazily up and down. "Good as a *bear trap*... when you don't have a bear trap," he added in his usual slow drawl.

Logan grunted as he exerted himself, trying to get the angle on the next stick just so. "How exactly does the thing work?"

"Well, it's pretty simple. The fella steps in there and his foot hits the bottom—VC sometimes put spikes there too. So now he's up to his knee in a hole. He's pissed and kinda stunned like he just stepped off a curb he wasn't expecting... and what's the natural thing he's gonna do?"

"After he shits himself?" Logan said, smiling at the visual. "He yanks his leg out, of course."

"Correct. That's why the Viet Cong angled their sticks downward. Picture it... so now the spikes are biting into his leg. They might be splintering, but the more he struggles the deeper they dig into the muscle. He can't pull it out," Duncan intoned, his eyes widening. "He's stuck now, like a kid that got hisself caught in a Chinese finger trap."

Then, as if someone had flicked a switch, some birds in the canopy above them suddenly came alive. Dull sleepy chirps, sporadic at first, that swiftly ramped up to a raucous chorus. Duncan went silent, gazing up through the spiderweb of limbs at the sky. The black was giving way to a deep purple as the sun prepared to make its first appearance of the day. He scanned the surrounding forest. Turned a full three-sixty, slowly, with his AR-15 held level. At the ready. After a few ticks he looked back at Logan, shrugged, and continued. "Most times the VC put their own *shit* on these things. Not quite a *million dollar* injury. Like a through and through gunshot wound could be. That kind of shit came with a Purple Heart and a jet plane ride home...

stewardesses and all. Still, sometimes the infection brought on was good enough to get a fella sent to Da-Nang... maybe even get laid by a horny nurse. Shave a few days off his tour if he's lucky."

"Back from your trip down memory lane yet?" Logan asked.

The question, though he was clearly joking, earned him a cold glare from his older sibling. "There are a few things this old hombre can teach you. Might come in handy when I'm no longer around to wipe your butt."

"That's right... you're so ancient you *did* wipe my ass. How could I have forgotten?" Logan slapped Duncan on the shoulder. "In all seriousness... I know there's no way those mindless rotters are going to notice this camouflage... but do you really think this is gonna fool a person?"

"We ain't up against the VC. I'm confident from what I saw when me and Phil tried to go to town... these folks don't cover their tracks. The gunfire I heard sounded to me like some fool shooting holes in the sky. Bottom line... they aren't very cautious. Either way... something *or* someone comes this way, they're getting stuck in one of these."

Logan pulled a laminated overview of his property from a cargo pocket, unfolded it and marked the location of the trap on the map in black ink. He twirled his mustache and looked at his brother.

"How many more you think?"

Duncan looked up at the rapidly lightening sky. Made a show of checking his watch. "As many as we can finish before noon," he replied. "Something tells me Chance and his kind *are not* early risers."

Chapter 44
Outbreak - Day 16
Near Driggs, Idaho

The first thing Daymon noticed when he snapped awake was the smile of an angel. He dug his fingertips into his eyes and cleared out the sleep, leaned over and gave her a peck on the cheek.

The second thing he noticed was that the deep furrows on his chest had stopped throbbing to a calypso beat. He pulled his shirt up, peeled away the bandage, and probed the wounds with his finger. The redness had subsided a little, and the green discharge seemed to have slowed but wasn't altogether gone. He wasn't home free, that he knew, but the topical equine medication Charlie had risked his life to get for him seemed to be working. And as a cherry on top of the sundae, the melodramatic side in him marveled that he didn't have the urge to whinny or a sudden hankering for a handful of oats.

"How are you feeling?" Heidi asked.

"Be better if we could get on the road."

"I mean your wounds."

"Night and day," he said, covering up the white bandages with his tee shirt. "How are you this morning?"

"Much better," she said.

"Judging by the sound of your voice I'd have to disagree."

"I'm better," she croaked.

"Save your voice. It's still early... so why don't you get a little more rest and I'll go downstairs and try and talk Charlie into leaving this dump *today*."

Heidi smiled briefly and then her hand went to her neck. He had seen her do this a hundred times over the course of three days, and he wasn't so sure that she was even aware that she was doing it.

"How's the neck?" he asked. "Thumbs up, sideways, or down?"

She put a thumb horizontal then rotated it a few degrees north. "Not as sore as it was yesterday."

Daymon gently put a finger to her lips and shushed her. He gazed into her blue eyes and willed himself not to look at the contrasting bruises encircling her throat.

"How does it *look* today?" she inquired while her hand continued the absentminded massage.

"Not *so* bad," Daymon lied. *Considering you were nearly dead a few nights ago.*

This time she remained silent, saving her voice for later.

He kissed her forehead and said, "Anything I can bring you when I come back upstairs... bottle of water? Anything?"

She stopped worrying her neck and put her head back down on the pillow. "No, but thanks hon. I'm good." She smiled and closed her eyes.

***

Downstairs, Daymon cracked a water. He did a quick count of the remaining bottles. *Eight. Yet one more reason to blow this joint,* he thought to himself as he took a long pull. Then, out of the corner of his eye he picked up movement down by the road. He pressed his face to the window above the sink and looked down towards the gate. Not liking what he saw, he walked his gaze down the feeder road to the main highway. The situation at the intersection was no better.

"Charlie!" Daymon bellowed. "Come here and see what followed you home yesterday."

Launching out of a deep sleep, Jenkins choked mid-snore and inadvertently kicked the La-Z-Boy's foot rest down. The violent action continued through the chair's mechanism, straightening the back up and nearly pitching him on his face.

"What the hell is it?" he said, wiping a slug track of drool with the back of his hand.

"Come here and see for yourself," Daymon pressed.

Jenkins muttered as he pulled his boots on. He lifted his pistol off of the coffee table, stuffed it in its holster and hustled over to the kitchen.

"Hell did you have to wake me for?" He looked at his watch. It read: 6:10 a.m.

"Because you are gonna want to see this."

Bellying up to the sink, Jenkins accepted the offered water, cracked the seal and then his eyes followed the length of Daymon's outstretched arm, past his fingertip.

"*That* is what the cat drug home—"

The water bottle slid from Jenkins's grasp, hit the floor and rolled under the kitchen table where its contents glugged out onto the floor. He stared at the amassed dead. He didn't need a pair of field glasses to see the situation was about to get worse. "Fuck me running."

"They'll fuck us shuffling and moaning if we give them a chance," replied Daymon in a low voice.

"How many do you think are down there?"

After a quick headcount and another moment of contemplation, Daymon ventured an educated guess. "Thirty... maybe forty," he said in a near whisper.

"Shit," Jenkins whispered back. "What do you propose we do?"

"I know one thing we're not going to do. We're not going to tell *Heidi* about them," Daymon hissed. "There is *no* sense in *freaking* her out any more than she already is. I still can't tell if she's going to get over the shit that that Robert Christian fucker put her through. She won't open up to me... and carrying that kind of baggage around will fuck a person up in the long run."

Shaking his head, Jenkins continued staring at the throng. "I'm no shrink. That stuff's between you and her," he said matter-of-factly. "It's those things down there that have got my panties in a wad. And to think there was only one of them down there yesterday and it was only a flippin' crawler."

"You mean it had arms and a head and that's about it?"

"Yeah, creepy as hell. Thing tried to eat my boots while I was locking up."

"Thought you cut the lock when we got here."

"I did. I just jerry-rigged the chain when I left. But when I came back I coiled it and secured it with a carabiner... should keep 'em out for the time being."

"What'd you do to the halfling?"

"Let it be."

"You didn't kill it?" said Daymon incredulously.

"No... I didn't have the heart."

"Better find your heart now, Charlie," said Daymon as he rifled through the drawers. His eyes widened as he slid out a twelve-inch knife. It was slender and came to a very sharp point, and had characters etched onto the blade that indicated it was probably of Japanese origin. With a smile on his face he handed it over to the former police chief.

"And what am I to do with this?" asked Jenkins.

"Use your imagination," replied Daymon. "Come on. We've got our work *cut* out for us."

The pun wasn't lost on Jenkins, who looked at the knife then stole one long look out the window. "Then what?" he asked.

"We get the hell out of Dodge before we get ourselves trapped. By the way, have you seen my machete?"

"It's in the Tahoe," rasped Heidi, who was standing, hand on hip, in the hallway that ran between the kitchen and living room. "I remember seeing it on the floor in the backseat area."

Caught off guard, both men froze like statues. Then they mechanically turned to face her.

Daymon cleared his dreads from his eyes and pinned them behind his ears. "*Stay*," he said to himself as if words alone could control the Rasta-inspired do. He swallowed hard, not sure what to say, then he cut to the chase. "How much of our conversation did you hear?" he asked sheepishly.

"Enough to know that I don't want to stay here, and more than enough to *piss* me off because you two were talking behind my back," she answered in a raspy-sounding voice that was barely above a whisper.

"What'd you say, Heidi?" Jenkins asked, wide-eyed as he skirted the kitchen table heading in her direction.

Heidi repeated herself slowly, enunciating every syllable while Daymon stared stone-faced.

Jenkins took a moment to process what she had just said, and then grimaced because he knew she was right.

"Well, first of all Heidi, I owe you an apology for not only talking behind your back, but also for not taking your opinions into consideration," Jenkins proffered. "What—if anything—can I do to make it up to you?"

"Drive us the eff out of here," she whispered. "*Now*."

"Well it looks like it's two against one," he muttered. Then he flicked his wrist and sent the keys to the Tahoe sailing across the kitchen. Daymon snatched them mid-flight.

Reflexes of a cat, Jenkins thought. "I'm going to check a couple of the outbuildings, see if I might find a couple of gas cans and maybe cut us a piece of hose. Why dontcha get your blade from the truck and I'll meet you out front."

***

Five minutes later, Jenkins returned to the Tahoe carrying two small plastic gas cans and a good-sized length of hose.

Heidi was already in the back seat, fully dressed and ready to go.

Jenkins hauled himself into the driver seat, and looked over at Daymon who was cradling the machete in his lap.

"Ready?" asked Daymon.

"I was born ready," Jenkins lied. Truth of the matter was, including the one he had stomped the day prior, he had only killed a few of the creatures, and that had been at range with a pistol or rifle—not one up close and personal with a blade. Shooting a human to protect another life or himself—no problem. The NA guards at the Teton Pass deserved to get headshot. But the dead were just poor souls in the wrong place at the wrong time—not bad guys or criminals. He threw a shudder thinking about what he was being asked to do. He started the Chevy, backed around, and began the solemn trip to the gate.

Chapter 45
Outbreak - Day 16
Schriever AFB
Colorado Springs, Colorado

The first out of place sound registered in Brook's subconscious. A second later she hinged up from the bed, planted her bare feet on the tiles and had her rifle in hand held at a low ready.

But before her eyes could adjust to the dark, a second sound—a joy-filled squeal—brought her to her feet, and she placed the M4 back where it had been, propped against the wall, muzzle aimed towards the rafters.

"Raven, sweetie. What's the *heck* is going on?" she called out.

"Quick Mom. Come here."

Brook stretched as she padded towards the front of the Grayson's billet where the sounds of happiness had originated. "Marco," she said as she navigated the forest of bunks.

"Polo," came Raven's reply.

A smile blossomed on Brook's face when she saw what had gotten her twelve-year-old so excited. Near the front door, shining in the warm morning light pouring in through the parted curtains, was a girl's mountain bike. Purple and white and chrome. Just the thing Raven had been hinting about back in

Portland before the madness known as Omega had been released upon the unsuspecting citizens of the world.

"Just the right size," she said.

"Where did Dad get it?"

"You know your dad's can-do attitude. Even when there seems to be no way... he wills it to happen. That thing is *nice*," Brook said stretching the word '*nice*' out for a beat or two. "How many speeds ya think it has?"

"No idea Mom. Can I take it out?" Raven said excitedly.

"Yes you may."

With that, pig tails bouncing, Raven was out the door. She mounted her birthday bike and slalomed between the paths connecting the living quarters, the big tires leaving furrows in the knee-high brown grass.

Brook laced on her boots and was about to go outside and watch Raven be a kid when she noticed the white silk rose sitting atop the stark white envelope on the table near the door.

Instantly her stomach lurched. She knew exactly what it was and what it meant. And the thing that scared her the most about its presence was that Cade hadn't left a death note since his final deployment to the *Stan*—slang for Afghanistan—more than two years ago.

He hadn't felt good about his prospects of returning in one piece from that tour, and for good reason. His unit had lost a handful of men in one chopper crash high in the mountains, and he had seen things and had some particularly bad scrapes of his own that he hadn't been able to open up about even to her. His body still harbored some shrapnel the doctors hadn't been able to retrieve. The ugly pink scars associated with the nasty sizzling chunks of lead were a visual testament to the rigors of war.

The fact that he had a bad enough feeling about this mission to leave the envelope scared the hell out of her, and if anything happened to him she didn't know if she would ever forgive herself. So she said a prayer to God. Not a foxhole type of prayer, but still it was one of desperation. The ill-advised type. The type where you *ask* for something rather than let His will be done. And as silly as it sounded to her as it bounced around in her head, she still had no regrets for asking. She only hoped that God had been listening and He used His direct line to Mister Murphy.

Chapter 46
Outbreak - Day 16
Logan Winters's Compound

Gus could just make out faint guttural growls, somewhere distant, riding the carrion-tinged breeze. He could see the creatures in his mind's eye, somewhere off to the west, stumbling along the tree-flanked stripe of roadway he was standing on.

Clearly the monsters had been drawn in by the noise the shovel produced each time it took a bite from the gravel-choked soil. That was a given he had already entered into the equation when he broke ground on the first hole. That he'd buried two cylinders before he had hungry visitors was a blessing. He figured he had a few more minutes before he'd have to make the decision as to whether he could handle the approaching rotters solo or if he would need to hail Duncan and Logan on the two-way and pull them in from their task.

So, he kept his ears pricked and turned back to the digging. He placed the sharpened blade next to the last cut and leaped off the roadbed, landing both boots simultaneously on the curled metal flanking both sides of the shovel's handle. Tempered steel on rock produced another harsh grating noise under the force of his two-hundred-pound frame as it cleaved cleanly through another foot of the densely packed shoulder. He tossed the ochre dirt over the barbed wire and made several similar cuts, widening the circle incrementally until it was the diameter of a manhole cover. Once he had dug out the hole to an eyeballed depth of eighteen inches, he placed the next to last cylinder on the bottom, and shoveled the dirt he had saved over the top and around the sides until it was no longer visible.

The former Salt Lake sheriff wiped his brow with the top of his forearm, and took a belt from his canteen as he gazed east at the sky. Overtop the tree line, billowing thunderheads struck through with bars of sunlight lent the impression he was looking at a stained glass in some cathedral in a thousand-year-old European city. It moved him, stirring emotions that had been dormant for quite some time. So much so, that he had a hard time tearing his eyes away when the moaning sounds behind him grew louder.

With the wind taken from his sails, he grudgingly turned westward where he could just make out a clutch of rotters trundling around the gentle curve in the road.

With renewed effort he worked the shovel. Biceps and back muscles burning, he made short work of the final dig, and by the time he was tamping dirt over the last cylinder, the group of lurching monsters had halved the distance.

A quick glance over his shoulder told him what he faced. Every one of the creatures were first turns—much slower than the newly turned—but every bit as deadly.

He recalled with crystal clarity how a hastily-erected triage center outside of Salt Lake had been overrun by the dead. How, as he watched on in horror, the infected corpses in the makeshift morgue had reanimated by the dozens and had breached the flimsy rip-stop nylon tents with ease. They played no favorites, attacking the infirm and healthy alike.

The heavily-armed soldiers seemed unable or more than likely *unwilling* to fire on their fellow citizens as the place fell to the blitzkrieg of tooth and nail in a matter of minutes.

What a bloodbath that had been, he thought to himself. It had been his tipping point. The one event that opened his eyes to the possibility that order could never be restored. *If the National Guard couldn't stop the dead*, he thought at the time, *what the hell good is one sheriff going to do?* And with that question and a fair amount of guilt hanging over his head, he hastily made his way to his good friend Logan's compound.

Gus propped the shovel against the barbed-wire fence and regarded the fresh scars in the dirt across the road. They stood out like two black eyes against the rest of the shoulder. He looked at the two on his side of the road, determining that all four of them would be visible to someone with half a watchful eye. But he had a hunch that as the day warmed up and the sun traced its normal east to west path directly over the road, the cover soil would dry out and become less conspicuous.

Gus's two-way radio crackled to life, bringing him back to the present. He stole another glance at the rotters as he fished the radio from his back pocket.

"Gus here."

"How is it going up there?" Logan asked.

Before Gus had a chance to answer, Jamie's voice sprang from the speaker. "Gus... if you let the rotters get any closer I'm going to start putting them down for you. You got a death wish or something?"

"No, Duncan says to leave them," Logan replied, sounding confused. "I'm right here with him... he says the rotters will pose more of a problem for Chance and his gang when they show up."

"Wait one," Gus said.

He stowed the radio in a pocket and snatched the shovel, using the digging end to keep the nearest zombie beyond arm's reach.

Seventy-five yards uphill, in the same hide where Chance had been taken prisoner, Jamie had the zombie bracketed in her crosshairs and was a breath away from sending a jacketed hollow point into its brain. *Safety be damned*, she thought to herself. Gus was dangerously close to being overtaken.

As her finger smoothly reeled in the small amount of trigger pull, Gus sprang into action. She watched him use the shovel to create some space between himself and the advancing throng. Then he took three long strides toward the fence and, using the shovel as a makeshift pole, vaulted himself cleanly over the top strand of wire. He landed upright and fetched his rifle from just inside the fence. It looked like he was pulling his radio from his back pocket when her own two-way crackled alive again.

"What's going on up there?" Duncan asked.

"I just about witnessed Gus get eaten," Jamie replied drily.

"Can you elaborate?" asked Duncan.

"He was sparing the rotters for you," Jamie snapped. "God damn it... can't we just cull these ones now? More will show up. They always do."

"Save the ammunition, we are going to need it. Stay put for now. When me and Logan are done here, we're going to need your help to conceal the Humvee."

"Give Logan a kiss for me," she replied in a husky voice, knowing full well he was listening in and his cheeks were about to turn several shades redder.

"Do it yerself," Duncan drawled. "And it's about damn time. Kid's more nervous around you than a long-tailed cat in a room full of rocking chairs."

Jamie smiled. She keyed the talk button—held it down for a second—but reserved her comment for later.

"Duncan or Logan, do you hear me?" Gus said, trying to get a word in edgewise over the chatter. "One of you needs to come and walk me back in. I don't want to be the first to test out whatever diabolical contraptions you two have dreamed up."

Gus took a couple steps back from the fence which was bowing towards him under the weight of the rotters. His eyes passed over the motley group. A younger male, probably high school-aged before it turned, bared its yellowed teeth and swiped across the fence at him. Gus stood still as the thing fought against the barbs even though every fiber in his body screamed, *Shoot it in the head!*

"Come on Winters," Gus muttered under his breath. "Get me out of here."

"I'm right here," said Logan, who had snuck up on Gus from behind. "Grab your shovel and come with me."

Gus did exactly that. He followed the younger man through the undergrowth, shovel in hand, matching him step for step, and as they transited the forest Logan pointed out each one of the covered traps as they happened upon them.

Gus whistled softly. "You guys have been busy," he said.

"Like little beavers," said Logan. "Neither one of us slept last night."

"I bet you wished you were doing something other than digging holes," Gus added.

"Don't we all," Logan said with a chuckle. The fact that there were only two single women among the small group of survivors wasn't lost on the younger men. And Logan had been the recipient of most of the ribbing among them, due to the slow approach he was taking at courting Jamie.

"Watch it," Logan said, pointing out another Punji stick-filled depression.

"How's Jordan?" Gus asked, trying to make small talk. "She coming out of her shell?"

Logan looked over his shoulder and shook his head.

"Nope... she's still keeping to herself," he said. "That whole thing at the cabin—messed her up real good."

"Too young for me anyway," the former sheriff added sourly. "Maybe her and Lev can find some chemistry."

The trail opened up into a small clearing ringed by scrub oak and mature trees. Duncan was eased up against a sizable trunk, legs outstretched, smoothing his moustache with deliberate strokes. The Humvee sat near the feeder road, squat and sinister looking with the .50 caliber Browning's black barrel protruding from the rig's top-mounted turret.

The sun was at an azimuth where its rays were still being absorbed by the canopy, so, following Logan's lead, Gus switched on his headlamp.

"That thing good to go?" Gus asked Duncan.

"It's low on fuel but loaded for bear."

"How long did it take Phillip to link the ammo?"

"Too long Gus... way too long," answered Duncan as he hauled his weary frame from the forest floor. "Lead the way Oops. Let's get these holes dug."

Gus and Duncan each put a shovel over their shoulder and followed Logan across the clearing and melted back into the forest.

Chapter 47
Outbreak - Day 16
Schriever AFB
Colorado Springs, Colorado

6:15 a.m.

The briefing that had started at zero-five-hundred hours lasted an hour and fifteen minutes.

Although the sunrise had been at 0604, by the time they stepped from the TOC at 0615 the low-hanging orb in the east had already brought the temperature to seventy-five degrees.

A freight train rumble rolled in from the west as the KC-130's four Allison turboprops—with a combined eighteen-thousand horsepower—handily pulled the refueling bird down the runway. And just when Gaines thought the sound couldn't get any louder, the fuel-laden aircraft gained more speed as the pilot pegged the throttles. The sonic tempest ratcheted up and the plane nosed up and easily cleared the fence at the far end of the runway. The landing gear disappeared into its flat underbelly and it made a graceful roll to port and cut a large half-circle around Schriever's south and east flanks before powering away on a northeasterly heading, leaving four tails of exhaust in its wake.

Gaines craned his neck looking to the left. Watched the gray airplane level off and climb into the rising sun. He continued tracking the first of the three accompanying tankers until it was a speck on the horizon, then stared daggers in the direction of the motor pool. Shook his head because the vehicles that *should* have already been here waiting when the briefing concluded were nowhere in sight.

"Going to be another hot one," he said to no one in particular.

"Already had too many of these scorchers in a row," Ari opined. "But I have a good feeling that it's going to be quite a few degrees cooler where we're going."

"One of the only reasons I decided to come along with you boys," Gaines shot back. "You didn't think I was tagging along for just some company and deep conversation, did you?"

"Our rides are here," Lopez called out as a pair of propane-powered golf carts juddered to a stop in front of the men and their mountains of equipment.

He looked at the carts and then glanced back at the gear baking in the sun.

"I think we better call a dead sled to follow us with our kit," Lopez said, as he began tossing his gear into the waiting Cushman.

Everyone but Gaines laughed at the stocky Hispanic's joke. Gaines wasn't in the mood. He hadn't been lucky enough to have the same two-days stand down time he'd ordered on the rest of the Delta team, and waiting in the heat for their ride hadn't helped matters any.

"Load em up," he bellowed as he tossed his own gear into the area behind the seats.

After everything was piled aboard and the operators were seated, Airman E2 Davis, who was Nash's personal errand boy, transported them to the flight line. Ari, Durant, and Hicks rode along with the general in an identical Cushman being driven by an Airman called Nealon, who looked barely old enough to enlist, let alone drive.

Cade closed his eyes and listened to the thrum of rubber tires on grooved pavement. A few minutes later he and the other operators were doing the same awkward dance with their bulky Pelican hard cases, fully stuffed rucksacks and weapons—only in reverse order—hauling them off the Cushmans and stacking them near the flat black helo awaiting the pilot's OK to move everything one last time and stow it aboard the ominous-looking aircraft.

While he waited for the OK to board, Cade watched the men who were busy getting their gear squared away. Except for the tall surfer-looking guy whom he recognized as the head of the President's Secret Service detail, he knew all of the other men who would be aboard the Ghost Hawk, which would once again be piloted by the usual suspects: Ari Silver in the pilot's seat on the right, and Durant in the co-pilot chair on the left.

Jedi One-One would have a total of five customers aboard. Somehow—though this time out the team would be hunting for scientists, not stray nuclear weapons—Tice, the former CIA nuke specialist-cum-honorary Delta member and holder of the not so coveted '*Puker Patch*' was coming along on the mission. Thankfully though, it appeared to Cade that Tice had given up trying to stand out—as all '*covert cowboys*' usually try to do when thrown in amongst the uniformed Tier One shooters. Gone was his usual Hawaiian print shirt and Detroit Tigers ball cap. Instead, he wore the same tactical gear as Cade, Lopez, and Gaines: digital ACUs in desert tan, full knee skids, padded gloves and the ubiquitous low-riding tactical ballistic helmets most of the Tier One guys preferred. And he guessed from the way Tice was fidgeting in the seat beside him that the spook also had a ballistic vest strapped on underneath his ACU blouse.

The President's man, on the other hand, had gone the Mission Impossible route. Head to toe, from his boots on up to his low-riding ballistic helmet, Special Agent Adam Cross was dressed in full black. His silenced MP7 machine pistol was black. His MOLLE load-bearing gear and the load it was bearing was all black—not a scrap of fabric, Velcro or plastic on the man was a color other than black. And black wasn't even a color, Cade mused as he approached the President's man.

"Cade Grayson," he said, offering his hand to Special Agent *Vader* who in turn reached out and met him halfway.

"Adam Cross," the agent replied. "Heard a lot about your recent exploits, Captain. And I've been meaning to say thanks for all you've done... not just from me but from the President as well. As you already know, she thinks very highly of you."

Cade nodded but made no reply. It was his way of testing to see how full of himself the new man might be. He watched for a reaction from the corner of his eye and was pleasantly surprised when the minor slight seemingly went unnoticed. Cross just removed the magazine and cycled the bolt on his HK MP7, inspected the chamber and looked the mag over. Seemingly satisfied, he snapped it back into the well, smiled in Cade's direction, and let the weapon dangle against his black body armor.

"You're welcome," Cade finally replied, nodding his head. "I know you from somewhere. But I just can't place it. Too many tours... worked alongside dozens of operators from every branch."

"I remember you too, Captain. Ramadi, Iraq... half a dozen years ago. Summer of the *Devil.*"

A look of recognition crossed Cade's face.

"That's right. You were with SEAL Team 3. You had a big bushy beard back then. That's why I didn't place you at first. Welcome to our cobbled-together Delta Unit."

Just as Cade finished speaking, Lopez displayed his knack for perfect timing.

"I noticed you got stuck riding bitch again," he called out to Tice. "You oughta call shotgun once in a while."

"Some sneaky *bastard* always seems to beat me to it," Tice replied boisterously.

Lopez grabbed his ruck from the Cushman, and slowly looked Tice up and down. "Now that I think about it, you *do* kinda look like an operator when you leave the Don Ho getup alone."

"Captain Grayson didn't like me trying to sneak it past him the last time. And I thought with Gaines along this time... I didn't want to take any chances."

"Hope you shoot as good as you look today... *honorary Delta*," Lopez said with a wry smile. He slowly turned and walked towards the angular black Jedi Ride that would be delivering the team into harm's way.

"Wheels up in five," Ari bellowed from the other side of the tarmac. Then he went back to inspecting the aircraft's flight surfaces. Jiggling this and that. Everything short of kicking the tires.

Gaines stepped from the lead Cushman, shouldered his SCAR—Special operations forces Combat Assault Rifle—and waved Cade over. Taking the younger captain's shoulder in a firm grip, he pulled him close. "I just want to let you know that I don't recognize that short amount of time in which Nash was holding onto those for you"—he tapped the cloth captain's insignia adhered by Velcro to Cade's ACUs—"I want to reaffirm what the President said... I don't question your allegiance. Not for one second."

"Copy that, General. But after this mission," Cade whispered. "*I am done.*"

Gaines nodded. "I know," he replied. He gave Cade's shoulder a squeeze and let it go.

The door to Whipper's office flew open and banged against the ribbed metal hangar wall, adding yet another blemish to its yellow exterior.

Simultaneously all eyes took in the first sergeant as he stepped from his tiny anteroom. A sheepish look was on his face as he closed the door. He raised one hand in a gesture Cade took as an apology, and shielded his eyes against the rising sun as he approached the flight line.

"General Gaines. Captain Grayson?" he said, offering up a precise salute which was promptly returned by the officers. He glanced at Cade apprehensively. Eyes flicked to the rank on the ACUs. He said nothing and scurried over to the Ghost Hawk, where he appeared to have a conversation with Durant before squirting off in the direction of the matte black Osprey sitting on the far apron.

Cade made a face. "What's gotten into him?" he asked.

Gaines wagged his head. Rubbed his shiny black pate. "Probably just the pressure of the times we're *living* in... *surviving* is probably the more appropriate word," he replied. "I've seen a lot of strange behavior these last few days. Really began to ramp up after word got out about how many Zs were coming our way from Denver. Then the nukes popping off... disconcerting to say the least. You know, Captain, we're sitting ducks out here. And after hearing first hand just how fast Fortress Bragg fell from the people who were there... in their own words. Can't say that I blame Whipper, or *you* for that matter. Hell, if I wasn't in the position I'm in now I'd be bugging out with you."

The sun washed the left side of Cade's face with a warm glow as he looked off towards Pikes Peak. He took a moment working up some kind of reply. "Truth be told Ronnie, it's not so much me as it is Brook who wants to *bug out*. I never run away. You know me, I run into the fire. I thrive on it. But Brook... Brook's *over* Army life. Was years before I quit the first time. She got spoiled and now she wants that life back."

Good luck with that, Gaines thought to himself. "When I said *bugging out* I didn't mean it in a cowardly manner. If it's any consolation, there is not one sane person on this base who could blame Brook for wanting to leave either. Every person here— myself included— is collectively holding their breath hoping for something positive to happen. To me, the guy who is stuck in the middle, it feels like I'm waiting for two tectonic plates to slip and release an enormous amount of energy. The problem is I've got no idea which way the scale is going to tilt. If we strike out on this one I'm certain morale is going to get much worse. And when the big one strikes... a 9.0 figuratively of course. I don't know how me, Shrill, and Nash are going to hold it all together."

"Two minutes!" Ari yelled from the far side of the helo.

Cade silently thanked the SOAR aviator for rescuing him from conversation—one of his least favorite pastimes. Then he looked over and watched as the compact muscular Night Stalker clambered into the black helo. Then he focused on the like-colored Osprey which was squatting on the apron fifty yards beyond, where a chalk of Rangers, thirteen in all, were busy hoisting their burdensome-looking rucksacks aboard. The craft suddenly emitted a sharp whine, and a puff of exhaust followed as the massive twin props spooled up. And as soon as the last of the Rangers and their gear was finally aboard and the rear ramp had powered closed, the engine noise picked up to a deafening roar.

In the Ghost Hawk, the operators had stowed their weapons and were cinching safety belts.

Durant looked back into the passenger compartment and received a thumbs up from Hicks, who had just closed the sliding door on the starboard side. His gaze passed over Agent Cross, Tice, and Lopez, who were occupying the seats backing up to the aft bulkhead. Cade was seated on the port side, and Gaines had also planted himself on one of the canvas seats near the port mini-gun.

"Launch in one mike," Ari announced over the onboard comms.

Hicks regarded the shooters in the back through his smoked visor, and placed a hand over his mike boom. "I see you got the bitch seat again," he said to Tice.

"Shotgun is not in the man's lexicon," quipped Lopez.

To answer would only fan the flames, so Tice said nothing.

The Gen 3 helo shuddered subtly as Ari pulled pitch. And as the carbon fiber blades grabbed the hot desert air and provided lift sufficient to overcome Earth's pull, the sudden G-force created pressed everyone firmly into their seats. Simultaneously the nose pitched down and the ground flashed underneath as Ari swung the tail around to starboard in a gut-churning maneuver that brought the Ghost around to the Osprey's port side.

Holding on to the seat and his cookies, Cade watched the Rockies spin by through the window next to Hicks' shoulder. "Never gets old," he said into his mike.

Gaines nodded and raised his right hand which was clenched into a fist.

Seeing this, Cade did the same and delivered a fist bump to the general. *Surreal,* he thought to himself. Then he swiveled his head and looked over his shoulder in time to see the black Osprey lifting off. In seconds, the northeast entrance, complete with the unmistakable winking of muzzle flashes piercing the predawn light, caught his eye.

"Looks like the numbers of Zs showing up overnight are multiplying," he said to Gaines.

"Good observation, Captain. Seems like there are a few more each night... some are *hot.*"

Cade continued to scrutinize the scene as it passed underneath the helo. There appeared to be forty or fifty Zs at the gate. The guards' fire raked over them, downing at least half their number before the viewing angle changed and all he could see was sun-drenched desert and the road to Yoder splitting the horizon to the east. With the word '*hot*' echoing in his head, he wondered silently to himself what percentage of the walking corpses were radioactive. A cold finger traced his spine as he pondered the ramifications of a two-sided attack. An irradiated herd from Denver would be disastrous. But add a large exodus from Pueblo, and Schriever would be caught in an undead pincer that would be hard to defend against and nearly impossible to escape.

"Say goodbye to our rotting friends," Ari said in his best Pacino. "Thanks for flying Night Stalker Airways. We will be cruising at two hundred knots at a sustained eight thousand feet AGL—above ground level—Major Ripley is going to throttle back her *Frankencopter* so we can keep pace."

Cade grinned at Ari's disparaging description of the Osprey. Clearly the SOAR pilot was one of the old school aviators—the kind who cut their teeth first on UH-1s and then the early Black

Hawk variants. To say he was biased would be an understatement of monumental proportions.

He craned his neck and watched the big Osprey off the port side for a few seconds. And as he closed his eyes to begin his mental preparations, he felt Ari change the Ghost's angle of attack which in turn sharpened their rate of climb. Though it was nothing like rocketing up the face of the Flaming Gorge Dam, his stomach still closed the distance with his scrotum, and in no time Jedi One-One had leveled out and they were cruising along smoothly. With the harmonic whirring of the rotors directly overhead and the baffled turbines off to his right providing a nice white noise, his chin hit his chest and he quickly fell asleep.

Chapter 48
Outbreak - Day 16
Schriever AFB
Colorado Springs, Colorado

The first airplanes had rumbled down the distant runway just before dawn. Their engine noise as they turned and roared overhead had been loud enough to snap Wilson from a blissful sleep. Whatever he had been dreaming about must have been good, he thought as he rolled over and faced away from Taryn in order to conceal his morning wood.

But as he tried to will the thing down, he had drifted back into another round of satisfying REM sleep which lasted only a handful of minutes before he was rudely jolted awake by a new, raucous noise that he couldn't place.

Outside, somewhere in the distance, the thunder of rotors beating the air rose to a sonic tempest. It was coming from the part of the base occupied by the large hangars where he had endured all twelve hours of his quarantine time.

He sat up and looked around the room, searching for his cargo shorts. A thin shaft of light speared through the cracked curtains and fell across the tangled khaki lump sitting on the floor five feet away. He untangled the thin sheet from his legs and looked down at his lap. His face colored as he realized he was buck naked. Then he pinched his nipple just to be sure he wasn't dreaming or imagining things. It hurt, so he surmised the situation he was in was not some figment of his vivid erotic imagination. That he wasn't somehow reliving in his subconscious one of those Forum stories that had kept him somewhat sane and *relieved* during those frequent months' long *dry spells* was indeed a welcome revelation.

Looking over his shoulder, he noticed Taryn's raven-black hair splayed across the pillow. The sheet was pulled up, covering her chest which he imagined was still bare. She was still sleeping, so he continued to drink in the sight. Her ears were pierced multiple times and the strange see-through necklace the thumb drive had been dangling on was nestled against her neck. The black and gray tattoos encircling both arms had at first seemed out of place to Wilson. The inked-on skulls, demons, and skeletons belonged on bikers and ex-cons, he'd thought, not on first year college students.

But that been before he had met the nineteen-year-old, and though she was younger than him by nearly two years, she seemed to have a poise and bearing of someone much older.

The aircraft noise outside picked up and the whole base seemed to be languishing under it.

Still, Taryn continued to breath steady. Rhythmically.

A pang of guilt twisted his stomach as he averted his eyes from her lithe form and focused on his discarded shorts. Suddenly the guilt was replaced by a sense of dread and a gut-churning dose of worry as his sagging self-esteem torpedoed the magical moment.

He darted to his shorts and quickly pulled them over his blindingly white backside, cinched the belt and pulled his sweat-stained black tee over his red mop. He located his boonie hat and crunched it down over his hair. *Who needs a comb*, he mused.

As he laced on his boots he wondered if this had been his one real shot with Taryn. He wouldn't trade the night for anything, but still he had a sick feeling it had been a fluke. *Or what was even worse, maybe*, he thought, *last night's events were a sympathy fling*. That was it. He knew it. He shook his head and grimaced as the thought of how out of his league Taryn was polluted his mind. Then he stole one last look. Locked it away—just in case. Taryn's face was placid and she seemed totally at peace. Angelic was the adjective that crossed his mind as he stepped into the humid morning air and closed and locked the door behind him.

Wilson heard the heavy chop of rotor blades approaching from the west, and in seconds the source of the racket was directly overhead. He shielded his eyes against the rising sun and picked up the matte-black hybrid-looking helicopter as it disappeared east over the nearby tents. Then he felt a sort of harmonic, breath-robbing pressure in his chest. He shifted his gaze towards the piece of sky the first craft had come from and picked up the near-silent angular black helicopter as it blazed directly overhead. It seemed close enough to touch and was following the same heading as the other aircraft.

Something is up, he thought as he unlocked the door to his humble abode. But that thought disappeared the moment he placed a foot inside the darkened room and found himself under interrogation.

"So I see you grew a pair, big brother," said Sasha. The disembodied voice caught him off guard and startled him a bit.

"Sorry if I woke you up, sis," he replied.

"You didn't, *Wilson* I'm *always* up before seven," she said sarcastically. "Truth is I couldn't sleep... something about being *alone* when a zombie outbreak can happen at any moment."

Wilson propped his Todd Helton Louisville Slugger against the nearest wall, strode across the room and parted the blackout curtains. "I said I'm *sorry* and I *meant* it. I woulda called but you know how bad the cell coverage is out here," he added jokingly.

Sasha covered her eyes and was silent for a second. Then she rose from her bunk and padded back towards the bathroom. "You *really* like her," she called back over her shoulder.

"More than any other girl I've ever known. But I don't want to talk about it... I don't want to get my hopes up."

Noticing the hangdog look on her brother's face when she returned, Sasha tried to cheer him up. "You know, Wilson, the way she shut me out yesterday says more than words. Take it from me. Most younger sisters try to get in the way of their big brother's suitors and she knows that," she said, nodding her head in order to validate the random line of bull she had just pulled out of the blue. "Besides, Wilson... what's not to like about you?"

He wasn't falling for it. Chances were Sasha was just trying to get him to let his guard down so she could kick him in the junk with one of her patented zingers.

"You are a *nice* guy, Wil..."

"Yeah, and you know what they say about nice guys... they always finish last."

"Newsflash, Mister Nice Guy, there are no other civilian guys here even close to her age. Sooo— apparently *last* just became *first*. Besides, Wilson, if she didn't like your company she wouldn't have inserted herself into the whole leaving Schriever fantasy that you and that Brook lady cooked up."

"It's no *fantasy*, Sash. She and her husband and their daughter are leaving today, and you and I are going too... *if* she can talk her husband into it."

"Big *if*... It's boring as hell here but I'm not holding my breath, *Wilson*. I'm going back to sleep," she added as she slipped between her sheets. "Wake me when you go to breakfast."

"I didn't sleep but a couple of hours since I snuck out on you, so breakfast is going to have to take a back seat to a few more minutes of shut eye," Wilson said sheepishly.

"Good for you, Mister Nice Guy... you grew a pair and apparently they work just fine," Sasha said, trying to keep a straight face. Then she pulled the covers over her head and muffled laughter filtered out.

Wilson threw his shorts on the floor and climbed into his bunk. *Amazing how fast Sash is growing up,* he thought to himself. *Fourteen going on twenty.*

"Sorry brother. I love you."

"I love you too sis."

Chapter 49
Outbreak - Day 16
Near Driggs, Idaho

When Jenkins stepped from the Tahoe to unchain the gate, nothing on the other side was moving. Earlier, he and Daymon had gone down the fence line and systematically killed the zombies one by one, he with the Japanese sushi knife and Daymon with a utilitarian neon-handled machete.

Though he had worked at a small chicken processing plant as a teen, and had sent his fair share of future McNuggets to the great coop in the sky, he had balked at using the knife. Just the thought of jamming a blade into a former human being's eye socket gave him a case of the heebs.

But due to the prospect of gunfire drawing even more of the walking dead up the feeder road, he had followed Daymon's lead, sucked it up, and started on the high side of the property. And by the time he and Daymon, who had started on the low side, had met in the middle, Jenkins had chalked up eighteen kills up close and personal while Daymon had culled twenty-four of the putrefying corpses.

"Easy peasy mac and cheesy," Daymon sang as he wiped the machete off in the tall grass.

"Says you," Jenkins spat as he fought back the bile rising in his throat. "I prefer a bullet to a blade any day."

"Still, you better bring along the Ginsu," Daymon said with a wink. "Who knows... it may come in handy down the road." He poked his head in the back window and checked on Heidi, who seemed to be feeling better by the minute. Funny, he mused, how the prospect of being trapped by a horde of dead could speed up the healing process.

Jenkins waited until Daymon was in the passenger seat and had closed the door, and then he eased the patrol Tahoe over the prostrate dead.

As the front wheels found purchase, Daymon clucked his tongue and said, "I'd gun it if I was you."

"You wanna drive?" Jenkins shot back. In fact, Daymon's attitude was starting to rub him the wrong way. So to show the younger man who was boss, he continued over the pile at a crawl, only to be greeted by the awful sound of gas escaping bloated organs. And as the rig bounced overtop, the gunshot-sounding cracks of bone snapping under the weight of the SUV emanated through the floor pan.

"See what I mean?"

Fuck you, thought Jenkins as he relented and pinned the accelerator to the floor, causing the SUV to slew sideways and the spinning rear tires to spew flesh.

"Better than dragging a ton of dead meat from the road and breaking our backs in the process, don't you think?" said Daymon. "Hell, at the least, I probably would have popped these cuts on my gut open again."

"Always thinking about yourself. Let's go. Now, now, now..." Jenkins said, shaking his head. "Like a spoiled brat only child."

"How did you know?" Daymon said sarcastically.

Jenkins wheeled the rig around a small knot of dead, hung a hard right, and laid down two black stripes as he buried the gas pedal. He took his eyes from the road for a second and looked Daymon in the eye. "If it walks like a duck," he said.

"Boys will be boys... I get that. But too much is at stake here," said Heidi. Her head and shoulders poked into the front of the SUV. She looked at Jenkins, then shifted her gaze to Daymon where it lingered for a long silent moment. "I didn't persevere while Christian and his wealthy *shitbirds* had their way with me just so I can ride along and listen to you two juveniles argue like a couple of fucktards."

Jenkins mouthed the word '*fucktard*' and tried to grasp its meaning. He'd never heard the term, though he figured she was right. He was acting like an exposed nerve and should have never let Daymon get to him. Time to drop the Officer Friendly *protect and serve* mentality, he told himself. Time to grow some hide, Charlie. In his peripheral vision he noticed Heidi retreat back into the middle row of seats. And without saying a word Daymon sunk into his seat and his head mechanically turned to gaze out his window. Charlie decided to join the silence party and keep his eyes forward and his words to himself unless he had something pertinent to add.

Chapter 50
Outbreak - Day 16
Near Pierre, South Dakota

The minute deceleration awoke Cade from his slumber a few seconds before Ari's voice resounded in his flight helmet. He looked out the port window as Ripley guided her Osprey to a perfect linkup with the white refueling hose extending behind the trailing edge of the KC-130s right wing.

"Nice..." Durant intoned. "She got the basket on the first shot."

Ari matched speed with the flying gas station and watched with one eye the delicate dance happening off the Ghost Hawk's nose. After what must have seemed like an hour to Ripley, but in reality had been only a couple of minutes, the fuel had been transferred from the Herc into the Osprey's puncture-resistant fuel bladders, and she had disengaged and put her bird in a position mirroring that of the Ghost Hawk—only on the opposite side of the refueling bird.

"Oil Can Five-Five, how copy?" Ari said to the pilot of the turboprop Hercules.

"Good copy, Jedi One-One," came the pilot's tinny reply.

"Seems like Whipper's turned over a new leaf," said Ari. "Word is he released enough fuel for the mission and then some. Any truth to that?"

"Pull up and find out," said the Hercules pilot. He had a familiar southern twang in his voice but Ari couldn't place where he had heard it before.

"Copy that," Ari replied as he matched airspeed with the Herc and finessed his own controls as the bigger aircraft's slipstream buffeted the helo momentarily. "In the sweet spot. Hitting the drogue," he informed the crew chief, who was in the rear of the refueling plane looking through a small porthole, and had, for very good reason, the best seat and view of the refueling procedure than any of them.

Sitting with his back pressed firmly to the bulkhead and his eyes shut tightly, Cade smiled at the comment about Whipper and his newfound understanding of a concept most people learned early on in life: Sharing is Caring. Then, through the ship's thinly-layered carbon fiber skin, he sensed the coupling taking place thirty feet in front of where he was. The slight *clunk* reverberated almost imperceptibly through the seat of his pants as the trailing hose mated with the retractable fuel probe sticking from under the helo's chin plexi.

Another few minutes passed and Cade felt the helo shudder and decelerate and lose altitude.

He looked out the port side window at the hardscrabble landscape gliding by. From the briefing two hours earlier, he knew their first refueling was set to take place seventy-five miles south and west of Pierre, South Dakota, and from what little he remembered from geography in school, the sparkling silver snake running off into the distance on the left had to be the Missouri River.

Meanwhile, in the cockpit, Ari flashed the boom operator a thumbs up that he hoped got noticed. "Jedi One-One. Going to the hard deck to recon Pierre," he said to Ripley in One-Two over a separate secure channel. Then, after receiving a *"Copy"* from Ripley's co-pilot, he switched over to the previous frequency—the same one on which he had been chatting up Oil Can Five-Five.

"Where the heck have my manners gone?" said Ari. "Thank you for the drink, Oil Can Five-Five."

"You got it, Jedi One-One," the pilot drawled.

"Looks like we'll be picking you up over Winnipeg for a top off," added Ari, who had just received updated flight data on his HUD—Heads-Up-Display—courtesy of Durant, who was also in the process of setting up a live satellite downlink to be shared between both the Ghost Hawk and the Osprey. "Maybe we'll take in a Jet's game and get a couple of Molsons when my *customers* finish their *transaction*," he added.

"Copy that," said the pilot, playing along. "And they had better be frosty. It's been too long since I've enjoyed a cold beer... or a *hot* woman for that matter."

"Copy that, I feel ya, Tex," Ari quipped as he nudged the stick forward and fought hard not to chuckle. "You know what they say... misery loves company, and beggars can never be choosers. And if you ask me... those two go together like OJ and his gloves."

The Hercules pilot laughed and then signed off and nosed the gray bird into a climb to get to a more fuel-friendly cruising altitude.

The SOAR pilot, being anything but demure, almost always left the shipboard comms open so that anyone wearing a flight helmet and had it plugged in would be privy to his ongoing banter. And it was no secret among his peers and the people he delivered into combat that the exceptional chopper jock considered his knack for comedy a close second only to his prowess at the stick. Desantos, in a roundabout way, had kind of contributed to these antics. The salty operator had always looked the other way when it came to the Night Stalker's penchant for ongoing chatter, because he knew from experience gained on battlefields all over the world that when the time came for Ari to do his job—which was flying a helicopter as if his nerve endings were grafted with the thing—the aviator was all business. So

Gaines had been content to just sit back and enjoy the dog and pony show. After all, the precedent had been set by one of his all-time favorite peers, so who was he to go changing the rules in the middle of the game.

Cade couldn't keep from smiling after hearing the last part of the conversation between Ari and the unnamed pilot who was flying the most important aircraft in the sky save the one that Cade was strapped into—the aircraft that was currently carrying enough JP8 to see everyone aboard both the Ghost Hawk and the Osprey home with some to spare.

He cast a sidelong look at Gaines and noticed he was smiling as well. Then, without making eye contact, he looked away in order to take in the countryside below. He estimated the helo was now no more than five hundred feet from the deck. The descent had been so gradual and quiet that he hadn't noticed the seventy-five hundred feet of altitude Ari had shaved off in just a matter of minutes.

Cade rested his eyes as the Ghost Hawk droned on for another fifteen minutes, and when he opened them the Missouri River dominated the terrain and a small city was scrolling into view. He watched Jedi-One One's shadow far off on the port side keeping pace as they paralleled a two-lane road that entered the city from the southwest.

Aside from a few squat office-type buildings, and one massive domed structure he took to be the capitol building, most of Pierre consisted of tightly packed residential neighborhoods radiating from a central downtown core. *Pretty unimpressive for a state capital*, thought Cade. Strangely enough, the blacktop below wasn't choked with cars or Zs like the highways near Colorado Springs and Denver had been after the outbreak.

He searched his memory, trying to recall how many people lived in Pierre. *Nothing.* Though he had impressed himself by remembering that Pierre was the state capital, he didn't know one other fact about the place.

"How many people in Pierre?" he asked over the comms to no one in particular. He received a shrug from Hicks, whose eyes were hidden behind the smoked visor of his flight helmet.

"No idea," Tice replied as he snicked a *Hubble*-sized telephoto lens onto the black Nikon camera body. He put the gear bag aside and panned the camera around the cabin, nearly decapitating Lopez in the process.

"There were less than twenty thousand before the event," Durant answered.

The city bumped up to the edge of rocky bluffs north of the Missouri River and was fairly flat, except for a few low rolling hills far away in the distance. Tice whirred away with his camera as the Ghost Hawk overshot the river and made landfall once again. Directly below the helo was a sizable National Guard presence complete with a dozen or so Humvees—half of them parked on a lonely bridge straddling the turbid brown water. Soldiers and citizens waved at them as Ari slowed the chopper and scribed a large arc in the sky overtop the aging iron bridge. With only two lanes, one going each way, the black span looked like it was built from an old discarded Erector Set.

"Looks like there are quite a few survivors down there," Cross noted. He stabbed a finger at the glass. "See the road-blocked streets? There... and there. Looks like the dead own a good chunk of downtown."

Durant's voice crackled through the onboard comms. "Damn smart of them to keep the bridge clear as an egress route."

"*Egress* to where... the desert? The great wide open?" Lopez asked. "Can't be much more than tumbleweeds and oil derricks out there." Then his voice rose an octave. "Madre," he said. "I see *demonios*... thousands of them."

Sure enough, pressed against the crude fortifications erected at the intersection of every street for five blocks on either side of the main road leading towards the bridge were too many walking dead to count, let alone guestimate.

"We need to get these folks some help," Gaines said, finally breaking his self-imposed silence. Then he quickly rattled off a series of orders. "Durant, see if you can get someone on the radio. Ari, take us as low as you can, and Tice, take some extreme close-up photos of the situation down there, then have Durant fire them off to Nash back at Schriever so she can light a fire under Whipper and have some ammo parachuted in to those fine Americans."

"Copy that," Durant and Tice replied nearly in unison.

"General, shall I deploy the mini-guns... and what *exactly* do you mean by *low*?" asked Ari, who, unless instructed to do otherwise, would have them riding the razor's edge, skimming main street between store fronts while nearly getting paint from the yellow centerlines on the helo's underbelly.

"You *know* what I mean, Ari Silver," Gaines replied testily. "I want a *closer* look. One hundred AGL should do the trick."

"Copy that," said Ari sheepishly. "If I'm good... on the way home can I fly low and fast?"

Shaking his head, Gaines said, "I will give it *some* thought. First we have to complete this mission." *You fly boys are all the same*, is what he didn't say.

After a mental fist pump celebrating what hadn't yet been fully decided, Ari nudged the stick to bring them within a hundred feet of the top segment of the bridge and the tan Humvees he presumed were protecting it.

Durant switched over so that only the general and the aircrew were on the same channel. "I have a man says he's Governor Boothe on another channel. Says they have been trying to hail us."

"Put them through shipwide," Gaines said. "We're all on the same team."

"Except Spooky and the President's manservant," Lopez mumbled to himself.

Before engaging the survivors on the ground, Gaines looked across the cabin and shot the stocky Hispanic operator a healthy dose of the stink eye.

Note taken, thought Lopez as he shifted his gaze forward towards the cockpit, where he could see between the pilots the areas of the city that were completely overrun by the Zs.

"I have Governor Jensen Boothe on the open line," Durant intoned.

Gaines nodded to indicate that he could hear, then he keyed his mike. "I'm General Ronnie Gaines, USSOCOM—United States Special Operations Command—operating out of Schriever Air Force Base in Colorado Springs. Who am I talking to?"

"Jensen Boothe here, Sir. I'm South Dakota's governor."

"Good to meet you, Boothe. Good to hear someone's still keeping the peace down there. I see you've got the Guard deployed. That right?"

"Yes Sir, but this is all that's left of the Guard. Got a captain in command down here. The adjutant general went missing when Madison fell to the dead. Sioux Falls was silent by the first Sunday after the outbreak. And Fort Meade and Ellsworth Air Force Base also are not operational. The B-1 bombers all flew out of Ellsworth early on. Good thing... Rapid City is full of those things too."

"I'm afraid there isn't much left anywhere, Governor," Gaines said. "I wish I had some good news for you."

"Two weeks and everything is gone. Just gone. We're hungry down here, Sir," Boothe said. Then, after a long silence. "Sir, are you there?"

"I'm still here," Gaines said. "I sympathize fully with you, Governor. D.C. pretty much fell apart on Z day. MacDill fell three days after. Bragg, Dix, Lejeune, Coronado... all gone. Can you put the captain on?"

"Sure, he's close by."

"What is his name?"

"Rodriguez... Captain Rodriguez," said the governor as a volley of automatic weapons fire filtered over the mike along with his words.

"Captain Rodriguez here."

Gaines introduced himself in the same manner he had the governor. "What can I do for you *right now*, soldier?" he asked.

"Sir, we need ammo and food... in that order. We're holding them off but I don't think we have long. I figure we have enough ammo to last half a day max, then we have to cut and run."

Gaines looked around the cabin at the ashen faces of his men. Cade nodded in sympathy. He had been in a similar situation with the survivors at the dam. Desantos had mentioned something about old folks leaping off of a multi-story building in order to escape the dead, and how the decision to mercy kill the lot of them had been one of the hardest decisions he'd ever had to make.

Cade watched Gaines come to some kind of decision. His features changed. Softened.

"Captain. I'm going to have a pallet of .223 ammo and some cases of rations airlifted to you before 1200 hours."

Cade looked at his Suunto wristwatch and did the math. *A little over three hours.*

"Copy that," said the captain. "I think we'll be able to hold out. Thank you, General."

"We take care of our own, Captain. Now you take care of your men. Let me talk to the governor."

"Boothe here."

"Listen to that captain. I'm going to have some supplies dropped... listen to that young man and work with him. How many survivors do you have down there?" Gaines asked as he craned his neck to see the ground from the orbiting ship.

"A couple of thousand. But we're having nightly outbreaks... lose a hundred a night."

"I'm certain you'll be OK," said Gaines. "Clamp it down and work together." He clicked over and spoke to Durant. "Get Whipper on the line and make it happen."

"Copy that," replied Durant.

"Let's go Ari. Can we catch up with One-Two?"

"Done," Ari said.

Cade leaned back once again and listened to the hum of the engines. *Three hours*, he thought to himself, *and we'll all be in Canada.*

Chapter 51
Outbreak - Day 16
Near Victor, Idaho

Four miles and ten minutes after the trio left the farmhouse in the rearview, the white colonial with the gigantic red barn loomed on the horizon.

Jenkins inclined his head towards the rolling green pastures and the buildings beyond. "Daymon, my man. You can thank the fine folks of Three Rivers Equestrian for the salve on your gut."

"Doesn't look like they needed it anymore," he said. "What'd they do? Take the horses with them?"

"No they didn't," said Heidi slowly. She was in the back seat behind Jenkins. Her window was down and the incoming wind was whipping her blonde hair back into her face. "The fucking beasts got to them."

Jenkins let out a soul-shuddering moan that caused Daymon to jump from his seat. "What's the matter?" he asked.

"Gimme the binoculars," Jenkins demanded as he slipped the truck into park. "*Now*," he barked without removing his eyes from the blurry red mounds dotting the rolling green expanse.

Calm down, thought Daymon as he placed them into the driver's upturned palm.

Jenkins removed his glasses, set them on the dash and reluctantly pressed the binoculars to his face. "No, no, no. You dumbass, Charlie."

"So what," said Daymon. "They're fuckin' horses."

"Those aren't just any horses. Those are the ones I rescued," Jenkins snapped. "Or what is left of them. Some fucking rescuer... I saved them from a slow death locked up in their stables. Let 'em go into the pasture and then I left the gate wide open."

"Don't be so hard on yourself, Charlie," Heidi said. "You were jumped by a couple of those things. Weren't you?"

"That's no excuse."

"Let me see those," Daymon said.

Jenkins handed over the binoculars and donned his eyeglasses.

After panning the pasture, Daymon said, "Listen up, Charlie. I think I have an idea that might help you feel better. We could drive up there and kill two birds with one stone."

Jenkins shot Daymon a skeptical look. "What are you getting at?"

"I say we roll up there and siphon the tanks of those two cars. Nose around the house for some food, and then kill those rotten fuckers." Daymon looked at Heidi, then shifted his gaze to Jenkins and continued where he had left off. "Horse meat? Really? Nobody eats effin horse meat."

"Those bastards will eat anything," replied Jenkins as he urged the Tahoe forward.

***

Daymon was able to siphon enough gas from the two compacts to top off the Tahoe's tank. Then he performed a quick calculation in his head and decided that one more refill somewhere along the way would probably get them to the GPS coordinates Cade had given him.

He stowed the hose and can and retrieved the crossbow and one of the AR-15s from the truck. He slung the rifle and started off towards the house on the knoll.

On the porch, Heidi was holding an animated conversation with Jenkins. She had come a long way since he'd first laid eyes on her at the Teton Pass, thought Daymon. But she certainly had a long journey ahead of her. Scratch that, he thought. *We* have a long journey ahead of *us*, and he gathered that he owed it all to Charlie. Then out of the blue, a mischievous grin cracked his face.

He retraced his steps to the truck and fetched the machete, then made his way back to the big white colonial, climbed the stairs, and joined Heidi and Jenkins on the wide wraparound porch.

"Been inside yet?" Daymon inquired.

"It's locked," said Heidi, referring to the wide oak door with the prominently displayed '*closed*' sign.

"First things first," Daymon said as his smile returned.

Jenkins eyed the weapons, then flicked his gaze to Daymon. "What'd you break those out for?"

Still grinning, Daymon placed the machete on the railing nearest Jenkins, set the crossbow against the wall next to the front door, and shrugged the carbine from his shoulder.

He received a perplexed look from Heidi, and one of resignation from Jenkins.

"Choose your weapons," he said.

Saying nothing, the former police chief took the machete, clomped along the wooden porch and down the stairs while calling out a challenge to the feeding zombies. "Come and get me. Fresh meat over here... no fillers."

Daymon wrapped an arm around Heidi and they watched the zombies, one by one, rise from the shredded horse carcasses and stagger towards Jenkins. "Time for a shooting lesson," he said with an added wink.

"What do you recommend?" she asked.

"Take the rifle. Low recoil... point and shoot." He showed her the basics. Then hefted the crossbow and rested it over his shoulder.

By the time they reached the bottom of the stairs, all of Jenkins's hooting and hollering had drawn quite a crowd. Half a dozen bloody-faced shamblers clutched the stark white fence, leaving crimson smears everywhere their hands went.

"This one is first," Jenkins said, pointing the machete at the first turn with a sloppy mess of tangled entrails swinging from its maw.

"That bushwhacker is *very* sharp. Be careful," Daymon said.

Jenkins set his jaw and raised the machete shoulder high.

"Time for some PETA street justice," Daymon said in a sing-song voice as he watched the machete trace a flat arc towards the zombie's temple. Although Jenkins hadn't put enough muscle behind the blow to cleave the thing's skull in half, the finely honed blade still sliced through the corpse's right orbit bone and became wedged in its ethmoid—the strip of bone separating the nasal cavity from the gray matter. With its brain now destroyed, the monster's jaw released, letting the intestines plop to the grass.

"Hell yeah. Feeling better?"

"I'll let you know in a minute," Jenkins said. Then he walked down the fence line, leaving split skulls and crumpled flesh eaters along the way.

"Save one for Heidi."

"There'll be more," Jenkins replied quietly as he buried the machete into the last creature's skull. "There always are."

Mission accomplished, thought Daymon. *Looks like the real Charlie is back.*

***

Twenty minutes later, after the trio had gone through the two-story house room by room, they stood on the porch with nothing to show in the way of food and water except for two cans of something a vagrant wouldn't eat and a glass jar of crap that a food drive would probably reject.

"Dibs on the marinated artichoke hearts," Daymon said, tossing the jar from one hand to the other. "That leaves sliced water chestnuts and"—he scrutinized the faded label of the third can—"lutefisk... what the hell is lutefisk?"

"Cod, I think," said Heidi.

Jenkins hitched a thumb in his belt. "Left in a hurry, didn't they."

"I think *bolted* is the word," Daymon replied.

"My appetite is returning and this stuff isn't going to cut it. What are we going to eat?" Heidi gazed at Daymon waiting for a response.

"The good news... we've got a full tank. And we've got a few waters left." Daymon paused a beat and looked out over the pastures where what remained of the dead horses had already drawn a ravenous murder of crows. And as they fed and cawed and carried on, he added in a low reassuring voice, "Don't worry hon, we'll rustle up some food. Promise."

***

As Jenkins maneuvered the Tahoe along 33, he remained silent, focused inward deep in thought. The question that had been nagging him since leaving the Three Rivers Equestrian Center was why the last ones out hadn't seen fit to let the horses go free. Then he reflected on the effect the monsters that used to be living, breathing citizens had on him. Young or old, male or female, even though they were infected by the Omega virus and were nothing but walking corpses, putting a bullet or a blade in them didn't sit well with him. And then the realization that his loved ones were still out there somewhere—monsters wandering around in search of human flesh—came to the fore and hit him like a mule kick. He said a silent prayer that someone, some survivor like him or Daymon or Heidi would come into contact with them and ease their pain. He didn't care how, so long as their suffering in this hell on earth ceased. Then he reflected back to the zombies he had just dispatched. How every one of them had had rough, cracked, and calloused hands, and wind-burned faces, indicative of a person who worked outside for a living—on a horse farm perhaps. Then he remembered the scuffed and worn cowboy boots one of them had been wearing and it clicked. Suddenly the anger and white hot rage that had pushed him over the edge and had driven him to hack the creatures to death morphed into a sense of serenity. His grip on the wheel lessened and his jaw relaxed. *Yes*, he thought, *the folks at Three Rivers were undoubtedly horse lovers just like him.* And, he guessed, they probably couldn't bring themselves to put down people they knew—who had become infected—just to spare a few horses. He still had the horror of putting his own wife down indelibly etched in his memory. The fact that even in his frequent nightmares he could smell the coppery tang of her blood as he placed her cold corpse in the bathtub made the idea of hating a person who had been put in the same position seem utterly absurd to him.

"Jenkins, slow the eff down!" Daymon bellowed.

Looking down at the speedometer, Jenkins noticed the needle pulling back from sixty. That meant he had to have been doing as least seventy while perseverating about his hand in the death of a few animals. "You drive, then," he said. He put the big disc brakes to work and brought the Tahoe to a sudden stop on the shoulder. "I'm fatigued as it is. Maybe even a little depressed... but I'm no shrink."

"So you're sleepy... and she's hungry. Then what dwarf am I?" Daymon said, trying to lighten the mood.

"Certainly not bashful," Heidi quipped.

Jenkins slipped the truck into park, popped his seat belt, and traded places with Daymon.

Once they were moving again Heidi spoke up from the rear seat. "You didn't answer the question, Charlie, which dwarf is Daymon?"

Not wanting to offer up an answer that would be taken the wrong way, he glanced over his shoulder and shot her a look that said, *Leave me the hell out of this.*

"Come on Charlie... play along," chided Heidi.

"Goddamnit, I just killed six of those things. And the only difference between me and them is that *I* haven't been bit *yet*. And the fact that I lost my cool and did them in with a machete makes me feel like some kind of serial killer." He looked away at the barren countryside flashing by.

"Get used to it, Charlie," said Daymon as he steered around an overturned car. "They aren't ever going to stop coming." And as if to confirm his statement, a pale arm reached out from the crushed passenger compartment, groping for the passing SUV.

Daymon suddenly slowed at the bottom of a long sweeping curve and pointed up the hill, where tendrils of black smoke curled into the air. At the end of a short drive that teed off of a narrow feeder road was a small plat of land, with a large oak standing sentinel over a pale blue garage and some remains smoldering where he guessed a house once stood. Milling about the property were more creatures than Daymon cared to count; some were charred black, but most were just your garden variety zombie—pale, shabbily clothed, and relentless. Suddenly, the gaunt faces turned at once and locked their milky eyes on the white and black Tahoe. Then, as if a switch was flipped, a ripple of movement coursed through the amassed dead and the herd began to shamble towards 33.

"Shit... there's gotta be a hundred of 'em," exclaimed Daymon. "And that is the same yellow Hummer I saw yesterday."

"There's not much left of the house," added Jenkins as he swapped his glasses for the binoculars. "Just a few bricks that *used* to be a chimney."

"I remember seeing that ugly yellow truck parked at the *House*," Heidi hissed.

"Yeah, I've seen it before," Jenkins admitted. "It belonged to that movie star prick who owned the *House*. He drove it around town whenever he decided to jet in from Hollywood and grace the little people of Jackson with his presence. We used to joke about the color... called it *'look at me yellow.'*"

"Fitting," Daymon said. "For a 5-foot-2 shrimp. Probably has blocks on the pedals so he can reach 'em." He rolled up his window, trying to shut out the stench, and eased his foot from the brake.

"I hope that whoever was in there died a painful death... no, make that a thousand painful deaths," Heidi spat. "Just the

312

thought that those animals who drugged me and did who knows what while I was under might still be running around out here makes me sick to my stomach." She slumped into her seat, blinking away tears. Although her memory of the events was like a patchwork quilt missing many pieces, the slices of time that she couldn't recall were filled in by her very vivid imagination.

"You're going to be just fine," Daymon said. "I won't let anything happen to you. Promise." He really wanted to tell her about Cade and how the soldier had scooped up Robert Christian, and that there was undoubtedly a gallows and a hangman's noose in the rapist's immediate future. But if just the sight of a vehicle linked to her ordeal was enough to bring everything to the surface, he reasoned, then letting the fact be known that the main culprit was still alive and kicking was totally out of the question.

They had only been moving for a minute and had covered less than a mile when Daymon stopped the rig abruptly on the centerline. "Lu Lu!" he cried. He'd thought he had been seeing things the night before, and yet, as he looked off into the distance at the green Scout with the unmistakable black E painted on her, he still couldn't believe his eyes.

"Who the hell is Lu Lu?" inquired Jenkins.

"My International Scout."

"Sure as shit is Lu Lu," rasped Heidi, who had composed herself and had her upper body wedged between the front seats again and the binoculars pressed to her face. "But there are a couple of those walking corpses hanging around."

Incredulous, Jenkins asked, "How in the hell did your Scout get here? We're what, ten... fifteen miles from where you left it."

"I don't know, but I'm sure as hell going to try and find out."

Heidi shook her head. "What are you going to do about those things?"

He put the truck in neutral and allowed it to coast down the slight grade. Then, once gravity had taken over and they were barreling silently towards Lu Lu and the zombies, he held his right hand out, palm up, like a surgeon in the OR demanding a scalpel. "Machete," he said, without taking his eyes from the road.

Jenkins obliged, and when the Tahoe had pulled parallel to the smaller Scout, Daymon secured the brake, put it in park, and then hopped out.

From inside the truck Heidi called out to Daymon. "Be careful," she hollered. Then she curled up on the bench seat, and covered her head with Jenkins's uniform jacket. She couldn't stand to watch. Between the zombie bodies Daymon and Jenkins had piled up at the farmhouse outside of Driggs and the head chopping spree at the horse farm, she had seen enough splattered brains to last a lifetime.

The first turns staggered from the road's shoulder and approached the Tahoe on the passenger side.

Daymon got as low to the pavement as his lanky frame would allow, and when he rounded the front end of the rig he was doing some kind of contorted duck walk, only the top of his dreadlocks visible to Jenkins. Scudding along, seemingly floating over the white hood, the tightly wound locks looked like some kind of mutant tribble from Star Trek.

In the back seat, Heidi jumped when the two creatures bashed into the sheet metal in an attempt to get at Jenkins.

Hurry the hell up, Jenkins thought to himself as the flesh eater swiped its bloated tongue along the window inches from his face. Then, in his side vision, the abomination's head disappeared from the nose up. When he turned his head to the right, he caught a glimpse of gray brain nestled in a honeycomb of white as the creature's chin bonked against the window channel on its way to the ground.

Daymon watched the ghoul collapse in a heap, and with the well-balanced machete in a loose, right-handed grip backpedaled to create some distance between himself and the other staggering mess. Minus one ear and missing a majority of its fingers, the hissing cadaver—whether male or female he hadn't a clue— looked like it had fended off one hell of an attack before dying and joining the ranks of the walking dead.

"Hey Stumpy. Over here," Daymon called out. Then, just as the zombie pivoted and set off headlong towards the new meat, the Tahoe's window lowered and Jenkins straight-armed his pistol and shot it in the head from less than a yard away.

Daymon winced as what seemed like ten pounds of gray matter exited opposite the bullet's entry point and splattered all over Lu Lu. God, how he'd missed his truck. He'd been so overwhelmed with emotion when he had abandoned her that he hadn't had a chance to say a proper goodbye. Now that she was wearing half a walker's brains, he didn't know if he even wanted to go near her.

"Thanks Chief," he said sarcastically. "Why did you have to go and do that for? I had it covered."

"Wasn't in the mood for any more head splitting," Jenkins replied as he slid out of the Tahoe.

The rear door creaked open and Heidi stepped out timidly, tip toed over the bodily fluids and bolted to Daymon's side.

As Jenkins looked on, Heidi gave Daymon more lovin' in the span of a minute than he'd seen her give the man in three days.

"Get a room," Jenkins said.

Daymon flipped him the bird and the couple walked arm in arm towards the gore-splashed Scout.

"If only you could speak, little lady," Daymon said to Lu Lu as he used the machete's rounded blade to scrape detritus from around the door handle. Then, as he went to open the door, the vehicle lurched once and then shimmied on its worn springs.

He looked over at Jenkins and cast his gaze to Heidi. Both were nowhere close enough to the vehicle to have touched it, let alone have caused the movement. And neither one of them seemed to have noticed the tremor. Daymon wondered if he had imagined the whole thing, then reminded himself that getting bit was usually the penalty for displaying a cavalier attitude. So before he opened the door, he decided to check the interior from the relative safety of the outside. He wiped a four-inch square of road grime from the rear glass and peered in. All he saw was his firefighting turnout gear. On them, the words *Property of JHFD* were stenciled in white, inch-high letters. Underneath the Nomex protective clothing he could see his old, double-bladed axe poking out.

Next he walked around to the passenger side and looked into the back seat area, where days ago three Delta Force operators had been sardined hip to hip with all of their weapons and gear and attitude. He didn't expect to find anything, and was shocked to discover what looked like a bruised and bloody corpse. Legs and arms drawn into a fetal curl, the slight man looked to have been of Asian descent. And the longer he stared at the man's profile, the more he felt like he had seen the man somewhere before.

"Jenkins, can you come here for a second?"

"A second is about all we have," Jenkins answered. "We got an undead posse heading our way."

"How far?"

Jenkins lowered the binoculars. "'Bout a quarter mile," he said. "Maybe a little less. Gives us about three or four minutes, I gather." He made his way around the front of the Tahoe. "What do you got?"

"This guy look familiar to you?"

Jenkins cocked his head and furrowed his brow. "What do you mean, *guy*?"

"Just look in there," Daymon said, stepping back from window.

"Well I'll be. Looks like he ain't going to be serving High Tea ever again," Jenkins said. "You haven't seen him move?"

"No... I'm pretty sure he's dead."

"Why don't you forget about him and forget about *Lu Lu*... and let's *go*."

"Lemme see those binocs," Daymon said.

Jenkins handed them over.

"We've got time," Daymon stated. Then he whistled. "Jesus... would you look at the critter in front, he's huge."

"I noticed him already. That *was* Lucas Brother, one of Ian Bishop's guys."

"What did you just say?" Heidi said sharply. She stormed over and snatched the field glasses from Daymon's hands. She adjusted them to fit her narrow feminine features and had a look for herself. As soon as the charred zombie came into focus, a week's worth of horrible memories came flooding back. Without a doubt it *was* Lucas—matted and singed blond locks and all. The mere sight of him caused her hands to shake uncontrollably.

While everyone's attention had been focused on the advancing throng, Lu Lu began to rock gently on her shot springs and the driver door popped open.

Daymon pulled Heidi behind him and looked to Jenkins, who had his pistol aimed over Lu Lu's roof in the general area where the thing was most likely to emerge.

"Save your ammo," Daymon barked as he stalked around the SUV, holding the machete loosely in his right hand. "Don't watch if you can't hack it." He chuckled at this. "Get it? *Hack* it."

Jenkins stared daggers at the dreadlocked former firefighter. *Smartass*, he thought. Then he returned his gaze to the abomination scrabbling from the vehicle, then back to Daymon who had the machete in the air, ready to bring it down for the coup de gras.

Muscles tensed, Daymon wondered how the hell a *zombie* had wormed its way from the back seats to the front and *then* managed to work the goddamn door handle. Hell, if he didn't know any better he was probably looking at the zombie evolution taking place right before his eyes. Then he about shit himself when the battered creature turned and uttered the words: "Help me."

Chapter 52
Outbreak - Day 16
Draper, South Dakota

Jasper steered the dusty old Chevy onto the shoulder. He didn't know why. Habit, he guessed. He could have stopped smack dab in the middle of the road without repercussions. Hell, he coulda jammed the brakes on without looking; there was no chance of getting rear-ended.

Truth was he hadn't seen a vehicle or a living soul traveling this lonely stretch of blacktop since July turned into August—a full week into this madness. By that time he had already put down his wife and his two kids. One of the wandering monsters had gotten to them while he had been out disposing of the human shells that had been his closest neighbors.

He had arrived back into town to find Delores, his wife and best friend of a dozen years bleeding out on the kitchen floor of their old house with the monster's face still buried in her guts. He decapitated the thing with one of Delores's prized Henckels, the ones they'd gotten as a wedding gift so many years prior. Two or three quick sawing motions and the serrated knife relieved the undead stranger of its head. After which Jasper buried the blade into his wife's eye socket when she began to reanimate.

In the backyard, in the shade of the elm under which two cats and way too many goldfish were interred, he found his oldest eating his youngest—Bobby with a mouth full of Jenny's entrails was a sight that would haunt him 'til the day he died—and he nearly did that day.

But in the end he couldn't bring himself to add another body to the gun that had put down his only two children. He buried his family that day, but not under the elm. He took the time and did it right. Three graves, each one of them three feet wide by six feet long, and dug six feet deep into the earth. It took him all day—backbreaking labor for certain—but his family deserved no less.

He sat in the truck with the engine running, thinking about his family and what he could have done different. Drawing a blank, he ran a hand through his chestnut-brown hair. It was short from the razor cut he'd given himself prior to conducting the solemn graveside service, and hadn't grown out much since. His face had a week's worth of reddish stubble working hard to cover up two weeks' worth of heartache and stress. He wiped the back of his hand across his brow and glanced in the rearview at the twisted limbs and contorted death masks worn by the dead—the same folks who had been his good neighbors.

Still, the Mathersons wouldn't receive the same courtesy as his family. Their moldering bodies would go on the growing pile in the cemetery with the rest of the townspeople—seventy-something in total—who had succumbed to this thing the people in Sioux Falls called Omega. The same desperate folks who had been so thoughtful as to have delivered it here, to Draper, a hundred and eighty easy miles due east, right down the I-90.

Omega, thought Jasper. *Couldn't have picked a more appropriate name. No coming back from this one. No way. Not breathing and possessing a pulse anyway.*

He looked through the back window at the white church steeple. Woulda been nice to have had a service for the Mathersons but it was only him now. No priest. No pall bearers. No choir. Just him and the birds.

319

He shifted his gaze to Dale. The extra puckered eye on his forehead was not becoming of him. It sure was amazing what a little deuce-deuce pistol could do to a zombie at point blank range, and the lead, Jasper supposed, was probably still hanging out with Dale's scrambled brains somewhere inside of his blood-slickened dome.

He had stopped short of the overflowing graveyard for a reason. Not because he wanted to gaze at his dead cargo. It was the sight and sound of the strange-looking whirly birds heading northeast towards the capitol that had drawn him to pull over. High in the sky they droned along. One black and angular. The other seemingly built out of spare parts. It had two forward facing propellers ten sizes too big. How the thing landed without chewing up the runway was anyone's guess.

He watched for a beat as they cut through the azure sky, and then when his personal airshow had concluded and they were out of view he jammed the truck into drive and headed for the mound. As the truck jounced over the rounded shoulder and back onto the smooth roadway, he put one hand on the shotgun on the seat next to him. *Just in case*, he thought to himself. Just in case disposing of the dead proved too hard to bear and he couldn't see the task through to the end.

He already knew what the muzzle of the little .22 pistol tasted like. Gun oil commingled with the mineral tang of cordite. If he used the shotgun he'd decided he wouldn't put the thing in his mouth. He'd already run this scenario through his head a hundred times. He'd park the Chevy next to the holes in the ground where Delores, Jenny, and Bobby were slowly doing the ashes to ashes and dust to dust part of the short service he'd performed for them. He'd stay inside the truck with a photo of them on the dash. Under his chin is where he would place the business end of the twelve gauge—then he'd pull the trigger. No way he'd chicken out. Not with the shotgun.

Three more houses to clear of the ones he knew were really dead. And nearly double that many that still had living dead inside. Then he'd be going home to see them. Two days at most, he hoped.

The organic hum emanating from the feeding birds was reaching his ears over the V8's soft throaty rumble. And as he left the road and wheeled north to the graveyard, the crows and ravens and buzzards took flight in a blast of black feather and murderous cries. Bracketed by the mature dogwoods planted decades ago on the west and east sides of the cemetery, the dark-feathered raptors all but blotted out the sky, dipping and diving over the sea of grave markers and putrefying flesh.

Ignoring the aerial display, Jasper reversed until the rear bumper met resistance with flesh and bone. He hopped out, skirted the truck, and quickly dropped the tailgate with a clang. *Oh to be young again*, he thought as he pulled on rigor-stiffened limbs in order to move the Mathersons to their final resting place. The three kids were the easiest of the six to remove, and Grandma Matherson might as well have been a kid because her frail body matched the little ones' weight. Dale and his wife Loraine were another story altogether. Both loved their food deep-fried and were easily north of two hundred and fifty pounds. Lugging their dead weight out of the Chevy nearly broke the volunteer undertaker's back.

He went around to the cab and punched open the glove box, retrieved his tattered King James edition and slammed the door. When he turned around, two of the walking corpses were within spitting distance. He reopened the door, clambered across the bench seat and clutched the scatter gun with one hand before popping out on the driver's side. The fact that the rotting pair had been able to sneak up on him was supremely disconcerting. *Maybe the things are learning*, he thought as an involuntary shudder wracked his body at the prospect.

He crunched a shell into the chamber and let the dead trudge closer. Thankfully he didn't recognize either one of them. *Probably from one of the big cities*, thought Jasper. *Lately, most of them were.*

He didn't relish the idea of seeing another dead body with a face full of buck, but he was left with no other alternative. He brought the muzzle up and pulled the trigger. The discharge punched the stock into his shoulder but the damage to the shambling creature was far worse—fatal, in fact.

The frail cadaver left the ground and flew backwards through the air a half dozen feet and came back down with a hollow thud. The gray matter that exited its skull travelled much further and painted the dry earth in a wide arc.

Jasper followed the same routine and pulped the other walker's face with a well-aimed shot.

He shifted his gaze to where the gravel road made a T with the blacktop to town and noticed a half dozen more of the rotten beasts traipsing across the open flat land about a half mile to the south.

Keeping one eye on the walking dead, Jasper read a passage from Genesis 3:19 for the unfortunate Matherson family. *"In the sweat of thy face shalt thou eat bread, till thou return unto the ground, for out of it wast thou taken: for dust thou art, and unto dust shalt thou return."*

He walked back to the truck, being careful to avoid the dusty clumps of brain. He slid behind the wheel and started the Chevy, cut a three-point turn and headed back towards town. He glanced down at the Bible and then at the shotgun next to it. *My work today is not finished,* he thought grimly. *Next stop, the Valdezes' casa de la muerte.*

***

Near Victor, Idaho

Daymon's jaw went slack and he slowly lowered the blade but kept it pressed flat against his right leg.

"Come again?" he said, craning to see into the creature's eyes.

"Help me," the thing rasped.

"Oh, hell no," Daymon said, shaking his head in disbelief. "I'm hearing shit." He looked over the top of the Scout, drawing eye contact with Jenkins, then shifted his gaze to Heidi and said, "One of you tell me I'm just hearing shit."

322

As if in response to his question, the group of walking corpses started in with their own chorus of moans.

Jenkins crabbed around the rear of Lu Lu with his pistol held in a two-handed grip, Heidi sticking to him closely.

Turning its blood-streaked face away from Daymon and towards Jenkins and Heidi, it uttered the same two words: "Help me."

"You heard it," Daymon spat as he backpedaled towards the Tahoe. "Help it. Put a bullet in its fuckin' brain so we can get the hell out of here."

Jenkins slowly lowered his gun.

Noticing this, Heidi stepped from behind Jenkins and angled for a better view. "That's Tran."

"I was thinking the same thing," Jenkins stated as he holstered his pistol. "Couldn't see the resemblance at first cause of the goose egg and all the dried blood."

"He was the *only* one of them who was nice to me," Heidi said. "Brought me wet wipes and warm washcloths after..." Her eyes turned glassy and tears welled up. "And when I came off the drugs he brought me food even though I said I didn't want any."

Jenkins stepped closer to the man and called out his name. There was no response. Then he touched Tran's shoulder. It was warm.

Heidi had just turned to get Tran a water from the Tahoe when a single shot rang out. She shrieked and whipped her head around, glaring at Jenkins and thinking the worst.

But his pistol was in its holster and he was hauling the bulky firefighting gear from the back of the Scout.

More gunfire, controlled and steady, sounded from the opposite side of the Tahoe.

Heidi crouched near the cruiser's rear tire and gazed down the road where one by one the undead herd was being thinned out. Finally, when there was a lull in the shooting, she hollered at Daymon. "This one's alive," she said, looking for some recognition. What she saw instead was a look of confusion on her man's face as he slapped home a fresh magazine. Then from behind she heard Jenkins tell her to get to the cruiser. She looked over and saw he was helping Tran to the vehicle.

Dressed in Daymon's old firefighting gear, the slight Asian man looked like a cross between one of the infected and a sad-looking scarecrow.

"Saved the worst for last," Daymon said as he charged a fresh round into the AR-15.

Heidi put herself between Tran and Daymon.

"No, not him," said Daymon.

Now Heidi wore the confused look.

A wicked smile formed on Daymon's face. With his off hand he corralled his dreads behind his ears. "I saved the Lucas bastard for *you*."

She looked beyond the rear of the Tahoe at the shambling giant. She regarded the pinkish half-moon where the blackened dermis was missing from its neck and looked into its milky eyes, then shook her head slowly. "No, let him rot."

That's my girl, Daymon thought. He lowered the rifle and slid behind the wheel.

Jenkins helped Tran into the back seat and clambered over him to take a spot behind Daymon.

"Next stop, Eden," Daymon said. Then he leaned forward in order to see around Heidi and stole one last look at Lu Lu.

Chapter 53
Outbreak - Day 16
Southwest of Winnipeg, Manitoba Canada

Give or take a tenth of a mile, Oil Can Five-Five was right where it was supposed to be.

Apparently the GPS birds are still talking to each other, Ari thought to himself. He had a feeling that his days of flying without a modicum of worry, being able to rely upon the information being provided by these wonders of technology, were coming to a close. *Was there anyone alive at Cape Canaveral?* he wondered. Because sooner or later the satellites that nearly every piece of equipment in the United States arsenal relied on for navigation, communication, and targeting were destined to fail. Orbits decay, and without aerospace engineers to design and build new birds and the necessary heavy lift capabilities to throw them into orbit, the prospect of navigation by compass and sextant was very real and probably in his immediate future.

"Jedi One-One coming to drink," Ari said into the comms as he maneuvered his ship into the refueling tanker's slipstream.

"We've got you covered One-One. But that'll be two beers for each of my crew," the Herc pilot replied.

"Roger that," said Ari in an agreeable tone. "But if I'm buying you a beer, at least tell me your name."

"Lieutenant Dover," the pilot replied. "Ben Dover."

"Well Lieut... should I call you Benjamin or Ben?" Ari asked without missing a beat. He then gazed to the left at Durant, and wide grins broke out behind their boom mikes.

"Ben," the pilot drawled matter-of-factly.

Either the Herc driver had already heard his fill of wisecracks concerning his name, or he didn't know the SOAR pilot's reputation as a ball breaker. *Probably a combination of both,* thought Cade as he caught Gaines eye.

Both men smiled.

Covering his boom mike with a gloved hand, Cade leaned across the cabin. "Hey— Agent Cross... is Ripley this loose on Marine One's comms when the boss is aboard?"

Cross shook his head. Pantomimed zipping his lips and throwing away an imaginary key.

"I heard that," Ari shot back into the shipwide comms.

Now, with a fully loaded fuel tank, the Ghost backed away from the refueling boom and climbed away to the port side of the Herc, where Ari flashed another thumbs up before reforming up next to the loudly droning Osprey.

Cade watched as the last link to the Desantos era busied himself with his M4. Lopez checked the batteries in the laser pointer affixed above and behind the suppressor. Then he took a microfiber swab, and for the third time in as many hours meticulously cleaned the lenses of the Eotech optics mounted atop his weapon's upper receiver. First he polished the flip-away 3x magnifier, a cylindrical scope about three inches in length which sat behind the square-topped holographic sight. Then he carefully wiped the imaginary accumulated dust from the latter, which had a floating red dot on the lens and was optimal for close quarters combat. The large lens, allowing for super-fast target acquisition, could be brought on target with just one or both eyes open—and whatever the operator trained that red dot on, his bullets were sure to strike. Ignoring the banter, Lopez seemed lost in his own world, no doubt perseverating over the multitudes of *demonios* he would soon be facing.

The entire Delta team, including Tice, who was their honorary member, was equipped similarly with anti-ballistic body armor, tactical helmets, knee and elbow protection, and to guard against bites to the hands and fingers they all wore tactical gloves that were constructed of thick Nomex fabric complete with Carbontek molded knuckle caps.

Each operator carried a suppressed M4 with identical optics, laser pointers and drop-down fore grips.

Agent Cross had the ubiquitous Secret Service suppressed MP7 dangling under his arm, as well as a semi-automatic sidearm strapped to his right thigh.

Suddenly Durant's voice boomed over the comms. "Ten mikes out," he said. "Once again good ol' Nash has worked her magic. Heads up, I'm patching through a satellite feed."

"Real-time?" asked Gaines.

"Roger that, Sir," answered Durant flatly. "Wait one." A half a minute passed and he added, "OK, it's coming up on the cabin monitor."

The LCD flat-panel, which was inset into the Ghost Hawk's aft-facing bulkhead, glowed blue for a few seconds before the real-time image being beamed down via one of the 50th Space Wing's remaining Key Hole satellites splashed onto the screen. The billion dollar Air Force bird was currently parked in a geostationary orbit over downtown Winnipeg so that the KH-12's powerful cameras were always trained on the Delta team's target.

As soon as the image hit the screen and the optics zoomed in closer, the resolution sharpened and the situation on the ground became crystal clear.

Lopez whistled. Then he said, "You've gotta be kidding me. Looks like Custer's last stand down there."

The static image they were looking at could only be described with two words: catastrophic failure. A dozen abandoned military vehicles were spread out around the eight-block perimeter just inside of the breached fence lines.

Another dozen ringed the center plaza of the National Biological Laboratory's campus. The facility was Canada's answer to the United States' CDC in Atlanta, and was equipped with laboratories ranging from biosafety level 2 on up to level 4, the highest, which were designed with multiple safeguards in order to contain the deadliest microbial killers known to man.

Looking a little bigger than ants as seen from space, wandering Zs choked the streets across the entire city. The facility suddenly appeared closer as the camera zoomed in a few stops and more details emerged. Dozens of living dead moved about the manicured grounds inside the perimeter fencing. And sitting idle in the central plaza, a dozen APCs—low-slung six-wheeled armored personnel carriers with turret-mounted cannons—were also surrounded by wandering throngs of flesh eaters. Some kind of boxy tracked vehicle occupied a grassy knoll that rose between four reflecting pools containing brackish water and splayed-out bodies of what looked to be dead Canadian soldiers. That the track bristled with multiple whip-like antennas meant it was most likely the command vehicle in which the highest ranking officer would have overseen the ground operation.

The desert tan APCs sat adjacent to sandbag emplacements, complete with heavy machine guns deployed facing outward with their lines of fire following the cement pathways that radiated away from the knoll, like spokes on a wagon wheel.

Cross piped up, "How did Nash come to the conclusion there are still live bodies in the facility?"

"Right here," Gaines said. He leaned in and touched the display, pointing out a few small white squares hanging off the side of the third story of one of the glass and metal buildings. "You can't see it so well here because of the angle, but in the footage Nash showed me you could clearly tell that these are sheets of some sort hanging from these windows. The messages on them were enough to make this mission more than just a shot in the dark... one of the messages read: *ALIVE INSIDE.*

Another read: *HELP US*. That alone was enough to convince me."

"How do we know that those sheets didn't go up there on Z day and the people lobbying for our help aren't already dead and gone?"

"Because," Gaines said evenly, "the one with *ALIVE INSIDE* painted on it also had yesterday's date on it." He let the fact sink in for a beat.

"Good enough for me," Cross replied. "Still think we can go in through the roof?"

Cade fielded the question. "The general and I went over that with Ari and Durant after the briefing. The Osprey is going to have to find a standoff location because that noisy beast will let every Z from BC to Quebec know that we're here."

"And the team? How are we getting in?" Cross pressed.

"Ari thinks he can infil and exfil from the roof provided there are no more than three survivors we have to transport... which I think is highly unlikely."

Gaines nodded in agreement.

"If those are the parking lots for the building," Tice said, alluding to the expanse of blacktop northeast of the plaza where the sun was dancing off of glass and sheet metal, "there had to be a lot of people inside there when the shit hit the fan."

Cade nodded but said nothing.

"Five mikes," Durant said over the intercom as he looked back and flashed an open hand for a visual cue.

"As soon as I get eyes on the target I'll know if I can put this bird down or not. Worst case scenario, you five have to work for it," Ari said.

"Four," Gaines said calmly. "Captain Grayson is running the show. I'm going to be the eye in the sky."

"Copy that," replied Cade.

Cross leaned over, looked Cade in the eye. "Did you know about this, Captain?"

"Not until two seconds ago."

"You're OK with that?" said Cross through gritted teeth.

"It's my job to improvise. In fact, it's something I learned from a man who is no longer with us."

Lopez performed a quick sign of the cross and pointed towards the helo's roof and heaven beyond.

After a few long moments of uneasy silence, during which time all eyes were riveted on Cade and the President's man, Cross broke out in his big surfer boy smile. "Just busting your balls, Delta. I've got your back."

"I had no doubt about it," replied Cade coolly. He looked toward the ground. It was rapidly approaching, and he could see a muddy body of water running serpentine through residential areas south and west of the downtown core where the target was located. Why anyone would build a level 4 facility in the middle of a city of roughly four hundred thousand was beyond his comprehension. *Hell*, he thought, *a level 2 or 3 in the city was still asking for trouble.*

Cade felt the helo change course and track around to the east. The river below merged with another turbid vein of dirt-laden water. Then the five-story main building that housed the level 4 containment lab in its basement loomed through the portside glass.

Major Ripley had already ruled the roof out as a landing zone for the Osprey due to the upthrust air-scrubbing apparatus and HVAC gear scattered about.

Jedi One-One, however, needed a flat spot the size of a postage stamp compared to the other ship.

"I was afraid of this, gentlemen," said Ari over the comms.

"What is it?" Gaines asked.

"The rooftop to your target *is not* flat. It's stepped and the terraces will get in the way of the rotor blades. And every edge where I'd usually rest a wheel to let you door kickers out is protected by concertina wire. Can't risk getting the bird snagged."

"Fast rope it is," said Cade, taking charge. "Let me help you, Hicks."

With Lopez and Cade pitching in, the two ropes, one port and one starboard, were attached, coiled, and ready to go.

As the near-silent helo cut an arc around the back of the cluster of buildings, sunlight blazed off of a glass-enclosed skywalk. Constructed entirely of white tubes, it was flat at the bottom and both sides angled in and joined at the top creating a very lengthy triangular passage linking the main building and the parking lot to the east.

"The fencing around the parking lot is compromised," Durant noted. "And what I presume is the main guardhouse looks to be unmanned."

"Roger that," replied Cade.

As Ari pulled the Ghost into a silent hover at a hundred feet AGL, just over the tree-lined northern perimeter, Cade spotted the white sheets Gaines had pointed out fluttering against the glass and metal background. "Camera," he said to Tice, who promptly handed over the Nikon.

Cade manipulated the focus ring and the shutter stuttered as he fired off thirty frames. He looked briefly at the mammoth LCD screen and then passed the camera to Gaines.

"Good intel from Nash," Gaines said, nodding subtly. "Someone's written today's date up there."

"Indeed they have," Cade answered. He shifted his attention to the parking lots near the outlying buildings scattered about the grounds, searching for a suitable rally point. A place where both aircraft could land in the event there were more survivors than the Ghost Hawk could safely accommodate.

Durant's voice filled the comms. "I've got movement. Third floor, three windows over."

"Taking us closer," intoned Ari as he side-slipped the helicopter toward the building, keeping the port side of the bird level with, and parallel to, the bank of windows. "Looks like they had to break a few windows in order to hang those."

Looking at the ground, Cade noticed a half-dozen battered filing cabinets lying amongst sparkling shards of safety glass that used to reside in the metal frames above. Files and papers began to blow from the open drawers and were propelled into the air by the down-blast caused by the whirring rotor blades.

By the time the quiet helicopter had moved in close, the sheets had been pulled inside, and a number of people stood waving their arms in front of the three broken panes, obviously very happy with the prospect of being rescued.

"How many?" Ari asked as he fought against the rising rotor wash to keep the helo steady.

Durant answered. "Thirteen on first count."

Gaines confirmed the number. "That's what I got... lucky number *thirteen.*"

Just as Ari was about to pull pitch and move away from the building, he noticed one of the survivors, a tiny Asian lady, furiously scribbling away on what he guessed to be a dry erase board. "Someone get eyes on the small woman in the middle window. She's working on a message for us."

"Copy that," Cade said. Once again he relieved Tice of the Nikon. "You can back her off, Ari. I've got the Spook's camera."

As Jedi One-One peeled away from the vertical face of the building, Cade trained the camera's telephoto lens on the dry erase board the woman was holding aloft.

"What's it say?" Tice asked, sounding anxious.

"You don't want to know."

"Tell us, Captain," Gaines said sharply.

"OK, you asked for it," said Cade in an *I told you so* voice. "Floors one, two, four and five... *overrun with infected.* Her words, not mine."

"No bueno," Lopez said. "You were right, Wyatt, I didn't want to hear that."

"Hold on. She's erasing—" Durant said. "Looks like she's writing something else."

"Come on lady," Cade said. He had the viewfinder pressed to his eye and he could see that the rest of her coworkers shared his sentiment. They looked like they'd run a marathon a day since this event popped off. *No doubt,* Cade thought, *that these people were the ones working around the clock to find a cure before the place fell to the dead.* And after it did, human nature probably kicked in and people fled the building in order to save themselves. Then, like falling dominos, once the panic had started it was hard to contain and nearly as infectious as Omega. He'd seen the same type of aftermath everywhere he'd been since Z day.

He fought against the bobbing of the chopper to keep the ungainly foot-and-a-half long telephoto lens locked onto the woman. Finally, mercifully, she finished scribbling.

"OK. Message to follow," said Cade as he read the chicken scratch. Then he relayed his interpretation of the message. "In not so many words she's telling us they are trapped in the large conference room on the northwest corner of the third floor. There are Zs in the stairwells and roaming the third floor. She indicates they are trapped."

"Madre," Lopez said under his breath.

A few expletives echoed in the cabin and over the comms as the rest of the team came to grips with the daunting task ahead of them.

"Fix your NVDs—night vision devices—and lock and load *gentlemen...* means you too, Tice," Cade said as he unplugged his flight helmet and swapped it out for the low-rise tactical helmet, on which he had already affixed a pair of the newest generation night vision goggles. When flipped into the down position, the four stubby stocks would protrude forward in front of the operator's eyes, making him look like something straight out of a sci-fi movie.

The rest of the four-man team swapped out helmets, checked their weapons, and cinched them down to their chest in anticipation of the rapid fast rope descent to the rooftop.

Cade looked at the men and smiled inwardly. He wished they had more time to get used to working together, but these were extraordinary circumstances that called for a lot of flexibility. The unit had lost a lot of dedicated shooters over the last two weeks, so he supposed he should be grateful for the guys he had.

The smell of death and hot exhaust instantly assaulted the cabin as Hicks wrenched open the starboard-side door and readied the fast rope.

After one quick final gear check, Cade pointed up with an index finger and bellowed to be heard over the turbine whine. "Take us to the roof, Ari." Then, as he gripped the anchored nylon rope in his gloved hands, he received a slap on the shoulder from the general.

"Go get 'em Grayson," said Gaines as he reached for the door latch on the port side.

Cade took some calming breaths, gazed at the mirrored building, and observed his own reflection as the helicopter rose to the rooftop.

Chapter 54
Outbreak - Day 16
50 Miles South of Victor, Utah

Tran recognized the woman in the passenger seat and the man to his left, but he had never seen the driver before, and given the African American man's exotic looks, if he had, he was certain he wouldn't have forgotten the encounter. He remained watchful and silent as the Tahoe ate up fifty miles of blacktop. In fact, everyone in the SUV seemed more than content to keep their thoughts and words to themselves.

He tore a strip from his tartan pajamas and wet it with a splash from one of the bottled waters.

Daymon peered in the rearview mirror. Scrutinized what his new passenger was up to and decided to break the silence. "I'll tell you a little known secret, Tran my man."

After making little progress at wiping the congealed blood from his face, Tran met Daymon's eyes and hitched his brows as if to say: *Let's hear it.*

"Fact... the only natural thing known to man that breaks down blood is... drumroll please... *saliva.*"

"Bullshit, Daymon," said Jenkins.

"Try it, Tran," said Daymon, shooting a quick glance towards the man.

"Keep your eyes on the road," Heidi said sharply.

"There is one catch. It has to be *your* saliva. I guess it has something to do with the enzymes in your own spit that breaks down your own blood."

There was a minute of silence as the Tahoe bounced along 89 South with the sun punishing everything outside of the air-conditioned ride.

Tentatively at first—as if he thought he was the butt of a cruel practical joke and didn't want anyone to know he'd been had—Tran spit on the tartan scrap and dabbed at his face. After a few minutes, he looked at his reflection in the window and said, "Works great. Thanks."

After that brief exchange, the floodgates opened. Tran explained his lengthy relationship with the billionaire. His voice grew soft when he began to describe the events that followed after the Omega outbreak, and how his boss's behavior and demeanor had changed overnight. He mentioned his friend Fredrick and how Christian had killed the man for the smallest offense. Tears filled his eyes and he choked up when he apologized to Heidi for not doing anything more to help her and the other girls who had been kidnapped, drugged, and taken advantage of at the *House*.

"It wasn't your doing," said Heidi. "It was a guy named Bishop, the brothers Lucas and Liam, and a little runt named Francis who kidnapped me from the bar."

Glancing at Tran in the rearview, the gears began to turn in Daymon's mind. And as he processed this new information, he resurrected the plan for revenge that Cade and his team of Army men had cut short just three days prior. Only now he set his sights set on a new target, and as the road clipped by he vowed silently to himself that he'd make Ian Bishop pay for kidnapping Heidi or he would die trying.

Tran dabbed at the deep fissure on his forehead, wincing as he did so. "Bishop abandoned Robert and a bunch of us at the mansion," he said.

Jenkins turned in his seat towards Tran. "What happened back there... at the torched house near where we found you?"

"They deserved what they got," Tran said without showing remorse.

"Ruthless... you burned the place down around them?" Daymon pressed.

"I don't know how that happened," answered Tran in a funereal voice. "I let the demons in the house. That's all."

"You did what?" said Jenkins incredulously.

Tran described in detail his flight from the mansion in Jackson Hole beginning with the explosions in the elk refuge, how he had found the keys in the Scout's ignition, and how the dead had all but ignored him. Finally he detailed how he'd led the dead to the house, where, because of the yellow Hummer in the drive, his gut told him the brothers were.

"You should write a book about that shit," exclaimed Daymon.

"Who's left to read it?" Jenkins quipped.

"I wasn't being literal..." Daymon didn't have time to finish the sentence. To keep from plowing into one hell of a roadblock, he mashed the brake pedal to the floorboards and stopped the big rig in a fashion that would have made the writers at *Road & Track* proud.

Smoke from the burning rubber wafted over the truck as it rocked on its springs.

"I told you to watch the road," chided Heidi.

Wide eyed, Daymon looked back at Jenkins. "Effin great brakes on this thing," was all he could think of to say. His mouth hinged open as the smoke dissipated and the odds they faced became evident.

Chapter 55
Outbreak - Day 16
Schriever AFB
Colorado Springs, Colorado

"Stay away from the fence," Brook called out to Raven.

Still wobbly on the new and much bigger bike, Raven risked taking one hand from the handlebars to wave an acknowledgement to her mom. Just then Max darted by and took a playful nip at the bike's knobby rear tire.

"She's just like Cade," Annie said quietly. "That's a fearless kid you've got there."

"She's been real resilient. I even had her shooting Zs again yesterday. Seemed to be no problem... and that kinda scares me," Brook said, wiping a tear. "Truth is, I want my innocent little *bird* back."

"My girls are *oblivious*," stated Annie. "Then again, they are much younger than Raven. You know the last couple of nights they've slept straight through. I think it's good that they are letting their guard down a little. It's a direct result of being inside here... behind the wire. Provides them a tangible sense of security."

The perfect opening presented itself, so Brook seized it. "Why don't you and the girls come with us tomorrow. Cade knows about this compound full of likeminded people just outside of Eden, Utah. May not be as much security as here, but it's not as close to a city the size of Denver either."

"Thanks for thinking about us, Brook. I'm sure Cade..."

Putting a blanket on the conversation, a large gray transport plane with Air Force markings roared down the distant runway and crawled into the sky. Jet engines working hard against gravity, and trailing black exhaust, the aircraft banked left and took on an easterly heading.

Both women watched in silence until it was a distant speck on the horizon.

The kids, who had also been frozen by the spectacle, resumed their game of tag as soon as the rumble had dissipated.

"As I was saying, Cade does not have to honor the pact he and Mike had. That was between them, so you needn't feel guilty." Annie's face tightened and her brow crinkled. "Me and the girls will be *just* fine here. Besides... I want to protect their innocence for as long as I can."

"The invitation's open until we drive through the gate. And there may be a couple of young adults and a girl a little older than Rave coming with if I can talk Master Grayson into it. I spent a couple hours talking with the kids... I guess I'm aging myself when I call them *kids*, but they're full of so much hope. I couldn't imagine being fifteen years younger than I am now and being stuck inside of here. It's just not my idea of *living*."

Annie said nothing.

As they enjoyed the peals of laughter and the occasional yelp out of Max, both women gazed across the field, pondering their future.

Brook finally broke the silence. "Are you *sure* you want to stay at Schriever?"

"I'm positive," Annie said, her voice cracking. "This way we can be close to Mike—the girls can visit him any time they want," she added, pinning a strand of graying blonde hair behind her ear.

There was another long moment of silence.

Brook turned and, probably for the last time, embraced her dear friend. "Time for a color," she said in a low voice as she stroked Annie's shoulder-length hair.

Annie pulled away slightly and stared at Brook straight away. "Time for a *frickin'* spa treatment," she replied as she shifted her gaze and tracked her twin daughters as they bounced through the brittle grass.

"And a mani-pedi," Brook added jokingly.

The ice was broken and their conversation morphed to the mundane. At least as mundane as talk can be with a dozen hungry Zs clutching the fence a hundred yards away.

Chapter 56
Outbreak - Day 16
National Microbiology Laboratory
Winnipeg, Manitoba Canada

Cade and Cross slid out of the hovering chopper in unison, and once they were on the roof they steadied the dangling fast ropes against Jedi One-One's vicious rotor wash.

Cade stared up at Lopez's size nines as they rocketed towards his face, and at the last moment released the rope and stepped out of the way.

A half second later Cross let go of the other fast rope and Tice was also safely on the roof.

"Clear starboard," said Hicks over the comms.

"Copy, starboard clear," answered Ari.

"Clear port," intoned Gaines.

"Copy, port clear," said Durant.

Cade went to one knee, brought his M4 up, and swept the barrel left to right. *Clear.* He gazed skyward and flashed a thumbs up at the black helicopter and watched the fast ropes free-fall to the rooftop and the portside door slide shut. In his earpiece he heard Durant calmly report back to Nash—who was monitoring the mission from the TOC at Schriever—that he, call sign Anvil Actual, was on target.

341

"Let's move," Cade said as he took off at a trot across the metal rooftop. Pitched to fifteen degrees and slick as snot, the going was precarious, and a fall equaled death at the hands and teeth of the Zs below.

Once he and his team reached the east side of the rooftop, they formed up next to a doorway inset into a sort of step-up on the building top.

Cade let his M4 hang on the center point sling and pressed his ear to the cool metal door. He considered having Tice scan the interior with a fiber optic camera, but seeing as how something was steadily scratching the other side of the door he saw no need. "We have Zs," he said, stabbing a finger at the door. Once again he took a knee, slid the lock gun from his cargo pocket, and went to work on the mechanism. After manipulating the tumblers for a short time, there was a soft click. Just to be on the safe side, he put his shoulder and all one hundred and eighty pounds of his body weight against the door while he stowed the lock pick tool and drew the Glock 17. He fished the suppressor from another pocket and threaded the flat black can onto the Glock's barrel, pulled the slide back an inch and saw the reassuring gleam of brass. *One in the pipe.* "Counting from three," he said.

"Copy that," came three near simultaneous replies.

He counted down, hit one, and pulled the door open in one fluid motion. The carrion blast was like nothing he had ever smelled. *Well, almost nothing,* he thought to himself. Stuck in a superheated attic with a bitchy Daymon and a sweaty Hoss and a hundred Zs a floor below would never be topped on the stench scale. But this blast of air from the darkened stairwell was a close second.

A heartbeat after the door hit the stop, the source of the scratching filled the doorway. Badly decomposed and trailing greasy ropes of lower intestine, the creature staggered into the light and hungrily eyed the operators.

"Engaging," Cade said as he swung the Glock on target and put two 9mm rounds through the creature's right eye, sending brains and blood blasting through the exit wound behind its left ear.

Immediately, another two moaning Zs ambled through the doorway and were tripped up by the prone body of the first creature. As they struggled to rise, Cade took a quick step to his right and pumped a pair of rounds point blank into each of their skulls. "Going in," he said, pulling the NVGs in front of his eyes. Without hesitating, he stepped over the leaking bodies and entered the stairwell with the Glock moving in a defensive arc to the left.

It was your standard-sized stairwell, four feet from wall to rail. Just enough room for the team to traverse one at a time while practicing proper spacing. Cade counted seventeen stairs from where he stood to the next landing where the run doubled back to the right.

He took the stairs slowly, keeping his Glock moving wherever his eyes went. Nearly to the next landing, he looked over his shoulder. Four stairs separated him from Tice. Similarly spaced, Cross was in the three spot with Lopez a few steps up from him keeping an eye on the team's six.

Satisfied everyone was inside, Cade inched over to the rail and peered down the well. On the next flight down, a corpse was wedged in the door, allowing natural light to filter in. He put his gloved hand on the handrail and felt subtle vibrations transferring through the metal. He shifted his gaze straight down between hundreds of feet of serpentine handrail where he could hear scraping noises echoing upwards as an unknown number of dead things negotiated the stairs.

He pressed forward, made the landing and stood over the headless corpse. Pressing his back to the wall next to the fifth-floor door, he flipped his goggles up and peeked around the door's edge. Ringed with windows letting in a copious amount of light, the expansive rectangular-shaped room spread out before him. There was sturdy gray carpet on the floor, and overhead a white drop-down ceiling housed scores of long dead florescent tubes behind frosted plastic panels. There were numerous offices fronted with opaque glass doors running away on the left. In the far right corner there was an immense glass enclosed meeting room with a long dark wood table and comfortable-looking high-backed chairs arranged around it. In the center of the office were row upon row of unoccupied desks in various stages of clutter.

In the center of it all, he counted a total of three zombies, all of which were not dressed in office attire. One had on a tee shirt and shorts, and the other wore tattered blue jeans and a bloodied tank top. The third creature was large by anyone's standards and wore a tent-sized floral muumuu revealing much more than Cade needed to see.

"Contact, three Zs. Going in solo," Cade said in a stage whisper. His voice was amplified and transmitted via his throat mike to the rest of his team as well as Gaines, who was monitoring the mission from Jedi One-One which was either at a standoff position close by, or orbiting the facility high above.

Cade pushed the door inward, fully flooding the stairway with bright light. Pistol clutched tightly in his gloved hands, he stepped over the dead body and padded into the room across the forgiving carpet. He picked his targets by order of awareness and proximity. When he had closed to within ten feet of the tee-shirt-and-shorts-wearing Z, he promptly put it down with two rounds to the back of its head, sending its skullcap and half a head of hair careening end over end across the room.

As he crabbed sideways cutting the room, he targeted the portly female Z that had obviously suffered a terrible attack at the hands and teeth of the dead. He made a face at the sight as the creature lumbered around on tree-trunk-sized legs and faced him. The muumuu that the woman had been wearing before she died had been reduced to strips of fabric where the feeding Zs had torn into her abdomen. Raised teeth-marks a vicious shade of purple peppered its pale abdomen. All of the organs needed to sustain life were missing, leaving only yellowed fat framing the empty chest cavity. Feeling more than a little sorry for the pathetic sight, he put a round in each eye and ended her hell on earth.

The third monster was still a few yards away and had turned at the sound of the first suppressed salvo. Simultaneously it snarled and raised its arms, then caromed off a desk and staggered towards the operator.

Keeping a three-desk buffer, Cade went to one knee, steadied his aim atop a computer printer, and caressed the trigger twice. The Glock rocked in his grip sending lethal lead into the walking cadaver's open mouth, and sending teeth, tongue, and blood erupting through a shredded cheek. The muzzle-climb from the first discharge changed the angle minutely, sending the second round into its left eye and peeling a flap of dermis and skull backwards as the bullet and its considerable kinetic energy was absorbed by bone and brain.

Ten seconds had elapsed between Cade's solo entry and the third Z hitting the ground. "Clear," he called out. "Last man through secure the door."

No effin way, el Capitán, thought Lopez when he heard this. He was rear guard, therefore he was the one whom Cade expected to manhandle the dead body out of the way. Still recovering from the ordeal of carrying the wriggling Alpha specimen up fourteen flights of stairs at the CDC in Atlanta, the prospect of touching another Z corpse—moving or not—didn't sit well with the highly religious operator.

Cade felt his heart rate returning to normal as he swapped magazines in the Glock and racked a new round into the chamber. He swept his gaze around the room, waiting for the rest of the team to file in.

"Clear," was called out by both Tice and Cross as they stepped over the decapitated woman and hustled through the doorway.

Lopez reached the landing last. He checked the stairway to ensure he was alone. *Clear.* He regarded the task waiting near his feet. *Fuck.* His nose crinkled at the sight of the shredded and decapitated body. Nonplussed, he swung his M4 behind his back, letting it hang on its sling, and reluctantly grabbed the clammy corpse by its bloated ankles. Muttering a few Spanish curse words, he dragged it the rest of the way inside and clicked the door shut, then announced that the door was cleared and secured.

Calling out more orders, Cade sent Cross to check out the fishbowl-looking conference room. He told Lopez and Tice to hang tight. He went down the row of offices on the left, checking them for survivors, then came back empty-handed with a look of resignation on his face.

"Clear," called Cross from across the room.

"Moving to four," Cade stated calmly. He flipped down his night vision goggles, approached the door to the stairs, and held up a fist.

The three other team members donned their goggles and quietly waited.

Cade put his ear the metal door. *Nothing*. He gently pushed the panic bar, and entered the well with the silencer on the Glock's business end leading the way.

The team made both flights of stairs and the landing in between without running into trouble.

Cade stood in front of the fourth-floor door with the team stacked up behind him. He cocked his head and listened to the sounds in the stairwell. They seemed to have increased in volume, though thankfully not in tempo. From past experience he knew stairs gave Zs trouble, so he figured the multiple flights might buy the team enough time to get to the third floor without having to fight a bunch of them in the close quarters of the stairwell.

He pressed his ear to the door. "Lots of movement," he whispered. He rose and motioned Tice forward.

Without a word Tice descended the stairs, crabbed past Cross and went to a knee in front of the steel door. He pulled a flexible fiber-optic periscope from a pocket and manipulated the lens with the small trigger at the base of the cable.

Cade watched through his NVGs as what resembled a glowing green eye on the end of a bendable stock swiveled around like something alive.

Tice squeezed the lens under the vinyl door sweep affixed to the bottom edge of the door, powered up the four-inch-square LCD screen and mated the display to the fiber optic mast.

"Contact," Tice called out as he swept the lens back and forth.

Master of the obvious, thought Lopez, who had glanced over the Spook's shoulder. Though the '*Contacts*' on the screen appeared but an inch tall, there had to be at least twenty of them stumbling around the sunlit room which looked to be identical in layout and furnishings to the one they had just cleared.

Still affected by his decision to abandon the survivors on the dam at the Flaming Gorge Recreation area, and with the desperate looks on the faces of the lady and her kids adrift on the sailboat still visiting him nightly, Cade weighed the odds and made the difficult call. "Wrap it up Tice... I've seen enough." He paused for a moment, second-guessing his decision, then continued. "Five and four are cleared... There are no survivors. Moving on to three."

"Copy that," replied Gaines.

Thank God, thought Lopez, pushing the flashbacks from the CDC mission to the back of his mind.

A few seconds later, when the team had reached the landing between floors four and three, Cade spied the source of the scuffing sounds. Glowing green in his goggles, on the flight below the door to the third floor, at least a dozen undead were climbing upwards on shaky legs, one stair at a time.

Holstering the Glock, he pressed his left shoulder to the wall, and using hand signals which only the team could see in the dark, ordered Cross to engage the rear of the pack and Tice and Lopez to hold fire and continue watching their six.

He swung his M4 around and thumbed on the infra-red laser pointer attached to the weapon's Picatinny rail. About the size of a pack of cigarettes, the device emitted a beam in the light spectrum that could only be seen with a night vision device.

Like a mini light saber, the green beam lanced out when Cade depressed the thumb switch. He flicked the weapon from safe to single shot and trained the bouncing dot on the nearest Z. He tensed his finger on the trigger, pulling up a few pounds of pressure, and said a silent prayer. He waited for Cross to activate his laser, and when the President's top agent had a Z painted with his beam, Cade opened fire.

Instantly the creatures looked upward toward the muzzle flashes which illuminated their ghastly features. Shadowy green gave way to a strobe-like effect as Cade and Cross pumped deadly accurate fire into their midst.

The lead creature caught a round from Cade's M4 between the eyes; its brains and skull painted a glowing Rorschach pattern on the cool cement wall. He shifted aim and double-tapped a couple of twentysomething shamblers. The fact that they wore tattered everyday street clothes sent a shiver of worry down his spine. *I sure hope the bottom floor isn't open to the dead in the plaza, because if it is,* he thought, *then this was going to be a long day.*

The time for noise discipline had passed. "Lopez, go back up and prop open the door to five. It'll give the Zs somewhere to go," Cade said. "Tice... watch our six and when Lopez returns scope the door."

There was no response. None was necessary at this point. Each man had been trained to operate autonomously and think critically.

Cross continued firing 4.6x30mm lead into the living corpses, and by the time he'd expended the entire twenty rounds in the mag he had put down seven or eight of them.

The echo of boots clomping down the stairs preceded Lopez's reappearance on the landing. "Done," he said over the comms.

"How many, Tice?" Cade bellowed.

"Not there yet."

"Hurry it up." Cade swapped out mags and added more fire down the stairwell at the Zs as they kept coming, scrabbling through the fallen flesh.

"Half a dozen Zs inside," Tice said from above.

"Pop the door," Cade said, handing over the lock gun. "You and Lopez start clearing the floor. Watch for collateral damage. The survivors should be in the northwest corner... inside the fishbowl."

A few seconds after Tice had defeated the lock and the two operators had disappeared inside, Cade tapped Cross on the shoulder and stabbed a thumb towards the open door.

Cross, understanding the hand signal, backpedaled up the stairs, watching as Cade commenced firing on the advancing pack.

A moment later the stairwell was drowned in silence as the bolt on Cade's carbine locked open. He blinked at the cordite haze hanging in the air and punched the mag from the M4. As it clattered to the stairs amongst the expended brass, he ripped the Velcro securing the fresh mag to his MOLLE gear and with a little tug let it fall into his palm. Finally, in one practiced motion, he slapped it home and charged a fresh round. Then, seeing that more Zs were clambering to get over their fallen, he turned and took the stairs two at a time, legs pumping like pistons. Once he made the landing and crossed the threshold into the bright room, Agent Cross, who had been waiting for him, slammed the door shut.

Cade put his back to the door, pushed the goggles from his face, and looked around the room. And as his eyes adjusted to bright sunshine, he noticed the dozens of shell casings scattered about the light gray carpet and then he spotted the leaking bodies lying in various death poses not five feet in front of his face. Then his gaze drifted to Lopez and Tice, who had their backs to him. Finally, he looked beyond them at the weary faces staring through the sheen of dried bodily fluids and bloody handprints smeared on the thick glass walls of the conference room. On those faces he saw a mixture of emotions: relief, fear, happiness, and for reasons unknown to him—a few of the faces displayed looks that seemed scathing and angry. Then, something else dawned on him—somehow the thirteen people he had counted from within the hovering chopper now amounted to, by his estimation, more than twenty.

Chapter 57
Outbreak - Day 16
Etna, Wyoming

Daymon slipped the transmission into park and reluctantly killed the engine. There were too many weapons pointing his way to do anything but.

He remembered the road sign they had passed a mile back promising that "Etna, Wyoming, Population 200" was a mere two miles ahead. *So close, yet so far*, he thought bitterly. Having not eaten for twenty-four hours and totally out of bottled water, they had pinned their resupply hopes on breaking into an uninhabited house on the outskirts of Etna.

Not gonna happen now, Eagle Eye G.I. Joe, Daymon thought. Truth be told, he was heated at himself for not being on high alert this close to a population center. And even more so because he hadn't noticed the roadblock before it was way too late to do anything but stand on the brakes.

He gazed along the full length of the looming yellow school bus and quickly determined there was no going over , under, or through it—there was no way to turn the Tahoe around. For a second he contemplated backing down the rise that had cleverly hidden the choke point and wrenching the police cruiser into a blistering J-turn and speeding away, but thought better of it seeing as how he was no stunt driver and outrunning bullets was always a losing proposition.

Blocking egress to his left was a large bulldozer and a half-filled mass grave. To the right was a sturdy guardrail, and beyond it a substantial copse of trees clinging to a hillside that fell off sharply.

He regarded the unsmiling faces and the muzzles protruding from the windows of the bus. He walked his gaze over the armed men and women, and then noticed the vivid red, white, and blue of Old Glory hanging limply from a standard planted near the front of the bus. The sight of it alone gave him a modicum of hope.

"What should we do?" asked Heidi, directing her question at Daymon.

Without answering her, he took matters into his own hands. He powered down his window and slowly stuck both arms outside of the vehicle where the people with guns pointed at him could see his empty hands. This sudden surrender garnered a frantic look from Heidi, who was still badly shaken from her first and hopefully last stint in captivity.

Daymon matched Charlie's gaze in the rearview. He figured since they were outgunned and between a rock and a hard place, at the very least they still had two things working in their favor: the fact that the vehicle he was sitting in was a bona fide black and white police cruiser complete with the low-profile light bar riding on top, and the words Jackson Hole Police Department plastered on nearly every flat surface was one. The other was the bona fide credentialed chief of police hailing from said city who just happened to be riding in the back of said police cruiser. Plus, with no fewer than fifteen rifles of indeterminate calibers aimed at the windshield, he thought by extending an olive branch on his end, the forced relationship might get off on the right foot.

Then the United States flag unfurled and a strong wind gust hit the Tahoe broadside. Daymon fought the urge to cover his nose and mouth as the sweet smell of death wafted in through his open window.

As soon as Daymon's hands came into view, a man in the driver's seat of the bus stuck a bullhorn to his lips and began his spiel. "*Driver*, keep your hands where they can be seen."

Duh, thought Daymon as he rested his forearms on the window channel.

Then the man belted out a series of nearly identical orders directed at the other three passengers. In a matter of minutes the Tahoe was inundated with the stench of death and there were four pairs of hands sticking out of the SUV's open windows.

After holding the posture for a couple of minutes with the sun tanning their forearms, the man who had been issuing amplified orders stepped from the bus, causing it to rear up noticeably on its shocks.

Another man with a Freedom Arms ball cap riding low over his eyes, clad in blue jeans and a tee shirt, mounted the bulldozer, fired it up and let it idle for a moment. Then with a belch of oily black exhaust the giant orange tractor reversed, providing a sizeable gap between its blade and the front of the school bus.

After a few seconds, the man who had been talking on the bullhorn lumbered through the opening, followed by four ordinary-looking men toting an assortment of shotguns and automatic rifles.

"Pretty good security," whispered Jenkins as he watched from his seat behind Daymon.

"Keep them where we can see them," the big man said as he approached the Tahoe on the driver's side. He walked with a slight shuffle and was nearly as wide as he was tall. He brought his mass to a halt a foot away from Daymon. He regarded everyone in the truck, pausing on each face for a beat. He dabbed some sweat from his brow and said, "That grave you see there." He stabbed his thick thumb over his shoulder. "That is where we put the walking dead when they wander in here. And if you all don't do as I say and cooperate fully you could find yourselves rotting away in there as well."

"Be ready," Jenkins whispered.

Suffering a severe charley horse, Tran fell back in his seat, causing his arms to retract into the cab.

In less than a second one of the security men had reacted and had jabbed his AR-15 inside the truck.

Jenkins stared down the muzzle and decided to stand down. Words were just that, after all. And the big man struck him as a talker. Not a killer.

Holding onto his spasming calf with both hands, Tran bowed his head and looked away from the weapon.

"State your business," the big man said, gazing at Daymon.

"Just passing through. That's all."

"How did you acquire the vehicle?" he demanded next.

Daymon said nothing. Instead he tilted his head toward the backseat.

The big man addressed Jenkins directly. "Why aren't you driving *your* own cruiser?"

"We were on the road between Victor and Alpine siphoning fuel when we were jumped by a large group... he just happened to be closest to the wheel," Jenkins answered as his gaze drifted from the apparent leader to the two armed men flanking him.

"Let me see your identification *and* your badge."

With slow precise movements, Jenkins complied without taking his eyes from the unwavering muzzles.

After a moment of scrutiny the big man returned the badge and credentials and the questioning resumed. "So, *Chief Jenkins...* where are you all headed and why'd you leave your jurisdiction?"

Jenkins eyed the rotund man and felt his blood run hot. Being on the other side of the questioning was uncharted waters for the Jackson police chief. "We're on our way to Salt Lake," he lied. "Daymon here has reason to believe his family is still alive. And my jurisdiction no longer exists... Jackson Hole is finished. The dead overran our roadblock. Hell, from the looks of yours I shoulda taken a play out of your book," he added, trying to remain on the big man's good side.

"How do you fit in with those contractor New American whackos that have been roaming all over *our* Wyoming?"

Finally a chance to tell the truth, Jenkins thought. "I distanced myself from them on day one, and I ran away as soon as the opportunity presented itself."

The big man studied Jenkins for a long minute. "I believe you, Chief Jenkins," he finally said. "In my line of work a fella has to have a finely tuned BS detector."

Jenkins said nothing.

"You do realize that you're taking the long route to Salt Lake," the big man stated.

Jenkins nodded slowly. "We had the 89 bridge over the Snake barricaded pretty good... or so we thought. The dead overran Jackson three days ago. We had no choice but to escape via the Teton Pass."

The big man attempted to bend at the waist. His upper body only hinged over a few degrees and his gut leapt from under his John Deere tee shirt. He looked past Daymon and locked eyes with Heidi.

Heidi's blood ran cold. But before she could act on her fight or flight impulse, the big man smiled and said, "I don't have the *heart* to send you all around the long way..."—Daymon and Jenkins exchanged glances but remained stoic. The time would come later when they could laugh at the inside joke—"... so when Harley moves the tractor I want you all to drive through real slow and follow the first vehicle you see. Follow it all the way through to the edge of town and they'll let you on through to the other side. We can't help you with supplies or fuel so don't ask."

Leaning out the rear window, Jenkins caught the big man's attention. "Can I ask you a question?"

"What is it?"

"First off, thanks for letting us pass."

The man winked.

"What's your name and what do you do here in Etna?"

"Name's Mr. Carter. I taught fifth grade at Etna Elementary."

Jenkins smiled at the teacher and powered his window shut. "Truth's stranger than fiction," he said.

"I couldn't help it," Tran said. "My calf knotted up. I thought we were doomed."

Heidi exhaled sharply. "Me too. But damn it feels good to know that not everyone is on the side of darkness," she said.

Daymon started the truck, and for some reason something that Cade had said days ago popped into his head. He vowed to himself he'd follow the man's sage advice and remember to *stay frosty* from this moment forward.

***

Daymon followed close behind the old slant-back Chevy Nova as they passed through the tiny downtown core of Etna, Wyoming. Nothing stood out. Every building and house looked to have been transplanted from another era. There were no traffic lights. There were no billboards, and most importantly, there were no dead.

"Want to switch places with me?" Daymon asked Jenkins.

"You go ahead. I'm going to kick back."

"After that screw up back there?"

"No Daymon... that was no *screw up*," drawled Jenkins. "I didn't see the roadblock neither. And I was *lookin'*." He donned his hat and pulled it over his eyes, then added, "You done good. You drive the rest of the way."

"How far?" Heidi asked.

The Nova pulled aside just prior to an old green bridge, crossing some anonymous creek. On the other side was a roadblock nearly identical to the one at the other end of Etna. The driver waved them across about the same time the bus pulled away from the far end of the bridge, leaving an inviting stretch of tree-lined highway beckoning.

Tipping his hat up, Jenkins looked at Daymon in the rearview and said, "That, my friend, was a *First Blood* moment. Only this time John J. Rambo was escorting old Galt out of town." He let the hat cover his eyes and slumped into the seat. He doubted if his comment meant anything to the other three, but to a small town chief like him—the leniency showed them by Mr. Carter was a Godsend.

Chapter 58
Outbreak- Day 16
Winters's Compound
Eden, Utah

Gus put his eye to the scope atop his Les Baer AR-15, aimed for the spot where the road cut into the forest, and braced his arms on his knees. He was sitting Indian style amongst the short scrub brush just inside the tree line, seventy-five yards uphill from the spot where earlier he had buried the canisters on the side of the road.

He could hear some type of vehicle approaching, and, judging by the high performance whine of its engine, he guessed it was either an exotic supercar or one of those Japanese made-crotch rockets; considering the fact that he was in Utah and not Southern California, his money was on the latter.

"Stand by," he said into the two-way. He listened intently and still couldn't determine what was approaching. "I've got at least one vehicle coming our way from the west."

Duncan swiveled the turret-mounted gun to the right a few degrees so that it was trained down the westernmost stretch of 39. He remained still, peering through the camouflage netting, and contemplated the possible scenarios. His first inclination was that his gut instinct had been right and the plan he had set into motion the previous day was about to pay off in spades.

Releasing Chance on his own recognizance had been a gamble that most everyone in the compound had not agreed with. However, Duncan thought fighting a large hostile group out in the open with the element of surprise and the luxury of preparation was preferable to adopting a defensive posture and eventually be forced to engage them, and possibly more rotters, in the woods.

"I want *everyone* to hold fire until I give the word," said Duncan. He figured it was about to go down one of two ways: whoever was approaching could just be a neutral survivor, however unlikely, and would pass on through, or, the interlopers would prove him right by either storming the compound or cutting the fence and once again letting the rotters in. *Either action in the latter category*, he thought, *will justify springing the ambush on them.*

In no time the source of the noise, a neon-orange motorcycle with black tiger stripes and a piercing blue headlight, rocketed from the forest's embrace. Wide and low and riding on fat performance rubber, Gus pegged it as one of the 1200cc models. He watched it crest the rise at high speed, jink around a shambling rotter, and then suddenly the front end dipped and the engine howled in protest as the rider simultaneously braked and rapidly downshifted, bringing the fiberglass-clad bike to a standstill fifty yards short of Duncan's *pet* zombies.

Balancing the idling bike between his legs, the rider, who was wearing a full-faced helmet painted to match, produced a pair of binoculars from inside his jacket, flipped up the mirrored visor, and glassed the entire valley. As the rider panned the field glasses over to the area where the Chance kid had been conducting his surveillance the day before, Gus noticed scraggly twists of blonde hair darting snakelike from under the bottom of the helmet.

Gus keyed his mike and said, "That Chance kid is back and I've got a clean shot on him." He tensed his finger on the trigger, drawing up a few pounds of pressure. *Come on Duncan, make the call*, he thought to himself.

"I've got him bracketed as well," said Logan, who was positioned the farthest away due east, and save for the Turret-mounted M2, wielded the most powerful rifle in the group. His finger also was itching to pull the trigger and send a .50 caliber projectile through the big Barrett sniper rifle and downrange through the rider's facemask.

"Stand down. He's just probing us," Duncan blurted. "I'd bet the rest of his posse is within spitting distance. Hold your fire Gus. Hold your fire Logan."

In fact, unbeknownst to the kid on the bike, he presently had seven sets of eyes and the same number of weapons trained on him. Jamie and Chief were on the high side of the hill, a little west of Duncan and not too far from the hidden entrance leading to the compound. And secreted in the tree line on the compound side of 39, at an oblique angle from the planted IEDs, Phil and Lev waited patiently in the low scrub.

Unaware that his life had just been spared for the second time in less than twenty-four hours, Chance stowed the binoculars and spun the bike in a tight one-eighty on the center line, leaving a half-moon of burnt rubber behind. In seconds the bike became an orange blur speeding away, its exhaust note taunting the hidden shooters.

Chapter 59
Outbreak - Day 16
National Microbiology Laboratory
Winnipeg, Manitoba Canada

The small Asian woman was first to venture from inside the gore-spattered glass prison. She took a few tentative steps onto the carpet, looked over the men clad in camouflage and body armor who towered over her. Then a tear traced her cheek and she rushed Cade and threw her arms around his neck. She planted a peck on his sooty cheek and broke down sobbing, clinging firmly to his MOLLE gear.

The others exiting the room at a slow trickle seemed to be in a state of shock. Cade had seen the reaction many times before, but it wouldn't take long for their brains to process what their eyes were seeing.

"Who is in charge here?" Cade asked as he looked over the disheveled group.

Silence.

A round and matronly-looking woman stepped forward. Gray hair clutched in a large plastic clip positioned at the rear of her head and a pair of bifocals perched on her nose, she looked like she'd be at home herding kindergartners for a living. She put her arm around the Asian lady and eased her away from Cade. She bent to the petite woman's level and looked her in the eyes. "Mary," she said softly. "This man has some questions for you."

"Screw that," said a man in the back. He was African American, and stood a head over the others. "I only listened to her cause she had a Level 4 clearance. I'm not even in her work group." He shook his head and his face tightened. "I shoulda left with the others when I had the chance."

"The others are dead, *Andy*. Don't you get that yet?" said a woman dressed in light blue hospital scrubs. "They were attacked before they even got out of the building, and they are still walking around down there."

"You guys are Americans, aren't you?" asked another man who was also dressed in utilitarian blue hospital-style scrubs. He furrowed his brow and stabbed a finger at Tice's chest. "It's all your fault... you didn't shut down air travel soon enough. And now look what we're facing."

Tice took a step back and let the man continue his rant.

After getting the lady named Mary seated and allowing her a few moments to collect herself, Cade asked her to start from the beginning.

Five minutes into her story, Cade had gathered that Mary's group had been composed of virologists and microbiologists who had been working to get a handle on the Omega virus in conjunction with the CDC in Atlanta up until the phones and the Internet went down. All of the bio level 4 personnel had been in the process of evacuating from the below-ground containment facility when the perimeter fell. She mentioned seeing the glass on the ground level implode from errant gunfire. Then the resulting tide of dead that had poured into the building split her group and she and two others had been forced to take to higher ground.

"Only the three of you worked with the Level 4 bugs in the bio containment facility in the basement?" Cade questioned as he pointed at Mary, the schoolmarm-looking lady named Rita, and a white man who appeared to be in his fifties and was wearing a name tag that read *Virgil.* "Where did the rest of the people on your team go?"

"The others followed the soldiers outside... we were right on their heels, then we got cut off and had no choice but to duck back into the stairway."

There was silence for a moment, then Cade hailed Gaines. "This is Anvil Actual, sit-rep to follow. How copy?"

Gaines answered at once. "Good copy, Anvil Actual. Go ahead."

Cade took a moment and explained the situation in detail.

"*Twenty-one...* did I hear you correctly, Anvil?"

"Roger that. Three principals. Eighteen survivors."

"Wait one while I consult with Ripley," Gaines replied.

"Roger that," said Cade.

"So you escaped the mayhem on the ground level and then you all made it back to the stairwell..." Cade took a second to think. "Are you certain you closed the stairwell door behind you?"

"Of course. I'm no dummy," Mary said. Virgil nodded in agreement. "Because the windows were shot out, the lobby has got to be filled with dead by now," he added.

"Ten of our group went out three days ago..." said Mary.

Cade pointed to the dead Zs on the floor. "And these ones?"

"Those are some of the ten that originally tried to run for it," Mary said as she rubbed her temples. "Three minutes... less than three minutes and they were back banging on the door." She broke down, sobbing.

"And you let them back in?" said Lopez incredulously.

Andy piped up. "We didn't know they were bit. No way to know that. And once they were back inside and seemed OK, nobody knew what to do." He shot an indicting glare at Mary. "And no one took *charge.*" Heads nodded in unison.

"It was my idea to go into the conference room," Mary proffered.

"You mean you got us *trapped* in the conference room," said someone from the rear of the group.

"I didn't want to let them back in," said Andy in a melancholy voice.

"Can't change the past," said Cade coolly.

"Don't have to make the same mistake twice either," Andy spat. "I'm done taking orders from her."

As some of the other survivors tried to calm the tall man, even tugging on his arms to encourage him to sit, Cade issued a couple of orders. "Cross, take a look outside, tell me what you see."

Cross made his way to the windows and looked down at the entry, which was flanked by a carpet of colorful flowers and cement planters with short well-manicured shrubs growing from them. The landscaping had been trampled and at least two dozen dead seemed to be able to enter and exit the building at will. Though he couldn't verify if the windows and doors below had been compromised, the movements of the Zs all but confirmed Mary's account.

"What do you need me to do, Captain?" Tice asked. He was sitting cross-legged on the floor with his M4 resting across his knees.

"Go scope the door to the stairwell," Cade replied. "I'm hopeful the Zs found the fifth floor door Lopez left ajar and are hunting for fresh meat up there."

"I'm going to have to use the low-light mode," Tice said, thinking out loud.

"Whatever it takes, make it happen," said Cade. Then he eyed Mary and fired a couple of questions at her. "From the air I saw a glass sky bridge attached to the east side of the building. How do we access it from here and where will it take us?"

"Second floor, northeast corner," she said, pointing towards the far end of the expansive room near where the Delta Team had emerged onto the third floor. "That stairwell lets out pretty close to the bridge off of the second floor mezzanine, and it's used mostly to access the parking lots without having to deal with the cars coming and going during a shift change. There are several hundred people who work in different buildings scattered all over the campus. The NML, in the sub-basement, where me and Rita and Virg worked, employs just a fraction of the workforce."

But your jobs are the most important, and the most dangerous, Cade thought. He suddenly realized that he was faced with a serious moral dilemma. One that no amount of extra training could have prepared him for. The cold, indifferent decision would be to leave most of these Canadian citizens to fend for themselves and hustle just the three scientists up to the roof and spirit them away in Jedi One-One.

But the *right* decision, which he had embraced almost instantly, would be to see all twenty-one of the survivors to safety. Though it was going to be difficult to pull off, and he doubted everyone was going to make it out alive, to make it happen he had to find an LZ—landing zone—where both the Ghost and the Osprey could land safely and exfil *all* of the workers. *Two birds with one stone*, he thought.

Chapter 60
Outbreak - Day 16
Winters's Compound
Eden, Utah

Duncan glanced at his watch. Less than fifteen minutes had passed, and by his estimation the people who had passively attacked the compound days ago should be rounding the bend down the hill at any minute.

He'd allotted five minutes for Chance to motor away and tell the rest of the group that he had taken a long hard look (a lie on the kid's part) and that the coast was clear. Then he gathered that another five minutes would probably be burned as the brain trust argued over who was going to do what, when, and to whom. And then, finally, Duncan presumed it would take at least three hundred more seconds for whomever the leader was to give a short pep talk, rally the troops, and make their way east towards the compound all full of piss and vinegar and ready to unleash hell.

Exactly sixteen minutes and thirteen seconds had gone by before Chance and his shiny motorcycle returned.

But this time he was not alone.

With the noon sun flaring from the flat windshields, two tan Humvees emerged from the forested stretch of road. Next, three large SUVs still sporting dealer plates materialized behind the former National Guard Hummers.

Duncan guessed the five vehicles were maintaining about a thirty-five mile-per-hour clip while keeping bumper to bumper in a single file column. *Looks good in the movies*, he thought darkly. *Deadly as hell in real life*. Vietnam, Iraq, Afghanistan, or ancient Carthage, it didn't matter where, the tactic of ambush—attacking from concealment and with an element of surprise—hadn't changed much over thousands of years. And travelling so close together, whether on foot, horseback, or in a modern vehicle was, for the people being ambushed, a recipe for disaster.

Duncan kept the field glasses trained on the convoy until the kid on the bike pulled off the road in virtually the same place as he had before.

The plan was coming together, Duncan thought. The zombies on the road near the compound's hidden entrance had precisely the effect on the bad guys that he was hoping for.

The lead Humvee stopped abreast of the motorcycle just as Chance dismounted.

Through the binoculars, Duncan watched Chance start a conversation with the driver, while at the same time another man, wearing woodland camo and carrying a large pair of bolt cutters, jumped out of the middle SUV and quickly went to work cutting the fence.

"Lev," Duncan said dryly. "Kill the guy cutting the fence first."

"Roger that," replied the former 11 Bravo-Infantryman, U.S. Army.

"You made your bed, Chance," Duncan muttered. "Now you're going to take a dirt nap in it." He tracked his gaze to the left to the fence post with the X scratched into it. Although the second Humvee wasn't fully bracketed in the kill zone, he decided to spring the ambush anyway. He traded the binoculars for the two-way radio and clicked the transmit button twice. His hands found the twin vertical grips of the Ma Deuce. He swiveled the barrel up and placed the sights a hair above the passenger-side headlamp on the black Toyota at the rear of the column. Then, he took a steadying breath and depressed the paddle-shaped trigger with both thumbs.

Chapter 61
Outbreak - Day 16
National Microbiology Laboratory
Winnipeg, Manitoba Canada

All twenty-one of the survivors were assembled in front of Cade as he paced the room, thinking about what to say first. He stopped and stood still directly in front of the three scientists, who were each sitting in plush leather chairs taken from the conference room. Before speaking, he looked over their heads and walked his gaze across the worry-filled faces of the others, who were mostly lab assistants and clerical workers.

"I have been sent here to rescue anyone with experience working with pathogens in a lab environment... particularly BSL-4—bio safety level 4."

At this disclosure, several of the younger people blanched and looked at one another. Cade could hear the gears turn in their minds as they asked themselves if they were expendable or not.

"If we *all* work together and do our part, each and every one of you will make it out of here alive." He cringed inside because he knew the probability of that statement coming to fruition was nearly impossible. He looked over the faces and picked out the most likely to become fodder for the Zs, and made a mental note to place them on the inside of the group when they got underway. "The second we step into the stairwell, you *must* keep quiet, and while we are in there you *must not* stop moving forward. Everyone on my team has got night vision devices and will guide us where we need to go, so just keep close to one another and pretend we are playing follow the leader. It will be *totally* dark, so use the handrail or your neighbor's shoulder for support. And most importantly—and this I *cannot* stress enough—*do not stray from the group.* You've already seen your colleagues *turn* in front of your eyes," Cade said, pointing to the dead Zs lying in the spreading pool of bodily fluids. "Once infected a person can turn in *seconds.* I have personally seen a man hold out for *hours* before succumbing to Omega. But as *all* of you know, it *will* happen eventually. So if you get bit, *I* will have no choice but to leave you behind." Cade let his words sink in for a beat and then said, "Any questions?"

Andy shot his hand into the air. "If I get bit I want one of you guys to finish me off. I watched my friends here go through the process... it's effed up. Turning into one of them ain't pretty." He paused, then realized he still had his hand up and put it down slowly.

"Remember what I just told you. Keep your wits about you and all of us will get out of here alive," Cade lied.

"Just shoot me right here," Andy said, pointing at his temple. He looked over his colleagues and then settled his gaze on Cade. "'Cause I'd rather die than become one of them."

You and me both, bro, Lopez thought as he paced the carpet.

"Just follow our lead, keep breathing, and don't panic," Cade said, trying to assuage the tall man's concern. "We *will* get you out of here."

"Where are you taking us?" asked another man. The same man who had implied that America had been the source of the Omega outbreak.

"Colorado Springs," Cade said, staring the man down. "You *will* be guests of the United States for a short time. Then you can go wherever you please," he lied. It sounded promising, but it was all he could conjure up.

"I'm not going to America," said Mister Conspiracy.

"Anyone who wants to stay here is more than welcome to," Cade shot back. "We leave *now*."

A woman standing on the periphery, who had been quiet until now, blurted out another question. "Why can't we use a flashlight in there?"

Cade tapped the NVGs attached to his helmet. "The dead are blind in the dark," he said as the lies piled on. The truth was the Z bodies had piled up two deep in the stairway and he didn't want any of the civilians to see the carnage he had wrought, get spooked, and start a stampede. Moving them along was going to be a clusterfuck as it was, and doing so if they were panicky would only make matters worse. "These goggles will give us the upper hand. You just have to have a little faith..."

Tice's voice crackled in Cade's earpiece. "We have a window. The landing is clear."

"Let's go," Cade bellowed. "I'll take point. Tice and Cross, you two play sheepdog in the middle. And Cross..." The black-clad Secret Service agent paused with one hand on his NVGs, looked over and caught Cade's eye. "You guard the *principals*." Cade's emphasis on the word principals wasn't lost on Cross, who figured out that he was expected to treat the trio of scientists no different than President Clay—and if that meant taking a bite for one of them, he was prepared to do so.

Tice looked up from the LCD screen he had been eyeballing. "Landing and stairwell is still clear," he said.

Though he didn't need to state the obvious, Cade looked at Lopez and said, "You get our six and close the door behind you."

"Roger that," he replied as he performed the sign of the cross over his tan MOLLE gear bristling with fully loaded magazines.

Cross took charge of the civilians, moving them over into the narrow hall near the door, and then he pulled Mary aside and whispered into her ear. "You and Rita and Virgil have to stick to me like Velcro. We will be in the *middle* of the pack and that's where we have to stay." He pulled away and locked eyes with the lead scientist. "*Understood?*" Mary just regarded him with wide eyes and delivered a subtle nod.

Thick and sweet, the odor of death invaded the room as Tice opened the door to the stairway.

Chapter 62
Outbreak - Day 16
Randolph, Utah

Daymon wheeled the Tahoe south on 89, following the rural highway as it wove across the border between Wyoming and Utah, transiting 30 in spots over the one hundred and twelve miles. They passed through long stretches of flat farmland dotted with nondescript dwellings and rusted farm implements, while the Bridger National Forest, lush and green, kept them company off the driver's side. Daymon negotiated a few small pileups with people dead and undead festering in the mangled vehicles. Heeding his earlier mental note, he drove cautiously, head on a swivel, staying frosty, through a number of small towns with names like Thayne, Grover, Smoot, and Cokeville. After having passed straight through without having any contact with other living, breathing humans (good or evil) Daymon was beginning to relax from the pucker-inducing encounter in Etna. Then, just outside of Randolph, Utah, he came to the realization that his eyeteeth were beginning to float and he needed to piss. He slowed as he came to the sign which he presumed marked the city limits, or at the very least the county line.

"Randolph... population four hundred and sixty-four. What do you think?" Daymon queried. "Stop and stretch our legs... get some water?"

"How far to the compound?" asked Jenkins.

After finding the correct button on the GPS navigation unit on the Tahoe's spaceship-like dash, Daymon waited for the number to display. "Says sixty miles... but I cannot wait. Can't tie it off. Can't pinch it while I drive one-handed either..."

"We get the point," Heidi said. "I'm not holding it for you either, so you pick the place."

He drove for another mile and pulled into a boarded-up gas station/repair shop called *Tony's*. He left the engine running and hopped out of the conditioned air, and was instantly blasted by a wall of humidity. It had to be in the low nineties, and suddenly he coveted an ice cold, unnaturally yellow-hued banana Slurpee. *What a thing to crave*, he thought as he attempted to write his name in urine on the superheated cement. Not a cold Silver Bullet or a Cadillac Margarita, but a Slurpee. What *has* the world come to. He smiled inwardly.

As he was in the middle of one of those two minute, *when the hell is it ever going to end* type of squirts, someone in the Tahoe honked the horn. He jumped and let go of himself, peeing on his boots in the process. *Very funny*, he thought. He glared back at the SUV and noticed Heidi in the midst of throes of laughter. He thought about throwing her the bird but decided to just be grateful she was making progress. When he turned to resume his business, he caught some movement from behind one of the broken-down cars that *Tony* was never going to repair. He backpedaled and zipped his pants at the same time as a flesh eater emerged from behind a Ford Econoline Van. By the time he had made it to the Tahoe and jumped inside, the abomination was making its way around the cruiser's tubular grill-guard.

"That's Tony," Heidi blurted out. "Says so on the nametag."

"Precious, but you almost fed me to Tony," Daymon barked.

In the late stages of decomposition, the creature was one of the quiet stalkers. Daymon had been seeing more of these lately.

He made another mental note to go over some of the finer points of surviving in the new world with his better half. Of which honking the horn was not one.

He reversed away from Tony, slapped the transmission into drive, and powered around the mute shambler. After consulting the GPS, he said in his best Ralph Kramden bus driver's voice, "Next stop fifty-five miles, Logan Winters's compound."

Chapter 63
Outbreak - Day 16
Logan Winters's Compound
Eden, Utah

Duncan aimed low and walked his fire up and to the right. Finger-sized .50 caliber bullets spewed from the Ma Deuce as the ambush he had just sprung unfolded in slow motion.

In the rear of the column, the black Toyota he was shooting at lost a headlight in a blossom of sparkling glass, and then yellow-green coolant gushed from the pierced radiator and began to pool under the front bumper.

The next two rounds carved foot-long silver channels in the sheet metal, then punched through and became lodged somewhere near the firewall. Finally, the last two shells in the salvo blasted fist-sized holes through the windshield and splattered the driver's upper half all over his backseat passengers. By the time the first burst—lasting little more than two seconds—had left the muzzle and hit down range, a number of bad guys had bailed from their vehicles.

While Woodland Camo Guy divided his attention between cutting the barbed wire and watching the rotters only a car length from him, he was nearly cut in half by a half-dozen rounds fired from the nearby underbrush. Holding in his guts with both hands, he went hard to the ground, face first. He screamed and writhed and pushed his toes against the road, attempting to crawl the short distance to the perceived safety of the Humvee.

Meanwhile, Logan was splayed out on his stomach in the grass three hundred yards to the east. The first vehicle in the column was bracketed in the scope atop his thirty-pound Barrett M82A1 sniper rifle. His initial shot was low, evidenced by the sparks and vaporized paint as the round, traveling 2,800 feet per second, pierced the steel bumper and the body directly behind it before burrowing under a metal plate next to the rugged vehicle's wheel well. After the miss, Logan adjusted his aim upwards, exhaled slowly and drew up the trigger pull. He caressed the trigger between heartbeats and then whooped when a geyser of steam erupted from the Humvee's ruptured radiator. If the .50 caliber round had performed as designed, he reasoned, there was a good chance the slug had also cracked the engine block, thus immobilizing the vehicle. He shifted his aim alongside the vehicle where the motorcycle rider was crouched. He still wore the orange helmet that all but screamed *AIM HERE*. So Logan did just that. The wedge-shaped muzzle brake was still dispensing wisps of smoke as he snugged the rifle to his shoulder. He went through the same breathing routine and then caressed the trigger. Through the ten-power scope he watched the helmet split like a robin's egg. One half flew off towards the fence as the other spun down the road, spinning like a gaudy top. His eye perceived Chance's bone, blood, and brain matter as a spreading pink mist as the near-supersonic bullet decapitated the dreadlocked kid.

Back in the Hummer, on the sloping hill north of the ambush, Duncan shifted his aim left, targeting the vehicle in the middle of the pack. At the same time, across the road on the compound side, Lev and Phillip raked staccato bursts of gunfire right to left along the sides of the thin-skinned SUVs.

"I've got a couple of squirters..." said Lev over his two-way, indicating two men who had just dismounted the second Humvee and were sprinting towards the lead vehicle. "But they just fucked themselves," he added as the men came face to face with the clutch of rotters.

One of the camouflage-clad men panicked and opened up with his AK-47, chattering out an entire magazine with no adverse effects on the monsters.

Dressed for war and clueless, thought Lev as he considered euthanizing the pair, but instead sprayed a full magazine into the occupants of the fourth vehicle.

For a brief moment the kill zone was dead silent, and then the two men who were just overrun began to scream. Their cries, carrying up the hill, sent chills dancing around Duncan's ribcage and up his spine. In a way, he wished they were on his side of the convoy so he could spare his ears and put them out of their misery.

Once again the telltale boom of Logan's Barrett reached his ears as his brother opened fire from the hide to the east. The first slug struck one of the buried propane tanks, causing an explosion that rocked the two Humvees on their springs and slapped the crotch rocket on its side.

Two more closely-spaced shots sent one of the canisters spinning heavenward, trailing flames like an oversize firework.

Down the road, Logan shifted his aim and—shoulder be damned—unloaded the remaining five rounds into the other two canisters which resulted in successive explosions similar to the first.

In the meantime, three men had exited the black Toyota at the rear of the column; they took cover behind its open doors and returned automatic rifle fire uphill at the camouflaged Humvee.

Sounding like angry metal hornets, rounds sizzled over Duncan's head and smacked into the plate surrounding the turret. One errant BB-sized piece of lead caromed off metal and burrowed under his skin, lodging somewhere above his right ear. *Close*, he thought as the pain began to spread.

Though the ambush, from Duncan's opening kill shot to his being fired upon just now, had happened in a few short seconds, it still felt to him like half a day had elapsed. Ignoring the throb in his temple and the warm trickle of blood, he popped his head up, aimed the M2 at the Toyota's driver door and squeezed off a three-second burst, walking it from the door behind the pulped driver to the gas-filler door. Twenty rounds cut through glass and sheet metal alike with ease. Two of the three men were killed instantly, shredded by flying lead and shards of glass and disintegrating body panel. The third man survived the initial onslaught only to die when the SUV's gas tank caught fire and exploded.

The middle vehicle, a silver Land Cruiser, managed to scrape past the Humvee in front and pull a partial U-turn. The desperate maneuver left his flank fully exposed to Jaime and Chief, who were tucked into the shadows up the hill.

Although Jaime had already killed in order to survive, she derived no pleasure in pulling the trigger on a living person. She aimed for the A-pillar to account for the Land Cruiser's forward movement, steadied her breathing like Logan had taught her, and squeezed off three closely-spaced shots.

The first 5.56 hardball slug passed through the driver's neck, severing his carotid, and then shattered the passenger window. The second round missed altogether. Her third bullet was a little low. It snapped his clavicle, then caromed downward and burrowed deep into the driver's left lung. Mortally wounded, the man's hands automatically went to his neck, and all control of the vehicle was lost. His foot inadvertently floored the accelerator, sending the big SUV plowing through two lengths of barbed wire before becoming wedged between two stately firs.

"Hold your fire," Duncan barked into the two-way. He snatched up his field glasses. *Gonna be a hell of a cleanup*, he thought as he scrutinized the burning and leaking vehicles. The orange motorcycle was also ablaze, the intense heat fusing its aerodynamic fairing to the pavement.

Duncan got on the radio and asked the group for a consensus on what their next move should be. He had hoped it wouldn't come to this, but when the fella started cutting the fence the line had been crossed. Duncan truly felt he had been left with no other choice.

Upon Gus's insistence, the group stayed in place for another thirty minutes; by then when nothing had moved, they opened fire on the handful of flesh eaters that remained in and around the kill zone. When that was done, Chief and Gus set off to track down the small number of rotters that found their way onto the property.

Duncan walked the road while keeping a good distance from the black Land Cruiser that was now sitting on bare rims in a pool of molten rubber.

"Mr. Winters... wait up," Lev called out. "I want to talk."

Slowing his pace, Duncan ran a hand through his thinning hair, Suddenly he felt at least a hundred years old. He looked at the row of bodies. A bunch of misguided men who had drawn their final breaths just minutes ago. He removed his glasses, plucked his handkerchief from a pocket, and wiped the cordite from the lenses.

"Yeah Lev, what's up?" Duncan asked.

"I think we just created a larger problem."

"Why do you say that?"

"I looked at the dead guys. I only recognized a couple of them from the attack on your neighbor's place."

Duncan donned his glasses and gave Lev's shoulder a gentle squeeze. "Well, that's a couple of them that aren't going to bother us again. And the rest are dead by association. I had a feeling that Chance wasn't going to be the last sacrificial lamb sent our way"—he gestured towards the corpses, then went on— "and those inept fools lying there alongside him pretty much proves my point."

There was a moment of silence.

Duncan watched Lev scan the bodies, maybe trying to come to some type of a conclusion. "Spit it out, Lev," he finally said. "What are you getting at?"

"There were a lot of hard-looking individuals down at the Gudsons. I've seen those kind of folks use some of the same kind of tactics in the *sandbox*. Send invalids, the infirm... even kids to do their dirty work. Soften the target so to speak. Then the hardcore jihadis join the fight... the kind that possess a modicum of discipline, not just the usual spray-and-pray type of jihadist."

"I would have to agree. We haven't seen their A game by a long shot." Duncan paused to collate his thoughts. "So we let them have Huntsville *and* Eden for that matter. We block the road and bolster our defenses. Then we take the helo up and go on a real foraging mission."

"That brings me to my last question," Lev said with a tilt to his head. "Who made you boss?"

Duncan shrugged. "If you had any better ideas you shoulda spoken up."

"Didn't need to," replied Lev.

A fusillade of gunfire rang out, then echoed into silence.

Duncan didn't acknowledge the sharp reports. "And why is that?" he asked. He let his arms fall to his sides and leaned against the silver Toyota.

"Because, without a Bradley fighting vehicle at my disposal, that's the same way I would have set up that ambush." He paused before he asked the burning question. "Where'd you learn that skill set?"

"Contrary to popular belief, Uncle Sam's sent fellas off to other wars," Duncan said. He looked away, remembering the fallen, and wondered how it was that he was still on this earth. "And just recently I found myself on the wrong end of a similar ambush outside of Boise. That one didn't end well for a few of the survivors in our group."

"Sorry to dredge that up," said Lev. "And as far as my *boss* comment... no worries on my part. As far as the rotters go... they are going to be a problem for us for a long time to come, but the good thing is they're somewhat predictable. It's the *humans* I'm worried about, and you and I both know this is only one battle in the coming war between the remaining." He turned to walk away, but Duncan grabbed his shoulder once again.

"I'm not trying to step on anyone's toes. As far as I am concerned, we are all equals here. But we are all going to have to sit down and decide how we want to proceed."

"What do you mean by *proceed?*"

"If we are ever going to enjoy any sense of security in our little neck of the woods, we will have to go on the offensive."

"Understood," Lev said.

"Lots of work still to be done here," Duncan said, changing the subject.

"Hopefully the fellas holding down the compound will save us a couple of *warm* ones."

The men shared a laugh and went back to work cleaning up their little stretch of 39.

***

Schriever AFB

The sun warming her face, Brook stretched out on a folding chaise lounge she had pilfered from the Family Resources building.

Raven was blazing around the cement walkways on her new mountain bike. She would zip by and rattle off the newest lap to her mom, then disappear from view and reappear from between another of the Quonset huts moments later, logging yet another notch in her belt.

"Twenty-three, pretty impressive!" called Brook as Raven blurred by with Max close behind.

She turned the white rose over in her hands and wished she knew what tomorrow was going to throw at her. It was after noon, and she had already tried to hunt down Wilson and the others and come up short. No matter. They would learn soon enough that today was a no go. 'Circumstances that were out of her control' is what she would tell them. Not a lie but not necessarily the whole truth either. Since the kids were not on a need to know basis, this didn't trouble Brook at all. With the terrorists still on the loose, Shrill had kept the base on lockdown. *Nobody was going anywhere*, Brook thought glumly. The thriving metropolis that Schriever was not, more than assured her that she'd bump into the others sooner or later.

Chapter 64
Outbreak - Day 16
National Microbiology Laboratory
Winnipeg, Manitoba Canada

As Cade picked his way along the blood-slickened layer of rotting corpses, every step he made forward caused the bodies to shift and slide atop one another. He paused equidistant to both landings with one boot grinding into a dead woman's neck and the other planted firmly on a first turn's bloated stomach. He glanced over his shoulder and saw Lopez enter the stairway behind the group. The stocky operator pulled his NVGs over his eyes and eased the door shut, enclosing them all in the tomb-like stairwell.

The civilians' frightened luminous eyes stared back at Cade, and one by one green beams lanced the air as Cross, Tice, and Lopez toggled on their lasers. And as Cade stood in the dark, tamping down his own rising fear, he toggled on his own laser and regarded the dead Zs underneath his boots.

Rendered in green by the NVGs, slack masks of death stared up at him like nightmares from a Boris Karloff flick. Hands frozen in death, skeletal and grotesque, seemed to be clawing at him from under the mass. And the stench, a thousand times worse now that the dead had been draining onto the stairs for several minutes, set his salivary glands off. With acidic fluids assaulting his throat and nose he swallowed, fighting off the urge to puke. Then a hand clapped his shoulder, mercifully returning his runaway mind to the task at hand.

Cade switched the M4 to his right hand and used the wall to steady himself as he leaped to the landing. He hit the cement like he'd been taught in basic training, letting his knees compress to absorb the energy of his hundred and eighty pounds, but when his boots made contact with the accumulated slurry of blood and bile his forward momentum brought him down to all fours.

With fluids dripping from his knee pads and the off hand which he had used to arrest his fall slickened with who knows what, he finally regained his balance and scrambled to his feet. *One more flight,* he told himself wearily as the footfalls from below grew louder and closer. Keeping his head near to the floor, he craned his neck around the handrail and eyeballed the next flight down, where he spotted a large number of zombies clambering towards him.

He turned and used hand signals to silently warn Cross, who in turn signaled Tice and Lopez of the impending contact.

With the possibility of having to scramble over another mound of rotting Zs looking more and more certain, Cade was determined to drop as many of them as he could as far down the stairs as possible. He picked the closest one of the Zs and painted its forehead with the laser. He calmed his breath and sent two 5.56 rounds tumbling into the monster's brain, which in turn pitched it heels over head into the undead mass below. He shifted his aim right and punched out a flesh eater's eyes with one impressive double-tap.

The mournful moans and hissing started a heartbeat later, and then increased in intensity after the second staccato volley from his M4.

Determined to get everyone out of the stairwell alive, Cade pushed forward, firing as he went. Over the constant softened reports of his suppressed carbine, he started to hear new sounds that let him know the strobe light effect of his muzzle flash, combined with the darkened claustrophobic confines of the stairwell, had begun to take a toll on the survivors. There was crying and whimpering and he could clearly make out more than one voice praying openly and loudly.

Standing three stairs up and to the right of Cade, Cross had leaned over the railing and was engaging the rear echelon of the undead throng. White-hot flashes lanced from his MP7 as he swept its laser overtop of the Zs, raking them right to left with 4.6x30mm dome shredders.

Cade looked up and right as he changed magazines and thought: *Good shooting, Agent Cross.* In the green glow he could also see the three scientists arm in arm and kneeling on the stairs behind the big-boned Secret Service agent. He shifted his gaze behind them and noticed that Tice and Lopez had successfully kept the civilians moving, and they too were nearing the landing.

"Let's move," Cade bellowed as he seated a new magazine, let the bolt fly forward, and worked his way further downstairs. When he made the final landing it was littered with spent brass and dead Zs. The door in front of him had a plastic sign embossed with a big letter M, and protruding below it were a series of bumps that he presumed spelled out mezzanine in braille.

He fired half a magazine—fifteen shells—blindly down the stairs into the dead, hoping that a few found their mark.

He heard Brook's voice in his head saying, "*Lift with your knees,*" as he reached down and hauled a cold corpse from in front of the door and sent it tumbling into the moaning Zs below. He tried the door handle. *Locked.*

"Back up a few stairs," he called out to Cross, who was swapping out for a fresh magazine.

There was no time to bring Tice forward to scope the door, he reasoned. Nor was there time to pick the lock. So he improvised. He backed up so that he was at an oblique angle to the door. He put the laser dot an inch to the right of the brushed metal handle and then fired a single round where he presumed the locking mechanism engaged the jamb. He tried the handle.

Still locked. The single shot had had no effect. So he took a step back and quickly squeezed off two more shots and was rewarded with a few slivers of light and a quarter-inch of give to the door near the bolt.

A guttural moan drew his attention away from the door to the flesh eaters on the stairs. A rowdy mop of black hair appeared first, and then a pallid forehead bobbed to and fro as its eerie green eyes darted about in the dark searching in vain for some sort of prey.

The laser sliced the air and the dot wavered between the Zs eyes for a tick before Cade caressed the trigger and sealed the deal. The thing's head snapped back from the impact and green flecks of bone and liquefied brain erupted rearward, peppering the wall behind it. Cade drained his magazine at more bobbing heads, slammed a new one in the well and charged a round, all in seemingly the same motion. Then, with a buffer of fallen Zs slowing down the column, he reared back and delivered a powerful kick to the door. With the resulting vibration still shivering his bones, the door flew open and he burst from the dark and into the wide open mezzanine full of windows and glorious sunshine. He recovered his balance, flipped his NVGs up, and took in the full scope of the loft built within an atrium.

Fifty yards to the fore, quad escalators that he guessed normally brought people up from the ground level were unmoving. As he watched, two Zs filed between the closely-spaced rubber handholds and stepped clumsily from the metal treads and onto the cement mezzanine level terrace. Seeing this, and fearing more were on the way, likely drawn by the gunfire and his door kicking, Cade looked around for the sky bridge.

Tice emerged from the stairway, followed closely by Cross and his charges. As soon as Lopez exited, he turned and planted his back against the gunshot door, slid down onto his haunches, and wedged his combat dagger between the door's bottom and the floor, effectively locking the creatures inside—he hoped.

As Cade moved forward, he studied the entrance to the glass sky bridge which branched off to the right thirty feet from him.

There didn't seem to be a gate or anything else that would keep them from crossing over to the parking lot side. Whether the other end was locked or not would remain to be seen. *And if it was locked, and couldn't be picked, no problem*, Cade thought. That's what he'd brought det cord for.

Behind him, a semicircle of walking dead, likely drawn by the door banging open and then slamming shut again, had rounded the corner and flanked the group on the left, catching them unaware.

One of the civilians, a mousy-looking redhead who looked to be in her late twenties, was caught in their clutches before anyone had a chance to react.

Tice brought his rifle to bear first, but not before he witnessed, simultaneously, the woman's throat being torn out and Andy bravely and inexplicably inserting himself into the melee.

Tice fired a dozen rounds into the Zs that were feeding on her supine body and then ended her suffering with one shot to her temple. Blood, ten shades brighter than her hair, instantly began to pool around her head as the rest of the dead largely ignored the living and pounced on her still-twitching body.

Andy unleashed a war cry and delivered a kick to the nearest of the creatures that did nothing but draw its interest. In seconds he was taken down by a handful of the snarling beasts. His shrill screams resonated off the glass ceiling above him as Lopez emptied a full magazine into the pig pile, making sure to walk a few into the would-be hero's clean-shaven head.

Cade shook his head in disbelief. He couldn't believe, how, in just a handful of seconds he had witnessed Mister Murphy—of Murphy's Law fame—throw a ninety-five mile-per-hour fastball at his chin. "We're about to be surrounded," he warned his team. Then he called for exfil. "Jedi One-One, how copy?"

"Gaines here," the general calmly replied.

"I need air support on station," Cade said. He let his M4 hang from its sling and drew the Glock 17, then dropped a number of Zs that had angled between the group and the sky bridge.

"Roger that. One-Two is two mikes out."

Somewhat relieved at the much needed good news, Cade waved to get Cross's attention, called him and the others forward, and then started off at a slow trot towards the sky bridge. Keeping his head on a swivel, he reestablished comms with Gaines. "We are going to shoot our way out of here, cross the road via the sky bridge, and somehow get to the entryway. The road running between the guard shack and the sky bridge, I believe, is the safest place for the exfil," said Cade as he dropped a couple more Zs at the top of the escalator.

"I concur," stated Gaines. Then Ari's voice crackled in Cade's earpiece. "Anvil Actual. This is Ari in One-One. *I* will have no problem putting my bird down there. But with those trees lining the drive there's no way One-Two can pull it off right there. Those two rotors give the Osprey a helluva wingspan. How copy?"

"Roger that," said Cade. "I'll take care of the trees. Just give me a couple of mikes to get down there, then watch our flanks with the mini-gun. I'll pop purple smoke when the LZ is prepped."

"Copy that," Ari replied as he wondered what the hell the brash operator had up his sleeve.

Gaines's voice edged in over the comms. "Anvil Actual, do you have the HVT's with you?"

"Yes Sir. We have three high value targets and sixteen others."

"Sixteen others?" Gaines said incredulously. "If you can't clear an LZ big enough for One-Two, then you *must* be prepared to leave them."

Glancing over his shoulder, Cade saw that Tice was handling the monsters to his left flank, and Cross and Lopez were busy ushering the civilians away from the feeding frenzy and towards the sky bridge.

"I'm not leaving them behind," Cade said sharply. He went into a combat crouch and rounded the corner with the Glock held in a two-handed grip. He stared down the triangular-shaped glass walkway—except for two Zs about twenty feet in front of him, it was clear the rest of the way to the elevator on the far end.

Wishing his cardio was a little better, Cade broke into a sprint, quickly closed the distance, and fired twice into the back of the first ghoul's head. He kept moving silently and double tapped walker number two at the mid-point of the bridge. Taking a knee, he turned and waited for the rest to form up. As he watched the three operators hustling the survivors towards him, Lopez suddenly stopped in place, raised his M4 and began shooting at the undead herd flowing up the nearby escalator. When all of the survivors reached his position, the woman named Mary broke ranks and stepped to him in a huff. "How the hell do you think we are *all* going to get out of here?" she barked. "Megan and Pete are dead back there. Shot up by *your* guys," she added, palming away some newly formed tears.

"Couldn't be helped," Cade replied quietly. "They got bit and those are the new rules. You worked with the Omega virus. You should know the score by now."

Mary harrumphed and crossed her arms.

A few seconds passed and Cade pointed skyward at the approaching Osprey. Then the glass above their heads flexed and began vibrating under the buffeting rotor wash as the craft cut a lazy circle overhead. "*That,* lady, is how you are getting out of here," he stated. "Time to go," he called to the Delta team. "Our chariots await."

Cade called Lopez off, and when he returned to the group Cade led them to the east end of the sky bridge and stopped in front of the elevator doors. He punched the down arrow and nothing happened. He turned towards Cross, arched an eyebrow, and shrugged his shoulders. "Worth a try," he said.

They located the stairwell just around the corner from the dead elevator. Tice moved forward and scoped the door. "Clear," he called out.

It took Cade almost a minute to open the locked door using the lock gun while Tice continued watching the LCD screen. "Still clear," he added.

Suddenly memories of Maddox, Desantos, and a host of other dead and gone shooters Cade had served with flooded his head. Not only did he miss Darwin's skills as a lock pick, he also missed the camaraderie and the operator's ability to always have the right quip or observation in the chamber and ready to go. Cade also lamented the fact that since that day in Grand Junction he hadn't been able to properly mourn the man's death. *Something I'll need to tackle back home*, he thought.

Tice retracted the flexible shaft and Cade eased the door open. Light streaming from the skylights above made their NVGs unnecessary.

Sweeping the Glock in order to cover the stairs to his right, Cade entered the stairwell and padded down them two at a time. Light on the balls of his feet, he cut the corner to his left in a combat crouch, keeping his elbows in and the polymer pistol at the ready. *Clear.* He silently motioned the others forward and covertly peered through the two-foot-square window inset into the metal door.

The east parking lot spread out before him. There was a large contingent of dead ambling among the abandoned cars baking in the high noon sun. He returned his gaze to the faces of the civilians packed on the rise above him and quickly laid out the rest of his plan. And when he had finished, the skeptical looks the survivors shot his way didn't surprise him in the least. Hell, he expected nothing less. After all, he and his team were for all intents and purposes kidnapping these folks from a friendly sovereign nation. That they had yet to put up any kind of a fight, let alone a full-on mutiny, had Cade scratching his head.

Tice craned his neck to get a look through the window. "How many out there, Captain?"

"A few dozen... *or more*," replied Cade. "*Pinche demonios*," added Lopez as he made the sign of the cross.

"At least you're not humping the *Alpha* right now," Cade said, flashing a rare grin.

In fact, it was the first emotion Lopez had seen the man exhibit since they'd left Schriever. *A good omen*, he thought to himself.

"Come in One-Two... this is Anvil Actual. I am in the stairwell at the east end of the sky bridge. I need you to lay down some fire in the parking lot ASAP."

"Copy that," said Ripley all business-like. "Rolling in."

The skylights above vibrated as an ominous shadow momentarily blocked the incoming light. Cade holstered the Glock and readied his M4. He peered out the window just in time to witness every one of the Zs stop in unison, turn their pallid faces skyward and fix their milky eyes on the noisy Osprey. As he watched it enter the airspace overhead, slowly the big propellers became rotors, and Jedi One-Two's forward momentum all but ceased. Then all at once, the dual nacelles finished rotating up and locked into the upright position, the black aircraft assumed a wavering hover, and the rear ramp motored down, exposing a chalk of eager Rangers and the crew chief behind a heavy machine gun.

Suddenly a buzzsaw-like sound filled the air as the remotely operated mini-gun on the craft's belly began belching hot lead into the seemingly hypnotized Zs. And a heartbeat later, the crew chief manning the M2 Browning on the tail ramp began hammering away at the undead below.

Using the cacophony created by the massive rotors stirring the air and the gunfire lancing down from the hovering craft as a diversion, Cade made his move. He hit the push bar and peeled left while keeping close to the wall, and at the next corner he curled left again with Lopez and Tice close on his heels. The trio ran under the sky bridge and moved single file along a sidewalk on the left that ran between a ten-foot-tall chain link fence to the left and a row of twenty-foot-tall trees, spaced roughly twenty feet apart, paralleling the road on their right. Cade stopped at the first of the six trees preventing the Osprey from setting down. While he coiled the self-adhesive breaching charge—a flexible type of explosive sprouting a length of det cord attached to an electrical firing device—around the tree's thigh-sized trunk, he noticed the other two operators split up, and each of them moved towards a tree across the narrow drive. He waited a few moments until both men were finished setting their charges. "Good to go?" he said into the comms.

With clackers in hand and a good standoff distance between them and the charges they had rigged, Tice and Lopez flashed Cade a thumbs up from across the street.

"Fire in the hole," Cade called out as he turned his face away from the impending blast and worked his clacker.

The three nearly simultaneous explosions resulted in a brief cloud of white smoke followed by all three trees lying down as if a giant invisible scythe had ripped through them.

"Holy weed-whacker Batman," said Ari as he tore his eyes from the destruction being wrought on the dead by the Osprey and watched the three trees nearest the sky bridge topple over in unison. Piloting the Ghost in a tight orbit above the Osprey, Ari watched Jedi One-Two circle the parking lot, hosing down wandering Zs while destroying a large number of cars in the process.

From the port side of the Ghost Hawk, Gaines spotted a legion of zombies streaming in from the plaza to the northwest. "Heads up Anvil," said Gaines. "You have Zs moving in on your six from the northwest. How copy?"

"Roger that, General," said Cade as he readied another tree for demo. "Should have the LZ prepped in two mikes."

"Make it quick, Grayson. You're in clear and present danger of being overrun."

Cade said nothing. When he'd finished wrapping the next tree, he glanced over his shoulder to the area under the sky bridge where a number of Zs staggered rigidly from the lawn onto the entry drive. Then he checked to make sure the other operators were finished setting their final charges. "Lopez... Tice... you ready?" he inquired over the comms.

Voices crackled in Cade's ear bud as the operators called back, indicating that they were good to go.

Clacker in hand, Cade backed away from the tree, and shifted his gaze between the diminishing amount of real estate separating him and his teammates from the advancing crowd of flesh eaters. "Fire in the hole," he exclaimed as he squeezed the clacker, sending electrical current into the det-cord leader.

Another series of explosions rumbled and echoed off of the metal and glass building, and the trees hinged to the ground in different directions. Cade watched as his tree canted over, hit the barbed wire atop the fence, and then rolled off without causing any noticeable damage. Satisfied with the newly created LZ, he adjusted his M4 so that it dangled behind his back and clambered over the splintered trunk, then crossed the sidewalk and the buffer of dried grass between it and the fence and fished out his last breaching charge. He adhered a three-foot length of the tape vertically, rolled out a dozen feet of leader and attached the clacker. When he fired the charge, the explosion ripped through the galvanized steel wire and left a smoking gash just big enough to admit a person.

Cade gave his handiwork a cursory glance, and though not as dramatic as falling a tree, he deemed the result acceptable.

Next, he called up Jedi One-Two and requested an immediate exfil for the nineteen survivors. Then he called to Agent Cross, who was presumably still sheltered in place with them in the sky bridge stairwell.

Cross acknowledged the call and listened as Cade brought him up to speed. Then he sprang into action, jammed the push bar and held the door wide with one hand and brandished his MP7 with the other. "Go, go, go," he bellowed at the survivors, and fired his machine pistol one-handed, stitching a decomposing first turn from sternum to forehead.

He looked over his shoulder, and when everyone was accounted for he lined up the three scientists on his six and set off at a slow jog inside the fence line.

Pushed along by fear and confusion, the scientists and civilians followed closely in his wake. As soon as Cross arrived at the breach in the fence, he helped Cade peel it back and hold it open while all nineteen Canadians filed through.

The guns on the Osprey went silent and the craft broke orbit and descended rapidly; in a matter of seconds it was wheels down and the Rangers were charging down the rear ramp.

Cowering amongst the fallen trees, the Canadians kept their heads bowed to protect against the flying debris whipped up by the whirring rotors.

Working against the clock, Cade first ushered the scientists into the yawning rear opening of the Osprey, making sure they were belted in securely. Then he waved the remaining survivors inside and passed them off to One-Two's strapping African American crew chief, who in turn showed them to the side-facing jump seats.

Cade raced down the ramp, and was pleased to see that while he had been in the aircraft the newly-arrived Rangers seemed to have slowed the advance of the burgeoning ranks of the dead. Staccato bursts of fire rippled along the phalanx of shooters as they fired and reloaded. Two Rangers from the 75th had taken up positions on either side of the road and, using the splintered tree trunks for support, were busily raking their SAWs—squad automatic weapons—across the Zs with deadly precision.

The turbine whine elevated as the dual thirty-eight-foot diameter rotor blades increased in speed, and Ripley's voice crackled over the comms. "Wheels up in one mike," she said.

Cade hustled over to the young Ranger master sergeant and motioned for him to have his men fall back to the Osprey. Then he got ahold of Ari in the circling Ghost Hawk and requested an emergency exfil.

He flicked his gaze up to the sky bridge where more Zs had amassed. They were now three deep and stretching from one end to the other. An icy ball formed in his gut as he watched the ashen-skinned monsters press against the aquamarine-hued glass, causing it to flex and bow in places. He feared that if Ripley didn't clear the LZ and make room for Jedi One-One quickly, his team would be facing a veritable waterfall of flesh eaters.

"Waiting," said Ari impatiently over the comms. Then Gaines's voice came onto the net over the SOAR pilot's, and with language unbecoming a general he urged the Marine major to get her bird into the air.

Sensing the Osprey lifting into the air behind him, Cade braced the M4 on a fallen tree, flicked the 3x magnifier up, and began picking off zombies. The rotor wash blasted his back with stinging debris and sent the piles of spent brass around his feet sliding away across the blacktop as One-Two thundered away to the south. Soon the rotor noise gave way to the eerie wails of the dead commingled with the reassuring sharp reports of steady gun fire. Cade looked over his shoulder to see the black craft bank and make a sweeping turn that once again brought it on station over the parking lot, where Ripley commenced a hover and the machine guns once again opened up into the dead below.

Tice, who was a few feet from Cross and shoulder-to-shoulder with Lopez, watched as Cade pulled a canister from a pocket and tossed it in the center of the drive near the mishmash of branches and fallen Zs. A soft pop sounded and smoke billowed out thick and purple, snaking into the air like something alive.

Cross changed magazines as he backed away from the moaning Zs and towards the drifting smoke. In his side vision he could see that Lopez and Tice took a cue from him and were also backpedaling in the same general direction.

Cade's voice crackled in the Delta team's ear buds just as the sonic reverberation of the Ghost's baffled rotor blades thumped deep in their chests. "Exfil in minus one mike," he stated calmly.

Suddenly a sharp sound, like a berg calving from a glacier, cracked off the building to the left. Then, like a wave breaking left to right over a reef, a cascade of sparkling glass and putrid corpses poured from the sky bridge.

Cade's stomach clenched as the heavy impacts of flesh and bone against the roadway vibrated through his boots.

The Ghost Hawk came in hot from the north and buzzed the top of the sky bridge with just inches to spare. Through the cockpit glass, Ari's grin was evident under his smoked visor, and Cade could see the hard set to Durant's jaw as the craft slid overhead, blocking out the sun.

Big black wheels emerged from the helo's belly and shells began to rain from Hicks's buzzing mini-gun as Ari presented the ship's starboard side towards the Zs. At the last second he flared and set the Ghost Hawk down softly in the same spot the Osprey had occupied seconds before.

Firing as he went, Tice broke from cover and made a beeline through the flapping branches. He emptied the mag and then let his smoking carbine dangle as he accepted a hand from Gaines and scrambled into the helicopter.

Cade watched in disbelief as an overwhelming number of Zs recovered from their thirty-foot fall, regained their footing, and plowed ahead oblivious of the drifts of glass crunching underfoot.

Screaming, *"Go, go, go,"* Cade stood fully upright and targeted the nearest of the snarling creatures. He fired round after round, sweeping the M4 in a deadly arc from left to right.

Simultaneously Cross and Lopez emptied their weapons, bowed their heads under the whirring blades and leapt to the safety of the waiting craft.

"Three in," Gaines called out.

Hearing this, Cade lowered the M4's smoking barrel and turned and bolted for the Ghost Hawk, which was now in a hover with the wheels already retracted into the fuselage.

Although eager to pull pitch and get clear of the compromised LZ, Ari held the Ghost rock steady three feet off the deck. He silently rooted for Cade as the Delta operator hurdled the crossed tree trunks while twisting and contorting his body in order to keep away from the flesh eaters' outstretched fingers.

As Cade neared the hovering helo, everything around him seemed to slow, and he could see a determined look on Hicks's face as the crew chief fired the clattering mini-gun into the dead. And as he lunged to grip Gaines's offered hand, he could feel intense heat searing his face and hear wet slaps as the streaking bullets found flesh behind him.

His boots left the ground and his body rose with the helicopter. Then, it felt like someone was sitting on his chest as the G-forces pressed him to the deck. He could tell that someone had a hold of one leg while Gaines maintained a firm grip on his gloved hand. The ground spiraled in his vision as the helo banked again and his organs returned to their normal accommodations. Finally someone helped pull him completely inside the helo and a gloved hand pulled the door shut in front of his face, mercifully blotting out the horrors he had just left behind.

Ari's voice crackled in his ear. "Close call, amigo."

Seeing as how his life had just flashed in front of his eyes, that was definitely the last thing Cade needed to hear. All the years in combat and the firefights he'd survived had never prepared him for something like this. As he'd struggled through the obstacle course of fallen trees, he'd seen Raven's face in his mind's eye, clear as day, and in it she'd been pleading with him to come home. Then, inexplicably he'd been standing in front of Mike's grave with Brook at his side—and he could have sworn the old warhorse had been there in the flesh trying to offer up advice or a warning, like some kind of Obi Wan Kenobi trick. Then the vision morphed and he'd found himself staring down at the scene, and Brook and Raven were all alone graveside; it had seemed so real in that millisecond flash that he'd thought he had died and they were mourning for him. *Pretty strange how a mainline surge of adrenaline affects the human brain*, he thought to himself as he closed his eyes, hoping that the hypnotic swishing noise from the rotors would somehow drive the unsettling visions from his mind.

Chapter 65
Outbreak - Day 16
Schriever AFB
Colorado Springs, Colorado

Security Pod

He was awakened by someone clutching a substantial handful of his silver mane and jerking his head from the table with all of the ferocity of a professional wrestler.

Before he could see his assailant, a thin tablet computer was cast on the table near his manacled wrists. The person standing in the shadows behind him activated the device, then swiped an icon that started a video running. After a few seconds a voice began narrating what he was seeing.

The first clip was taken in night vision mode which rendered everything in shades of green. It ran for four minutes and documented a group of men with high tech weaponry as they flowed silent and effortlessly through a nicely appointed mansion.

By the end of the tape the efficient killers had eliminated a host of people and were in the process of defeating what looked to be a thick ornate door.

Soon, a flash of light marred the feed from the point man's helmet-mounted camera, and when it returned to normal the door was hanging open on only one hinge.

Then the image jounced and a man was removed forcibly from a very large bed, leaving a woman behind, struggling to cover her naked body.

As Robert Christian watched the feed wind down, he recognized the man as former President and Guild member John Cranston. Then the point man pulled in for a close up and asked the man his name.

"You know who I am. I'm John Cranston. Former President..."

Suddenly a silenced pistol entered the frame, and Cranston was shot twice in the head. He fell to the carpet and the camera followed, then went black.

Soon a second video played a montage of scenes. The first casualties recorded were the father and son Presidents from Kennebunkport, Maine. Their vehicle was ambushed near a bridge, and they were dragged from a late model SUV and questioned briefly before being executed. Mark Buchannon, dot-com billionaire was next—executed in his Napa Valley bug out retreat by another team of ruthless killers. The video ended with Texas oilman and Guild member Hank Ross leaving the earth on the receiving end of a precision drone strike.

"Seen enough?" the disembodied voice said.

"Fuck you," Christian spat.

The blow to his temple came from out of nowhere and made him momentarily lose consciousness.

When he came to he saw stars, and the voice said, "Your Guild is dead, and the President sends her condolences."

Christian bit his tongue because lashing out verbally would only bring him more pain.

"She wanted to make sure you were aware just how far you have fallen before you fall one final time tomorrow—through the opening in the gallows."

The interrogator removed the iPad and strode from the room, leaving Robert Christian as alone and helpless as he'd ever been.

Chapter 66
Outbreak - Day 16
Winters's Compound
Eden, Utah

Luckily, the Land Cruiser had been at the rear of the column when its fuel tank erupted. Three hours after the ambush, the thing was still smoking and too hot to touch. Duncan decided to leave it where it was, sitting on melted rims in the middle of the road at the far west end of the gradual curve—a warning to anyone else who thought about coming around and causing trouble. He made a mental note to sit down with the rest of the survivors—the men and the women—and brainstorm on better ways to protect them against further intrusions.

The engine groaned as he used the Humvee as a makeshift wrecker and pushed the other bullet-riddled vehicles onto the shoulder. He slid out of the driver seat, walked over to the fence and retrieved the length of hose and the empty gas can from where Lev had left it.

Not looking forward to the prospect of the foul-tasting diesel touching his lips, he trudged over to the Hummer with the destroyed engine block. *Good shooting. Oops*, he thought to himself as he watched the vehicle's lifeblood dripping onto the cement. He noted how the black oil and antifreeze-tinged water refused to mix. It reminded him of how he and his little bro were before the apocalypse threw them back together. He had always wanted to foster some kind of a bond with his brother when Logan was a kid, but the drastic age difference had made it all but impossible. Now they were thick as thieves and he vowed to make up for lost time.

He put the hose to his lips and sucked. *Never works on the first try*, he thought to himself. He tried again this time, sucking harder, and before he could pull away the familiar foul taste was in his mouth.

After the five-gallon can was full, he put the hose aside and searched his pockets for the Zippo. Though he'd quit smoking years ago—for a woman, of course—he still carried the prized lighter he'd picked up in Da Nang.

While Duncan was dealing with the destroyed vehicles, Lev and Logan heaped the rotters into the ditch along with the others from the day before.

Duncan walked from one end of the moldering pile of corpses to the other, letting the thick diesel glug from the can. He didn't discriminate—whether they used to be men, women, or children—all were anointed with their fair share of accelerant. And when he was done, he lit the Zippo and touched it to the nearest fuel drenched rotter..

He watched the blue flame jump from body to body as the unmistakable stench of burning hair wafted over the funeral pyre. Soon the entire lot was fully engulfed.

He watched the bodies sizzle and steam as fluids cooked off and vaporized. After a short time, a smell he remembered all too well assailed his nose. It was the same smell belched out of any flame-broiling burger joint or at home from the BBQ grill on a hot summer day. Burnt flesh was burnt flesh. Cow, lamb, or man—it all smelled the same.

Having seen enough death for one lifetime, Duncan trudged up the hill to about the halfway point, and without saying a word took the shovel out of Jamie's hands. He pushed the blade through the grass and began to dig into the soft topsoil. Before long the grave was big enough to accommodate the dead humans. Silently the shooters went about the grim task of burying the burned bodies from the Toyota, as well as the other bullet-riddled corpses. For an hour, they scooped dirt over the fallen, and when the staring eyes and contorted faces were covered, they tamped down the dirt.

Then, starting with Chief, one by one the six men and one woman traded their shovels for a weapon. Before long, the engine noise that Chief had detected coming from the east became more pronounced and drew nearer.

With the vehicles still sitting on the shoulder and the zombie bodies cooking in the ditch, there was no chance in hell that the approaching vehicle was going to pass by the scene without stopping to investigate.

Duncan started off down the hill, sprinting for the operable Humvee, his sights set on the fully-loaded heavy machine gun. He parted the barbed wire and squeezed through, leaving a good-sized chunk of flesh behind.

He reached the tan rig, climbed into the turret, and had just brought the machine gun to bear when a black and white SUV emerged from the east where the road curved to the right and disappeared into the trees. He kept one hand on the .50 cal's handle and fumbled for the binoculars with his free hand. As he pressed the field glasses to his face, the words *Jackson Hole Police Department* leapt out at him. He steadied his arms on the bullet-pocked metal plate and focused on the driver.

"Well, I'll be damned," he said in a low voice. He recognized the dreadlocked driver, but the blonde woman who was riding shotgun was another story. "Hold your fire!" he bellowed.

***

"Duncan!" hollered Daymon as he stepped from the Tahoe and stretched his long legs. "Ain't you a sight for sore eyes. It's been awhile, hasn't it?"

"Yeah, last I remember I was watching you from a hundred-foot hover back in Driggs... scalping zombies and jumping

SHAWN CHESSER

fences." He clapped the taller man on the shoulder. "Good stuff."

"Some help you were."

"At least I hovered and distracted them and made sure you got inside your house... felt like a dad watching his kid walk off to school alone for the first time."

Daymon went silent. He looked at the wound on Duncan's face, then his gaze shifted to the remnants from the lopsided battle, the oily smoke drifting from the ditch where the bodies had been reduced to misshapen human-like forms. He looked at the bullet-pocked vehicles. Then he regarded the hard faces of those he didn't know or failed to recognize. "I thought you said the compound was in *Eden*, Utah."

"Not technically. It butts up against federal lands on one side. Eden and Huntsville are about the same distance as the crow flies. Methinks my little bro just liked the ring Eden has to it." Duncan smiled and pointed at the Tahoe. "Get in your rig. I'll show you to the compound where you and me can play a little catch up and the others can get acquainted."

"What about this?" Daymon said, making a sweeping gesture at the burned and bullet-riddled vehicles.

"We're finished here for now."

I'd hate to see what the encore looks like, thought Daymon as he walked back to the Tahoe. He smiled to set Heidi at ease as he slid into the driver's seat. "Thank God for GPS," he stated. "The compound is close to here."

***

Somewhere west of the Colorado Rockies

Ian Bishop gazed across the crystalline waters lapping at the sand near his feet, then considered the razor-edged upthrust peaks filling his view and the forces that had shaped them. He took another long pull from his Corona and crunched it back into the overfilled ice bucket, thinking there wasn't another place he would rather be.

So far the occupants of the nearby towns and all of the survivors scattered about tending to their own little fiefdoms hadn't seemed bothered by his arrival and the added activity. That he and his men helped to keep the undead population down by sending out patrols of their own seemed better than a few promises or treaties filled with hollow words.

But that will soon change, Bishop thought. When the men returned from their foraging missions, the balance of power in this alpine nirvana was going to shift noticeably. And when it did, the folks would either be *with him* or against him—no middle ground.

He brought the bottle to his lips and listened to the generator hum in the distance. Suddenly the Iridium sat phone in his pocket rang.

He looked at the incoming number, then at his watch, noted the time and thought to himself: *Just like clockwork. Time to sink or swim, Elvis. If he couldn't figure out a way to get to the coordinates I provided, then the man doesn't deserve to be part of the new venture.*

With a no nonsense look on his face, Bishop silenced the phone and fished another cold beer from the ice.

Chapter 67
Outbreak - Day 16
Near Pierre, South Dakota

"I've got you on visual, Oil Can Five-Five," Ari said. "Right on time once again."

"Roger that, One-One. Five-Five maintaining altitude and speed."

"Copy that," Ari replied. He switched to the shipboard comms. "General Gaines, please remind me to give Whipper a big fat sloppy kiss when we get back to Schriever."

"Forget Whipper," Gaines intoned. "Captain Grayson here is the one who should be on the receiving end of that affection."

Cade had been lost in thought, staring out the window, watching the multicolored plats of land slide beneath the helicopter, but as soon as he heard his name mentioned he glanced over at Gaines, shook his head and returned his gaze to the landscape below.

"Want to tell them what transpired between you and Whipper?" Gaines asked.

Cade said nothing in the hopes that Gaines would drop it.

"You tell them or I will."

Gritting his teeth, Cade wondered who'd told Gaines about the scuffle. Then he decided it didn't really matter—it was done. Water under the bridge, so to speak.

Cade turned his gaze to the general. "I knocked his dick in the dirt," he said slowly over the comms for all to hear. In the background, he noticed Hicks turn from the starboard gunner's seat and flash a thumbs up as a broad grin creased his face.

"Wait one, Captain," Ari said, cutting him off. He tapped a button on the glass display that caused a noise underfoot as the refueling boom extended from the Ghost's snout. "After we refuel... I'm all ears."

Ari maneuvered close to the Herc and expertly plugged the probe into the bobbing drogue chute. Then, fighting against a minor side wind, he kept the helo level and steady while a considerable amount of fuel was transferred. Next he uncoupled, eased away, and then retracted the boom into the helo's belly.

"Next," Ari said, indicating it was Ripley's turn to commence her final refueling of the flight.

"Roger that. One-Two moving into position," Ripley said. Effortlessly, she hooked the Osprey up with the lumbering Hercules. A couple of tedious minutes later, hundreds of pounds of fuel had flowed into the Osprey's tanks, Ripley bled her airspeed and backed off from the drogue.

"Jedi One-Two, why don't you go ahead and get your passengers back to Schriever. I'm going to the deck to check on our friends in Pierre."

"Copy that, One-One. Jedi One-Two is RTB—returning to base."

"Roger that. Meet me at the mess tent, Ripley?" Ari asked in an amorous tone.

"Don't bet on it, *Night Stalker*. This aviator doesn't see other aviators."

"Copy that," Ari said, putting on a sad act. "Too good for us *commoners*," he added in his best British accent.

"One-Two out. See you back at Schriever."

Ari watched the *Frankencopter* accelerate and climb while at the same time he did the exact opposite.

"Durant has been on the horn with Schriever," said Ari. "Whipper came through again. I'll go low so we can see with our own eyes."

"Did he arrange an ammo resupply?" Cade inquired.

"And then some. Beans, bullets, and bandages. The whole nine yards," Durant answered.

"Dang, Captain," Lopez piped up. "What did you do? Give the old first sergeant a couple of titty twisters and force him to say uncle?"

"I heard it was a reach around," added Cross, who had been silent and brooding since they went wheels up in Winnipeg.

Cade shot him a murderous stare that softened somewhat after a beat. "You're not Delta yet, Cross. That means you don't have the pedigree to bust my balls like that. Now put a couple more missions under your belt riding along with us on... what does Ari call his new venture?"—Cade thought on it for a second—"*Night Stalker Airways*. You meet those requirements, then, and only then, will you become an honorary Delta shooter and be able to crack on me like that. Right, General?"

Gaines turned his head to the Secret Service agent and nodded. "How bad do you want to be a member of Delta?"

"Am I being recruited?" Cross asked incredulously.

"No... we're just fucking with you," said Cade.

"Sorry to break up the love fest, ladies," quipped Ari. "But we're two mikes out from Pierre."

The operators shifted on their canvas seats to get a better view.

Tice readied his Nikon.

Lopez couldn't resist. "Preserving visions of hell for future generations, eh, Spook?"

"Following orders, *pendejo*."

Lopez bristled then stood down. "I almost forgot Mister Puker Patch here is honorary Delta now. I prefer *asshole* over *pendejo*... asshole."

***

As Ari held the Ghost Hawk in a tight orbit over the battlefield below, Durant called up the commander on the ground. A subordinate fielded the call, and then after a few ticks of silence a new voice came over the comms. An upbeat-sounding Captain Rodriguez thanked whoever arranged the drop and then explained how—in just the span of a few hours since the resupply—he and his men were finally beginning to make a dent in the number of walking dead.

"It was nothing," Gaines replied. "I'm sure you would do the same for us if the tables were turned."

The captain didn't reply, but his mike stayed hot for a moment and gunfire and men yelling to one another somewhere in the background came through loud and clear. Finally Rodriguez came back on and said, "Tell the folks at Schriever we owe them one."

"Will do soldier," Gaines said. "Godspeed to you."

***

Twenty minutes later

With Gaines's permission, Ari took the Ghost Hawk close to the deck, "Any of you guys seen Top Gun?" Ari asked.

"Who hasn't?" came Durant's stock answer for every obvious question Ari posed.

Heads bobbed an affirmative throughout the cabin.

With the rocketship-like E-Ticket ride up the eighty-degree face of the Flaming Gorge Dam fresh in his mind, Cade merely grinned. He doubted Ari could top that one for *wow* factor, but he knew better than to put anything past the hotshot pilot.

"Well Goose," Ari quipped. "It's time to buzz the tower."

Cade felt his back press to the bulkhead as the Ghost accelerated. He nudged his ruck under the seat Gaines was occupying, cinched his safety harness, and held his rifle tightly between his knees with the muzzle facing the decking.

"Hold on to your hats, ladies," Ari said over the shipwide comms. He eyed two rows of trees running parallel one on either side of the helo's flight path, spaced about a hundred yards apart, just on the other side of what appeared to be a centuries-old church. "Ride's going to get bumpy," he added as he took the ship closer to the ground.

Through the window Cade saw nothing but a brown and green blur. It was like he was staring at a blender as someone whipped up something way too healthy for consumption. He looked at Tice, who was turning whiter by the second. Then he regarded Hicks, who seemed to be dozing—though he couldn't see the crew chief's eyes through the smoked visor and couldn't be certain.

Next to Cade, copying what he had seen the other Delta boys already do, Cross was cinching himself in tighter. He'd ridden into combat on a Little Bird's platform and in a Black Hawk a hundred times while he was in the Teams, but his sixth sense was telling him he was in for a treat.

After signing himself for the tenth time during the mission, Lopez eased back next to Tice and clopped his new buddy on the shoulder.

Performing a maneuver he'd pulled off hundreds of times in Middle East wadis, forests over the Fulda Gap in Germany, and a hundred other places around the globe, Ari leaned the Ghost on its side so the rotors looked like a giant circular saw about to slice through the rapidly approaching church. Then, at the last second, he leveled the craft and popped it up and over the black-shingled roof, narrowly missing the white thirty-foot-tall steeple before hugging the terrain on the back side of the building.

Tice blanched immediately.

Cade could see the Spook's eyes searching for a safe place to deposit a stomach's worth of MRE. Then he smiled at the recollection of the former CIA man *earning* his Puker Patch over Grand Junction Airport just days ago. *Keep the door closed*, he thought to himself. Another whirlwind of regurgitated spaghetti was the last thing he wanted to experience. As he turned his eyes forward and peered between Ari and Durant, he noticed the looming canyon of trees, their skeletal branches reaching for the helo's skin on both sides.

410

"Splitting the goalposts," were the last words the occupants of the Ghost Hawk heard from Ari.

As Cade kept his eyes glued to the cockpit glass between the pilots' heads, the ground suddenly tilted up at him and was black as night. The speeding craft juddered as a handful of thunderous impacts rocked the fuselage and cockpit glass.

Simultaneously, Durant said matter-of-factly, "Bird strike," and Cade heard the turbines above and behind his head make an out-of-place sound—a groaning dirge as an eight-pound black bird was sucked through the baffled intake shroud and into the titanium and magnesium blades spinning at 15,000 revolutions per minute.

The impact with the ground was unlike anything Cade had ever experienced. He felt the butt stock on his M4 spear him in the gut and steal his wind. In his peripheral vision he saw an angel or cherub flash by. Then something resembling the Washington monument, tilted at a crazy angle, vanished into dust before his eyes. In one brief snippet of time he saw pallid corpses—wearing slack faces of men, women, and children— glide by outside the port window.

Fighting the unloading G-forces, he turned his head by a degree and witnessed Gaines seemingly fold in half, his flight helmet arcing down towards the helo's buckled floor. To his right, someone's arms and legs chopped at the air, weightless, like a bronco rider being thrown from his mount. His ruck levitated before his eyes, and then a slipstream of carrion-scented air blasted him and a cacophony of sounds assailed his ears: human voices crying out, carbon fiber shredding the earth, and metal groaning somewhere behind and below him.

Then the all-too-familiar copper smell of spilt blood commingled with the caustic odor of burning electrical hit his nose.

All of this sensory bombardment was followed immediately by silence and darkness.

###

Thanks for reading *Allegiance*. Look for Book 6: *Mortal*, the forthcoming novel in the *Surviving the Zombie Apocalypse* series in December of 2013. Please Friend Shawn Chesser on Facebook.

ABOUT THE AUTHOR

Shawn Chesser, a practicing father, has been a zombie fanatic for decades. He likes his creatures shambling, trudging and moaning. As for fast, agile, screaming specimens... not so much. He lives in Portland, Oregon, with his wife, two kids and three fish. This is his fifth novel.

CUSTOMERS ALSO PURCHASED:

  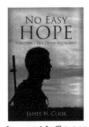

T.W. BROWN
THE DEAD
SERIES

JOHN O'BRIEN
NEW WORLD
SERIES

JAMES N. COOK
SURVIVING THE DEAD
SERIES

 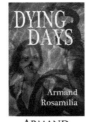 

MARK TUFO
ZOMBIE FALLOUT
SERIES

ARMAND ROSAMILLIA
DYING DAYS
SERIES

HEATH STALLCUP
THE MONSTER
SQUAD

Made in the USA
San Bernardino, CA
17 November 2013